Nightbirds

Nightbirds

Lawrence M. James

Library of Congress Control Number: 2013909533
ISBN: Hardcover   978-1-4836-4598-8
                 Softcover   978-1-4836-4597-1
                 Ebook   978-1-4836-4599-5

This book was printed in the United States of America.

Rev. date: 06/06/2013

To order additional copies of this book, contact:
Xlibris Corporation
1-888-795-4274
www.Xlibris.com
Orders@Xlibris.com
133610

It is said that there is a bird that sings only at night and only after sex. In the dark, hidden in the branches of a large tree, its song can be heard. In the morning, it looks common and ordinary like any other bird, waiting to sing again that night. They are called nightbirds.

PROLOGUE

SHE HELD THE cage in the air. "What is it?"

"She's a present." He looked at the bird.

"Why?"

"It's just my way of saying that I'm happy we met," he answered.

"Thank you."

"And that I believe we have a future."

She set the birdcage down and hugged him. "So do I."

They had met only a few weeks ago, and this was their fourth date. He respected time; he didn't like to waste it.

"What kind of bird is it?" she asked. "I don't recognize it."

"She, not it, dammit," he almost shouted.

"I'm sorry, she."

It was the first time he had raised his voice to her. They'd had sex for the first time on their last date, and he had been a considerate and indulgent lover, trying to learn about her body and her mind and her desires. But that didn't mean he could yell at her on their next date.

"I'm sorry," he said. "I didn't mean to shout, but I raised her from a baby. I cared for her and fed her and took care of her when she was sick."

She looked confused. "It . . . she's just a bird."

"No." He gritted his teeth. "They're quite precious and quite rare. They are called nightbirds, and they sing only at night and only after they make love. They are the only birds you can hear singing in the middle of the night."

"I'm sorry, Evan. Thank you very much."

"I just thought"—he looked away again—"after the last time, you know."

"Yes, thank you."

He was shortish and compact, and she hadn't recognized his strength until she felt his arms and back as he moved above her.

"You raised her?"

"Yes." He nodded. "The genus is . . ."

"Genus?" she asked. "She's so dark like a raven, but smaller. What does 'genus' mean?"

"Family, but it doesn't matter," he said impatiently. "They're very strong for their size. In their world, they're like pit bulls. They'll fight any other bird, no matter its size. But at night, they are very gentle and very private, almost shy."

"Like you." She smiled.

"Maybe."

"Do you have others?"

"Yes." He nodded. "I have an aviary. I'm an amateur ornithologist, birds."

"And she won't sing tonight?"

"They'll sing for me because they trust and love me. We'll see."

"You should have told me about your birds."

She undid the latch on the door to the cage.

"They mate for life. They are loyal."

He watched her hand move slowly toward the bird.

"Be careful," he said as the bird attacked her and pecked her hand three times.

"Ow!" She withdrew her hand quickly from the cage.

"Here." Evan held her hand and wiped off the blood. "Do you have some peroxide?"

She nodded. "Yes."

As he dabbed the peroxide on her hand in the bathroom and watched it bubble over the three wounds, he smiled and said, "It will be okay. She just wasn't quite ready to sing yet."

After they made love, he walked into the living room and stopped next to the birdcage. Slowly, he put his right hand inside and waited until the bird stepped off her perch onto his right index finger.

"It's time now, isn't it?" he said to the bird. "It's time to sing."

He set the bird back on her perch, walked into the kitchen, and looked through the drawers next to the convection oven until he found what he needed.

"Are you coming back to bed?" she asked, then yawned and stretched. "That was nice."

"Yes, I'm coming back."

"Thank you for the bird." She smiled. "I'm sleepy now."

"Good."

He took the rolling pin from behind his back and slowly lifted it over his head.

She squinted in the dark room. "What is that?"

"You never know, do you?"

"What?"

"You never know when you're going to meet someone like me."

"No," she whispered, "please no."

"It's time to sing."

He could feel the concussive impact in his arm and shoulder each time he smashed the rolling pin down on her face and skull. He could hear the sounds of her dying gradually become a whisper until there was no sound from her at all.

"It was time to sing."

In her bathroom, in the master bedroom, he washed the blood off the rolling pin in the bathtub and wiped it clean. Carefully, he set it down next to the bed.

In the living room, he lifted the door to the cage and waited until the bird stepped off her perch onto his index finger.

"It's been a long time," he said to the bird, "almost two years of work."

He stroked the bird, then said, "I'm sorry for what I have to do. Sing for me."

For a few moments, he heard the bird's plaintive warble, until he slowly crushed her in his hands, then set her back down on the floor of the cage.

"I'm sorry," he said and felt tears on his face. "I had to do it. I'm sorry."

He reached into the inside pocket of his sports coat, and his fingers curled around the hoof nipper that he had learned to use one summer when his father sent him to camp for six weeks. In the bedroom, he lifted her left hand and cut off her ring finger, then placed it in the pocket of his slacks.

"It's like we're married now," he said to the face he could no longer recognize as he lay on top of her. "Our love was short, but it will last forever."

Afterward, he folded her hands over her abdomen like a corpse at a funeral.

In the living room, he stopped for a moment and stared at the dead bird lying on the floor of the cage and began to cry again.

"I hope you understand," Evan said to the bird. "From now on, I'll be good. I promise."

CHAPTER 1

"**WE HAVE VACANCIES.**" The old man, who was wearing a brown cardigan sweater, gestured at the front door. "You must have seen our sign."

"Steven Matthews, FBI." He reached inside his coat, then showed the motel clerk his badge. "This is Lou Mark. He works for me. We're looking for five men that checked in within the last ten days."

He had been trying to catch these men for nearly two years. The media called them the Mall Bandits. They robbed jewelry stores, taking expensive watches and high-quality stones, and then fenced them in another state. During the course of their robberies, they had killed seven people. Yesterday, in a small jewelry store in a suburb of Boston, they shot a security guard in the throat and killed a female clerk by repeated blows to the head with the butt of a handgun.

"Lou?" The old man pointed at the man standing next to Matthews.

"Mark," Matthews said impatiently. "Lou works for me."

It was the first time he had worked with Lou Mark, who had joined the FBI a little less than two years ago. Mark was only thirty-two years old, but Matthews had heard he had a gift, the ability to visualize the crime at a crime scene as if it were happening again. At the last crime scene, Mark had found a matchbook from a topless bar called Babes, and at the club, he had talked with a deaf stripper who had gone out with one of the Mall Bandits. Her name was Chloe, and after sex, he had hit her, then given her a diamond pendant. She had said that they were staying at the Sundown Motel just outside Boston.

Matthews looked at the motel clerk, then Mark. The clerk was about five six, and Mark was six one and 190 pounds, with black hair. He remembered what Chloe had said about Mark—or rather, signed—which the manager of the bar had translated.

"You have beautiful blue eyes. They're like lights on a Christmas tree." Her fingers rapidly moved some more. "I trust you."

"I don't know nothing about the people here." The clerk shook his head. "I just check them in. I only do this because Social Security and Medicare isn't enough for us—me and my wife."

"Five men checked in here a little more than a week ago," Matthews said. "Give me the room numbers."

The old man glanced at the black phone on the counter.

"Yeah, maybe I do remember now." He nodded slowly. "Yeah, they came in together."

"What are the room numbers?" Matthews asked again.

"Let me look." Matthews watched him turn the old-fashioned folio rack on the counter with numbers above each of the slots. It was about two feet high, like a Rolodex in a way, with guest register cards in some of the slots.

"You don't have this on computer?" Matthews asked.

"This thing is our computer," he answered. "Yes, now I remember—rooms 24, 23, and 22." He looked at the phone again.

"Thank you," Matthews said, then turned toward the door to the office.

"Wait, sir." Lou Mark held up his hand. "He's going to call them."

"How do you know that?" Matthews asked.

Mark shrugged. "He looked at the phone twice while you were talking to him."

"I don't know what you mean." The old man lifted his arms in the air and shook his head. "I'm just here because Social Security . . ."

"Were you going to call them?" Matthews asked him.

"Tell me what they said to you, now," Mark demanded.

"Am I in trouble?"

"Not if you tell me what they said," Mark answered.

"He said something about child support, that he hadn't paid it, and he gave me some money to warn him."

"When they checked in?" Mark asked.

"No, just a few days ago."

"How much did he pay you?"

"Just twenty bucks."

"What does he look like?" Mark asked.

"A big man." The clerk spread out his arms, and Mark thought about Chloe. "Brown hair, black glasses."

"Did he bring a woman here?" Mark asked.

"I don't notice what our guests do." He shook his head quickly. "We respect their privacy."

"Sure. What else is there for you to do here at night?" Mark said.

"I don't . . . We respect privacy."

"Tell me, now," Mark said impatiently.

"She was young, hot, big tits." He started to smile. "In my younger days—"

"Of course," Mark said, then looked at Matthews. "What room is he in?"

"Twenty-four."

"Please step out from behind the counter, sir," Mark said.

"Am I under arrest?" He walked toward Mark. "He said child support, that's all."

"It's not about child support," Mark said, looked around the room, and saw the word "Men" on an old wooden door across the counter.

"Should I put him in there, sir?" Mark said to Matthews.

Matthews nodded.

"Come with me, sir." Mark grabbed his left arm firmly.

Inside the men's room, Mark saw the sink outside the stall and handcuffed him to the plumbing underneath it.

"I promised him," the old man whined.

"Integrity, an endangered species today," Mark said.

"But—"

"My father would have said something like that to you."

"I told him." The old man lifted his arm, and Mark heard the handcuffs grind against the steel pipe underneath the sink.

"Don't worry. I'll keep your promise," Mark said, then walked outside.

"Boston PD is on the way," Matthews said.

Behind the counter, Mark saw a key hanging on the wall just under the word "Master." He took the key off the hook.

"They don't expect us now," Mark said to Matthews, "and they're probably sleeping."

"All right."

At the door to room 24, Mark nodded, then inserted the master key. To his right, Matthews waited with his gun in his right hand. Off to his left, Mark heard the clanging sound of solid ice cubes landing at the bottom of the old, rusty ice machine.

"Wait," he whispered until he heard the ice machine again. He turned the key and heard the vacuum-like sound as he shoved open the heavy metal door.

From the low-wattage lightbulb just outside the room, he saw a man turn toward the nightstand and the lamp bolted down on top of it.

"Lou Mark, FBI." He pointed his gun at him. "You're under arrest."

The man turned away from Mark and struggled with the covers and the heavy comforter as he tried to get off the queen-size bed. At its foot, he set his right leg down on the floor and tried to free his left, but Mark stomped down sharply on his right foot, then shoved his face into the worn carpeting.

Mark stuck his right knee on his back, then placed the muzzle of the gun against the back of his head.

"Not a word," Mark whispered to him, "not a single fucking word."

"What—"

"Not a fucking word. Sir, I think Boston PD can move in on the other two rooms now."

Mark heard Matthews speak softly into the cell phone and, minutes later, heard the SWAT team break through the doors on the adjoining rooms.

"Let me up, goddammit." The man wheezed. "I can't breathe."

"I need your handcuffs, sir," Mark said.

"Wait," Matthews said as he saw the SWAT team bring out four men. "We got them," he added as he walked toward Mark and handed him the handcuffs. "I can't believe it. After two years, we finally caught them."

Matthews turned on the light inside the room and saw a small open suitcase on the dresser next to the television, filled with expensive watches and diamonds. On the carpet next to the television, Matthews saw two suitcases.

"They were about to leave," Matthews said.

"Yes, sir." Mark cuffed him, then looked around the room. He saw a gun, black-rimmed glasses, and three packs of cigarettes on the nightstand next to the bed.

Mark remembered the videotape of the last robbery.

"He's the one." Mark pointed at the man lying on the floor. "He's the one who shot the security guard in the throat. Ballistics should match the bullet. And he hit that woman three times before she fell to the floor and her brain hemorrhaged."

"How do you know it was him?" Matthews asked.

"I can see it."

"How?" Matthews asked. "Some of the others were his size, and they were all wearing ski masks during the robbery."

"He likes to hurt people." Mark shrugged. "That deaf girl, Chloe, was right."

"But how could you see it?" Matthews asked again.

"The way he moves. How he tried to get away from us here, and I remembered the videotapes we watched of the other robberies."

"I didn't see it," Matthews said.

"It's just something I learned to do a long time ago."

"Fuck you," the man muttered into the carpet.

"I want to go back to Babes and tell Chloe that she doesn't need to be afraid anymore."

"Why?" Matthews shrugged. "Why do you care? She's just a stripper."

"She's just a fucking hooker," the man said, "and she's the reason you caught us. It's the only mistake I've made in two years. I should have killed her after I fucked her."

"You won't have that chance again," Mark said quietly.

The SWAT team picked him up and led him from the room.

"If the old man had called them," Matthews paused, "they would have killed us."

"Maybe, but he didn't know who they were."

"I won't forget."

"Thank you, sir."

"You told me when we started this case that you wanted to work in Behavioral Science, for Joe Mosely. Why in the hell would you want to do that?"

"I don't know—maybe because my father told me about them a long time ago."

"Serial killers?"

"Yes, sir."

"Your father was a cop?"

Mark nodded.

"I'll call Joe, and I'll call Tom Anglen. Do you know Tom?"

"I met him at the Academy."

"He's Joe's senior field agent. He's tracked serial killers on and off for twenty years. He killed a few of them. Maybe you'll work with him one day, but I heard he was leaving Behavioral Science. I'll call tomorrow."

"Yes, thank you, sir."

CHAPTER 2

E VAN SMILED. "I think you're the first Royce I've ever met."

"A lot of people say that."

She looked around the place. They were at a small bar and restaurant in a place called the Flats in Cleveland, Ohio. They had only met a few days ago.

"Tell me what it's like being a court reporter."

"Interesting sometimes." She shrugged and looked around, checking the place out. "It depends on the lawyer and the case."

"Why . . . ," he started to say and stopped. "You don't seem to be comfortable here."

"I'm sorry, Evan. I should have told you on our first date."

"What?"

"I have a boyfriend, sort of, but it's not working out. He's a real estate lawyer. I met him at a deposition. He comes here sometimes."

"Do you want to go somewhere else?"

"No." She shook her head.

"Maybe you'd feel more comfortable if we got a table in the back of the dining room."

"That's a good idea."

In the booth, he stared at her blonde hair and her green eyes. "Do you want to talk about it?"

"I don't know." She shook her head. "I mean, we just met a few days ago."

"All right."

They ordered appetizers, and she picked at them, then pushed the plate aside.

"I shouldn't say this because you know I write for a magazine about birds, but that's how you eat."

"I'm thirty-eight"—she shrugged—"and it's just harder now to stay in shape."

"You're in great shape. Why did you become a court reporter?"

"My dad. He used to be a lawyer, then he became corporate counsel for a local company that went public. Now he runs the company."

She looked around the dining room. It was a Monday night, and there were about twenty tables in the middle of the room and a half-dozen booths around it.

"We can still go somewhere else," he said. "Or you can go if you need to."

"My dad wants me to be safe. He wants me to have what I want."

"What do you want?"

"I told him about you." She took a sip of her wine, then set it down.

"Really? My name?"

"No," she shook her head. "Would it matter?"

"No, of course not. You didn't tell me what you want."

"A family," she said simply.

"Children?"

"Yes." She nodded.

"And that's the problem with the real estate lawyer?"

"Maybe," she said. "He works a lot, and he's committed to that."

"Family is important," he said, then nodded. "I agree with you. They made me what I am today."

"What does your father do?" she asked.

"He's retired now."

"Your mom?"

"She died."

"I'm sorry."

"I like your voice." Evan reached across the table and touched her hand. "It reminds me of something from a long time ago."

"And I like your voice, "Royce slowly withdrew her hand from his. "I noticed it when we talked the first time. It's deep and a little bit hoarse, like a voice you might hear on a radio station."

"My mother said something like that a long time ago."

"Really?"

"I got you something, a small present," Evan said.

"What is it?"

"Can I give it to you at your condo?"

"I don't know." She shook her head slowly. "My dad taught me to be careful. He said you never know . . ."

"If you want, I'll leave after I give it to you."

She smiled. "All right."

He paid the bill in cash, and they drove to her condo. Inside, he looked at the pictures on the walls.

"Erte." He nodded. "I always liked him."

"I think his work is so elegant."

"I'll be back in a minute," he said.

Outside, he opened the passenger door to the rental car and lifted the black sheet over the birdcage. She was sleeping, and when he lightly tapped on the cage, she opened her eyes.

"It's time to sing," he whispered, then dropped the sheet and lifted the cage in the air.

"Thank you, Evan," she said after she lifted the black sheet over the cage. "What kind of bird is it?"

"They call them nightbirds. They mate for life. They're loyal to each other. They are the only bird you can hear singing in the middle of the night."

He stepped behind her and rubbed her shoulders, then her arms, as she looked at the bird.

"You never told me why your father named you Royce."

"It was his paternal grandmother's name." She leaned back against him, then turned. "Thank you. I like the bird."

"You have to be careful," he warned her. "Until they get to know and trust you, they're aggressive. They are the pit bulls of the bird world. They'll kill and eat each other. But once they're your friend . . ."

"Friends are so important." She kissed him, lightly at first and then deeper.

In the bedroom, he lifted himself above her, then moved slowly until he felt her body stiffen, then relax, beneath him.

"That was good," she said. "My father . . ."

He saw the tiny beads of sweat on her face and her breasts.

"That feels good," she said as she felt the edges of his fingertips stroking her arms. "I love to be touched. It's been so long since someone touched me."

She moved her hips slightly on the bed when she felt his hand. "Since my divorce, there's only been one man until tonight."

"What about the lawyer?" He asked.

"It just hasn't quite happened."

"Why?"

"I couldn't trust anyone for so long," she whispered. "My father told me to be careful. To make sure I trusted you. But I liked the bird."

"Good." He started to pull away.

"Hold me," she whispered.

He lay on his side with the side of his face against hers and felt the sweat. After a few minutes, he pulled away and sat on the edge of the bed. With the back of his left hand, he wiped the sweat off his face and on her sheets.

He saw the display cabinet on the left side of her bed.

"I like that." He pointed.

She sat up. "The crystal?"

"Yes, I like the train."

"It's my favorite piece. What is it, Evan?"

"I want to check on her"—he stood up—"make sure she's comfortable."

"All right. You love the bird, don't you?"

"Yes."

At the open doorway to her bedroom he said, "I do like your voice."

"Thank you."

In her kitchen, he put his hand inside the cage and slowly moved his fingers up and down until he felt her feet on his index finger.

"You like to play, don't you?" He smiled.

At last, he set the bird back on the perch inside the cage. "It's time now, isn't it? It's time to sing."

In the kitchen, in a drawer under the microwave, he found what he needed and walked back into the bedroom.

She stretched. "Are you going to sleep now?"

"Soon," he whispered.

"What is it?" she asked.

"What did your father tell you?"

"That you never know . . . what do you mean?"

"He was right." He lifted the claw hammer over his head. "You never know when you're going to meet someone like me."

"No," she begged, "please, no."

"It's time to sing."

Next to the bed, after the hammer slipped out of his hand, he looked up at her as he tried to catch his breath.

"You're beautiful," he whispered. "Your voice . . ."

In the kitchen, he lifted the door to the cage and moved his fingers slowly in front of the bird until it hopped down on his right index finger. "Thank you. Sing for me."

"I'm sorry," he said afterward as he set the dead bird back in the cage.

"You are so beautiful," he said as he lay on top of her.

Afterward, he folded her hands over her abdomen and placed her ring finger wrapped in tissue in the inside pocket of his sports coat.

"I like the train." He set it in a plastic bag. "I like the train. I could see it when we made love. Sparkling in the light."

"From now on." Evan nodded. "I'll be good. I promise."

CHAPTER 3

"IT'S ALMOST LIKE** crawling back into the womb, isn't it?" Tom Anglen pointed at the narrow entrance to the cave, shaped like a spiked, distorted half moon.

"I suppose, sir. Where do you think he is? Mexico?"

"I don't think so. The bounty hunters have already looked for him there. He left his SUV about a hundred yards from here?"

"Yes, Mr. Anglen." He nodded. "And his dog on a leash tied to the bumper of the SUV with food and water close to him."

"You can call me Tom, Lieutenant," he said, then squatted down in front of the narrow opening to the cave. From the angle of the sun, he could only see a few feet inside.

"Where does this cave end?" Anglen asked.

"I don't know." The lieutenant shrugged. "It's called by the locals as the Rock Springs Cave. It's a network that winds through the mountain."

A few hours ago, Lieutenant Nielsen had picked him up at the Phoenix Airport and driven them to Payson, Arizona, where Robert Allan Sherman had disappeared a few years ago after he murdered his family.

"I didn't expect you to be this tall," he said to Anglen.

At six four and 240 pounds with salt and pepper hair, Anglen was a good seven inches taller than Lieutenant Nielsen.

"What did you expect?" Anglen smiled.

"I don't know." He shrugged.

In the lieutenant's Explorer, he had read the file John Oliver, an analyst at the FBI, had compiled before he left Washington. At the beginning of the file was the Wanted poster.

> *FBI Ten Most Wanted Fugitives*
> *Unlawful flight to avoid prosecution—first-degree murder*
> *(three counts), arson of an occupied structure.*

"What happened to the dog?" Anglen asked.

"His secretary took him. She lives in Scottsdale with her husband. Do you want to talk with her?"

"Yes." Anglen nodded. "What's her name?"

"Candence Read. They call her Candy."

The Wanted poster read,

CAUTION

Robert Allan Sherman is wanted for allegedly killing his wife and two young children and then blowing up the house in which they lived in Scottsdale, Arizona.

Considered Armed and Extremely Dangerous

The FBI is offering a reward of up to $100,000 for information leading directly to the arrest of Robert Allan Sherman.

"The reward is substantial," Anglen said. "After he disappeared, have you received any reports on him?"

"There have been over three hundred purported sightings of the suspect in the last year in Canada, Mexico, back East. We and your Phoenix office have investigated those leads, but nothing panned out."

The case file prepared by John Oliver described a man who had what appeared to be an ideal life. He was in his early forties, a successful engineer, with an attractive wife, a nine-year-old daughter, and an eleven-year-old son. He was a member of an evangelical church in Scottsdale and was respected in that community. Yet one night after his family had gone to bed, he shot his wife in the back of the head, then slit her throat with a fishing knife. A few minutes later, he had gone to his children's bedrooms and slit their throats while they slept. The next morning, the house exploded and burned nearly to the ground. Anglen wondered what had gone wrong with this particular version of the American dream.

"Tell me what else you know about him," Anglen said.

"He was an engineer. He was the outdoors type, hunting, fishing, and he liked to explore caves. What do you call it?"

"Spelunker," Anglen answered. "Did he explore this cave?"

"I don't know." Lieutenant Nielsen shrugged. "Arizona has a lot of famous caves. The caves at the Grand Canyon are the best known, I think. This is a smaller cave, but he could have. He's also in excellent shape, works out."

"Why would he drive here—what is it, an hour and a half from Phoenix—and leave his car and his dog near this cave?"

"I don't know, sir. We couldn't figure that out either."

"How did you find the SUV and the dog?" Anglen asked.

"A local resident called us, and we ran the license plate. The car was registered to his wife."

Anglen looked at the lieutenant's Explorer on the dirt road about one hundred yards from the cave.

"How much time did you spend looking for him here?" Anglen asked.

"Weeks, sir. We learned that there's a national society for people who explore caves and we called and they put us in touch with three, uh, spelunk, whatever, and . . ."

"Civilians went in there after a man who killed his entire family?" Anglen interrupted him.

"Yes, with officers."

"And were you one of them, Lieutenant?"

"Yes, sir." He nodded. "I have two kids. I wanted to catch him."

"What was it like in there?"

"Damp, cold, wet. It snakes around, and it sometimes opens up into small rooms. And there are bats living in those rooms. Some of it is so narrow, that you have to crawl slowly through it single file. I learned that the famous large caves are mapped out like a city, but there were no maps for this cave. We finally sent a sewer camera down, kind of like a colonoscopy, but we never found him."

Anglen laughed, then looked back toward the opening to the cave.

"What was funny, sir?"

"Your analogy of a sewer camera in this cave to a colonoscopy," he answered. "But I'm impressed that you tried so hard to catch this man. You couldn't pay most people enough money to crawl inside there."

"Thank you, sir."

Anglen looked at the barren Arizona landscape.

"What is it, sir?" the lieutenant asked.

"He's very bright," Anglen said finally. "He planned this for a while. Why, I don't know yet. He has been in this cave. He knew what you would encounter. But he never went inside it the night he killed his family."

"How do you know that, sir?"

"Because he knew how much time you would spend here looking for him while he escaped."

"But what did he do after he left the car and the dog here?" Lieutenant Nielsen asked.

"He had an accomplice. Someone followed him here after he killed his family. Did you see another set of tire tracks?"

"It rained hard that morning," he answered. "There were no tracks."

"My god"—Anglen looked up—"he even planned for the weather. Now I understand why he's on our Ten Most Wanted List and why Joe sent me."

"Joe?"

"Joe Mosely, the director of the Behavioral Science Division at the FBI."

Anglen felt the dry desert breeze on his face.

"We can go, Lieutenant. Robert Sherman hasn't been living in these caves for years. It was all a red herring. You can tell me more about him on the drive back to Phoenix."

At the car, he opened the passenger door for Anglen.

"I wanted to tell you, sir, that's it's an honor to work with you on this case."

"Thank you, Lieutenant."

"I mean you're a famous FBI agent. I read about your cases where you caught serial killers. You're here because Sherman is a serial killer?"

"No," Anglen answered. "I'm here because my boss went to law school with your governor and he asked for help."

"Sherman's not a serial killer?"

"No." Anglen stepped into the SUV. "He killed three people in a matter of minutes. At the FBI, we consider a serial killer to be a person who kills three or more people with common characteristics in more than thirty days."

"Are you tracking a serial killer now?" the lieutenant asked.

"No, I don't do that work anymore."

"Why not?"

The lieutenant closed the door after waiting for Anglen to answer him, walked around the car, then inside, started the engine.

"You didn't answer me," he said.

"I." Anglen paused. "I couldn't live in their world anymore."

"Did they scare you?" he asked.

"They scare everyone."

"What's it like to be close to them?" the lieutenant asked.

"Serial killers?"

"Yes, sir."

"In some ways"—Anglen paused—"it's like when you crawled into that cave."

Anglen heard the gravel pop up under the tires as the lieutenant turned the car around on the dirt road.

When he had told Trish a few days later that Joe had given him an assignment in Arizona, she had looked away, then asked if it was another serial killer. After he had said no, she sighed in relief.

"Can you find him?" the lieutenant asked.

"Maybe. He couldn't stand his life anymore, so he burned it to the ground. Most men just get a divorce, pay child support, and find another woman to spend time with. I saw in the case file that he came from a divorced home and that his brother killed himself. I don't know what that means yet. You'll have to tell me more about him."

"He was an amateur artist. He drew pictures of his wife, kids, his dog."

"What else do you know?"

"We think he disconnected the gas connection on the furnace, then rigged the house to explode. He also poured accelerant on the bodies and throughout the house," the lieutenant said.

"He poured gasoline on the bodies of his family after he killed them?"

"Yes, sir. He was hoping to burn up any evidence of the crimes." He turned onto the freeway. "Can you find him?" the lieutenant asked again.

"Did he paint any pictures of his secretary?"

"Not that we know of."

Anglen adjusted the seat to recline backward and stretched out his long legs.

"We'll be back in Phoenix in a little more than an hour. Are you going to sleep, sir?"

"Yes."

"You didn't answer me, sir."

"He created his future before he killed his family, but he didn't destroy everything from the past," Anglen answered.

"I don't understand, sir."

"The dog and the accomplice."

"So you think you know where he is?"

"Yes." Anglen nodded. "He set you up to believe he was here years ago, then I think he came back, knowing you would never look here again."

"You mean he's in Payson?"

"Or close by. But the answer is in Phoenix. Wake me when we get there."

At Quantico, in Joe's office, he had watched the video segment several times about Robert Sherman on a national television program devoted to catching fugitives. On the second broadcast of that story, Robert Sherman had called in.

"I had to do it. I just wanted everyone to know that. I did it for them."

"Who is this?" the host had asked.

"I just wanted people to know that what happened in Scottsdale had to be done. That's all."

"Is this Robert Sherman?" the host had asked. "Is this the man who killed his family?"

The television show had traced the call to a small town in North Carolina, but Robert Allan Sherman had escaped yet again.

"Why would he call?" Anglen mumbled.

"What, sir?" the lieutenant asked.

"Nothing, Lieutenant. I want to go to his former secretary's home about the time she and her husband get home from work."

Anglen closed his eyes and remembered talking with his wife a few days before Joe had given him this case and he had left for Arizona.

"I have only two months left on this rotation in Behavioral Science. I just do profiling now and some work in the lab. I told Joe today that I was going to take my life back, that in two months I was finished with the Serial Killer Division."

"Then will you retire?"

"Yes"—he nodded—*"in a year or so. I'll work in another division for a while or in the office. We're okay financially, aren't we?"*

"Yes. But what about the work?"

"I'm forty-nine now. I've done this long enough. I want to spend more time with you, Sean, and Mary."

"Mrs. Read," he said at the door, "I'm Lieutenant Nielsen with the Scottsdale Police Department, and this is Mr. Thomas Anglen with the FBI."

"Robert again?" She shook her head.

"Yes, ma'am. May we come in?"

"I've talked to the police and the FBI before," she said to them. "Why now?"

"He's still at large, Mrs. Read," Anglen said.

"All right, come in. We were having dinner."

The house was small and worn, like the furniture in the living room inside.

"Do you have a new lead?" she asked.

"Who is it, Candy?" her husband shouted from the dining room.

"Maybe," Anglen answered her.

She was, he guessed, about five foot five and maybe 120 pounds, with brown hair. She was in her late thirties. In many ways, she looked like the photographs he had seen of Sherman's wife in the case file.

"The police and the FBI, hon."

"Sherman again?" he asked.

"Yes," she said.

"I wish you had never worked for him."

"So do I."

Anglen saw her husband sitting at the dining room table, a young child in a high chair, then the painting on the wall over the couch. He motioned toward Candy Read. "Did Robert Sherman paint that portrait of you?" Anglen pointed at the picture over the couch.

"Yeah, he did," her husband answered. "It's kind of a conversation piece now when neighbors come over, but I'm going to sell it on eBay after he's caught. I figure it will be worth something then."

"Mrs. Read, could we speak outside?"

She gestured toward the front door. "All right."

After they were outside, Anglen took a file from his briefcase.

"Does your husband know?" Anglen asked.

"Know what?" She nervously rubbed her hands together.

He took a series of Visa bills from the file and handed them to her.

"What is that?" She thumbed through the bills. "Robert's credit card?"

"They are bills for restaurants and hotels prior to his disappearance," Anglen answered. "We have several witnesses who say you were with him at that time."

"I've waited for this day for over a year," she said finally.

"I saw your son's eyes," Anglen said. "Does your husband know?"

"No." She shook her head quickly. "He can never know that. You know he's crazy," she continued.

"Yes. I'll make sure he doesn't hurt you or your family."

Her eyes darted around the front yard of her home for a moment. "Will you tell my husband?"

"I will if you don't help us," Anglen answered.

"I don't know what to do," she whispered. "He's crazy. He'll kill me."

"When was the last time you saw him?"

"He took me hunting once," she said. "He killed a mountain lion, then smeared its blood on his chest."

"Where, Mrs. Read?"

"If he finds out Joey is his, if my husband finds out . . ."

Anglen watched her turn toward him.

"You promise?"

"Yes."

"He's in a little town near Payson. Camp Verde, it's called. He delivers pizzas at night."

"When you followed him that night to Payson, did you know he had killed his family?" Anglen asked.

"No, of course not." She shook her head quickly. "He said he was going away for a while, disappear, and then we could be together. I didn't know until the next day."

Anglen heard a siren, then a dog howling behind the house.

"His dog?" he asked.

"Yes." She nodded.

"Your husband never thought that you and Sherman . . ."

"We got married right out of high school, when we were eighteen," she explained. "Life becomes just a routine. We watch the same television programs together, you know American Idol, whatever, have sex a couple of times a month. No, he never thought I'd have sex with anyone else. That's why I did it. Robert had energy. I thought he cared. It was different."

"Do I need to leave Lieutenant Nielsen here?" Anglen asked.

"You think I might call and warn him?"

Anglen nodded.

"If he found out I talked to you, he'd kill me. What do you think?"

Anglen reached inside the pocket of his sports coat, then dialed Joe's number.

"I know where he is," Anglen said into the cell phone.

"Where?"

"Camp Verde in Arizona. I need a helicopter. I'll have him tonight. He won't escape this time."

"It will be ready for you when you get to the airport," Joe said.

"You won't tell my husband?" Mrs. Read asked after Anglen closed the cell phone.

"Why would I?" Anglen shrugged.

"After I knew what he did, having sex with him was like having sex with something cold, like death. I was scared. I didn't know someone could do what he did."

"What's the name of the pizza place?" Anglen asked impatiently.

"Roselli's. You're not going to arrest me, Mr. Anglen?"

"No, Mrs. Read, I'm only interested in him. What name is he using?"

"He created five new identities before he did it, new driver's licenses and social security numbers. He's using the name James Wilson now," she answered.

"And where does he live?"

"In a small apartment complex called the Pines."

"Why didn't you turn him in?" Anglen asked.

"I thought he would do to my family what he did to his that night."

"Thank you for your help."

Roselli's was in a strip shopping center just off the highway. On one side was a used bookstore and on the other side, a massage parlor that, according to the sign, had licensed masseuses available at virtually anytime, day or night. Inside Roselli's, Anglen counted twelve tables with customers at five of them, saw the small bar with four stools in front of it and the TV just above the bar. Near the front window, Anglen sat down at a table, ordered a small pepperoni pizza, and waited. Occasionally, he could hear the phone ringing and watched an older man that he assumed was Roselli taking a delivery order. He had not yet seen anyone who matched the description of Robert Sherman.

"Do you like the pizza, sir?" the waitress asked.

From the kitchen behind the bar, he saw a man walk in wearing a green army jacket and faded jeans. He looked like the guy who delivers a pizza on a Saturday night whom you never really see and never remember.

Lieutenant Nielsen was waiting in an unmarked car across the street from the small parking lot in front of Roselli's, and in the back were two FBI agents in separate cars.

He left fifteen dollars on the table, stood up, and walked past the waitress to the bar and sat down on the barstool next to Sherman.

"Mr. Roselli?" Anglen said.

"Yes."

"I'm new in town, from Phoenix. Could you get me a Bud Light?"

"Sure, sir."

Roselli had a heavy Italian accent, some of which he was sure was an affectation designed for customers. He heard Sherman shift nervously back and forth on the barstool and saw the gun under the green army jacket tucked into the waistband of his faded jeans.

"Can I buy you a beer?" he turned toward Sherman.

"No, I'm . . ."

With his right hand, Anglen reached slowly for the beer Roselli had set on the bar in front of him, then grabbed the back of Sherman's hair and tried to push his face down on the bar. Sherman fought back and reached for the gun in the waistband of his jeans. Anglen felt his strength as he twisted his neck back and forth and pushed against the raised edge of the bar with his left hand. For a few moments, Anglen stared into the absolute insanity of his eyes, until he felt the barstool tilt, released him, then smashed the beer bottle into his face as he toppled backward. The sound of Sherman's head hitting the hardwood floor in the normally quiet restaurant was like a gunshot. Anglen stood over him, then stomped down on his face three times with the heel of his shoe before he reached down and took the gun from the waistband of his faded old jeans.

"Tom Anglen, FBI." He held his badge in the air and looked around the room.

"He was my delivery guy," Roselli said, this time without even a hint of an Italian accent.

"He's a fugitive," Anglen said as he saw the blood flowing from Sherman's broken nose.

After he called Lieutenant Nielsen, he watched him handcuff Sherman, then walk him out of the restaurant.

"It was Candy, wasn't it?" Sherman spit blood on the asphalt parking lot. "I'll kill her."

"They have the death penalty in this state," Anglen said. "I don't think you're going to kill anyone else."

Inside the car, on the way to the airport, Anglen dialed Joe's home number.

"We got him, "Anglen said. "We're on our way back to Phoenix. I should be home tomorrow."

"Thank you, Tom," Joe said. "I'll see you tomorrow at Quantico."

Anglen turned away and looked out of the windshield of the car at the desert and the mountains.

"I made a promise," Anglen said.

"What, sir?" Lieutenant Nielsen asked as he turned onto the road leading to the airport.

"I made a promise to Candy Read."

"What do you mean, sir?" The Lieutenant asked.

"Tomorrow, call Candy Read," Anglen said. "And I'm going home."

"Yes, sir, I'll call her and tell her he's in custody."

CHAPTER 4

JOE MOSELY LOOKED at the six photographs John Oliver had tacked to the bulletin board in his office when he had come in a few minutes ago.

"The women in the first two photographs lived in San Francisco." Oliver pointed at the photographs on the left side of the bulletin board. "The second two photos, Chicago, and the last two photos are of women who lived in St. Louis. All of them were killed over an eleven-week time span, in roughly ten—to fourteen-day intervals. The last one was killed three weeks ago."

"They don't have faces," he said slowly as he studied the photographs.

Each photograph was of a young woman in good physical shape lying on a bed. With the exception of the blood splatters on their breasts and arms, their bodies were untouched.

"Six in a little less than three months in three different cities?" he asked.

"Yes and no, sir." Oliver shook his head.

In the first photo, the orbital bones over her eyes, as well as her eyes, nose, and cheekbones were crushed, and he could see brain tissue underneath the dried blood on what had once been her face. In each photo, he saw blood splatters on the wall behind the bed, stretching out like long, jagged fingers.

"What do you mean, no?"

"There are more, sir. Those are just the last six."

"I'm sorry." He turned away from the bulletin board and stared at Oliver. "You said there are more?"

He nodded.

"How many?"

"Forty-seven, sir."

Joe Mosely walked to his desk and looked out the window of his office at the training facilities at Quantico and the students who would soon be FBI agents. He had been the director of the Behavioral Science Section, better known as the Serial Killer Division, for more than twenty years. John Oliver was an analyst who had worked for him for the last five years. His job was to evaluate homicides on the FBI computer and find serial killers.

"Did you say he's killed forty-seven women?" he said slowly.

"Yes, sir."

"In San Francisco, Chicago, and St. Louis?"

"No, sir. He's done it all over the country."

"Over a long period of time?" Joe asked.

Joe, who would be sixty-three years old in a few months, was five foot eight, weighed 155 pounds, and had thinning gray hair. He had been born in Georgia, in a small town near Atlanta, and still had, at times, the remnants of a Southern drawl in his measured speech. Oliver was several inches taller, a good fifty pounds heavier, and only thirty-one years old.

"Not really, sir. He's killed forty-seven women in about two years."

"Are they hookers?"

"No, sir." Oliver shook his head. "They have regular jobs."

"It's not possible." Joe turned his attention to Oliver. "These women had families, friends, people who cared about them and who would have wanted the man caught. Are you sure it's the same man?"

"Yes, sir."

"It must have taken you a long time to do this," Joe said.

"I've been working on it for the last ten weeks, eighteen hours each day."

Before he joined the Bureau, John Oliver had been an accountant at a medium-sized firm in Cleveland. He had a gift for doing research, which was the patience to sit for days at his computer once he thought he had found evidence of a serial killer.

"Tell me how you did it," Joe said.

"I found her." He pointed at the first photo on the left side of the bulletin board. "Because she was killed in her apartment in bed, I assumed it was domestic, a boyfriend, husband, or ex-husband. Then, by accident, I found a second one in San Francisco. I looked at the photos of both of them before he did it and noticed that they looked like sisters."

"You're saying the profile is the same?"

"Yes, sir. Blonde, tall, in good shape. Thirty-five to forty years old. Divorced. No children."

"What did you do after you found her?" He pointed at the second photograph on the bulletin board.

"I created a general profile in terms of the age and appearance of the victims and their marital status and searched local police computers in large cities. I found lots of women who fit that general description, but they were killed by boyfriends or ex-husbands who were in custody. I refined the model and then found the first one in Chicago, then the second one, but I still wasn't sure"—he paused—"until I found two other common elements."

"What were they?" Joe said slowly. His speech pattern was a mixture of his training, his mind, and his Southern upbringing—deliberative and respectful, halting, at times.

"The birds," he answered.

"What do you mean?"

"They all had birds as pets, and he kills them too. He crushes them in his hands."

"What was the other common element?"

"He takes a body part with him"—he lifted his hand—"the ring finger on the left hand. A trophy, I suppose. I haven't figured out yet what kind of tool it is—carpentry, farm, whatever—but there's a nick in the cutting edge, and it's the same on every victim. Then I found the two in St. Louis and, over the last few weeks, found forty-one more, all across the country."

"How does he kill?" Joe asked.

"He smashes their skull with something I think he finds in their kitchen. He's used a rolling pin, ball-peen hammer, claw hammer, you name it—whatever he finds."

"You're saying"—Joe paused—"that he brings with him the tool he uses to cut off their ring finger, but he doesn't bring the weapon he uses to kill them?"

"Yes, sir, that's right."

"Why would he do that?" Joe asked.

"I don't know, sir."

"He has sex with them?"

"Yes. The victim is always naked in her bed. There are no defensive wounds, her hands aren't crushed or broken. They trusted him. It's almost like they wanted or expected something from him."

Oliver looked at the photographs on the bulletin board, then shook his head.

"What is it, John?"

"I enjoy doing the research," he answered. "Once I think I've found one, it's hard for me to stop working on it. But I never get used to what I ultimately find. I never understand why they do it."

"The United States produces more serial killers than any other country. Nearly 85 percent of the world's serial killers are here. Right now, there are anywhere from twenty to fifty active serial killers in this country. After more than twenty years in this job, I don't understand either, John."

"Any prints, semen, or DNA? Anything we can use?" Joe asked after a few minutes.

"No, sir. He's careful, neat, clean. I even think he washes off the murder weapon in the bathtub before he places it next to the bed, next to her. In some of the reports from the local police, they found trace elements of the victim's blood in the bathtub."

"You found the murder weapon next to the bed in each case?"

"No, sir, but in a lot of the crime scene photos I saw it. In the cases where I didn't see it, it was, I think, because of the angle of the crime scene photos taken by the local police photographer."

"He uses a condom?"

"I'm sure he does." Oliver nodded.

"You're good," Joe said. "I should make you a field agent."

"No, sir"—Oliver shook his head emphatically—"this is as close as I want to get to these people."

"Of course."

"There's one other thing," Oliver said.

"What is it?"

"I think he has sex with them again after he kills them."

"After he crushes their skulls?" Joe looked again at the photographs on the bulletin board.

"Yes, sir. It's the way the body is positioned on the bed. The . . . I can't explain it, but I'm sure."

"Amazing." Joe looked away. "Do we have a profile on him yet?"

"No, sir. I just figured this out, and I didn't want to wait."

"The last one we know about was killed how long ago?"

"Three weeks."

"So he's due now or he's already killed again?"

"Yes, sir."

"It doesn't make sense." Joe shook his head. "How does he find his profile so fast? I mean, he has to look for them, find them, then stalk them, doesn't he? Like every other serial killer I've seen in the last twenty years."

"Apparently not, sir."

"One more, and he'll match the Green River Killer, but he only killed prostitutes. How the hell did we miss this for so long?"

"He's smart," John Oliver answered. "He never kills more than two in the same city, then moves on. He must know that we don't get notified until there are three victims."

"Go to our profilers and work with them. Tell them to make this a priority," Joe said.

"Yes, sir."

"And now I have to decide who I'm going to send to catch this one."

Oliver walked to the door of Joe's office and, after he opened it, stopped and turned back toward Joe.

"Tom Anglen?" Oliver asked.

"He is the best, but I don't know." Joe shook his head.

"You were thinking about the new agent, Lou Mark, weren't you, Mr. Mosely?"

"In part, but he's too green. He just joined us."

"He just caught the Mall Bandits. He volunteered for Behavioral Science, and almost nobody does. And wasn't his father a legendary cop in the Midwest?"

"I know all that. I met his father. Go to work, John. Thank you."

"What else were you thinking, sir?"

"I just met with Tom before he went to Arizona and caught Robert Sherman. You did good work on that file."

"Thank you, sir."

"He said he was going to retire to spend time with his family. I promised him he wouldn't have to do this again." He looked up. "I want to hear from you in two hours."

"Yes, sir."

After Oliver left his office, Joe turned back to the window behind his desk and remembered when he'd met Mark's father. He had been a field agent then, working on a case involving a serial killer in Des Moines. The legend was that at the crime scene, Mark's father could visualize the crime as if it were happening again. It was his gift.

"You should come to work for us," Joe remembered saying to Mark's father many years ago.

"No." Mark's father had shaken his head. "I can't stand the images or the feelings. I can feel their energy, cold like death before they kill, then hot as the sun when they do it, then cold again afterward. They are the monsters of our time. And they always come back."

"I don't know if I believe completely in what you can see, but I watched you catch this man, and I think your talent is wasted as a detective for the Des Moines Police."

"I was born not far from here." Mark's father had ignored him. "It's about an hour commute to the farm, but I have an apartment in town. My son and my wife live there, and I see them on the weekends. He's only seven now, but he can see already, as I can, and I think he's smarter than I am."

"Are you sure you don't want to think about—"

"He may fight it for a while," Mark's father continued, "but in the end, it won't matter how hard he fights. It's in our family."

"Did you fight it?"

"No, it was different for me. But maybe someday he'll knock on your door."

I can't send him on this case, Joe thought, remembering Mark's eyes, deep blue and ice-cold, like oval-shaped diamonds, just like his father's eyes. But how can I ask Tom to do this again?

Joe leaned across his desk, pushed the intercom button on the telephone, then paused.

"Mr. Mosely, what is it?"

I made a promise, he thought.

"Julie, call the director and tell him I need to meet with him today."

CHAPTER 5

"IT'S A LITTLE Italian restaurant in Rocky River on the west side called Mancuso's. I haven't been there, but friends tell me it's terrific," Evan said.

"That sounds good, Michael. I live in Lakewood, which isn't far. I'll meet you there at seven-thirty?"

He had used the name Michael when they'd met. It was their second date, and this time he was certain they'd have sex.

"Yes, Monica. You looked good the last time," he added.

"Thank you."

"I want to get to know you better"—he hesitated—"with time of course."

"I think I do too," she answered.

She was thirty-eight years old, had been married once, and had no children. She worked as an account manager for the largest seller of frozen foods in Ohio. They shipped all over the country, she had told him the first time they met. He remembered he had trouble focusing on her words as he saw her long blond hair sway across her shoulders.

"I'm looking forward to it," he said.

Evan was sitting on the bed in the hotel room, and, for a moment, he stared at the crystal train on the dresser next to the television. The light from the lamp was shining inside it. It had been thirteen days since he had last seen Royce and taken the train.

"I have a present for you, tonight," he said. "Nothing expensive, I just think you'll like her."

"Her?"

"You'll see."

After he had made sure the blinds over the window were tightly shut, he had turned on the light in the bedroom and noticed the crystal, again, near the window in the bedroom of Royce's condo. The train was on the top shelf, and he had set the hammer down on the hunter-green carpeting. As he looked at it, he felt a drop of blood roll slowly down his face and land on the Plexiglas top.

"We probably should get going," she said, "I need to get ready."

He had opened the latch on the side with the claw portion of the hammer, then gently pulled the door open with it.

"I want to see this," he had said as he reached inside and lifted the train off the tracks carefully, then the tracks underneath it, making sure he didn't touch anything else.

"Thank you," he looked over at her lying on the bed.

With a Kleenex from her nightstand, he dabbed twice at the blood until it soaked through onto his fingers.

"You're right. I'll be on time."

"I'll see you soon, Michael."

"Good-bye."

Evan turned off the phone and dropped it lightly on the bed.

Next to the train on the dresser was a birdcage with a black cover over it. He lifted the cover and smiled.

"I'm going to give you to a friend tonight." He reached his hand inside, and the bird dropped onto his outstretched index finger.

"Are you going to sing tonight?"

The bird pecked lightly on his left thumb.

"Of course you are." He set the bird back on its perch and pulled the black sheet over the cage.

In the shower, he thought about Royce. *She looked more like her than any of them,* he thought as he rinsed the shampoo out of his hair. Her voice was almost the same.

He looked at himself in the mirror, fogged over at the top and bottom from the heat of the shower. When he was home, he worked out nearly every day, and when he was gone, he would use whatever they had at the motels he stayed at.

With the hair dryer attached to the wall, he slowly blew his hair dry. When he walked out and looked at the train, he knew where he would put it when he got home.

"I'll have to put it in the office at home," he said. "On top, yes, on top of the cabinet."

He looked in the tiny open closet area and the luggage rack underneath.

"You always have to present yourself well." He nodded. "My father taught me that and so many other things."

He selected a white shirt, a pair of blue slacks, and a navy sports coat. He remembered the last time he had seen him. Now he was old and gray, but he had been strong a long time ago.

"I need to be early," he said, looking in the mirror. "I need to show respect."

At the dresser, he adjusted the collar of his shirt, then picked up the cage next to the train.

"I'll be leaving here soon," he mumbled to himself as he set the birdcage in the backseat of the rental car.

It was about a twenty-minute drive from his motel to the restaurant, and he talked to the bird while he watched the bright lights from the oncoming traffic.

"I know you won't sing until I tell you to."

He heard his bird moving around in the cage each time he hit a depression or small pothole in the road.

"Cleveland." He laughed. "I'm only here because of you, Monica."

Through the light rain, which was becoming sleet, he missed the entrance to the restaurant twice before he pulled in the parking lot behind it.

"I won't be long."

Inside, he sat in the small bar, which had five tables and only four worn barstools at the bar. He ordered a glass of red wine and watched the front door.

Sex with Royce had been exceptional, Evan remembered. He wondered what it would be like with Monica.

His glass of wine was half full when he saw her walk through the door and wipe her feet on the rubber mat just inside.

"Monica." He stood up and hugged her. "It's a pleasure to see you again."

He waited while she took off her coat and sat down. She was wearing a black off-the-shoulder top with a skirt that stopped just above her knees.

"What would you like?" he asked.

"What you're having." She pointed at the glass of wine.

He nodded at the waitress, then ordered a glass of Merlot.

"I'd forgotten how bad the weather can be here this time of year," he said.

"We try to ignore it. Cold winters, hot, humid summers."

She turned when she heard a sound from the dining room. "I heard a baby." She smiled.

"Do you want a family?" He thought about the crystal train in his hotel room and the light sparkling inside it.

"Tell me about the present." She smiled as she ignored his question and listened to the sound of the baby crying in the dining room.

"Not now. I'll tell you when the time is right."

"When?"

"Later. When it's time to sing." Evan smiled.

"What do you mean?"

"You'll see."

CHAPTER 6

TOM ANGLEN KNELT down before the altar and bowed his head. He loved the old Catholic church, and, with the exception of an old woman in a pew a few rows behind him, he was alone. After a few minutes, he lifted his head and looked at the statue of Mary, then lit a candle and placed it on the altar near her feet. It was early afternoon, his favorite time to visit the church. On a hot day, the air was cool and fresh, and the light coming through the stained-glass windows was soft and ethereal. On a cold day, he felt the warmth and strength of the old oak pews. As Trish would say, he always felt safe there.

He focused on his family—his son Sean, who would graduate from high school in a few months and, in the fall, start college, and his daughter Mary, who would start high school next semester.

"Blessed Mother," he whispered, "thank you for the peace and comfort you provide."

He heard the rustling sound of the old woman's dress as she stood up, then her limp as she walked out of the room. *It's her left leg*, he thought, without turning. His hearing had saved his life more than once. He thought about the Cat Burglar. His name was Allen Richard Matthews, and during the day, he worked as a handyman in the suburbs of Chicago. He was pleasant, sociable, gracious, and attentive while he worked, until he returned one night after he felt he knew them well enough to kill them.

"No, I can't do it again," he had said to Joe a few hours ago. *"I made a promise. You made a promise."*

"I need you."

I can't, he thought, *I can't go back into their world again.*

Most of the time, he remembered, Allen Richard Matthews would simply knock on their front door after he made sure they were alone, and they always let him into their home. Befitting his role as the neighborhood handyman, he was short, a little overweight, with thinning dark hair and a beard that looked like it hadn't been near a razor for days. Polite conversation was the only foreplay he knew, and after a while, he would knock them out, strip off their clothes, and tie them up. While he waited, he took off his own clothes and sat in a plush chair a few feet away from them until he heard them moan through the gag he had shoved in their mouth. Of the eleven victims, six were older than fifty-five, and two were in their seventies. The youngest was only twenty-two years old.

After victims six and seven, the chief of police called Joe and said he thought he had a serial killer. The double murder that night made it even easier for him to walk through the front door of the next victim's home. But it was the beard, the two-day growth, through which Anglen ultimately found the Cat Burglar.

"Blessed Mother," he whispered, "help me take my life back."

He tried to focus again on his family, but he couldn't stop thinking about the work or his meeting with Joe a few hours ago.

"Tom," Joe said, "Oliver found this one. He has killed forty-seven women in about two years. I need your help."

"You don't mean going back into the field after a serial killer?"

"Yes." Joe nodded. "I'm sorry."

"I'm not going . . . ," Anglen said. "Hold on a minute. It doesn't make sense. You said forty-seven in two years?"

"Yes."

"Do they fit the same profile?"

"Yes. They are nearly identical. They could be sisters. Blonde, attractive, in good shape, mid—to late thirties, divorced, childless."

"Are they real people? I mean the Green River Killer killed forty-eight prostitutes that nobody missed," Anglen said.

"They have regular jobs and families, Joe answered. "They're missed."

"Where does he do it? What city?"

"All over the country. Two in each city, never more, then he moves on. One other thing."

"What?"

"They all have birds as pets."

"The same kind of bird?" Anglen asked.

"They look the same. We're checking. And he kills them too."

Anglen stood up.

"Will you do it?"

"I don't know." Anglen shook his head. "I have to think about it. I don't even want to see the file now."

"I'm sorry, I know I made a promise, but you're the best field agent I have. You're the best at forensics I've ever seen. Look what you did with the Cat Burglar."

"I'll call you."

"Blessed Mother," he whispered, "what should I do?"

Birds, Anglen thought. *Why? Does it have something to do with the birds?*

There had been four more victims, he remembered, before he caught the Cat Burglar. Based on the condition of the victims' necks, Anglen had assumed the killer's hands were dry and chapped from his work and must have felt like sandpaper to the women he killed. There was one other thing he noticed in the crime scene photos. All of the women's faces were red and raw, as were their breasts, with red streaks across them as if made with a dull blade. Three more women died before he knew what it meant, and one more died before he knew it was the handyman.

"Joe, it's his beard," he had said. "Like a cat, he rubs it against their face and breasts."

"During the rape?"

"I think so." Anglen nodded. "Can we map the scratches on their faces with his beard?"

"I don't know, we've never tried that. But it changes, it grows, he shaves."

"Some," Anglen said, "but not much. He's playing a role. Like a stage actor putting on his makeup each night. He's the handyman. He thought about this. He studied it."

"Don't we have enough now?"

"No."

Anglen had looked down at the body of victim number 11.

"She's just like the others," he said. "The force of his hands fractured the cartilage in her neck and ruptured blood vessels in her brain. It's almost like a stroke, isn't it?"

"Yes."

For two days, Anglen had waited outside the small home of Allen Richard Matthews. With the exception of a candle downstairs and one in an upstairs window, the house was completely dark. After two days, he heard from Joe.

"It's not definitive, but it's close," Joe had said. Assuming his beard is similar now, we can have one of our forensic experts testify about the scratches on the victims' faces, how they matched his beard.

"I'll call you after I have him in custody."

"Do you want help?"

"I'm not going to wait."

At the front door, he had picked the lock and slowly pushed the door open. Inside, he could smell the smoke from the candle in the room that was no longer burning. *He knows*, Anglen had thought, *he knows I'm here. He's been watching me.* After his eyes adjusted, he could see the blurred outline of furniture in the small living room and the staircase about six feet in front of him. At the landing, he thought he heard something, stopped, turned and saw nothing. A few steps later, he heard the sound again like socks gently brushing across a hardwood floor. He had waited until he heard the sound again, turned quickly, and fired. In the dark house, the spark from the hammer striking the bullet had spotlighted the man's face and the kitchen knife he held next to his head. The bullet had entered his face near his jawbone through part of his beard and exited through the back of his neck. He had dropped the knife and fallen face forward. After he kicked the knife across the hallway, Anglen had found the candle in the upstairs bedroom and set it down next to the body. With his gun aimed at the back of the man's head, Anglen had turned him over and saw the blood on his lips and face.

"How did you find me?" His voice cracked.

"Your beard. Why did you do it?" Anglen asked.

"My beard?"

"I asked why!" Anglen shouted.

"Liked them," he whispered. "I knew them."

"You killed them."

"Yes, sometimes I got angry, carried away. You know."

"No. Why the darkness here?"

"I can see in the dark better than most."

He coughed, and Anglen saw the blood land on his dirty white T-shirt near his chest. He coughed once more, and he was dead.

He had almost quit after the Cat Burglar, he remembered, but then there were others, and the work had become his life.

Anglen slowly stood up and noticed the old priest standing behind the altar.

"Tom," he said, "how are you?"

"Good," he mumbled.

"Your family?"

"Good."

"You have a new case, don't you? You always come here before."

Anglen nodded.

The old priest looked at Anglen's six-foot-four-inch frame and the salt-and-pepper hair.

"A serial killer, again?" the priest asked.

"Yes, Father, if I take the case."

"I don't know how you do it." Father Caliterri looked down.

"It's my job."

"Do you know why they do it?"

"I'll get a profile if I do this. I've looked at so many of them. Ultimately, I don't know. I just know that they need to be stopped."

"How many have you killed?" Father Caliterri asked.

"Three." Anglen thought about the Cat Burglar.

"In the Bible, in the New Testament, it is said that in the beginning there was the word, and the word was made flesh. John was referring to God's words, Jesus's words, and how they grew into Christianity. These people you pursue hear a different voice, and that word becomes flesh to them."

"You're right, in a way," Anglen said.

"I've known you for a long time. You're still strong. Come and see me when you're finished. Godspeed."

"Thank you, Father."

With his left hand, he took the cell phone from the inside pocket of his sports coat.

"Joe, I'll do it, but it's the last time."

"Thank you."

"Did you tell local law enforcement?"

"Of course not," Anglen heard his slight Southern drawl. "The director reports now to the president's intelligence chief. If we can't catch one man, how could we possibly win the war against terror? Politics."

"You met with the director?"

"Yesterday." Joe sighed. "He didn't give me a choice. He said you had to catch him as fast as possible. Thank you, Tom."

The church was five miles from his home, and, as he drove away, he thought about when he had met Trish more than twenty years ago in his last year of law school. With the exception of some gray hair she colored once a month and the shallow outline of crow's feet around her eyes, she really hadn't changed much. She was nearly a foot shorter than he was at a little more than five four, with dark hair, emerald-colored eyes, and a tight body she had maintained through regular exercise. They had met at a bar across the street from the law school after an exam. After they had gone out several times, she had told him what she wanted to do after she graduated from college.

"I want to help children, help them find a place where they can feel safe. If you think about it, psychologists really can't do much more than that."

"I think most of them believe otherwise," he said.

"They're wrong," she said simply.

"Do you have a place where you feel safe?"

"I did, a long time ago." She looked away. *"But I feel safe with you now."*

"Good."

"You're like a tall strong bear. And you have an acute sense of hearing. I could tell that the night we met. I could see you turning your head and listening to us talk. You can hear people behind you. You think I'm crazy, don't you?"

"No." He had shaken his head. *"Trying to find a place where you feel comfortable, safe, is about as healthy as you can get."*

Her father had died when she was a child, Anglen thought as he turned onto the street where they had lived for more than twenty years. *That's why she needed a place where she felt safe.*

Anglen parked in the garage and closed the door behind him, then walked into the kitchen. Trish was standing at the sink, preparing dinner.

"What is it, Tom?" she asked. "You're home early."

"When will the kids be back from school?"

"You know." She laughed. "Why are you so early today?"

She had been cutting a tomato with a paring knife and she dropped them in the sink. Anglen watched the tomato roll until it stopped at the edge of the opening to the garbage disposal.

"I knew it wasn't true," she said, her hands trembling. "You're going back to work, aren't you?"

"I'm sorry." Anglen nodded. "This one has killed forty-seven women." He walked toward her and put his arms around her.

"You were just at church. You saw Father Caliterri?"

"Yes, Trish. I promise this will be the last time."

"You said that before," she whispered. "Promise me you'll come back this time."

"I always do."

She nodded, then turned and hugged him.

"Where are you going?"

"I don't know yet. We have to wait for him."

"It's not in the same place, the same city." She looked up.

"Not this one." He shook his head.

"I don't understand."

"I don't either."

She pushed him away, turned, and walked back to the sink.

On the edge of the opening to the garbage disposal, she saw the tomato, pushed it inside, and turned on the garbage disposal.

"Can you have dinner with us tonight?" she asked after she turned off the garbage disposal.

"Yes. I have a meeting with Joe tomorrow morning at seven."

"I'll pack a bag for you."

"Thank you."

"You know I hate Joe. You know I hate that old man."

"I know."

Mark turned and felt the warmth from Cara's body next to him on the queen-size bed. She was lying on her left side with her back toward him. He gently stroked her reddish-brown hair.

He twisted under the weight of the comforter until he could see the half-open curtains over the window in the bedroom.

"Are you all right, Lou?" she whispered.

"Yes, go back to sleep."

"Good."

He closed his eyes, saw the image of his father sitting in a wheelchair, then opened them and shifted his legs underneath the comforter. When he closed them again, the image was gone and his legs felt heavy as if they were in warm water.

"You have to guard against the monsters, son."

In his dream, he could hear the gunshot downstairs years ago, hear his father's voice, and then saw portraits of famous serial killers from the past in what appeared to be an art gallery—John Wayne Gacy, Jeffrey Dahmer, Bundy, Mengele. At the end of the art gallery, he saw a blank canvas without an image, color, or even lines.

For a moment, it was dark and he could no longer see the paintings or hear the hushed voices in the art gallery. Gradually, he could see light and, finally, a man standing next to a bed holding a claw hammer above his head. On the bed was a woman with reddish-brown hair looking up at the man.

"Cara," he mumbled, "Cara."

"Lou, wake up." She pushed him hard enough that he felt the edge of the bed on his right side. "What's wrong?"

He sat up, slowly, and felt the sweat on his face and in his hair.

"Nothing." He wiped the sweat off his face with the back of his hand. "Just a bad dream."

"About what?" Cara asked.

"Work."

"Your new job?"

"In a way."

Mark pushed the comforter off, got out of bed, and walked over to the window. It was nearly sunrise, and the sky was a light shade of gray.

"I got a new assignment today. Joe asked me to work with Tom Anglen on this case."

"Tom . . . ?"

"Anglen. He's the senior field agent in Behavioral Science. He's the best. I met him once while I was going through the Academy."

"A serial killer?"

Mark turned toward her and nodded.

"How many?"

"Forty-seven that we know about now."

She sat up abruptly, then walked toward him. "Forty-seven." She hugged him and placed her hand on his chest "How could anyone do that, kill forty-seven people?"

"We don't know yet." He put his arms around her waist and held her. "We don't know anything about him yet, other than the profile of the women and how he kills them."

"Don't tell me." He felt her arms tighten around his shoulders. "Don't ever tell me how they do it."

"All right."

"I wished you had stayed with Mr. Matthews's division."

"I know."

She pushed against his chest and looked up. At five foot six, she was seven inches shorter than he was and weighed about 115 pounds.

"I wanted to try working in Behavioral Science," he added.

"It's about your father again."

"I suppose."

She walked across their bedroom and sat down on the edge of the bed. "Forty-seven." She shook her head. "You'll be careful."

"Yes."

Five years ago, she remembered, after they first had sex, she'd asked him about his eyes.

"I don't know what you mean. I don't know how they're different."

"Yes. They're deep blue and ice-cold like diamonds."

"People said the same thing about my father, but we never noticed anything different about them."

"I know your father was a cop, but what did he really do?"

"He was a detective with the Des Moines Police Department, but he consulted on murder cases with other law enforcement agencies. He was the best. He could see the crime again at the crime scene. They called him the man with the eyes because of his gift."

When they had met, he had just graduated from law school and was working for a medium-sized law firm, learning to be a criminal lawyer. He was cocky then, but in a few years, he opened his own office and won several high-profile criminal cases. They were married a year after he left the law firm, and the cockiness was replaced with a sense of confidence about what he could accomplish in a courtroom. But one night, she remembered, he came home and said he was through.

"He said he'd heard that Lou Mark wins all of his cases and that he needed my help. Cara, I know that he's guilty."

"How?"

"He's an old man, and he molested a young girl. He offered me a lot of money, but I sent him out to another lawyer."

"What are you going to do?"

"Work for the FBI."

"You're chasing the monsters." She paused. "Like your father."

"Maybe."

"I knew this day would come." Cara looked up at him. "It was the old dream, wasn't it?"

Mark sat down next to her on the bed.

"Yes."

"Your father had dreams like this?"

"Not the same kind, but he'd have nightmares until he caught them."

Mark remembered what his father had told him a long time ago.

"Everything you need to know is at the crime scene, if you can see it, Louie."

When he was growing up, he would watch his father working in the den. At night, after his mother put him to bed, he would sneak downstairs, lie behind the couch, and watch his father work through the double glass doors to the den. Once, when he was seven, he had seen something in a crime scene his father hadn't yet understood, and his father had told him he had the gift. Later that night, he heard his parents arguing.

"*Lou saw something I didn't see,*" *his father had said.*

"*You showed him photos of a murder,*" *his mother had shouted.*

"*No,*" *his father had answered.* "*He just came into the den and pointed at something in one of the photos.*"

"*Then you did let him see photos of the dead woman.*"

"*I told you, he just came in,*" *his father said again.* "*But I think he has the gift.*"

"*It's not a gift, it's a curse,*" *she answered.*

"*My father taught me that if you have the gift and you don't use it, that would be the real crime.*"

"*The women, bringing death into my house!*" *she shouted.* "*Is this what you want for your son?*"

"*He has it, I know it.*"

"He has your eyes," she said after a few minutes. "Maybe you're right."

"What do you mean?"

"I saw it years ago. I just tried to ignore it."

"He has blue eyes like me. So what?" His father had shrugged.

"They're different. And I watch him rub his face like you do when you're thinking."

"You know what my father said?" Mark looked at Cara.

"What do you mean?"

"At sunrise, the monsters run away, hiding from the light, but at sundown, as the light wanes, they return."

"Right." She sighed. "I wish I could have known him. Maybe then—"

"He bludgeons them to death with something he takes from their kitchen." She saw him look up at the ceiling. "And he kills their bird after he has sex with them."

She watched Mark slowly rub the palm of his right hand across the left side of his face.

"What is it, Lou?"

"Wait."

In his mind, he scanned the crime scene photos he had looked at earlier that day at the office.

"It's about the birds. They're not pets, they're gifts. It's about the birds."

"How do you know?" Cara asked.

"I can see it," he answered. "I think I'm right. It's simply not possible that all of them could have had the same kind of bird."

"What's different about the dream this time? For the last three nights, you put your father's gun under the bed."

"Nothing." Mark shrugged.

"There's something you're not telling me."

"It's the same, Cara. I promise."

She walked over to the walk-in closet, reached up, and took a small wooden box from the top shelf.

"I have two things for you." She sat down next to him on the bed and set the box on his lap.

He opened the latch, lifted the lid, and looked at the gun.

"It's a .32," she said. "The man at the gun shop said it was accurate from short to midrange distances. He said it was reliable."

"I have my father's gun."

"I want you to get used to carrying both."

"What else?"

"This is the worst possible time to tell you," she answered. "I can't imagine anytime—"

"What? Tell me."

"I'm pregnant. I was going to tell you three days ago, but—"

Mark set the box on the bed next to her and hugged her.

"Do you know?" he asked.

"Boy? Girl? No, it's too soon."

"I can't believe it. We've been trying for more than a year, and now when—"

"I know."

"This is great news, Cara." He hugged her. "I don't know what to say."

"When was the first time you had the dream?" Cara touched his face.

"You know," Mark mumbled.

"The night your father died."

"Yes. When I could fall asleep."

"I love you, but you have to let this go. It's not your fault."

"I wish I could. I should have seen it. It was obvious to everyone else."

"You're haunted by a memory . . . I used to think I could fix this, but I can't."

"It's part of my family." Mark looked away. "It's part of me. Something happened a long time ago."

"What?"

"Someday, maybe . . . But I have to tell Mr. Mosely. This case is about the birds—they're not the victim's pets."

"I'm sorry." Mark turned back toward Cara.

"The case." He smiled, then shook his head. "I'm going to be a father, aren't I?"

"Yes." Cara nodded. "You have to be careful."

CHAPTER 7

MARK CAREFULLY EXAMINED the photographs tacked to the bulletin board in Joe's office. The first two photographs had San Francisco scrawled underneath them, the next two, Chicago, and the final two on the top, St. Louis. Underneath the two photographs of the women who had lived in San Francisco, he saw a single photograph of a woman with a stunning body and no face.

"How did he find you?" he whispered.

He turned one of the side chairs in front of Joe's desk so it faced the white-colored board, sat down, and studied the photographs.

He arrived early, and Joe's secretary, Julie, had told him to wait in his office. At six-thirty at Quantico, candidates were eating breakfast in the cafeteria or training on the obstacle course. For months, he had lived in the dormitory about a mile away from the main campus and the cafeteria. He had heard back then that despite being offered an office in the J. Edgar Hoover building in Washington, Joe had elected to work at Quantico so he could be close to students training to be FBI agents. Occasionally, Mark would see him standing at the window behind his desk and wondered if he would ever sit in that room.

The Behavioral Science Division was something candidates rarely talked about. The rumor was that a rotation in Behavioral Science was always voluntary and would never last more than three years because the psychiatrists at the FBI believed that no agent could stand it beyond that time. Tom Anglen was the exception, having done four rotations in Behavioral Science since he became an agent nearly twenty years ago. One rotation, Mark remembered hearing, had lasted two years, and after, Anglen had taken six months off with his family and then had come back. Once, while at the Academy, Mark had attended a lecture in one of the stadium-type auditoriums. He remembered the deliberate, halting speech pattern Joe had, as opposed to the crisp delivery of Tom Anglen. He had met them both after the lecture, but he doubted that either would remember him.

He returned to the photographs. In two of them, he could see a hammer on the floor near the bed and blood splatters on the wall and headboard stretching out like long jagged fingers. Their arms were folded across their abdomens like a corpse in a coffin, and their legs were spread open slightly as if they felt safe and relaxed after sex.

How does he do it? Mark wondered. *How does he make them feel comfortable?*

Most dates bring flowers, but what does the bird mean? Why am I even here now? Mark thought. *Why am I doing something even my father refused to do again after he caught two serial killers?*

"I want to see the monsters, Daddy. I want to see the monsters."

On the second photograph in Chicago, he saw blood after he had crushed the cartilage in her nose, running like train tracks across her mouth, neck, and breasts. Just above her folded hands, he saw caked blood in the small valley between her breasts and her abdomen.

He could feel the killer's rage each time the head of the hammer landed on her face and then felt the blood land on his face and chest.

He waits for these moments, Mark thought, *but who is he really killing? He doesn't even know these women.*

"Other than the physical similarities, I doubt he even remembers their names," Mark said softly. "They're all the same person to him, and they all have the same name. Who is it?"

Mark looked at the right hand resting on top of the left hand in each of the photographs, then nodded.

"He keeps the fingers in a display case, or something like that. The trophy means something to him. What is it?"

Mark closed his eyes and squeezed his left hand with his right. "Now I know why you didn't want to do these cases," he whispered and remembered what his father had said about serial killers.

"What do they look like, Daddy?"

He remembered his father had reached for his wallet and pulled out a dollar bill.

"They look like George Washington?"

"No." He laughed. "They look as common as a dollar bill. You can't see them coming. I'll never work on a case like that again."

It was the case he had worked on with Joe a long time ago. The man had killed twelve women before his father had found him hiding in a small walk-in closet in an apartment in Des Moines. Years later, after the accident, his father told him that the man had been crying and apologized repeatedly until he reached up and stabbed him in the stomach with a kitchen knife. At close range, his father put three bullets in the man's chest, and he died instantly in the closet where he had been hiding.

Every day after he killed him in the walk-in closet, he had gone to the hospital with his mother and seen his father on a respirator and the hole in his stomach.

When he heard the door open to Joe's office, he thought he could hear the gunshot downstairs once again.

"Tom," Joe said slowly, "this is Lou Mark. He just joined us."

"Mr. Anglen." Mark stood up and shook his hand. "I'm looking forward to working with you on this case."

"So am I." Anglen nodded. "I heard you did a good job for Steve Matthews on the Mall Bandits."

"He's in Cleveland," Joe said in his halting speech and the slight Southern drawl, "and that's where you're going this afternoon."

"Her name is, was, Royce, Royce . . . I can't remember her last name." Joe pointed at the photograph. "I guess it doesn't really matter now. She lived in a suburb of Cleveland called Shaker Heights. The crime scene is taped off and hasn't been touched by the local police. I want you to call me after you process the crime scene."

"Thank you, sir," Mark said.

"For?"

"The chance to work with you and Mr. Anglen on this case."

"You might want to reevaluate that after we catch him," Anglen said dryly.

At the door to Joe's office, Mark stopped. "You knew I'd be here early, didn't you, sir?" Mark asked.

"I thought you might." Joe nodded.

"And you wanted me to look at the photographs alone. That's why you told Julie to let me into your office."

"Tell me what you saw," Joe said.

"He keeps their fingers as trophies."

"We know that."

"He . . ." Mark paused and pointed at the bulletin board. "In his mind, he's not killing them. He's killing someone else he knew a long time ago."

"What do you mean?" Joe asked.

"The insanity has been inside him for a long time, and something triggered it about two years ago."

"What?" Anglen asked.

"That I don't know yet. There's one other thing."

"What?" Joe asked.

"The birds are his gifts, not their pets. It creates a bond or trust between them, which is why there are no defensive wounds on their hands or arms. They were surprised."

"Did you see anything else?" Anglen asked.

Mark remembered the dream from last night and the man standing over Cara.

"No, not yet," he answered.

Joe walked toward him and shook his hand.

"I met your father years ago when I was a field agent."

"I know, sir."

"We caught a serial killer together in Des Moines. Actually, your father found him. Your father was in the hospital for a month afterward."

"I know, sir. He nearly died."

"I respected his work and his gift," Joe said. "I even asked him to join us, but he said he couldn't do this work."

"He told me the same thing," Mark said.

"I think you can. Tom's the best man I have. I think you can learn a lot from him."

"Thank you, sir. But we need to find out what kind of bird he gives them. It's about the birds," Mark said.

"I'll have Oliver look into that," Joe said. "Call me from Cleveland."

"Yes, sir."

CHAPTER 8

"WHAT DID SHE do?" Anglen asked.

"She was a court reporter," the local agent answered. His name was Robert Evans, and he worked in the Cleveland office of the FBI.

"Do they make that much money?" Anglen walked toward the bed.

"Her family has money," he answered.

They were in her condo in Shaker Heights, an upscale suburb on the east side of Cleveland.

Anglen surveyed the room, then crouched down next to the bed. "Who found the body?" Anglen asked.

"Her boyfriend, yesterday. He's a local real estate lawyer," Evans answered.

"How?" Anglen asked.

"He said she didn't return his calls for two days. He has a key and came in and found . . ." He pointed at the woman on the bed.

Mark looked around the room. The furniture appeared to be new and expensive, and on the walls were hung three lithographs signed and numbered by an artist named Erte. Across from the bed, near the dresser, was a door leading to an L-shaped balcony.

"Time of death?" Anglen asked.

"Three and a half days ago, roughly around midnight," Evans answered.

Mark looked at the dried blood on the headboard and the wall behind it.

"The local police haven't touched this crime scene?" Anglen asked.

"They were here, obviously," Evans said, "but I received Mr. Mosely's memo and called a captain at Cleveland PD, and he notified me. I don't think they disturbed the crime scene."

"Did he ask why?" Anglen said.

"Of course." He shrugged. "But I've known him a long time. He didn't push it."

In the corner of the room on the far side of the bed, Mark saw a Plexiglas display case with crystal objects inside it. He walked over and knelt down beside it. He saw a swan, several bears, and assorted replicas of famous structures like the Eiffel Tower.

"You didn't find anything here, did you, Mr. Evans?" Anglen asked.

"No, sir. No semen on the bed, no DNA. We're still analyzing the fingerprints, but I don't think we'll find anything. He's careful."

"You looked in the wastepaper baskets in her condo and the Dumpster outside?" Anglen asked.

"Yes, sir, nothing."

"Who have you interviewed?"

"Her boyfriend. Three girlfriends."

"And?"

"She had a date that night, one of her girlfriends told us. But she didn't know his name or how she met him."

Mark stood up and stared at the victim, the blood in her blonde hair and what was left of her face, her hands folded across her abdomen, and the missing ring finger on her left hand. He could see the struggle before she died in the twisted bedsheets wrapped around her body.

"Do you have a photograph of her?" Mark pointed at her body. "I want to see it again."

"Yes." Evans looked in the file, then handed it to him.

Mark looked at the photograph, then over at her body. "She was beautiful," Mark said.

"So?" Anglen shrugged.

"Think of the photographs in Joe's office and in the file. The faces, what's left of them, look pretty much the same. The violence was measured in a way. He would hit them four, five, six times until they were dead. He liked this one more. He got excited. Look at her face."

Anglen looked down at her.

"He crushed her forehead," Mark said. "Her eyes are like crushed grapes. He even knocked her teeth out, and they'll find them in her stomach when you do the autopsy. He hit this one ten to twelve times, then dropped the hammer next to the bed from exhaustion."

"You're saying that this one looks more like her than the others," Anglen said.

"Yes, and he took two things from this one."

"The finger and . . ."

Mark turned to Evans. "You didn't dust the display case with the crystal."

"No," Evans answered defensively. "It was self-contained. We didn't see the need."

"The dust is disturbed in two ways," Mark said. "On the top of the case is an oblong distortion. It is either a tear or saliva."

"What else?" Anglen asked.

"He took one of the objects. This is expensive crystal. There is thousands of dollars in that case. I can't pronounce it, Swarovski, I think. My wife likes it, I just can't afford it. I think it was the train. There's a locomotive, a coal car, and two other cars on crystal train tracks."

"Why that object?" Anglen asked.

"I don't know yet, sir."

"How the hell did you see this? I didn't."

"It's sundown, sir." He pointed at the half-opened blinds over the window. "The light."

Anglen nodded at Evans. "Mr. Evans, process the display case carefully. We may have DNA and even fingerprints. And have the bird taken to Quantico."

"Is he still in Cleveland, Mr. Anglen?" Evans asked.

"Yes," Anglen said, "until we find the next one."

Outside her condo, on the balcony overlooking the lake, Anglen said, "Do you think he was crying? Is that what you saw on the top of the display case?"

"No." Mark shook his head. "I think he was excited."

CHAPTER 9

"MICHAEL, THIS IS a nice place," she said. They were in one of the best restaurants in Kansas City, Missouri, in a corner, by a floor-to-ceiling window that overlooked the city.

"It is," Evan answered.

It was their second date, and he had looked forward to it since they had met only a few days ago. He watched her blonde hair sway slowly across her shoulders as she turned and looked out the window.

"It's a great view," she said.

"It is."

They'd had good sex on the first date, and she had told him how hard it was to meet someone who fit her needs. She had talked to him during sex, driving him crazy with her words.

"It was great the other night. I was afraid if we, you know, that you might not call again." She looked away.

"There was never any doubt," he answered.

"I hadn't had sex in a long time. I was just attracted to you. Maybe I came on too strong."

"It was terrific, don't worry."

She looked at his longish brown hair and hazel eyes, with flecks of gray in the pupils. He wasn't particularly tall, maybe five nine, and when she wore heels, she was slightly taller than he was. But she had liked the way he looked and how he felt above her the first time. He had told her he wrote articles for bird magazines about rare birds and rare bird diseases.

"Stop it," he said and touched her left forearm. "I'm glad we met."

During sex, she had reached down and touched him, then whispered in his ear. Her voice was a little bit hoarse, like a mild, but chronic case of laryngitis. She reminded him of one of the newscasters on a local morning show he had discovered when he had first arrived in Kansas City. Next to the television in his hotel room, Evan had placed the two birdcages he had brought with him.

The waiter had brought steaks for both of them, and she rubbed her foot against his leg under the table as they ate.

When he had asked the waiter for a bottle of ketchup, she'd thought it was strange.

"Ketchup? For a good steak?" she watched him pour it all over the steak.

"I put ketchup on most everything. In a way, I learned it from my father. I buy it by the case. Old habits."

Kathy was thirty-seven years old, divorced once, and childless.

"You know I want to have a child. I hope I'm not scaring you away. But I do. It's important to me and my family."

"Maybe," he answered, "we should give ourselves some time to know each other."

"Of course." She set down her fork and looked out the window, and he felt her foot on his left leg again. "I want to put a chair next to the bed tonight. Try something."

"Sure."

Evan had checked out the morning newscaster he watched as he listened to his birds, and she seemed perfect, but after the next one she would make three, and he hadn't violated his rule in almost two years.

After the waiter took away the plates, he said, "I have a present for you."

"What is it?"

"You'll see when we get back to your place."

He had told her he was in Kansas City for a bird seminar, but that he lived in a small town in the Midwest.

"Are you going back home soon?" she asked. "I'll miss you."

"No, you won't," he said quickly.

"What is it?" she asked again.

"You'll see."

He paid the check, and at her home, he removed the black sheet from the cage and handed it to her.

"Thank you," she said. "What does it mean?"

"That I'm happy we met. She's rare. She's loyal. She mates for life. The common name for them is nightbirds because they sing only at night and only after they have sex with their mate."

"That's nice. Thank you."

In the bedroom, she slowly sat down on him in the chair she had carried in from the dining room, and afterward, in the bed, he had held her for a few minutes, then went out and talked to his bird. In the kitchen, he found a claw hammer and held it behind his back as he walked into the bedroom.

"Are you coming back to bed? I want you to hold me." She smiled.

"You never know, do you?"

"What?"

"You never know when you're going to meet someone like me."

"What do you mean?"

"It's time to sing."

Evan smashed the claw hammer into her forehead and watched her eyes rotate upward and then hit her again and again until he could no longer hear her breathing. He looked down at his chest for a moment and saw the blood splatters from her face that were like small irregular tracks. Slowly, he moved his left hand across his chest, then looked at her blood on his hand. In the bathroom, he washed off the hammer and set it next to the bed, and in her living room, he listened to the bird sing until he crushed her lungs in his large hands.

"Our love was short, but it will last forever," he said after he cut off her finger and lay on top of her.

Before he left her bedroom, he folded her hands neatly over each other, like a corpse lying in a coffin.

"Teddy bears." He smiled as he looked at her collection on the chair next to the bed.

In the living room, he stopped at the birdcage and felt tears on his face as he looked at his bird. "From now on, I'll be good. I promise."

CHAPTER 10

"**WHAT WAS HER** name?" Anglen asked.

"Monica Phelps. She . . . ," Robert Evans, the agent in the Cleveland office, said.

"Wait." Anglen held up his hand and drew a circle with his index finger around the victim's face. "He did it again, didn't he?"

"Yes, sir," Mark answered. "He seems to enjoy it more each time he does it."

"Jesus Christ, there's blood everywhere," Anglen said. "The local police haven't been here yet, Mr. Evans?"

"They haven't been in the room"—Evans shook his head—"but the captain I know at Cleveland PD is now sure we're looking for a serial killer in his city."

"Our forensics team?" Anglen asked Evans.

"They'll be here in a few minutes."

"Lou, look around and see if he took anything other than her finger this time."

"Yes, sir. But he's gone. He only does two in each city."

"So?" Evans said.

"You can tell your friend at Cleveland PD that he won't see another body here," Mark said.

"I want them to do everything," Anglen said. "Look for carpet fibers from his shoes. I want every inch of this place dusted for prints. I want luminol and a blue light on the bed and around it and in the bathroom. Nothing is overlooked this time."

"Yes, sir." Evans nodded.

"And I want interviews of her neighbors." Anglen sighed. "Maybe they saw him."

"I don't think we're going to find anything here, sir," Mark said. "He gets better each time."

"Nobody could kill this way and leave no trace," Anglen said firmly. "What about the last one, Mr. Evans?"

"The bodily fluid on the top of the crystal case was her blood, and the only prints we found inside were hers also," Evans said. "We did find scratches on the latch that we think were from the claw hammer. It's how he opened it before he took the train."

Mark closed his eyes. "I was wrong. It wasn't his saliva or a tear. It was a drop of her blood on his face."

Mark slipped on latex gloves and inspected the room. On the walls, he saw poster art that she had probably purchased from a local frame shop. In the dresser drawers, he found neatly folded sweaters, socks, undergarments, and hosiery. On top of the dresser, he saw several knickknacks and a jewelry box. Through the mirror over the dresser, he could see her in his mind. He could see the naked man standing next to the bed, holding the hammer over his head, and her mouth opening to scream until the head of the hammer smashed into her forehead. He could see her head turn and the second blow land on her temple and the third on the bridge of her nose. Just before she died, he could see her body shaking as if she were having a stroke or a seizure, then she was still.

Mark rubbed the palm of his right hand across the left side of his face, then crouched down in front of the dresser so he was at eye level with the jewelry box.

He dropped the hammer, Mark thought, *caught his breath, then looked around the room and saw the jewelry box.*

Mark stood up, lifted the lid on the jewelry box, and heard "Brahms's Lullaby." When he glanced at the mirror, he could see Anglen and Evans watching him. Inside, he saw one tier with small compartments containing costume jewelry, rings, and earrings. He lifted it out and set it on the dresser. Underneath it, he saw a pearl necklace, a ticket stub from a rock concert about ten years ago, a white-colored golf tee, a shiny silver dollar, and a few small diamond stones. *For her,* Mark thought, *the false bottom of the jewelry box was like a safe deposit box or a burial crypt for her memories of a failed marriage.*

"How long ago was she divorced?" Mark asked.

"A little more than seven years ago," Evans said.

"Mr. Evans," Anglen said, "would you please check on the forensics team and leave us alone for a few minutes?"

After Evans left the room, Anglen walked over to the dresser. "What did you see?" He asked. "I saw your eyes in the mirror."

"I saw him killing her."

"In the mirror?"

"No." Mark shook his head. "My father taught me to visualize the crime from the evidence at the crime scene. That's all."

"What did you see?"

"I saw him hitting her with the hammer. I saw her trying to avoid the blows, and I saw her body twitching out of control before she died. Each blow did more brain damage. After a while, she couldn't see, then she couldn't feel her hands or her feet. It was like a massive stroke. She finally choked to death from the blood in her mouth and throat."

"How does he know about this?" Anglen touched Mark's shoulder.

"Yes." Mark nodded. "In some way, he saw or experienced this before."

"You're saying that he could have taken a knife from their kitchen, shoved it through their heart, and it would have been over quickly."

Mark nodded. "Comparatively, his way is a slower and more painful death. Each time the hammer hits their skull, they lose another function—sense, sight, hearing, feeling. They slowly drop into a black hole from which they never return."

"What did he take in addition to her finger this time?" Anglen asked.

"Something from her marriage, I think."

"It was in the jewelry box?" Anglen asked.

"Yes, she kept the good memories from her marriage in there. But I didn't see an engagement ring."

"She could have sold it."

"Maybe, but she kept a ticket stub from a rock concert years ago and a golf tee probably from when I think they played golf together the first time. I think she would have kept the engagement ring."

"Mr. Anglen," Evans said at the door to the bedroom, "the forensics team is here."

"Thank you, give us one more minute. What else did you see?"

"He can continue to kill for a long time. He's smart, maybe brilliant, and there are a lot of women like Royce and Monica to choose from."

"Why is he taking something else now?" Anglen asked.

"To remember them, I think," Mark answered. "It's hard to remember forty-nine women."

Anglen looked at Mark's eyes. "There is something else, isn't there?"

"Yes, sir." Mark nodded. "I'm not sure what it is. A sound I think. Something she heard the night he killed her."

"What is it?"

"Look at the black dress on the floor next to the bed. They were out, at a restaurant or bar, and she heard something then, and it meant something to her," Mark explained.

Anglen sighed. "When I was your age, I wanted to stop these people. Now I hate this work because of what it does to me and my family. Now we wait for him to kill again."

"Yes, sir."

CHAPTER 11

"**H**OW LONG?" JOE asked. "The director called me his morning. So far there hasn't been any publicity."

Anglen sipped on the scotch. "I don't know." He took a cigarette from the pack on the small circular table next to the bed. "Soon, I hope."

"Where?"

"We have no idea." Anglen lit the cigarette, then looked around the hotel room. "What did forensics find at the last crime scene?"

"A partial thumbprint on the jewelry box. We know it wasn't the victim's. We ran it through the computer, but there were no matches. We found some cat hair in the living room and the bedroom."

"She didn't have a cat," Anglen said.

"I know. We think he has a short-haired black cat and that he brought that in on his shoes or his clothes," Joe said.

"That's it?" Anglen asked.

"Unfortunately," Joe said slowly, "yes."

Anglen looked around the room again and saw the twenty-one-inch TV bolted to the dresser, the light green carpeting, the plaid-patterned bedspread, and the inexpensive prints on the walls.

"In the last twenty years, I have spent so much time in rooms like this waiting for them to kill again. They all look the same to me now."

"What is it, Tom?"

"Nothing."

"You're smoking and drinking scotch."

"Yes, I always do when I work."

"There is"—Joe paused—"something else, isn't there?"

"There are a lot of things I'm thinking about." He sipped on the scotch. "How long is it going to take to catch this one? How long am I going to be away from my family? And I wonder if I have the focus I had twenty years ago, even ten years ago."

"I know you didn't want to do this again," Joe said, "but we have to stop them."

"And you're right, as you usually are. Since I started doing this nearly twenty years ago, we have developed better ways to catch these people. Think about the sniper case. It took, what, six weeks to catch them after they killed ten people. We now have thirteen markers for DNA testing. We have the best lab and the best forensic teams in the world. And we have geographic profilers who can locate where they live within a city block if they kill in the same city."

"What are you saying?" Joe asked.

"I don't know if any of that science will stop this one. He's smart, maybe brilliant, and he leaves nothing behind. He's like a ghost holding a hammer over his head, leaving nothing but a dead body behind."

"You'll find him," Joe said, "you always do."

"Unless he makes a mistake, we won't catch this one in six weeks. And I'm not going to spend another six months or a year of my life living in these rooms."

Anglen looked around the hotel room again, then poured another glass of scotch.

"You're saying"—Joe paused—"that if we don't catch him soon, you're going to leave the FBI."

"Yes." Anglen nodded. "Mark can handle this."

"Are you sure?"

"Yes. Mark saw that this serial killer now takes more than just the ring finger on their left hand. He takes something personal to them."

Joe remembered Mark's father and how he had caught the serial killer in Des Moines a long time ago. He remembered his eyes and his pale complexion after he had been released from the hospital.

"You don't look good," Joe had said.

"How do you expect me to look after he stuck an eight-inch kitchen knife in my stomach?"

"What happened?" Joe had asked.

"I got careless. I won't again. I should have just killed him when I found him crying in the walk-in closet."

"Why didn't you?"

"That's a question I'll ask myself many times as I heal. You believe we should keep them alive, don't you?"

"Yes." Joe had nodded. "To study them. So we can understand them."

"That's a waste of time and money. How long are we going to house Charles Manson, and please tell me what you have learned from him."

"Nothing. I still want you to work with us."

"No."

"When I sent you to interview the serial killer in Northern California, what did you learn?" Joe asked.

"Not much." Anglen shook his head.

"I watched the videotapes of your interview with him again."

"What do you mean?"

"Is this one anything like him?" Joe asked.

Anglen sighed and remembered sitting across from him in the small interrogation room with the solid concrete floor.

"He wanted to kill me. I could see it in his eyes. He was handcuffed to that table, and every few minutes he would pull on the cuffs and test the strength of the steel. You want me to think about him?"

"No," Joe answered, "unless it helps."

"What happened to Lou's father?" Anglen asked.

"He got careless one more time, and that time it wasn't a knife."

"I'm going to call Trish."

Anglen set the phone down, for a moment, then dialed the first five numbers to his home, and then set it down again.

"I'll call her tomorrow," he whispered, "she'll only ask questions I can't answer."

He sipped on the scotch, lit a cigarette, then picked up the paperback book and started reading.

Trish watched television while he read and reread books. In his mind, he could hear Sean and Mary upstairs in their home and see Trish sitting on the love seat next to the couch.

He set the book down, paced around the room, and remembered his interview with the Taurus Killer. His name was Vincent Crea, and he had killed fourteen women in Northern California before he had caught him torturing number 15 in a cheap motel room just outside Oakland. Vincent Crea liked them young, and this one, he remembered, was only eighteen years old.

"My god," he whispered and sat down on the bed, "how could I have spent most of my adult life in their world? I believe in God and the church, and each time, they test my faith."

Joe's policy, which he had started fifteen years ago, was to interview serial killers after they were caught and incarcerated. The data was then uploaded into a computer software program and was used by FBI profilers. The questionnaire was, in part, specific to the particular serial killer and, in part, a modified and shorter version of the MMPI, a test designed by psychologists at the University of Minnesota to determine personality disorders. He thought about the interview with Vincent Crea.

"I have some questions." Anglen sat down across from him in the interrogation room.

Vincent Crea was five ten, weighed 215 pounds, and had thick muscular forearms. His hair was longish, curly, and black, and his skin was olive colored. He had been forty-one years old when he killed and had driven a truck for the largest wholesaler of beer in the Bay Area.

"You put me here for the rest of my life." He clenched his fists and pulled on the handcuffs on the table.

"You put yourself here," Anglen answered.

"Fuck you, Anglen."

"You killed fourteen young women." Anglen ignored him. "You raped and tortured them, then stuck a knife through their hearts."

"Did I?" He smiled.

Anglen remembered that when he had come through the door with two detectives from Oakland PD, she had been tied to the bed with duct tape over her mouth. He'd had a knife in his right hand, and he'd shot him in the chest and watched him fall off the side of the bed.

"I saw you, remember? I shot you."

"Fuck you, Anglen." He felt the spit on his face. *"You took away my life."*

"I stopped you from killing any more women."

"The bullet collapsed my lung. I almost died."

"I should have killed you when I had the chance."

"It's too late now. I have a new business." He smiled. *"Do you want to know what I do?"*

"Yes."

"They educate us here. They try to rehabilitate us." He laughed. *"I took a fine arts class."*

"So?" Anglen lifted his hands.

"I learned to draw. I learned I have talent. I'm an artist now."

"What do you draw?" Anglen asked.

"I remember things." He lifted his left hand toward his face, but the handcuff stopped him about six inches from his head. *"Dammit."*

"Go on. What do you draw?"

He lowered his head and scratched it just above his left ear.

"We do seriographs," he explained, *"it's like lithographs. I draw them, my brother signs them for me, he prints them, then we sell them on the Internet. My brother has a website."*

"What things do you remember?"

"Just things. Do you want to buy one?"

"Why did you kill these women?"

"I liberated them." He shook his head. *"I liberated them from their fears of sex and intimacy. I helped them."*

"This is a waste of time." Anglen stood up.

"But for you"—he clenched his teeth—*"I could still be helping them. Fuck you, Anglen, fuck you."*

At the door to the interrogation room, Anglen heard him say, "Wait, please. I want to talk. I spend all of my time in isolation now."

Anglen sat down on the bed in the hotel room and lit a cigarette, then set the disposable lighter down next to the pack of cigarettes. Vincent Crea, who had left the symbol of the zodiac sign from Taurus on the chest of each of his victims, had answered every question, and several hours later, as he was leaving, Vincent Crea had asked him a question.

"Why do you do this?"

"My job?"

"Yes." He nodded.

"That's a question I ask myself every day."

"I liked what I did, my job." He smiled again. *"Do you know what I liked best?"*

"No."

"It wasn't the sex." He shrugged, and Anglen heard the handcuffs *grind against the table. It was fine, good. But they'd do anything I wanted just for the chance to live a few more minutes. I could do anything I wanted to them. I was like God. Fuck you, Anglen, for taking that away from me. Now I live through my art.*

Anglen sighed, sipped on the scotch, then called Joe.

"I remembered the interview with Vincent Crea."

"And what did you remember, Tom?" Joe said slowly.

"Two things. He said he was liberating his victims. Ignoring the insanity for a moment, this serial killer is destroying something, a memory, and it was dormant, incomplete, until something triggered it. Mark's right."

"What else?"

"Have our profilers look at Vincent's artwork. Do you remember it?"

"Yes, it wasn't art. It was just drawings of women spread-eagled on a bed, and he always drew himself sitting next to them. I can't believe anyone bought them."

"I can't either," Anglen said impatiently, "but that's not the point. Have the profilers focus on how he drew himself."

"Do you want me to e-mail you copies of the drawings?"

"You don't need to do that. Those images, I'll never forget."

"Thank you, Tom," Joe said. "I'll call you tomorrow."

Anglen closed his eyes, and the images of Vincent Crea in his art flashed through his mind. He had done over one hundred, and his brother had converted them into thousands of signed and numbered seriographs.

"Unbelievable," Anglen mumbled, then thought about Trish. "She needed to feel safe after what happened a long time ago. And this man has a place where he feels safe. I need to take that away from him, and then I can stop him."

CHAPTER 12

TOM ANGLEN STOPPED at the doorway to the bedroom and slowly scanned the room. With the exceptions of bloodstains on the surface of the old mattress and dried blood on the wooden headboard and the wall behind it, the room was clean. After Cleveland, he had sent Mark home to spend time with his wife while they waited. Three hours ago, Joe had called him and said they had found a body in Kansas City, Missouri, that matched the description of the other victims.

"Didn't you get a memo from our office on this type of murder?" Anglen asked.

Her body was in a steel drawer at the morgue, and the dead bird had been disposed of shortly after the body was found.

"No, sir." The police captain shook his head. "What were we supposed to do?"

"Who found her?" Anglen asked.

"Officer Woods." The captain nodded, then tapped the man standing next to him on the shoulder.

Captain Walter Richards was, Anglen guessed, in his late fifties, while Officer Woods was maybe thirty years old.

"How did you find her, Officer?" Anglen asked.

"The neighbor. He said he smelled something coming from her room, knocked on the door, then called us, and I was the closest squad car."

"Tell me what you saw."

"Her." He raised his right hand and pointed at the bed. "It made me sick. I threw up in her toilet. I've never seen anything like that."

"Sure." Anglen nodded. "Did you clear the apartment first?"

"No, sir." Officer Woods looked down. "It's just . . . I didn't expect this."

"Of course. What did you do then?"

"I checked her pulse to see if she was dead, then moved the chair out of the way."

"What chair?"

"There was a chair facing the window in this room," he answered. "Then I closed the blinds."

Anglen looked at the gold-colored, horizontal miniblinds over the window.

"They were open?" Anglen looked back at Officer Woods.

"Yes, sir."

"I didn't see that in the report, Captain."

"I didn't think it was important." Officer Woods shrugged. "I mean, you really couldn't see much through the slats."

"Show me how they were," Anglen said, "when you came in here."

Officer Woods walked over to the window, adjusted the horizontal blinds until each slot was open to about a sixty-degree angle, then pulled down on the cord until they were wide open at the bottom, six inches from the windowsill.

"That's how they were, Officer?" Anglen asked.

"Yes, sir."

"And where was the chair?"

"Facing the window"—he pointed at the bed—"near the edge of the bed."

"What does it mean?" Captain Richards asked.

"I'm not sure," Anglen answered. "When your forensics unit processed this crime scene, did they find anything?"

"No." Captain Richards shook his head.

"Did you find anything on the body?"

"Such as?"

"Blood or skin under her fingernails or semen in her vagina?"

"No."

"Captain, leave the crime-scene photos on the dresser and give me a few minutes alone in here."

"You said something about a memo from the FBI," Captain Richards said at the doorway.

"It's really not important now," Anglen said.

"Your name is familiar to me, I just can't place it. But tell me why the FBI would be interested in the murder of a thirty-seven-year-old woman in Kansas City."

"I really can't talk about it, Captain," Anglen answered.

"Will there be more?"

"How could I possibly know that? Please give me a few minutes, Captain."

Anglen surveyed the room slowly, stopping at the queen-size bed with the wooden headboard, the nightstands on each side. Across from it stood a dresser with the mirror above it, and the chair in the corner had more than twenty teddy bears on it. At the dresser, he picked up the crime-scene photos taken by the police photographer from Kansas City PD and flipped through them until he found a photograph taken from the foot of the bed. With his hand, he held it out, looked at it for a moment, then back down at the empty bed. Her body was lying at about a forty-five-degree angle across the bed, the sheets twisted around the body, with her legs slightly open and her hands crossed over her abdomen.

Anglen slipped the photo behind the others and looked for close-ups of her head. In each one, her face was crushed, covered with blood and matted hair.

He repeated the process with each photograph as he walked slowly around the bed, then into the bathroom, where, in the photo, he saw trace amounts of blood.

"It's him," he whispered, "there's no doubt."

Standing near the bed, he could still smell the faint odor that had alerted her neighbor to her death. After death, the body released chemicals into the air, which had permeated the small bedroom, then her apartment, then the hallway outside.

He walked over to the window and opened the blinds. Behind her apartment, to the south, he saw three single-family homes. He took his time observing the lights inside the homes, the blurred image on a big-screen TV in one of them, and the occasional movement of people inside. *Maybe*, he thought, *one of them saw something when she was having sex with him on the chair facing the window. This couldn't have been the first time. No, she liked people to watch her.*

He turned to the blood splatters on the wall behind the bed and then the photographs.

"They dried at different times," he whispered. "This time he started, then stopped, then hit her again. Why?"

He knelt down in front of the beige-colored chair in the corner and checked out the bears. Some of them were normal-sized stuffed animals and other miniatures. He picked one up and saw a brown thread in the back and wondered if she had made them herself.

"Is this what you took this time?"

Anglen stood up when he heard his cell phone ringing.

"Joe, it's him. There's no doubt," he said. "They didn't get the memo here. The body was in the morgue when I got here. You have to make sure this doesn't happen again."

"I'll do what I can," Joe said slowly. "But the director will never agree to any media coverage on this. It would create a panic in this country."

"Women are being murdered," Anglen said. "The director's concern should not about people panicking. They have a right to know."

"Tom"—Joe paused—"you know there's nothing I can do about this. Tell me about this one."

"She liked people to watch her having sex or maybe walking around her apartment nude. The blinds were open in the bedroom that night and she had sex with him on a chair facing the window. I assume she was facing the window."

"Why would he do that? Someone might see him."

"He knew they really couldn't see him through partially opened blinds. But there are three homes behind her apartment. Have agents interview those people and her neighbors in case they did see something."

"The bird?"

"Incinerated," Anglen answered. "Hold on. There must have been blood all over him. He must have taken a shower before he left here."

"Hair in the drain? Is that what you mean?"

"Yes." Anglen nodded. "Have our local forensics unit process this crime scene again. Maybe they'll find his hair."

"What are you thinking, Tom?"

"He's bright, meticulous. He plans every move, like a ritual. He's not likely to make mistakes. He's not going to be easy to catch."

"You mean he scares you more than the others?"

"They all do," Anglen answered. "My religion tells me one thing, and they teach me something else."

"What was her name?" Anglen asked at the doorway as he looked at Captain Richards and Officer Woods waiting in the living room.

"Kathy Rogers," Joe answered. "Did he take anything else this time?"

"A teddy bear, I think. I'll call you in the morning."

Anglen closed the cell phone and set it in the inside pocket of his sports coat.

"Is this a serial killer?" Captain Richards asked.

"It takes more than one," Anglen answered.

"Officer Woods recognized your name," Captain Richards said. "If it's a serial killer, I have to notify the commissioner."

"Give me a little bit of time, Captain. Then I'll tell you why I'm here."

"How long?"

"A few days, maybe less."

In the hotel room, Anglen set his gun on the nightstand, turned on the television, and found the local news. The first story was about the unexplained and brutal death of Kathy Rogers. After that story, as he sipped on a glass of scotch, he saw a promo for the local morning feel-good show and saw the image of one of the morning newscasters.

She looks just like her, Anglen thought, *she looks just like Kathy Rogers and the others. Could she be the next one?*

CHAPTER 13

*T*HE FBI DEFINES *serial killing as three or more killings with common characteristics in more than thirty days,* he had read on his computer screen.

After Officer Woods got home to his small, two-bedroom apartment, he had turned on the computer, and while he waited for the painfully slow dial-up service, he set his gun and baton on the kitchen table and took a beer from the refrigerator. Spy blocks, Adware Protection, and the connection time later, he had finally logged on to the FBI's website.

"Three," he said, "but Kathy Rogers is the only one here."

The more organized the killer is, he had read on, *the more likely he is intelligent, ritualistic, and attentive to the most minute details of the crime. Historically, this type of serial killer will be able to avoid detection for longer periods of time. The chances of his making a mistake or losing control are minimal.*

Why would the FBI, he wondered, send Tom Anglen for one murder?

The developmental histories of serial killers can include childhood sexual or physical abuse, parental deprivation, rejection, or abandonment, or, in some cases, exposure to violent role models.

"Violence as a teaching tool." He sipped on the beer.

Serial killers, he had read on, *are abnormal and demonstrate one or more personality disorders, such as antisocial behavior, sexual sadism, borderline personality, and, in some instances, pedophilia or necrophilia, but few organized serial killers are psychotic when they kill.*

"They're not crazy," he said to himself, "not legally crazy. Is that what they mean when they kill and have sex with dead people?"

We can only estimate the number of serial killers in the United States today. The FBI tries to monitor multiple murders, but it is difficult, if not impossible, to track them or predict where or when they will kill again. To a large extent, the FBI is dependent on local law enforcement officers for the initial determination. For serial killers, the FBI distinguishes between instrumental violence, where the violence is the means to an end, money, or property, and affective violence, where the death of the victim is the ultimate goal. The ultimate effect, in most instances of serial killing, is generational for families, and the motivational aspects are multifaceted and difficult to detect. A serial killer could be your next-door neighbor, apparently normal in all respects.

He left the FBI website and typed in Anglen's name in the space at the top of the screen, saw a number of matches, and stopped at the fifth one.

"Serial killers—New York News—Tom Anglen is the best at catching . . ."

He clicked on the match and found six articles written by a crime reporter in New York named Pete Westport. Until the final article, Anglen refused to comment on any of his cases, but in the last article concerning his testimony before the Senate Appropriations Committee, he did comment.

"Budget cuts in Behavioral Science will strip us of invaluable resources needed to catch very real and very dangerous men."

He went back to the list of matches, clicked on the one that said Senator Duffy and Tom Anglen, and looked at the photograph.

"I worked with a famous man tonight," he said.

He picked up the telephone and dialed his girlfriend's number. At thirty-two, she was a year older than he was. They had met at a bar about three months ago and had been dating since then.

"Cindy, did I wake you?"

"Yes, Rick," she answered. "It's after eleven."

"I'm sorry, but I worked with a famous man tonight."

"Who?" She could hear his excitement.

"You know the woman who was killed?"

"Kathy Rogers? Yes, I saw it on the news. People were talking about it at work."

She had completed school a few years ago, had a paralegal certificate, and worked at a medium-sized law firm.

"His name is Tom Anglen, and he works for the FBI. A reporter wrote articles about his cases, and he had his picture taken with a senator."

"That's good, hon. What did you do?"

"Not really anything much," he answered. "Talked about the evidence a little. I think he believes I screwed up the crime scene. You know, I told you I threw up when I found her body and I touched some stuff. Moved the chair away from the window."

"What chair?" she asked.

"It was from the dinette set."

"Why was it in the bedroom?"

"I don't know." Rick Woods shook his head. "I also don't know why the FBI would send its best man."

"Could there be others we don't know about?" she asked.

"Not here. We, the cops, would know, and the media wouldn't miss this."

"You think the FBI knows something they're not telling anyone, that this one has killed others in Missouri and Kansas?"

"Yes." He nodded. "It's the only thing that makes sense. Maybe Jefferson City or St. Louis or Topeka in Kansas, who knows?"

"What are you going to do?"

"I don't know. Maybe do some research on other similar murders? Maybe it will help me get a job with the FBI."

"Why don't you just talk to the famous FBI agent?" she said sarcastically.

"He won't tell me anything. I mean, he was nice to me tonight, but the FBI isn't going to tell me anything."

"Do you think it could be more than just Missouri?"

"I don't know, but why would Mr. Anglen be here, waiting for the next one?"

"You're scaring the hell out of me, Rick."

"I'm sorry. Go back to sleep."

"Good night."

I'll start with the newspapers, he thought, *track common characteristics of the murders, women who look almost the same, like on the FBI website.* Out of curiosity, he went to the Census Bureau website and read the information:

Projected population:
291,609,481
One birth every . . . . 8 seconds
One death every . . . . 13 seconds
One international migrant every . . . 25 seconds
Net gain of one person every . . . . . . 11 seconds

One death every thirteen seconds, he read again. On the calculator on his computer, he multiplied sixty times sixty for the number of seconds in an hour, then times twenty-four for the number of hours in a day, and divided that by thirteen.

"Six thousand six hundred forty-six people die every day in this country. What if he kills every two weeks? In fourteen days"—he clicked on the calculator again—"ninety three thousand forty-six people die in the United States.

If he's killing all *over the country*, he thought, *if they're not lucky, they'll never find him.*

CHAPTER 14

MARK KISSED HER neck and heard her moan softly in his ear.

"Turn me over," she whispered.

He leaned back, looked at her for a moment, then turned her body so she was facedown on the bed.

"That feels good," she gasped. "Lou, I'm almost ready."

He felt her muscles tighten and watched her arms stretch slowly toward the headboard as she arched her back, then heard her take a number of long, deep breaths before he quickened the pace again, then lay on her back.

"I love it when you do it right after me. Stay there."

After a few minutes, he pushed away from her and rolled over on his back.

"Are you sure this was okay?" he asked.

"Don't be silly, Lou." She turned and looked at him.

Strands of her long reddish-brown hair had fallen across her face.

"But you're pregnant." He pushed the hair away from her face.

"I said don't be silly, it's fine."

He lay back and looked at the ceiling.

"What is it, Lou?"

"He does this, or something like this, before he kills, then he does it again. This is as close as two people can get physically, yet for him it always ends in the same way. Why is he killing? Who is he killing? He doesn't even know these women, or does he believe that he does?"

"Do you have a profile yet?" she asked.

"Mr. Mosely said we'd have it soon." He stood up. "I have to work tonight."

"On this case?"

"Yes."

Mark put on a pair of sweatpants, then pulled a polo shirt over his head.

"I'm sorry," Mark said at the doorway to the bedroom. "I know I've been away."

"It's all right. I'm just glad you came home for a while."

Mark turned on the light in the den downstairs and sat down in front of the computer As he waited for the Internet connection, he looked around the room. They lived in a small two-bedroom condo just outside Quantico, which he had purchased shortly after he had become an FBI agent. It was in a midlevel suburb in Virginia about twenty miles from the FBI's primary training facility, which housed the Academy and the FBI lab.

In the den, which he had made his office, he looked at the plaques on the east wall. The first four were awards his father had won as the top detective in the Des Moines Police Department. Next to the plaques were a series of newspaper articles his mother had framed about his father's work. He read the headline on the first one.

JOHN MARK, THE MAN WITH THE EYES, SOLVES A TWENTY-YEAR-OLD CRIME

Twenty years ago, he had read on, *a wife and mother disappeared one night, as did a local man who owned a small business in Davenport. The woman was the wife of State Court Judge Tom Lewis, known as the Hanging Judge for the stiff sentences he regularly dispensed in his courtroom. In this case, which the police describe in a ghoulishly accurate way as a cold case file, Judge Lewis claimed he had no idea why his wife had suddenly disappeared. For the next twenty years, Judge Lewis continued to preside over the criminal bench . . .*

"Lou, it's nearly two o'clock in the morning," Cara said at the doorway. "Shouldn't you sleep for a while?"

"Soon . . ."

"You obsessed this way when you practiced law before a trial." She stood behind the chair and put her hands on his shoulders.

"What are those?" She pointed at the drawings on the small table on the left side of the computer.

"You really don't want to look at those, Cara."

"They're primitive. What do they mean?"

She looked at the pen-and-ink drawings of a woman tied to a bed, with a man sitting on the edge of the bed next to her.

Mark stood up and turned her away from the drawings on the table.

"Do you really want to know?"

She nodded. "They scare me."

"It's serial killer art, if you want to call it that. Mr. Mosely asked me to look at them."

"This one?"

"No." Mark shook his head. "His name is Vincent Crea, and Tom Anglen caught him years ago, then interviewed him. He's an old man now, and he'll be in prison until he dies."

"These are pictures of . . ."

"Yes. He killed fourteen women. Now he draws pictures of the crime scenes, and his brother sells them on the Internet."

"People buy them?"

"Yes. I'll be more careful in the future so you won't have to see these kinds of things." Mark held her. "I'm sorry."

"I thought there was a law that prevented them from making money on what they did," she said.

"You're right," Mark answered, "they're called the Son of Sam laws based on David Berkowitz, a serial killer in New York. But third parties can sell their work and profit from it."

"I don't understand the difference." She shook her head.

"There isn't any difference. There's a movie, a documentary, called *Collectors*, about two men who collect and sell serial killer art and, in some instances, evidence from crime scenes. They call what they sell murderabilia. They contact and communicate with imprisoned serial killers and encourage them to create so-called art that they sell on the Internet. For a long time, you could buy serial killer art on Internet auction houses."

"How do you know all this?"

"It's my job." Mark shrugged. "I watched the movie at Quantico. We have the DVD. The two collectors in the movie have what they call "Death Row Art Shows." They have some celebrity clients who buy the art. After the serial killer is executed, the value of the work increases dramatically."

"Like real artists?" Cara asked.

"Yes." Mark nodded. "Most of it is common, still lifes, flowers, self-portraits. You remember John Wayne Gacy's self-portrait as Pogo the Clown?"

"Yes."

"Vincent Crea's art is truly art imitating life in a way. Every drawing depicts one of the fourteen crime scenes from different angles. He titles the drawing with the first name of the victim. In the Joanie series, the first drawing is titled *Joanie, Scene One, Her Bedroom.* The second is titled *Joanie, Scene Two, the Seduction.* There are ten separate drawings in the Joanie series alone. Vincent Crea is the best-selling serial killer artist in history."

"How do the families of the victims react?" Cara asked.

"Just the way you would think. They relive the crime when they hear about his art."

"These people in the movie *Collectors* sell that." She pointed at the drawings on the table next to his desk.

"No"—Mark shook his head—"his brother is his agent and he's made a small fortune."

"How can you . . ."

"I'm going to take you to bed now." He clasped her hand and led her out of his office.

"You're not afraid of these people, are you?" Cara said at the door to his office.

"Of course." Mark shrugged. "Everyone is."

"You don't have to do this. You could work for Steve Matthews again, catch people like the Mall Bandits, or practice law."

"No, I can't now," Mark shook his head slowly.

"It's about him." She pointed at the framed newspaper story in his office. "And you're not afraid of them."

"It's about something that happened a long time ago."

"And you won't talk about it."

"Not now."

"It's the only thing you're really afraid of."

"You should go back to bed." Mark gently touched her right elbow.

"This is about him, your father."

"He thought he could hear their last thoughts. It drove him crazy, finally."

"Can you do it?"

"I don't know yet." Mark shook his head. "You have to go to bed."

"Why do you have those things, the drawings" Cara asked.

"Mr. Mosely wants me to meet with him and talk about this case."

In their bedroom, he lay down next to her and held her.

"I don't want you to do this work, Lou," she whispered. "You were a good lawyer."

"My father taught me a lot of things," he said. "He taught me how to protect myself, how to read a crime scene. I'm just learning what I can do now. Give me time, please."

"But . . ."

"Just give me time to see if I can do some things he couldn't or wouldn't do."

"What do you mean?" Cara asked.

"Go to sleep."

He waited until he felt regular breathing, then slowly turned to the edge of the bed until he felt his feet on the carpet.

In the den, he read the rest of the newspaper article his mother had framed years ago.

> *John Mark discovered that the Hanging Judge, Judge Lewis, had learned about the affair his wife was having with the local businessman, followed them to a motel in the suburbs, and waited until they were asleep after having sex. He then drugged each of them with a syringe full of morphine and buried them alive at a landfill site just outside the city. John Mark found an old guest register at the motel, saw the crime, and confronted Judge Lewis with the facts. Judge Lewis confessed and now is awaiting sentencing by a judge he has*

known for more than twenty years. Usually, as the cliché goes, Justice delayed is justice denied. In this case, Justice has been done twenty years later.

Mark turned on the desk lamp on the table next to the computer and, for a few minutes, scanned Vincent Crea's art until he found the last one in the Joanie series. Joanie had been nineteen years old the day Vincent Crea had abducted her in a parking lot at a grocery store not two miles from her home. She was a freshman at a local community college studying marketing and lived at home with her parents and three teenage brothers. Her parents had called the police the night she didn't come home from school, and by the next morning, when the police began to look for her, it was already too late.

Mark picked up the last drawing in the Joanie series, titled simply as *Joanie, the End*. In the drawing, she was tied to a bed with silver-colored duct tape covering her mouth. Anatomically, the drawing was childlike—her body was too small for the disproportionately large head and the wide-open eyes on the depiction of her face. Sitting on the left side of the bed, Vincent Crea held a long kitchen knife in his right hand, poised over her torso. This self-portrait of sorts appeared to have been sketched quickly with sharp strokes from the nub of the pen he dipped into the inkwell on the desk in his cell as he worked. After he finished one drawing, his brother would sell the pen on an Internet auction house. With the exception of the silver-colored duct tape and random drops of red blood on her breasts and stomach, the drawing was done entirely in black ink.

"What can I learn from this?" Mark set the drawing down, then stacked them together and put them in his briefcase.

"What do they have to do with this serial killer?" Mark rubbed the palm of his right hand across the left side of his face.

In their bedroom, he lay down carefully next to Cara so he wouldn't wake her and gently put his arm around her waist.

"Sometimes you talk in your sleep," Cara mumbled.

"You've told me that before."

"Sometimes I can understand the words, and sometimes it sounds like a foreign language."

"You shouldn't listen. You should just sleep." Mark held her.

"You don't like talking about this." She turned slightly toward him.

"No."

"Why?"

"My mother told me a long time ago that it just gets worse with time and age."

"The nightmares? Your father?"

"I'll hold you until you fall asleep," Mark whispered in her ear.

"I want to know. I want . . ."

"Sleep."

"Please don't leave me." She hugged him.

"Why would I? I love you," Mark answered.

"I mean the way your father left your mother."

"He never left her, Cara. He found women in town, but he always came back."

"Why did he . . . ?"

"I don't know. We really don't talk about it."

"What? What was it?"

"He got careless," Mark answered. "But I think it was one case. He caught a famous criminal no one else could find. And that man ended upon on the cover of *Time* magazine."

"The man he caught?"

"Yes."

"Who was it? You never told me." Cara turned on the bed.

"We really don't talk about it." Mark shook his head again.

"Why?"

"It almost killed him, and then finally it was the reason he died. He told me that spending time with him was like spending time with the devil."

"Who was it?" Cara whispered.

"Joe called me late today." Mark ignored her question. "He's in Kansas City. I leave in the morning."

"When will you be back?" she asked.

"I don't know."

"You didn't answer me about the man your father caught," she said.

"When my father caught him, he was an old man, decades away from what he had done. Go to sleep."

CHAPTER 15

"EVAN"—SHE GASPED—"YOU FEEL so good inside me. I'm so close."

Her eyes were closed, and she was breathing heavily through her mouth. As he continued to move slowly above her, he looked around her small bedroom at the fancy decorative pillows she had set carefully on the chair next to the bed before they started, the photographs of her family over the bed, the little figurines around the room, and the jewelry case just above his head. *Just junk*, he thought.

Evan placed his hands on her narrow shoulders and moved faster above her, until he felt her body stiffen. After, she reached down and touched him while she whispered in his ear. When he finished, he felt her body moving again beneath him until she relaxed, then kissed him.

"That was nice, but I wish you would stay just for a minute after . . . you know," she said.

"Yeah." He had pulled away from her almost immediately after he felt her lips on the side of his face. He was lying on his back looking up at the ceiling.

Almost all of them, he remembered, did it voluntarily, but some of them he had to convince in other ways.

"Do you like your gift, Nancy?"

"Yes, she's beautiful. Like a raven, but smaller. But my hand hurts where she pecked me. I hope it doesn't get infected."

"Your hand will be fine. They're tough birds, aggressive. And she's a little cranky right now because of her condition."

"What do you mean?"

"It's not important. Why all the pillows?" he looked around the room again.

"You don't like them?"

"No, they're fine, but why?"

"It makes this place, this apartment, like a home," she explained. "I had a home when I was married. Don't you have a home?"

"Yes." Wanting to leave, he sat up on the edge of the bed. "Back east."

"Do you have other birds there?"

"Yes." He nodded with his back to her. "I have an aviary."

"A what?"

"I have a lot of birds." He turned toward her. "Sometimes they're born prematurely. They are called incubator babies, and I have to keep them in a safe, sterile, and warm environment, like the womb, until they are strong enough to live on their own."

"That's interesting, Evan," she said, her voice softening. "You care for them."

"Yes." He nodded and felt her hands slide up and down his back. "But sometimes they die. Sometimes, they were just born too early to survive in this world."

"Someday I want to see your birds."

Evan picked up her glass of wine from the nightstand and handed it to her, then picked up his.

"Drink," he said.

He watched her sip from the champagne flute, then hold it against her right side.

"I don't tell many people this." He swallowed the wine and set the glass down on the nightstand. "But I was an incubator baby."

"Really?"

"Yes." He nodded. "My father told me I was delivered a month early, covered in blood, my mother's blood. He said I looked like a tomato with tiny arms and legs, like a bottle of ketchup had been poured over my head. At delivery, I was only four-and-a-half pounds."

"What happened to your mother?" she asked and rested on one elbow on the bed.

"She died giving birth to me."

"Oh, I'm sorry." She set the wineglass on the nightstand, then tried to comfort him by moving her hands across his back and stomach, reminding him again of something he really couldn't remember but had never forgotten.

"My father said how I was born is the reason why I put ketchup on everything I eat." He laughed.

"Is that supposed to be funny?" She leaned away from him.

"He thought so."

"Where is he now? Do you see him?"

"Yes, I see him. He's in a safe place." He stood up and heard the bird moving in the cage outside the bedroom. "I'm sorry if this bothered you. I just wanted you to know."

"It's all right," she continued and changed the subject. "Did you like the way I talked to you during . . ." She looked up at him.

"Sure"—he shrugged—"but you all do it. You think that's it. But loyalty counts, like my birds."

"What do you mean all?" She sat up in bed.

"Nothing." He waved his hand in the dark room and looked at the figurines on the dresser. "I like those." He pointed at them. "I want one."

"I don't know," she said. "My mother gave me . . ."

"Perfect," he mumbled, then walked over to the dresser.

With his fingertips, he gently touched the three—to four-inch figures, starting with their heads, then moved slowly down their bodies. "You should dust these more often. What are they?"

"Disney figures from the cartoon movies. Cinderella, Snow White, you know."

"You mean animated features," he corrected her.

"Yes, Evan, animated." She sighed. "My mother gave them to me when I was a child, and despite all the times I moved, they've never been damaged."

"You have the woman from *Beauty and the Beast*. Your mother didn't buy you that when you were a child."

"No, you're right. My ex-husband bought that one for me," she said annoyed. "Why do you care?"

"I like that one." He picked it up but held it for only a moment before he was reminded of something else.

"I want to check on the bird." He set the figure back down on the dresser. At the doorway to her bedroom, he stopped. "Do you have a hammer?"

"Yes. Why?"

"I want to hang the birdcage for you. Where is it?"

"It's in the kitchen, next to the refrigerator, bottom drawer."

"I'll be right back."

In the living room, Evan held the bird in his hands for a moment and whispered to her that it would be all right. "It's time to sing, isn't it?"

In the bedroom, he saw her lying on her left side with her back to him. From the sound of her breathing, he thought she must be nearly asleep.

"You remind me of someone." His voice was hoarse.

"What?"

He stopped next to the bed, holding the hammer behind his back.

"You remind me of someone," he said again.

"Who, Evan?" She turned toward him and smiled.

"I was close to her for a while. She taught me about the birds. She taught me about loyalty."

"Who?" she asked again.

"My stepmother. She was about your age then, and childless like you."

"Was she a good person?"

He gripped the handle of the claw hammer hard and shook his head quickly.

"What did she do?"

"She got pregnant, like my bird, and my father smashed her skull with a claw hammer."

She sat up and crawled backward until she felt the edge of the headboard on her back. "Get out of here!" she yelled.

"It's time to sing."

Before she could raise her hands, he smashed the claw hammer down into her forehead and heard her skull crack, then hit her again and again until he could no longer recognize her face.

In the bathtub, he washed off the hammer, then, holding it with a hand towel, set it down next to the bed. In the living room, he listened to his bird sing and talked to her for a few minutes before he set her body back inside the cage. In the bedroom, he cut off her finger, lay on top of her, and when he was finished, folded her hands across her abdomen.

At his home, Evan kept their fingers in a lighted glass display case in the den across from his computer. Underneath them, after he put plaster around them and hardened them in a kiln, he would write their names and the dates it happened.

At the birdcage on the kitchen counter, he stopped.

"I'm sorry," he whispered to the dead bird, "but I have her figurine."

He whispered good-bye to his bird at the door to her apartment and locked it behind him when he left.

CHAPTER 16

"**S**OME OF THESE** witnesses, if you want to call them that," Joe said slowly, "say he was short, some say tall. One said he was an Arab and believes that this is part of the international terrorist conspiracy. Most of them said they didn't see anything and they didn't want to get involved."

Anglen looked at the television in his hotel room. It was seven-thirty in the morning, and he was watching the news.

"You're talking about Kathy Rogers, the first one here?" Anglen asked.

"Of course. We're still interviewing potential witnesses on the second murder."

"Hold on a minute," Anglen said and set the phone down on the bed.

For five mornings now, he had watched her on television. *She's the same*, he thought, *she could be their sister.*

"Go on, Joe."

"What it is, Tom?"

"The newscaster."

"What do you mean?"

"There's a local newsperson here who looks just like Kathy Rogers and Nancy . . . What was her last name?"

"Grace, Nancy Grace. What's your point?"

"I'm just thinking about it. Go on."

"The people who live in the two homes behind her apartment with indirect views claim they never saw anything and didn't know who she was," Joe continued. "But the guy who lives directly behind her did see something and . . ."

"She had Disney figures on her dresser," Anglen interrupted him. "I think she had some of them since she was a child."

"Kathy?" Joe asked.

"No, Nancy . . . what was her last name?"

"I just told you, Grace. Are you all right?"

"No." Anglen looked down at the carpet and scratched his forehead with the fingernails on his left hand.

"What is it?"

"Focus, I think."

This time, Anglen remembered, Kansas City PD hadn't removed the body or disposed of the bird. They were sure now, because of the two murdered women and his presence, that there was a serial killer in Kansas City, and someone had leaked it to the press.

"Tell me about the interviews," Anglen said.

"I will, but first you need to tell me if I need to bring you back and let Mark handle this case."

"I'll finish this." Anglen sipped on the glass of scotch. "I always do."

"This guy who lives behind Kathy Rogers is a computer programmer. He lives alone, and he's been watching her since he moved in. She liked to get dressed and undressed with the blinds partly open. She was, according to him, fairly sexually active, but not a "slut," to use his word. He did see the killer, but only brief glimpses. He was sitting on the chair, and she sat down on him, facing the window. He was looking at something else."

There was blood all around the bed, Anglen remembered, and after a few minutes, Officer Woods had excused himself politely and walked into the living room of Nancy's apartment.

"What about the rental car?" Anglen asked.

"We did get a partial plate from the super in her apartment building. Apparently, he was watching her too. We ran it through the computer, and I think we found the right rental car company. We think he rented the car through a Nevada limited liability company. There were no names. Nevada is a haven for people avoiding judgments and tax liens and the like. The attorney who holds the interest in his name won't disclose the equitable owner. We're trying to use the Patriot Act on him."

"You said he might be a terrorist?" Anglen laughed.

"We tried to make him believe that, yes."

"The birds?"

"I'm having two university ornithologists look at them for identification purposes, but they're badly crushed. We'll see."

"Can they tell if they're male or female?"

"I don't know. Why?"

"I'm not sure."

"Mark asked the same thing," Joe said.

On the television screen in the hotel room, he saw her again.

"Joe, how many women do you think are in Kansas City who fit this man's profile?" Anglen asked.

"A lot. Hundreds anyway."

"But he didn't see them," Anglen said. "He must have seen this news woman."

"You think he may go after her? He's already killed twice there."

Anglen remembered standing in front of the dresser in Nancy Grace's bedroom, looking at glass figurines, then looking up and seeing her body on the bed. *What were her last thoughts*, he wondered, *as she felt the hammer on her face?*

"I don't know," Anglen paused. "Maybe. Her name is Tanya Richards. She's on one of the morning feel-good shows."

"He's probably left, Tom."

"Maybe, but he's been here for what, three or four weeks now, and every morning he wakes up to her face and her voice. Her voice is distinctive, throaty, deep, slightly hoarse, like a mild cold. I think he might be hearing her in his mind and wondering if he could do three here."

"I'll find out everything I can about her," Joe said.

"Thank you. Call me when you have the information on Tanya. If she fits his profile, he already knows."

Anglen heard the beep on his cell phone and looked at the window. "It's Trish. I'll call you back later."

"Joe told you I was in Kansas City," he said as he sat down on the bed.

"Yes, Tom," Trish said. "I know you don't like to call me when you're working."

"It's not that," he answered. "It's just that I'm never sure when it will be over. How are Sean and Mary?"

"Good. They ask me every morning when you'll be home."

"We might have a lead. It might be sooner than I thought a few days ago."

"You've said this before," she said cautiously. "Do you mean it?"

"If I don't catch him here, I'm finished with this case," Anglen answered. "Is that good enough?"

"You've never said that before. Yes, it is."

"I'll call you in a few days."

"I love you. Please be safe."

"I love you."

"When will Mark be back?" Anglen said after he dialed Joe's number.

"He's on a plane now. He should be there in a few hours."

"I want his thoughts."

"You respect Mark?"

"Yes. What did they call his father?"

"The man with the eyes," Joe answered.

"Right," Anglen said, "I'll call you soon."

"Could Tanya be the next one?" he whispered. "Maybe this will be finished soon."

CHAPTER 17

"TANYA"—HER PRODUCER NODDED at her in the hallway—"good show today."

"Thank you."

It was four thirty in the afternoon, and she would be leaving work soon. Tomorrow, in addition to her duties as coanchor of the morning show, she was interviewing a woman who had invented a cardboard device that snapped around the handle on grocery carts. They cost ninety-nine cents each, could be reused, and were designed to stop the spread of bacteria and viruses. *Fascinating*, she thought sarcastically.

In her office, she looked at the computer, then leaned back in her chair. *I have to do something important*, she thought, *maybe the women, the serial murders. How many more before he's caught? Why these women?*

"Tanya, are you going to the Cavern tonight?" he asked.

It was Ray, the weatherman, whom she had gone out with last week, and he was leaning against the door to her office. The sex hadn't been spectacular, but it hadn't been bad.

"I haven't decided yet."

"Come with us." He smiled.

"Maybe. I'll tell you in an hour. I need to talk to Ron."

A few years ago, the channel had lost its network affiliation, and she had thought then that she had lost her opportunity to move up. *I need a real story*, she thought again, *like the murders*, but that was nighttime news and had been the lead story for the last four days. Because they were killed in virtually the same way, the speculation was that the same man had committed both crimes. The words "serial killer" were mentioned on every major station, but the police refused to comment. The lead-in to the news last night, read by anchor George McCoy was "Does Kansas City have a serial killer? The deaths of these two women are frighteningly similar. You'll want to know."

She got up, walked down the hall to her producer's office, and knocked gently on his open door.

"Yeah, Tanya."

"Ron, can we talk for a minute?"

"Sure."

"I want to do hard news—the serial killer story," she said.

"George does that at night, you know that."

"What if I get a lead?"

"Then we'll talk." Ron shrugged.

After she got back to her office, the weatherman leaned inside the door. "Tanya, are you coming with us?"

The sex, she remembered again, hadn't been spectacular, but it hadn't been bad.

"Yes, for an hour or so." She smiled.

"Good."

"Sir, would you like more coffee?" the waitress asked.

"Yes, thank you."

She had blonde hair, was probably in her early thirties, and had a wedding band on her left hand.

"How long have you been married?"

"Just six months."

"First time?" Evan asked.

"Yes, the first time for both of us."

"That's wonderful. Any kids?"

"We're trying now."

"Good luck."

"Thank you, sir."

Nice ass, Evan thought as he watched her walk away. It was a wireless room, and he looked around him and saw mostly laptops next to cups of coffee. His voice was deep and distinctive according to his stepmother and the various women he had known, and he had noticed the waitress's reaction when he spoke. His stepmother had told him that with time and age, it would just become deeper and richer and that he should think about going into religion or radio, which she had said was really the same thing. His stepmother, he remembered, was about sex in every movement, glance, and touch, but she was jealous and angry and had driven his father to the place he was today.

Should I approach the newscaster, or is it too dangerous?

Evan watched the waitress bend over and serve another customer. *Nice tits*, he thought, *my father would love fucking you.*

Gathering information on her hadn't been that difficult. From newspaper archives and a few telephone calls placed from pay phones to garrulous receptionists at the station, he had learned that Tanya was thirty-eight years old, had been married once for a little more than year to a man named Mike Richards, and had no children. He had been shaving one morning before he met the first one in Kansas City later that night, heard her voice, and stopped, knowing that she was right. He had followed her and learned her routine, even the bar she went to after work several nights a week. In the few weeks he had been in Kansas City, moving from one hotel to another using a different alias each time, he had come to know her and looked forward to the early-morning newscast. He had even followed her on a date once and from his car across the street watched the light go off in the bedroom of her condo and the man leave several hours later.

"Sir, can I get you anything else?" the waitress asked.

"Just a little more coffee and a check. Your husband is a lucky man."

"Thank you, sir. Why?"

"You're attractive, but I can tell you're loyal to him. That's important."

"I love him." She shrugged slightly, then poured the coffee.

"It's still important."

I feel loyalty to my birds, he thought. He loved his birds and hated what he had to do after he killed women who should never have the opportunity to raise a child. After he returned home, he would take the mate of the bird he had given as a present, walk upstairs to the kitchen, and quickly snap his neck. Each time, he always cried a little as he felt them die in his hands.

"Here." He set two ten-dollar bills on the table. "Good luck."

"Thank you again, sir."

With the exception of his women, he rarely looked anyone directly in the eyes. He knew it didn't make a lot of sense, as his eyes were hazel and ordinary, except for the gray flecks, but he thought it might help someone recognize him someday. He could always feel eyes. *I can feel their eyes looking at me, seeing me.*

It was late afternoon, and he drove across town in the rental car until he saw the Cavern, hoping he would find Tanya there. Inside, he saw her sitting with three men at a table near the bar. A few tables away, he ordered a Merlot and waited to talk to her. He sipped on the wine and heard a cell phone, then watched her reach into her purse.

"She'll meet with me," he heard her say as she walked to the opening between the bar and the restrooms. "Good. I'll change my career if I can interview the sister of one of these women he killed. Tell her I'll meet with her anytime she wants."

He walked slowly past her and put his hands on the door to the men's room.

He turned when he heard her close the cell phone.

"I know you." He lifted his right hand and pointed. "You're on TV. The news, the morning and midday shows."

"Yes."

"You're Tanya."

"Yes, thank you for watching the show," she said indifferently.

"I always watch you in the morning." He smiled.

"Thank you, again, but I need to get back to my friends."

"Sure, I understand. My name is Evan. Would you like to have a drink later?"

"I really can't tonight." She looked toward the opening between the restrooms and the bar. "Maybe another time."

"Of course." He nodded. "I'm sure you get this all the time."

"It's just that I don't know you," she explained. "You look like a nice guy."

"Thank you. I thought I might have a story for you."

"Really? What?"

"I'm a photographer. I work part-time for Kansas City PD. I took the photos of the crime scenes, the women, you know."

"And you'll talk about it?"

"To you. I can't be quoted. I can't be revealed as your source. I'd lose my job."

"Tell me what you know. I'll keep your name out of it."

Evan stared into her eyes. "You look so much like her."

"Kathy?"

He nodded. "And some others."

"What is it?"

"I was just remembering something." He smiled.

He noticed she was rubbing her arms as if she were cold and that she wouldn't look back at him. *She knows*, he thought.

"Maybe another time," he said slowly and nodded at her.

"Sure." She smiled easily as if she were on television.

As she sat down across the room with her friends, he thought, *She's an arrogant bitch. I will break my rule this time.* As she walked out of the bar, he saw she was on her cell phone again. He couldn't hear her words as he walked outside.

"Ron, I just got hit on by a guy at the bar," she said.

"This is news?" he said sarcastically.

"No, it was different." She stood up and turned away from the table.

"How?"

"There was something about him. I don't know."

"You think . . ."

"Maybe. Do I look like the victims of this man?" she asked.

"You could be their sister."

"I'm scared, Ron. He scared the hell out of me."

"A friend of mine at Kansas City PD told me that Tom Anglen is here from the FBI."

"Tom Anglen?"

"He catches serial killers. I'll call him, or I'll call his boss. Don't go home tonight. Go home with the weatherman. And be careful."

"I will." She closed the cell phone.

CHAPTER 18

"SHE FITS," JOE said, "in every way that we know of at this time."

"Tell me about her," Anglen said.

"Thirty-eight, married once, divorced, no children. You know the profile."

"Family?"

"The parents were divorced when she was eleven. The mother lives here, the father died a few years ago. She has one brother who lives out west."

"Tell me what she does after work."

"Several days a week, she goes to happy hour at pretty much the same bar. It's called the Cavern. It's trendy—professionals go there. She stays for a few hours and goes home alone most nights."

"Dating? Might she be with someone tonight?"

"She went out with the morning weatherman last week. She's staying with a friend."

"Anything else?" Anglen asked.

"You were right. He's smart. He planned this. For the first victim here, he used a different rental car and, apparently, a different disguise than for the second one. On the second car, the cell phone number belongs to a New Jersey corporation."

"Payments on the credit cards, cell phones?"

"Offshore accounts, we think," Joe answered. "We haven't been able to find an account yet in the U.S. or a signature card."

"He had to have some money to do this," Anglen said after thinking about it for a few minutes. "Not a huge amount, but some. And maybe he had some help before he started. Maybe someone else changed his name a long time ago."

"Why?"

"I don't know yet." Anglen shook his head. "I need more time. But I do know you're going to tell me something now."

"I don't know if it means anything or not. I got a call from Tanya's producer. His name is Ron. She was approached by a man at the Cavern yesterday. She thinks it might be him."

"What . . ."

"He's about five nine, bulky, muscular. He has a beard and wore a hat. That's the best I could get. Your hunch might have been right. What do you want me to do?" Joe said.

"I think it was him." Anglen looked around the hotel room. "I want one agent in the back and one out front of the bar. And

I want Mark inside dressed like a businessman who just got off work. I'll tell him. I want one agent at her condo so in case . . ."

"She's not there," Joe answered. "She's staying with a friend."

"Call me when she gets there," Anglen said. "Maybe we'll get him tonight. Otherwise, it could take a long time, and you're not going to get another year of my life."

"I understand."

His room was on the fourth floor of the Midtown Marriott, and for a moment, he looked out at the overcast sky and sensed the humidity.

"Rain," he said softly, "rain this afternoon or tonight."

He turned on the television and waited for the midday show.

"This morning," she said, "we showed you a local inventor who found a way to stop the spread of disease from something as innocent as a grocery cart. My producer thought we should run it again for those who missed it."

He turned down the volume, then picked up his cell phone.

"Trish, are you all right?"

"Yes, Tom. You're not calling to tell me it's over."

"No, but if we don't catch him tonight, I meant what I told you in the last call."

"Then you are coming home soon?" she asked.

"Tomorrow or the next day, at the latest."

"Can I believe you this time?" she said slowly.

"Yes. I'll quit if I have to, but Joe will let me go. Mark can do this."

"I'm scared because I want to ask you what you saw and what Mark saw, but I'm afraid of the answer."

"It's about the birds, and it's about their hands in a way, I think. They are always neatly folded across their abdomen like a . . ."

"Don't," she interrupted him. "Don't say anything more. And I'm scared because I'm about to get what I've prayed for, wanted for a long time—you're coming home."

"Why?"

"Because I never thought it would happen. I still don't believe it," she answered. "Tell me how you're going to catch him."

"Instinct, a hunch. There's a woman on the local news who fits his profile."

"And you think he'll go after her?"

"I think he will tonight," Anglen said. "I'll call you tonight, and I'll see you in a few days."

Anglen showered and dressed and then sat on the end of the bed in his hotel room and waited for the next call.

CHAPTER 19

SLOWLY, EVAN TOOK off his hat and held it by the brim at his waist as if he were carrying flowers for a date. Gently, he knocked at the door.

"Ray, I'll be ready in a minute." He heard her unlock the dead bolt.

He turned the doorknob and lightly pushed on the door. When he stepped inside, he saw her disappear in a hallway dressed only in a white bra and thong panties.

"Just give me a minute, Ray!" she shouted from her bedroom. "I'll be dressed, and we can go."

He looked around the living room of her condo, at the modern-style furniture, the beige couch and loveseat, and the big-screen television.

"Nice," he mumbled.

He waited until he heard the sound of her heels on the hardwood floor.

"Ray." She looked up and stopped abruptly a few feet away from him.

"I wish we'd had more time." He shook his head as he crushed the brim of his hat with his fingers. "I should have had a present for you. She was a bird, a nightbird. She's loyal."

"You're him. Please don't hurt me," she begged.

"You know they mate for life."

"Tom Anglen from the FBI is here," she warned him. "My producer told me."

"Tom . . ."

"Anglen. He catches serial killers for the FBI."

"They know," he whispered to himself. "They finally know."

He saw her eyes darting around the room, looking for a way out.

"Don't try." He shook his head. "Who's he working with at Kansas City PD?"

"I don't know." Her voice cracked. "The police report said Officer Rick Woods found one of the . . ."

"Thank you." He saw her take a deep breath and covered her face with his hat before she could scream. Under the hat, he felt her cheekbones on the first two knuckles of his fist and watched her tilt backward until she fell on the hardwood floor. Gently, he picked her up and carried her into the bedroom.

"She's dead, Tom," Joe said slowly.

"What happened?"

"The weatherman, Ray whatever, dropped her off so she could change. He went out to buy a pack of cigarettes. When he got back, the door was open, and she was in the bedroom."

"The same way?" Anglen asked.

"Yes. There's a claw hammer next to the bed. Where are you now?"

About ten minutes away from the Cavern to catch a serial killer who will never walk through that door again," he answered. "How did he know?"

"I don't know that he did."

"How could we have prevented this?"

"Obviously, we couldn't."

"You said the door to her condo was open," Anglen asked as he saw the Cavern in front of them.

"Yes."

"He's always been so meticulous in the past, carefully locking and closing the door when he leaves. Was there a bird?"

"I don't think so," Joe answered. "Are you going to the crime scene now?"

"No. Mark can do it. He reads a crime scene better than I do anyway. I'm not going to another one unless it's the killer's."

"You're quitting, Tom. You've said this before," Joe said.

Anglen walked through the front door of the Cavern and saw Mark sitting at a table in the middle of the room with a half-full glass of wine in front of him.

"I want one of our sketch artists to interview patrons." Anglen ignored Joe's question. "Someone saw him, and I want it given to the media and local law enforcement. I don't care what the director wants. Have Kansas PD take it to every hotel within a ten-mile radius of here. I want to lock him in. I want a forensics team at her condo with Mark. I'll tell him. He lives by his rituals, that way he doesn't make a mistake. This time he was careless."

"You didn't answer my question, Tom," Joe said.

"Yes, absolutely."

He closed the cell phone and sat down at the table with Mark.

"What happened?" Mark asked.

"Do you want something to drink, sir?" the waitress asked.

"Scotch."

"She's dead," Anglen answered.

"How?"

"She stopped at her condo to change her dress or whatever, and he was there."

"What do you want me to do?" Mark asked.

"I know what you're thinking. She wasn't supposed to be there. She was staying with a friend, so we didn't put an agent there. My mistake."

"Do you want another scotch, sir?" the waitress asked.

"Yes. Were you working yesterday, and do you know Tanya Richards?"

"Yeah." She shrugged. "She comes in all the time."

"Did you see a man approach her yesterday?"

"Yeah. I waited on him, and he ordered a Merlot."

"Do you remember what he looked like?"

"His eyes. I saw his eyes. Gray things, I saw gray things in his brown eyes."

"What do you mean?" Anglen asked.

"Spots, specks. Otherwise, he looked ordinary."

"Thank you."

"What do you want me to do, sir?" Mark asked again.

"One of our sketch artists will be here shortly. I want you to help him interview witnesses like the waitress. People saw him. I want a portrait of him. Then I want you to process the crime scene."

"You're not going?"

"No, Lou." He finished his scotch, then stood up.

"Have you told Mr. Mosely?" Mark asked.

"Yes."

"Thank you . . ."

"Don't thank me. I'll talk to you later."

As he slipped the plastic card into the slot and saw the green light activate, Evan thought, *How do I find Anglen? How do I find out what he knows?*

Inside, he turned on the television and found the news. "This is late-breaking news," the man said. "Tragedy has struck Kansas City again, and this time it is too close to home."

In the left-hand corner of the screen, he saw a photograph of Tanya, smiling.

"We lost one of our own today," the man said. "Tanya Richards was murdered—I'm sorry, give me a minute."

"As you all know," the man continued, "Tanya was coanchor of our morning and midday newscasts. She'll be missed by all of us. The FBI is searching for the killer who has now killed three women here in the last five weeks."

"Anglen," he whispered.

"Does the FBI have any leads?" the newscaster asked the reporter at the crime scene.

"I talked to Officer Rick Woods. He only said that the FBI is pursuing a number of leads."

"Thank you, Judy. Our sources tell us that the lead FBI officer is Thomas Anglen, an experienced agent on these kinds of cases. I hope . . ."

Evan saw a black-and-white sketch of a man wearing a rain hat with a beard on the television screen.

"This is a sketch by the FBI of the killer. If you have seen this man, please call this station, the Kansas City Police Department, or the FBI.

He pressed the mute button on the remote and poured a glass of wine.

"What leads?" Evan said. "What does Anglen know? How do I find out what he knows?"

Evan turned off the television and whispered, "I can find him, I can find Anglen. He'll use his own name at the hotel where he's staying because they never think we'll target them." On the way to his hotel room, he had walked past the Business

Center. *Computers*, he thought. *Yes, I can find Anglen. I have to know what the FBI has learned about me.* As he heard the door to his room close and lock behind him, he thought, *I have to leave here by tomorrow afternoon, but I should be safe until then—they think I'm already gone.*

CHAPTER 20

ANGLEN KNELT DOWN at the altar and bowed his head.

"Forgive me, Father, for I have sinned," he whispered to the statue of Jesus above him. "There is a man who kills, and I have to stop him, and I don't know how to do it. I don't understand why he does it or how. And this time, he killed three more people while I worked and . . ."

Behind him, he heard the wooden kneeler creak slightly as the old woman, who was in a pew behind him, struggled to get up.

He leaned forward and bowed his head.

"I asked you a long time ago if I should do this work, if I could do it. And now I know I can't anymore. At every crime scene, I leave part of myself behind."

Anglen heard the old woman struggle with her weight and the awkward positioning required to worship God before he

heard her feet shuffle slowly away from him. He was then alone
with the statues of Jesus and Mary.

"I'm sorry," Anglen whispered after he heard the bass sound
of one of the front doors closing behind the old woman. "I chose
this work, I chose this life. It's a little late to second guess those
choices."

He lit one candle and looked at the statue of Mary, "Blessed
Mother, please remember Tanya Richards."

He set another candle down on the altar at her feet, "Blessed
Mother, please remember Nancy Grace."

He lit and set the third candle down on the altar. "Please
remember Kathy and the others. They are all missing souls who
died before their time. Please embrace and comfort them."

Through the stained-glass windows, the broken lines of light
streamed onto the chapel's stone walls. He had been in Catholic
churches when his children were born, and he had been there
when people died—first his father, then his mother, and his sister
from breast cancer. He had spent time alone at altars like this one
asking why and praying for guidance. In the last twenty years, he
had given three eulogies, he remembered, for family members,
and he had always said the same words at the end.

"I trust your judgment and my faith."

His father had given him his faith. His father had told him
that life didn't make sense without it. But now nothing made
sense. Ten years ago, he remembered, cancer had spread like an
army of killers in his sister's body, and yesterday, Tanya Richards

had been bludgeoned to death. Nothing made sense, he thought again.

"I have to focus," Anglen whispered, then looked up at the statue of Mary. "I have to finish this job and then go home."

He had been afraid, he remembered, each time he saw family and friends die, as if the clock was ticking on his own fictional invincibility. *Can I still do it?* he would ask himself, *can I still hear them coming when they are only inches away from me?* But he would always go back to work, back to the world of men who killed for no reason at all.

"I have to focus," Anglen raised his voice slightly. "I have to, or I won't . . ."

He thought about Trish and Sean and Mary and smiled for a moment. *No matter what happens, I go back home tomorrow,* he thought, *and I'll never do this again.*

"My son," a priest said, standing next to the statue of Mary, "are you all right?"

"I'm sorry, Father, yes."

"I don't recognize you," he said. "You're new to our parish?"

"That's right." Anglen stood up. "I live back East. I'm working here, but I wanted to visit this church before I left."

"You are always welcome here," he said.

"Thank you."

"You lit three candles. Do you have friends in trouble?"

Anglen looked up at the priest.

"Their deaths were premature, but I want to believe that they'll be okay now. I'm sure they are."

"We all want to believe, my son. I'm sure they are fine where they are now."

"I know. Thank you, Father."

At the entryway to the chapel, he felt the drops of holy water on his fingertips, then crossed himself before he pushed open the door. In the bright sunlight, he squinted for a moment, then saw a young boy reaching into a storm drain a few feet away from him.

"Mister, could you help me? I dropped the keys to the lock on my bike."

"Sure," he said, then heard the sound of shoes scraping gently across the concrete behind him.

"We're friends," he heard a man's deep voice and knew who he was. "He thinks this is a joke I played on you."

"Mister, can you help me?" the boy said again.

Anglen reached for his gun.

"Don't do it," the man said. "Tell him it's just a joke, or he'll never ride his bike again."

"I . . . I," Anglen stuttered and thought about Sean and how Trish's father had died a long time ago.

"Don't be stupid," the man said. "I have a gun."

"Will you let him go?" Anglen asked.

"Maybe, after . . ."

"No, now," Anglen said firmly.

"All right, tell him he can go."

"Go, son, it was just a joke. Let me see you run."

When the boy hesitated, Anglen shouted, "Run now, as fast as you can!"

Anglen watched the boy run across the parking lot.

"I need to know what the FBI knows about me," the man said.

Anglen watched the boy disappear around the corner of the church, and then he turned.

"How did you find me?" Anglen asked.

"It wasn't that difficult. Tell me what the FBI knows."

"What do you want to know?"

"Do you know my name?" Evan asked carefully. "Do you know where I live? Can I go home?"

When Anglen didn't answer, Evan stepped toward him and said, "You have to tell me. Do you know what happened a long time ago?"

The man looked different from the sketch he had seen. Now he was clean shaven and looked a good ten years younger.

"We can talk next door," he said. "But I need to know what you know about me."

"I know that the man with the eyes will catch you," Anglen said, "and kill you."

"The man with the eyes?" He looked scared. "I don't like people staring, looking at me that way. The man with the eyes? What do you mean?"

"He's going to kill you. He's going to stop this," Anglen said again.

He lifted the gun and gestured with it at the vacant convenience store.

"Go. There you can tell me about the man with the eyes."

Anglen shook his head and thought about the priest inside the church. *I don't want to die here, I don't want to die now.*

"No, "Anglen said and shook his head again.

"Go!" he shouted.

"No."

"You have to." He sounded frustrated. "I have a gun."

"I won't hurt you," he said, "please just tell me what you know. And the eyes, tell me—I always feel them."

Anglen turned his back on him and reached slowly for his gun. "No."

"Tell me!" he screamed.

Anglen felt the handle of the gun in the palm of his left hand just seconds before he felt the first bullet rip through his lungs. The second bullet, he felt near his heart.

In front of a church, a sanctuary he had known since he was a child, he dropped to his knees and heard the metallic clatter of his gun drop next to him on the concrete steps. He felt the third bullet in his back and fell facedown on the steps. He couldn't see or feel the bright sunlight around him anymore.

"You should have told me," he barely heard the man say, then heard the sound of his footsteps as he ran away.

Just beyond the corner to the church at the street, the boy heard the first shot and stopped. He heard two more before he ran for his life.

CHAPTER 21

EVAN PARKED THE rental car between the two biggest SUVs he could find in the parking lot of the largest superstore in Kansas City, Missouri, and walked for what seemed like miles until he was at the front of the store. In a world of bright red carts, howling children, angry parents, noise, people, frequently announced specials, and more noise and more people, he waited impatiently for the cab he had called about an hour ago.

Now he looked nothing like the sketch he had seen after he had killed Tanya. Now he looked younger, clean shaven, wearing a sports coat, jeans, and dark tennis shoes. In this world, he would never be noticed—he was anonymous.

I don't think the FBI knows how yet, Evan thought. He smiled. *I killed an FBI agent, and I'll get away with it just like I have with women who should never have children.*

Through the thousands of cars in the parking lot, he saw the color yellow moving slowly across the lot. He walked to the curb and waited. When he saw the car drive down the center lane, he waved and then watched the cab driver place his bag in the trunk of the car.

"Where to?" he asked.

"Take me across the river to the First National Bank Building," he answered. "Do you know where it is?"

"Sure."

His plan was to be dropped off in Kansas City, Kansas, then take another cab to the airport in Topeka and fly to Omaha.

"You're here on business?" the cabdriver asked.

"Yes."

"What kind?"

"Birds. I write for bird magazines. There was a convention here."

"Really, I didn't know."

"Yeah, there were a lot of us here."

"Why not just fly out of the airport here?"

"I promised a friend I would see him before I went home," he answered.

"Did you read about the killer?" the cabdriver asked as they crossed the bridge.

"Yeah, it was terrible. I hope they catch the guy."

How did you find me? he remembered Anglen asking him.

It really hadn't been that difficult. In the Business Center at the hotel, he had typed in Anglen's name on one of the two computers in the small room off the lobby. He had been alone there the entire time. He read stories about two of Anglen's cases—the Cat Burglar and Vincent Crea. He had seen the photograph with the senator when Anglen had testified. In one story, he learned that Anglen was married with two children and was a devout Catholic. The story said that Anglen always visited the same Catholic church before he started a case. He had killed three here, and Anglen hadn't been able to stop him. Evan had wondered if Anglen would light candles for those three lives.

"And they think he killed that FBI agent. Did you hear about that?"

"No, I'm afraid I didn't."

He could still see Anglen's body freeze for a moment when the first bullet hit him, then drop to his knees when he felt the second bullet. He could still see the blood on the church steps. After Evan had made three telephone calls to the television station where Tanya had worked, a young-sounding woman told him that she had heard from a policeman that Anglen was staying at the Midtown Marriott. All he had said was that he thought he had information on the killer that he wanted to tell the FBI agent.

"We're in Kansas now," the cabdriver said. "It should only be a few minutes."

"Thanks."

"Why do you think he killed the FBI agent?" the cabdriver asked.

The third bullet, he remembered, had driven Anglen face-first into the concrete, and he had turned, slightly to his left, trying to breathe through a broken nose. There was only one Catholic Church within walking distance of the Marriott, and he had waited in the vacant convenience store for a few hours, checking the old Bulova watch his father had given him years ago until he saw a tall man walk into the church. From the photograph on the computer, he knew it was Anglen instantly. The boy had ridden his bicycle into the parking lot while he was waiting for Anglen to come out.

"Isn't that the First National Building on the right?" Evan asked.

"Yes, sir."

"My friend works there."

He paid the cabdriver, waited until the cab was gone, then walked around the building and stopped in front of a dumpster. Carefully, he wiped off the gun, then dropped it inside. Then he walked to a bar he had seen on MapQuest about a block away.

"How are you today, sir?" the bartender asked.

There were only two other people sitting in the bar.

"Good. Give me a glass of Merlot. Also, can you call me a cab?"

"Sure."

"Thank you."

The next flight to Omaha would take off in two hours, and he already had his ticket.

"He'll be here in minutes."

"Thank you." He paid the bartender.

"Business trip?" the bartender asked.

"Always. It's always business."

"I know what you mean."

Before he turned and ran away, he saw the spasming of Anglen's right hand as he tried to reach for his gun, which had dropped behind his head. He was lying on his left side, and the muzzle of the gun was pointed at the large oak doors to the old Catholic church.

Through the window at the front of the dive bar, he saw something catch the attention of the bartender.

"That's your cab."

"I know. Thank you."

"Come back and see us the next time you're in town," the bartender said.

"It will be a while, but sure, I will."

"Where to?" the cabdriver asked.

"Topeka airport."

"Topeka? Why not fly out of the airport across the river?" he asked.

"I'm meeting a friend there."

"Sure." The cabdriver nodded.

CHAPTER 22

MARK KNELT DOWN next to the body with his back to the doors of the church.

"Have you finished here?" He looked up at the woman from the FBI's crime scene unit in Kansas City, then shielded his eyes from the sun setting in the western sky.

"Are you Agent Mark?" she asked.

"Yes. You didn't answer me."

"Yes, sir. Do you want us to take him now?"

"No, not until Mr. Mosely gets here."

"Do you want me to tell you what we found?" she asked.

He shifted slightly, away from the sun. "No. Please leave me alone with him for a few minutes."

Mark watched her until he saw her reach the car in the parking lot, where two other agents from the crime scene unit were waiting, then stood up and walked around the body until he was just behind Anglen's feet. He had been at the bar, the Cavern, interviewing witnesses when Joe called from an FBI plane and told him Tom was dead. He had asked where, then drove to the old Catholic church around the corner from Anglen's hotel. The crime scene unit had been taking a few final photographs when he arrived. He guessed Joe would be there in about an hour.

Anglen lay facedown except for his head that was twisted to the left with his right cheek resting uncomfortably on the concrete in front of the church. His eyes were still open, and it almost looked like he was squinting into the harsh sun in the western sky.

"Fuck!" Mark shouted, then turned away from the body and noticed the woman who had been near Anglen when he arrived staring at him, along with the other two agents. He turned his back to them, then crouched down and slowly rubbed the palm of his right hand across the left side of his face. Mark lifted Anglen's pant leg and touched his ankle gently while he looked at the blood surrounding his torso. It had happened about two hours ago, he guessed, as Joe had told him. The priest had called the local police after he heard the shots and had seen the body. Now Mark was alone at the top of the stairs leading to the church, and the killer was long gone, almost certainly in another city now.

He closed Anglen's eyes, then gently touched the left side of Anglen's face. His body was under the cross over the church, and his face felt cold on his hand.

"Fuck," he said again, but quietly. *I have to focus. This is only the second time,* he thought, *that I've been at the crime scene of someone*

I knew. Did I meet Mr. Anglen, Tom, two weeks ago, or was it three?
No, it was at the Academy, he remembered. Just a few days ago, Tom
had said he was leaving the work, the FBI, because he couldn't
do it anymore. He felt pain over the loss of someone he barely
knew; he felt fear because he was alone in a world he didn't yet
understand.

"Am I ready?" He mumbled. "Am I ready for all this? Am I
ready to catch a man who has killed fifty women and a man with
far more experience than I have?"

He could feel the agents in the parking lot watching him,
listening, wondering what he was doing.

"I have to focus," he said a little louder. "I have to focus.
What can you tell me? What did you see? You're the only one of
us who has actually seen him, heard his voice."

Anglen's right arm was pointing straight at the doors to the
church, twisted so his right palm was facing upward with his gun
about a foot away from his hand. Mark saw three distinct bullet
holes in his back, two through his lungs and one apparently
through his heart, in the shape of a long narrow triangle.

He can shoot, Mark thought. *How did he learn?*

"These are entry wounds," Mark said, then stood up and
walked around the body several times, stopping every few feet.

"I know you were facing him before he shot you, then
turned. Why?"

Mark walked in nearly a straight line south until he was about
ten feet from the body.

"He was here," Mark said quietly and pointed at the ground. "You were standing here, waiting, when Tom left the church. But there was someone else here. Who?"

"I can almost see it," he whispered, but he couldn't stop the memory from a long time ago. He closed his eyes and could hear the shot downstairs as if it were happening again. When he got downstairs, he saw his father's head lying on his right shoulder with his eyes open as lifeless as Tom's eyes were now. His father had been left-handed, and his gun and the empty bottle of Jack Daniel's were on the floor to the left of his wheelchair. He had stopped at the door to the den and saw his mother standing silently next to him with her hands on her face and her eyes wide open. Then it had seemed like hours, but it could have only been minutes, when she started screaming, then mumbling words which made no sense.

"I was only away . . . He was . . . He was good . . . What did he . . . Why? Why this . . . but . . ." Then she had stopped and stared at Mark and asked, *"What do I do now?"*

His father had never been the same after he caught the serial killer who had been a fugitive for decades. He had taken some time, then tried to go back to work but had been careless. It had been, in many ways, a basic crime—a man killed his wife and a friend, then fled. Six months after the man had disappeared, the Chicago Police Department had asked his father to review the file, and he found the man in a cheap apartment on Chicago's south side. On the night it happened, his father had picked the lock, then turned when he heard a noise in the parking lot and felt the bullet pierce his spine. His father had killed the man but had never walked again. His father had tried to work, but he just didn't think he could see the crime scene from a wheelchair, so after many years of heavy drinking, he ended it.

"Lou, I got here as quickly as I could."

"I'm sorry, Mr. Mosely." Mark turned toward him. "I didn't hear you, I was . . ."

"I know," Joe said. "I knew him for twenty years. I will blame myself for this death for the rest of my life. I never should have given him this case. I should have listened to him."

Joe sighed deeply, then took off the sunglasses and looked at Anglen's body.

"My god," he whispered.

"Do you want to be alone with him, sir?"

"No, not now. I'm taking him home. I'll do it on the flight back. I want you to work. I want you to see everything that's here. I want you to use everything your father taught you. Then we'll talk about what we're going to do."

"All right, sir."

"I'm going to leave you alone. I'm going to talk with our crime scene people. Tell me when you're finished."

"Sir," Mark said after Joe had walked a few feet away from him, "they don't do this, do they?"

"What?"

"Target us—agents, law enforcement."

Joe shook his head. "I've never seen it, I've never even heard of it."

"They never hunt outside their profile. Why did he do this? There is too much risk," Mark said.

"I really don't know."

"How do I explain this to Cara? She'll ask me."

"I'll tell her that Tom was apprehending him when it happened."

Mark shook his head. "I don't think it will work. She's smarter than I am in many ways. She'll ask."

"I'll lie to her," Joe said simply and put the sunglasses back on. "Now go back to work."

"Yes, sir."

Mark walked back to the spot where the killer had been standing, then looked around the exterior of the church and the parking lot. At the foot of the steps, he saw a boy's bicycle on its side near a storm drain.

"It was a child, a boy." Mark pointed at the bicycle with his right index finger. "The killer used the boy to distract Tom. How?"

Mark walked back to Anglen's body, stopped, then walked into the chapel of the church. Inside, he saw an older priest sitting in the last pew, leaning forward, with his head in his hands.

"Sir, I'm Lou Mark with the FBI."

The priest looked up quickly, then nodded. "How can I help you, son?"

"Did you talk with Tom before?" Mark asked.

"You mean . . ." The priest pointed toward the front door.

"Yes," Mark said.

"Yes, he seemed troubled. He said people had been hurt. I think he felt responsible."

"Did he tell you who he was?"

"No, he didn't"

"His name, Father, was Thomas Anglen. He was an FBI agent. He was the best in the division he worked in. He was killed by a man whom I think visited your church today."

"Was it the serial killer?" The priest looked scared.

Mark hesitated, then said yes. The story was either already on the news or would be in an hour.

"The man . . . he was here?"

"Without doubt," Mark answered. "Was anyone else here when Tom was inside the church?"

"There was an older lady, Mrs. O'Neill. She comes here from . . ."

"It wasn't her," Mark said impatiently.

"She was the only one when Tom, is that his name, was here."

"You're sure?"

"Yes." The priest nodded.

"You heard the shots?"

"Yes." He nodded emphatically. "I was scared and I waited a few minutes, then went outside. I've never seen anything like that." the priest shook his head.

"Did you see anyone else?"

"No, there wasn't anyone there."

"I saw a relatively new bicycle in front of the church on its side at the bottom of the steps. It's a boy's bike. From the size of the bike, I'm guessing the boy is nine or ten years old. Do you know who it might belong to?"

"I don't know." The priest shook his head.

"Is there a boy that age who comes around here during the day? Please think, Father."

"There a number of them. We have a choir, yes." He nodded.

"He would have to live close by."

"It could be Richard." The priest turned his head. "Maybe, yes."

"Can you get me his last name?"

"Yes. The killer was really here?" the priest asked again.

"Please, Father, I need the name."

The priest handed him a small piece of the paper which had the name Midtown Diocese printed across the top next to a cross, with a single name he had written on it.

"I think it's him," the priest said. "Richard Carson. If not, he might be able to tell you who it is. He lives around the corner on . . ."

Mark wrote down the information, then thanked him.

"I'm sorry again. I'm afraid I wasn't much help. I've been a priest for thirty-five years, and I often think that, wonder if what we do . . ."

"You have helped, Father"—Mark shook his hand—"but now I need to talk to my boss."

"Can I come out now?"

"No." Mark shook his head. "Wait about an hour."

"He's still . . . ?"

"Thank you. Wait an hour."

When he pushed open the door, he saw the sun on the horizon, which was now bright orange. He shielded his eyes and saw Joe talking with the agents next to the car. On the other side of Tom's body, he crouched down next to his face.

"I really wish I'd had time to know you better," he mumbled. "You reminded me in some ways of my father. You left your wife and kids, but you know . . ."

Mark realized he didn't know what to say or why he was saying anything.

"Oh yeah, I didn't get the chance to tell you, I'm going to be a father soon, first time." Mark nodded toward Anglen. "How do I tell Cara about this? How do I explain this? How do I make her believe I'm safe?"

Mark looked away, then rubbed the palm of his right hand across the left side of his face. "If I don't catch him soon, this could happen to me. What else can you tell me?"

Mark closed his eyes and sensed something. "Were you thinking about your family when you left? You were thinking about feeling safe. Is that what you were trying to tell me? What does that have to do with the man who did this?"

Mark stood up, then walked down the steps toward Joe.

"You're finished?" Joe asked him.

"Yes, sir."

"Please take care of him"—Joe gestured at the three agents—"and leave us alone."

"What did you see?" Joe asked after they left.

"The man shot him three times after he left the church. There was a child here, and he used him. The priest gave me his name. Tom died protecting that child."

"Anything else?"

"Not yet." Mark shook his head. "I'm going to visit the boy later today or tomorrow. First, I'm going to Tom's hotel room and see if he left anything there."

"I'll have a captain with Kansas City PD take you to Tom's hotel room and to visit the boy. I am going to take Tom home now."

"That's what he was thinking about, I believe his family, his home, safety. Somehow it's related to the killer."

"Can you do this?" Joe looked at Mark.

"I think so, sir."

"All right, I'm either going to make this easier or more difficult for you. When you catch him, you're going to kill him."

"Sir?" Mark sounded surprised.

"You heard me. I'm not going to wait years for trial, appeals, new trials while he sits on death row. And then watch him live in an institution for the criminally insane. You do understand me?"

Joe was speaking much faster now, and the slight Southern drawl was nearly gone.

Mark nodded.

"This man is not going to outlive me. He's not going to do interviews, television, sell art. He's not going to do anything. We can do pretty much what we want with these people, particularly this one. And he's going to die."

"You really want . . ."

"Yes, goddammit!" Joe shouted. "This is an order, understand it. I think you were remembering your father's death when I got here. They were both senseless deaths. Use it. Justify it any way you want, but this man is going to die."

"Yes, sir."

"I'm going to take Tom home now," Joe said. "The funeral will be in two days. Call me after you see the child."

Mark watched the agents place Anglen's body gently in the trunk of the car.

"My god"—Joe put his sunglasses on—"he's really gone."

Mark watched the darkness envelop the black-colored bag as the agent closed the lid of the trunk on Anglen's body, as if he had never been.

CHAPTER 23

MARK KNELT DOWN in front of the boy. He was nine years old and lived three blocks from the church where Tom Anglen had been killed. The Kansas City Police had called him a little more than an hour ago, and he was in the living room of their modest, three-bedroom home with a captain standing behind him.

"He didn't do anything wrong, did he?" the boy's mother asked.

"Of course not," Mark said, "I just want to talk to him."

"I . . . I didn't know," the boy stuttered.

"I know you didn't." Mark touched the boy's left shoulder. "Just tell me what happened."

"I . . ."

"He was so close to that man, the killer." His mother started to cry hysterically. "He could have been killed too. I saw the pictures in the paper."

"You're not helping," Mark said quietly to the woman.

The boy looked confused and started to cry along with his mother.

"Is she always like this?" Mark whispered to the boy.

The boy wiped his eyes, then nodded.

"Is he still here?" the mother asked. "Are we safe?"

Mark sighed and pointed at the police captain. "Help her, would you? I'm going to take the boy in the kitchen for a few minutes."

At the door to the kitchen, Mark said firmly. "He's long gone, don't worry. I don't believe he'll ever come back to Kansas City again. You're safe."

He sat across from the boy at the kitchen table and heard a dog barking in the backyard.

"Do they call you Dick or Richard?" Mark asked.

"Dick," he answered.

"I know this isn't easy, but I want you to tell me what happened."

"I was riding my bike by the church when a man waved at me. I rode over to him," the boy said slowly.

"Had you ever seen this man before?"

"No." The boy shook his head.

"What did he say?"

"He said a friend of his was inside the church and he wanted to play a joke on him. He gave me ten dollars and asked me to wait in front of the church and pretend that I was looking for something and ask for help."

"How close were you to him?"

The boy shuddered. "Right in front of him when he gave me the money, sir."

"Tell me what you saw. What did he look like?"

"He wasn't as tall as you. Brown hair. And he had things in his eyes."

"What do you mean?" Mark asked.

"Dots, spots, gray colored. I could see them in the sun."

"Good." Mark touched his arm. "What was he wearing?"

"Coat, jeans." The boy paused. "Oh yeah, and a hat."

"You still could see his eyes?"

"Yes." The boy nodded. "He looked up at the sun."

"Okay, did he scare you?"

"No, sir. He was just meeting his friend, he said."

"Sure." Mark nodded. "What about his friend?"

"He was a lot bigger, taller." The boy raised his arms. "And he told me he wanted to see me run."

"Did you?"

"Yes, sir."

"So you were scared then?"

"Yes, sir." The boy looked down.

"What scared you?"

"I don't know. They didn't seem to be friends then. I just felt scared."

"What about your bike?"

"I left it in front of the church, and when I went back to get it the next day, it was gone."

"Did you hear shots?" Mark asked slowly.

"Yes, sir, three."

"And then what did you do?"

"I ran home. I'm sorry."

"No, there was nothing you could do. Don't be sorry. Do you remember anything else?"

"The tall man looked scared when the other man talked to him."

"And that scared you?"

"Yes, sir." The boy nodded.

"And that's why you ran when Tom . . . the man told you to?"

"Yes, sir."

"Anything else you can remember about this man?" Mark asked.

"He had big, strong hands. When he gave me the ten-dollar bill, he squeezed my hand, and it hurt a little. But he said he was sorry."

"Thank you, Richard." Mark stood up.

At the door between the kitchen and the living room, the boy stopped.

"I saw something else," he said.

"What did you see?"

"Part of his hand that he gave me the money with was red."

"Burned?" Mark asked.

"Yes, red."

"Thank you."

In the living room, Mark saw the police captain sitting on a chair next to the couch, talking to the boy's parents.

"He'll be all right," Mark said. "He was very helpful. I appreciate your patience."

"Are you going to catch him?" the mother asked.

"Yes. Dick"—Mark looked at the boy—"we have your bike. I'll make sure you get it back."

In front of the home, Mark stopped and listened to the dog barking.

"Did he really help you?" the police captain asked.

"Yes." Mark nodded.

"Can we do anything else?"

"You can take me to the airport. I need to get back to Washington for Tom's funeral."

"Of course."

At the airport, while he waited for his flight, he called Joe.

"Mr. Mosely, I interviewed the boy," Mark said.

"What did he say?"

"A few things. The killer has gray flecks in his eyes. That means he has hazel eyes. They call them chameleon eyes because their shade changes based on the color of what he is wearing. It's genetic. Most likely one of his parents had or has them. But the one thing that caught my attention was the boy's comments about the marks on his hands. The boy said they were red."

"And . . ."

"He has burn marks on his hands."

"What does that mean?"

"You know he takes the ring finger on the left hand of each of his victims?"

"So?"

"I think he puts plaster around them and hardens them in a kiln. They're his trophies. We'll find a place where he displays them when we find his home."

"You mean he gets excited when they're hot, when he takes them from the kiln, and burns his fingers?"

"Yes, sir."

Joe listened to the silence on the phone.

"You're thinking about something," he said. "I'm starting to understand you better. What did you see in Tom's hotel room?"

Mark coughed. "A half empty bottle of whiskey, a pack of cigarettes, and a book."

"What was the book?"

"Fitzgerald. But it wasn't *The Great Gatsby* or the other famous ones. It was a compilation of essays called *The Crack-Up.*"

"Is it significant?" Joe asked.

Unlike yesterday, his speech was now normal for him, measured and careful, with a slight Southern accent.

"He left some notes. They just called my flight. Can we talk after the funeral?"

"Sure. Kansas City PD found his rental car in the parking lot of the largest retail store in Kansas City. We believe he took a cab across the river. We don't know where he went. Come back here, Lou."

"Yes, sir."

CHAPTER 24

"TOM ANGLEN WAS my friend," Joe said, "and the best cop I ever knew. He was only forty-nine years old. This is a tragic loss for his family, friends, the FBI, and me. It is a loss I will never find peace with, for a man I will never forget."

At the front of the chapel was the coffin. In the front pew, Trish sat with Sean and Mary on each side of her; two rows behind them, Mark sat next to Cara. The Catholic church where Anglen had worshiped for years was full with FBI agents, policemen he had known, and all of his friends.

"Tom took on the most difficult cases we had and saved lives," Joe continued, "and that's how his life ended, saving someone else."

"I'm sorry Lou," Cara whispered. "I know he meant a lot to you, even though you only knew him for a short time."

"He did," Mark whispered to Cara.

"You couldn't have prevented Tom's death. You weren't there when it happened."

"I know that, but we'll talk about it later."

Cara nodded.

Mark listened to Joe talk about Tom, his work, his family, what had mattered to him. He had spent more than an hour in Anglen's hotel room in Kansas City, sitting at the small laminated table about five feet away from the bed, sipping Anglen's scotch. He had started looking at the book and found what he was sure were Anglen's notes a little less than halfway through the book.

"Lou." Cara grabbed his leg, then whispered, "Promise me something."

"What?"

"That I'll never be in a church like this, I mean, like . . ."

"I promise," Mark whispered.

"I'm scared." She looked up at him.

"Don't." He placed his hand over hers and shook his head. "Don't. I promise I'll be safe."

Mark looked up at Joe. Without any significant details, he was talking about a few of Anglen's cases and how Anglen's work had saved lives. It was true, Mark thought, but now in so many ways only an afterthought. Mark remembered Anglen's words in the book:

*To say he is evil is too easy and obvious. To look for the
reasons for this extreme behavior is simply a waste of time
because they'll never stop coming.*

When he read it the first time, he remembered his father's
words when he was a child asking what a serial killer was, what
it meant, what they looked like. His father had talked about
them and said they looked as common as a dollar bill. He'd said
at sunrise, the monsters run away, hiding from the light, but at
sundown, as the light wanes, they return.

He remembered again Tom's words in the book:

*This one has a place where he feels comfortable, safe—his
home. He travels to kill, but he goes home each time with
his trophy, a finger, and leaves it in a special place, almost
like a shrine, as an offering. I need to find that place he calls
home and drive him away. Then I'll catch him. But how?*

Mark thought, *He's right, but how do I do it, and what am I
going to do when I catch him?* He wondered if Mr. Mosely had
been serious.

Mark looked up at Joe.

"The last thing he did"—Joe paused and looked around the
room—"was to save the life of a young boy at the expense of his
own. As hard as this day is for everyone, Trish, please remember
that, and Sean and Mary, you remember that too. Your father
saved a nine-year-old boy named Richard. Please don't ever
forget that."

Mark watched Joe take off the bifocals, brush back his thinning gray hair with his left hand, and look away from the notes he had written the night before.

"I'm sorry," Joe said. "Last night, I was at my desk at my house, and I thought about a lot of things. Why do we do this work? Why do good men like Tom Anglen have to die as part of that work? I made a promise to a friend that I couldn't keep because of these people, and he's gone now. Lou Mark, one of my new agents, reminded me of the nine-year-old boy in Kansas City who is only alive today because of Tom."

"I lied to Tom," Joe continued. "I didn't intend to, but I did. I told him he would never have to go into the field again. But I had to ask him one more time."

"He really does blame himself for this," Cara whispered in Mark's ear.

"Yes." Mark nodded.

"But it's not his fault."

"You're right," Mark answered.

"Trish, Sean, Mary, Tom Anglen was a good man, a good husband, and a good father. His time here was well spent. If there is anything I can ever do for you, all you have to do is ask me. Now I'd like to take a private moment for each of us to remember our friend in our own way."

After a few minutes, Joe looked up. "Thank you for your thoughts."

Mark and Cara stood up as the family walked down the center aisle of the church.

"Promise me again," Cara said.

"Yes."

"Say it please."

"I promise," Mark whispered and gently touched her slightly distended stomach. "I promise this won't happen to me."

In the backseat of a pitch-black car, Mark sat with Cara as they were driven to the graveside service.

"Joe said Tom was killed while apprehending the killer," Cara said.

"Yes," Mark answered.

"It doesn't make sense." She shook her head. "You said he was the best. Why was he alone?"

"I don't know that, Cara. What I think is he followed a lead and he knew he was close. He didn't want to wait."

"Did this man come after him?"

"They never do," Mark answered quickly.

Mark looked out the window and saw the signs and the green lawns of the cemetery.

"We're here," Mark said.

At the graveside service, Mark listened to a priest talk about Tom Anglen as if he were still there, as if he were still alive, and then watched the coffin being lowered slowly into the ground.

"I want to talk to Trish now," Mark said to Cara.

"I'll be here."

Waiting just outside the rotunda, near the grave, Mark watched until Trish looked toward him, then nodded.

"Mrs. Anglen, I'm Lou Mark. I worked with Tom."

"He told me about you," she said.

"I have something of his to give you," Mark said, "a book Tom was reading."

"Yes, he always took one book with him when he worked." She felt the hard edge of the paperback book in the palm of her hand. "Fitzgerald, yes. Fitzgerald and Hemingway were his favorite writers. Thank you."

"He wrote something"—Mark pointed at the book—"in the margins on pages 116 and 117. I think those were the last words he wrote. They're ideas about how to catch this man."

She turned to page 116 of the book.

"He was still working then," Mark explained. "He expected to come back to the hotel room."

Trish turned the page, read Anglen's notes, then closed the book.

"I know," she said. "I thank you for this. You remind me of my husband in some ways."

"He told me something when we were working in Kansas City, after the newscaster was killed. It wasn't his fault, but he felt responsible."

"What did Tom say?"

"That you needed to feel safe. That it had something to do with the past. I think it relates to his words in the book. If I can drive this man away from the place he knows and feels safe, he'll make a mistake and I'll catch him."

"What else do you know?" Trish asked carefully.

"My father believed that he could hear a victim's last thoughts. I don't know if he really could or if he was just reading the crime scene. I don't know if I can do it, but I believe he thought about you and his children just before he died and he thought about something else and that I can't see." Mark shook his head.

She looked down and clutched the book against her stomach, then looked up into Mark's eyes. "Tom was right about you. Making people feel safe was his real gift. I would watch him stand up, and it was like a grizzly bear standing up, ready to fight. I don't know what happened. I don't know how this man was able to kill my husband."

"It was the child," Mark said. "He saved the boy's life."

"What about his own children? What about me?"

Mark nodded. "Can you tell me now?"

Mark saw the tears in her eyes.

"I was eleven then," she said and looked up at the sky. "My father was a big man, like my husband, and I always felt safe around him and in our home. One night, three men broke into our house. They were criminals. They just wanted things, property, but my father was too proud to give them anything, and he fought with them. We didn't have that much, but it was ours."

For a moment, she paused. "One of them hit my father in the face, and he stumbled backward and hit his head on the edge of the dining room table. From the sound and the way he fell, I knew he was gone. The three men ran out the front door, and we moved to a new house a few weeks later. Eight years later, and after God knows how many appeals, all three were executed under the . . ."

"Felony murder rule." Mark saw Joe and Oliver walking toward them about fifty feet away.

Mark hugged her and said, "Thank you, and I'm sorry."

Trish put her hands on Mark's chest and gently pushed him away.

"My husband was right. Take away his home, take away the things he knows and values, and put him in a place where he feels uncomfortable. Then he'll make a mistake, and you'll catch him."

"Thank you again."

"I'm sorry, Trish"—Joe walked up beside them—"but we need to talk to Lou for a few minutes. I hope my words today meant something to you."

"They were good, they were fine," she said and hugged him. "Tom always appreciated your friendship. It wasn't your fault. I need to be with Sean and Mary now."

"There's another one," John Oliver said after Trish walked away. "In Seattle. Counting Tanya in Kansas City, I believe its fifty-three now."

"How long ago?" Mark asked.

"Four days," Oliver answered.

"Call them now, and make sure they don't dispose of this bird."

"I told them to preserve the bird," Oliver said.

"Good. What do we know about the birds now?" Mark asked.

"Nothing definitive yet," Oliver said. "I searched the Internet, and I talked to three ornithologists at the university and showed them crime-scene photos of the dead birds. They said it looked like they were in the raven family, just smaller. I only have one lead. There's a legend in the bird world, or bird-lovers' world, about a nightbird. They sing only at night, and only after having sex with their mate. They mate for life. The legend is that they're loyal."

"Lou, what do you want to do?" Joe asked.

"We have three people who got a good look at him. Two people at the bar in Kansas City, and the boy. I hate to do this to the boy, but get our identity-recognition people to meet with them, get good sketches, and find common characteristics. I already know about his eyes. Let's see if there's anything else. Something he can't change or doesn't think he needs to change."

"All right," Joe said.

"Who is that?" Mark saw a man walking toward them.

"Pete Westport," Joe answered. "He's a crime reporter with the *New York News*. He wrote several stories about Tom."

"Joe, I'm sorry about Tom." He shook Joe's hand. "I'm sure he appreciated your words today."

"I'm Pete Westport." He extended his hand toward Mark. "I'm a reporter with the *New York News*."

Mark nodded, then shook his hand. "Lou Mark."

"And he is John Oliver," Joe said, indicating Oliver at his side, "they work for me."

"And one of them is taking over for Tom?" Pete asked.

"No." Joe sighed. "But you know I can't talk about that, Pete."

"I'm assuming a serial killer took Tom's life. Is there something the *New York News* should know about?"

"You know I can't talk about that either."

"I had to try." Pete shrugged.

"That's all, Pete," Joe said firmly.

"I'm sorry." Pete lifted his hands. "I didn't mean to intrude."

"Will he do a story?" Mark asked after Pete left.

"On you?" Joe shook his head. "I don't think so, not now."

"If he does, he could learn about Cara. That man could lead him right to my front door."

"I'll have someone watching your house."

"No," Mark shouted, then looked away. "I'm sorry, sir. I think I'm going to fly her to my father's farm in Iowa. My aunt lives there now."

"Won't he look there first?" Oliver asked.

"No. He'll assume we've taken her to a hotel with guards, and it will be difficult for him to approach my father's house without being seen if he does figure it out. Send your best man with her in terms of protection," Mark said.

"That would be Schaeffer."

"Good, thank you. I need to talk with Cara, and then I'll go to Seattle and, after, if I have time, meet with Vincent Crea in prison."

"You think he can help?" Joe asked.

"I won't know that until I meet with him."

"John, give us a moment," Joe said.

Joe waited until Oliver was a good ten feet away.

"Do you want someone to go with you?"

"Of course, yes, sir. But I think I have to do it alone. I'm not sure a lot more people will help. Besides, I'll have our local agents and the police department."

"Do you want me to go with you?" Joe asked.

"Your work is here, isn't it, sir?"

"Yes. Are you going to be able to finish this assignment?"

"I hope so, sir."

CHAPTER 25

"**P**ETE WESTPORT,** *NEW York News.*"

"Mr. Westport, would you be interested in a story about a serial killer?"

"Sure," he said cautiously. "The *New York News* is in the news business. Who are you?"

"I work for a government agency."

"Your name?" Pete asked.

"I can't tell you now. It's an ongoing investigation," he answered.

"You're saying you want to remain anonymous?"

"Yes, for now."

"All right, talk to me," Pete said.

"He's killed fifty-three women that we know of now. He's killed them all over the country."

"Fifty-three. Over what period of time?" Pete sat up in his chair.

"About two years."

"I haven't seen any stories about this"—Pete shook his head—"and I've been covering the crime section here for more than twenty years."

"You could ask the FBI—they're handling the case."

"If they are," Pete said slowly, "we'd be interested in this story. But I need to know who you are."

"I can't tell you now."

"If it's fifty-three, he's killed more women than the Green River Killer did," Pete said. "I don't know how we would have missed this."

"We did until a few weeks ago," the man said.

"The FBI?"

"I can't say."

"Didn't it take almost twenty years to catch the Green River Killer? He was just caught a few years ago," he continued.

"Something like that," Pete said.

"Think of the possibilities," the man said, "if he's already killed fifty-three in two years."

"You must be from Behavioral Science at the FBI." Pete leaned back in his chair.

"He's found a way to profile these women," the man said, ignoring Pete's question, "so he can kill about two every month in different cities all across the country."

"Go on." Pete wrote on the notepad on his desk. He thought as he wrote that it wasn't possible.

"The victims are virtually identical. They could be sisters."

"Every two weeks?" Pete asked.

"Yes. He gives them a bird as a present. We call him the Birdman. After he has sex with them, he . . ."

"The Birdman?"

"Yes," the man said impatiently, "then he bludgeons them to death and has sex with them afterward."

"Who the fuck are you?" Pete laughed. "We would have seen this."

"You didn't," the man said.

"What do you want?"

"I know how he does it," the man answered. "I'm writing a book. I could do it with you. You could help. We could make a lot of money. People love this stuff."

"Can I call Joe Mosely to confirm this?" Pete asked.

"I'd rather you didn't. You could compromise my work, my position, and the book."

"Anything else you want to tell me?" Pete asked.

"Do we have a deal?" the man asked.

"I need to confirm your story, but, yes. If it's true, factual, we do," Pete answered.

"I'll call you in the next few weeks."

After he heard the dial tone, Pete Westport looked around the room and thought about the call. It was nearly midnight, and he was working late, as always, and there were only a handful of people in the newsroom.

One of them was Debbie Billings, a researcher who had worked at the *New York News* for about four years. They had worked together on a few stories, but he really didn't know much about her other than she was divorced and that she worked at night. She was attractive, blonde, and somewhere in her midthirties.

"He didn't tell me the profile on these women," he said to himself. "What is it?"

He looked at the phone book on his computer and found Joe Mosely's home number.

"Hello."

"Joe, this is Pete Westport at the *New York News*. I just got a call from a man who claims he works for you. He told me that there is a new serial killer who has killed fifty-three women all across the country. Can you confirm that?"

Pete waited for a response and heard nothing.

"Joe, we've known each other for a long time. Is there a serial killer who has killed fifty-three women?"

"I can't talk to you, you know that," Joe answered.

"You won't confirm the story?"

"No."

"My caller said he gives them a bird, after sex, that you at the FBI call him the Birdman."

"I still can't talk about this," Joe said. "It's late, call me tomorrow."

Pete walked over to the managing editor's desk after a few minutes, leaned over, and said, "I think we have a story."

CHAPTER 26

MARK LOOKED AROUND the living room and the kitchen of the small apartment and saw an inexpensive couch, a dinette set, copies of modern art, including a large copy of two lilies on a black background, and the dead bird in a cage on the kitchen counter. *She had worked hard*, he thought, *to create the image of a home she'd had or she wanted, and somehow this man had found her and many women like her. Why*, he wondered, *how?*

"Lou, what is it?" Joe asked from the doorway, standing next to Oliver.

"I'm just wondering how he does it. John, we have a bird. I want you to take her to the lab, and I want to know right away what she is."

"She?"

"I think you'll find that it's a hen, female, whatever, and that she's pregnant. We can test your theory about a nightbird."

"Yes, sir." Oliver walked across the room and covered the cage.

"The Seattle Police processed this crime scene?" Mark asked Joe.

"They've been all over it," he answered.

"Look at the pictures. Everyone except for one picture is a little bit off."

"He's right, sir," Oliver said. "Except for this one with the flowers, they all hang slightly off level on the left side."

"I think she was very nearsighted in her right eye and not nearly as nearsighted in her left eye."

"So?" Joe said.

"Another set of eyes adjusted the large picture with the lilies," Mark said.

"Why didn't he adjust the other ones?" Oliver asked.

"He didn't have time," Mark said.

"Fingerprints," Joe said. "Him?"

"Right." Mark nodded. "Maybe you can get a partial latent print if the Seattle Police didn't touch it."

"That's good work," Joe said.

"Thank you, sir."

Mark remembered talking to Cara at the funeral.

"I want you to go somewhere for a while," Mark had said to Cara, "until this case is finished."

"Why, Lou?"

"It's just precautionary. You don't have to worry."

"I'd be stupid if I didn't. Tell me why."

"I want you to go to my father's farm and stay with my aunt. It shouldn't be too long."

"You didn't answer me, Lou. I hate it when you do that."

"I met a reporter from the New York News a few minutes ago. I'm afraid he might mention my name. That's all."

"I don't believe you." Cara looked up at him. "There's something you're not telling me."

"Really"—Mark lifted his arms—"that's it."

"He's after you, isn't he?"

"He doesn't even know who I am. Who would? I'm not Tom Anglen."

"I still don't believe you, but I'll go, and I want you to call me every night."

"Sure."

"We need to go home now and pack. I have to go to Seattle tonight."

"He killed again?" Cara asked.

"Yes. Mr. Mosely is going to send someone with you, so you feel safe."

"A bodyguard?"

"An FBI agent."

"You're not going to tell me now, I know." She hugged him. "Please be careful."

At the hallway leading to the bedroom, Mark stopped and looked at Joe.

"Sir, please leave me alone with her for a few minutes."

In the bedroom, he turned on the light and saw her on the bed. Her head, or what remained, was wedged between two of the gold-colored bars of the headboard, her right foot was resting on the carpet, and the left side of her hip was twisted toward the other side of the bed. Over the headboard, he saw a family photograph, where she was smiling.

He squatted down next to the bed near her right foot and rubbed the palm of his right hand across the left side of his face.

Mark stood up, saw the hammer next to her right foot, and walked around the bed.

"Who?" Mark said. "Who is he talking about? Who did his father kill? What else can you tell me?"

He saw the missing ring finger on her left hand, underneath her right hand, crossed over her abdomen.

Mark crouched down and again rubbed the palm of his right hand across the left side of his face.

"Who did his father kill with a claw hammer and why? It's the only thing that makes sense. He learned from his father, or someone close to him. Where is his father now?" Mark stood up and saw Joe standing at the doorway.

He could hear the sound of her heart beating, weak and irregular, even after he closed the front door of the apartment behind him.

"Jesus Christ," Joe muttered. "What did you see?"

"A fairly slow death and a lot of memories. He talked to her, more than with the other ones, I think. Each time he kills, he becomes more confident that he'll be able to do it again."

"What do you mean?"

"Her brain was pretty much dead, but her heart kept beating for a while after he left this place."

"What else?" Joe looked away.

"He talked to her a lot, about his life, I think. I think his father killed someone with a hammer—I imagine it was his stepmother. His father is in prison, or he's dead. Check for husbands who killed their wives with a claw hammer, twenty to thirty years ago. Qualify it by the wives being pregnant, like the birds."

"That could take forever," Joe said.

"Please start, sir."

"Anything else?"

"Is Cara at my father's farm?"

"Yes, with Schaeffer and your aunt. She's safe."

"I don't know Schaeffer," Mark said. "What's his first name?"

"Jeff."

"If he figures out where she is, I don't know if Jeff Schaeffer will be able to stop him."

"He's strong, physically, and has martial arts training in multiple disciplines. She'll be safe."

"Maybe." Mark nodded. "My father studied the martial arts for a while, then created his own system that he taught me on the weekends when he was home. I learned in the barn on an old heavy bag held together with duct tape. It's still there."

"And?"

"It didn't stop the bullet in his back."

"Cara will be safe."

"Tell Schaeffer to be careful."

"I will."

"Monsters," Mark thought, the title of his grandfather's best short story, the last one he wrote before he died.

"What are you going to do?" Joe asked.

"Wait, here, for the next one. It should be within a week or so, and wait until you have the report on the birds and the forensics team processes this apartment."

"Oliver and I are going back to Quantico tonight. Are you going to be all right alone?"

"Yes." Mark nodded. "You can drop me at the hotel, and I'm going to call Cara."

"Did he take anything this time?" Joe asked.

Mark pointed at the west wall of her bedroom.

"She had a crucifix on the wall. You see the shadow from the sun?"

"Yes." Joe nodded.

"It reminded him of when he killed Tom in front of that Catholic church in Kansas City."

On the balcony outside the apartment, Joe watched John Oliver get in the car in the parking lot.

"There's something else, isn't there, Lou?"

"You remember Tom's notes in the book he was reading before he died?"

"Yes."

"Tom wrote to find the place where he feels safe and take it away from him," Mark said.

"You told me."

"He's trying to do the same thing to me. He's after me and my family. I could feel it all over her bedroom. He's smart, maybe smarter than I am, and if he can distract me, he can continue to do the only thing that matters to him."

Mark watched Oliver pull the car up in front of her apartment. "Killing the same woman over and over again. The one he blames for wherever his father is today."

"I'll tell Schaeffer to be careful." Joe touched Mark's shoulder.

"Please, sir."

CHAPTER 27

HIS FOREARMS WERE like gnarled and twisted roots from an old tree barely visible above the ground.

"Who the fuck are you?" He reached up and wiped some saliva from the corner of his mouth.

"Lou Mark, FBI, Behavioral Science."

"Why"—he lifted his thick forearms—"why did you have them take off the irons?"

"I want you to feel free to talk with me."

"Anglen's dead." He smiled. "You took his place."

"No one ever will." Mark spread copies of his artwork on the metal table. "I want you to look at these."

"I drew them." He shrugged. "So what?"

"Take off the handcuffs and the leg irons," Mark had said to the warden when he saw Vincent Crea being led into the interrogation room.

"*Are you crazy?*" *the warden had asked.* "*He attacked two of my guards, put one in the hospital for two months. He nearly beat the prison psychologist to death. The only time he has free use of his hands and legs is when he's alone in his cell. I won't be responsible . . .*"

"*You're not. Mr. Mosely called and told you to do what I wanted here today.*"

"*Yes,*" *he answered,* "*but . . .*"

"*And turn the camera off inside the room.*"

"*Why did you choose the only interrogation room with a window?*"

"*For the same reason I want the handcuffs and leg irons removed.*"

"*I read the story. I know Tom Anglen is dead. I don't know why we keep these people alive, but you can't kill him.*"

"*I don't intend to.*" *Mark had looked through the glass after the warden told the three guards to remove the handcuffs and the leg irons.*

"*He tortured and killed fourteen women,*" *the warden had said.*

"*I know, but Tom stopped him. I didn't.*"

"It's Joanie." Vincent smiled. "My last one before Anglen shot me."

"I know," Mark answered. "How did you find them? How did you profile them?"

Mark remembered the videotape of Tom Anglen's interview with him years ago. Vincent Crea had killed fourteen women in Northern California between the ages of seventeen and twenty-four. He liked them young. Now he was in his sixties, five ten and about 215 pounds, with gray, thinning hair. He had driven a truck for the largest beer wholesaler in the Bay Area.

The media had called him the Taurus Killer because he carved a primitive image that resembled a bull on the chest of his victims, like cave drawings. When he was working, delivering beer to grocery stores, restaurants, and bars, he would see a woman and stalk her for weeks before he killed her. The prison psychologist had done a series of tests on him until the day he ripped the handcuffs out of the metal table and nearly beat him to death. The results of those tests were that he had an exceptional IQ. Now he was the best-selling serial killer-artist in history.

"It wasn't the sex," Mark remembered from Tom Anglen's interview, *"they'd do anything I wanted just for the chance to live a few more minutes. I could do anything I wanted to them. I was like God."*

Anglen had found him in a cheap hotel room in Oakland with an eighteen-year-old girl tied to a bed and shot him in the chest.

"Why." He stretched. "Why do you want to know how I found them."

"You need to answer me," Mark said.

"He's like me, isn't he? There's another one, and you think he's like me."

"I haven't forgotten my question."

"You talk like Anglen." He stood up. "You were a lawyer first like him, weren't you?"

"Mr. Crea, sit down now," Mark said firmly.

"I was in a different room when Anglen talked to me." He walked slowly toward the single window in the room and saw the cars on the freeway just outside the prison and the parking lot outside. "You set it up this way."

"Yes." Mark nodded.

"Fuck the warden and this place." He turned. "What do I have to lose here? They have to feed me, house me for the rest of my life."

Mark saw him clench his fists.

"I'll send you back to your cell, back to isolation. I saw Tom's interview with you."

"I haven't been able to look outside in more than fifteen years. That's why you took off the irons."

Through the window, he saw a young woman with two small children walking toward the entrance to the prison, with the barbed wire over the fence about one hundred yards behind them.

"You're like him. Did you work with him on this case?" He lifted his arms and held them parallel to the concrete floor for a few minutes.

"Yes."

"You're younger, what, twenty years?" He turned slowly.

"Yes. How did you . . ."

"I'll tell you in a minute. Your father was a cop." He sat down across from Mark.

"Yes."

"I'm glad Anglen is dead. He stopped me." Vincent Crea paused. "I wanted that woman I just saw through the window. She looked like the others."

"I need an answer now, Vincent. Look at the drawings."

He looked down. "It's Joanie, so what?" He shrugged.

"I saw something. The way you were looking at her on the bed. How did you find her?"

"I just saw her." He shrugged. "I saw her in the parking lot of a grocery store when I was delivering beer."

"You killed them all in the same city. How long did it take you to find them?"

"Weeks, sometimes months." He shrugged. "Why?"

"He kills every ten to fourteen days all across the country. I saw something in your drawings . . ."

"Art."

"Whatever." Mark shook his head. "The way you're looking at them. They reminded you of someone. That's what I want to know."

"No." he shook his head quickly. "You want to know how he does it."

"Tell me."

"What makes you think I know?"

"The drawings." Mark pointed at them.

"Anglen thought he could figure us out, and now he's dead." He smiled.

Mark stood up, gathered the drawings into a pile, and picked them up.

"Do you know or not?" Mark stared at him.

"It was a stepmother for me"—he paused—"and probably for him. It's what I saw every time. It's what I drew."

"How does he do it?" Mark asked.

"I've been locked up here for more than fifteen years. How the fuck would I know?"

"You do know, don't you?"

"Gods don't answer questions, do they?" Vincent Crea laughed.

"That's from John Updike, his baseball story about Ted Williams's last game, isn't it?" Mark asked.

"I like baseball, and we read a lot here. But if you think about it, I was like God just before I killed them. They'd do anything I wanted just for a chance at living."

"You're not going to tell me."

"I'm glad Anglen is dead. I read the papers. One of the bullets went through his fucking heart."

Mark set the drawings down, then grabbed him by the hair on the back of his head and smashed his face into the metal table three times before he saw the blood from his broken nose on the copies of his art.

"That's three times for each time you said you were happy my friend is dead."

"You're going to lose the light." He sneezed blood on the table. "You have bright blue eyes, but you're going to lose the light. You're going to end up like Anglen. Someday, it will be last light for you."

"Tell me!" Mark yelled as he heard the door open behind him.

"Fuck you! Fuck you!" he shouted.

He watched three guards handcuff him, then put leg irons around his ankles.

"I told you," the warden said. "I told you that he nearly killed one of my men."

Mark rubbed the palm of his right hand across the left side of his face. "What does he know?"

Mark watched him being taking out of the room by the guards.

"I can't control my anger now," Mark whispered. "Is it Tom, my father, this man, what?"

"I'm sorry," the warden said, "I couldn't hear you."

"I was thinking. But what does he know?"

CHAPTER 28

MARK SAT WITH his legs crossed under him in the middle of the bed in the hotel room. At the last crime scene, Joe Mosely had given him a composite profile of the killer prepared by five FBI profilers. He reached for the phone and ordered room service. This hotel room was virtually identical to Tom Anglen's room in Kansas City, he thought, cold, colorless, and empty much of the time. He sipped on the glass of scotch and began to read:

> *Target victim. Age 35-40, blonde, and in good shape. Each of them was married once for a relatively short period of time. Each of them was childless. Although we don't have a complete report on all the victims, we believe that there may be a history of serious dysfunction in the victims'*

families. This may make them more vulnerable to this
particular serial killer.

He heard the quiet knock on the metal door, picked up the
.38, and saw his hand shaking slightly, then looked through the
peephole in the middle of the door. Room service.

For a few minutes, after he set down his father's gun, he
sat at the circular table next to the bed and picked at the steak,
wondering what he would do when he finally met this man if
the gentle knock of a harmless waiter scared him.

He picked up the profile again.

"Fine," he said, "now tell me how he finds them, profiles
them."

Sex is how they hope to achieve their goals. Most of these
women are not shy about sex. The chair next to the bed and
the open blinds in the case of victim no. 50; the handprints
on the backside of victim no. 36, which we believe occurred
during sex, etc. On some of the victims, we noticed bruises
and contusions that appear to be inconsistent with casual,
even rough sex. Victim no. 26 was killed in the usual way,
this time with repeated blows from a ball-peen hammer to
her skull; however, her appendix was ruptured, we believe,
from a blow prior to consensual sex. It just simply would
have been too painful. Victim no. 31 had severe bruising on
her arms, which again is not consistent with consensual sex.
Victim no. 28 had a broken jaw, which could have come
from the claw hammer used in that crime; however, all other

trauma from the hammer was around her eyes and forehead.
In other words, some of these women said no for whatever
reason, and he wasn't able to persuade them to change their
minds.

Mark flipped to the back of the report and read the names of the profilers: one psychologist, one psychiatrist, two retired field agents, and one forensic pathologist—four men and one woman.

Mark got off the bed and stood next to the table while he ate cold steak. *All of them didn't say yes*, he thought. *Is it possible that one got away, survived? It would only take one voyeuristic neighbor, and one loud scream.*

Mark sat back down on the bed and picked up the profile.

Those who consent provide fantasies. Whether they are
intelligent or not, they maintain themselves through exercise,
cosmetic surgery in many cases, and a plentiful sexual
imagination. However, they are reaching the end of their
ability to conceive, and many of them must believe their
clock is ticking. This is somewhat anecdotal evidence fits two
different sets of profiles, the serial killer's and the victim's
profile. We believe the serial killer is single, midthirties
to midforties in age, never has been married, and has no
children. We'll talk more about him later in this report.

Restless, Mark got off the bed, squatted down on the carpet, and quickly did forty push-ups on his fingertips. After he caught his breath, he stretched slowly into a nearly 180-degree splits. As he did a series of punches and kicks, he remembered when his father had taught him how to fight in the barn on weekends. His father had been obsessive when he found anything interesting. Through reading and simplifying the mechanisms of a lock, he had taught himself how to pick most locks within a few weeks. Although it took substantially longer with the martial arts, he studied various disciplines, hard and soft, finesse and timing, and had created a hybrid discipline that he had taught Mark when he was a child.

"*Watch the target, Louie,*" *his father had said.* "*Always find and watch the target.*"

He remembered looking up at the heavy bag with the gray-colored duct tape around the holes in it in the barn, pulling back his arm and missing it completely.

"*No.*" *His father had smiled.* "*Short punches, and watch the target, son.*"

"Find and watch the target," Mark whispered to himself and sat down on the bed.

> **Nature of the Crime.** *The perpetrator gives the victim a present after having sex with her, a bird. We have not yet been able to determine what kind of bird it is. John Oliver has done some research on a bird called a nightbird, but we simply don't know as we have nothing but crime-scene photos of crushed birds. Obviously, if Mr. Oliver's theory is correct, or some variation of it, and the bird is rare, it could*

assist us in finding this man. The killer has sex with them, consensual or not, then takes a weapon from the kitchen, walks back into the bedroom, and bludgeons them to death. He has used rolling pins and hammers to crush their face and skull. We don't believe he brings any weapon. He just finds something convenient in the victim's home. He then kills the bird by crushing it in his hands. We believe that he has a private aviary and he has raised these birds. Killing the bird is symbolic for him, a sacrifice of sorts, and our belief is that he chooses a hen that is pregnant. In a way, he is reenacting a memory. After he kills, he has sex with them again and takes the ring finger on their left hand, which we assume he keeps somewhere in his home.

Mark set the profile on the bed and sipped on the scotch. For about fifteen minutes, he continued to exercise, feeling the sweat on his face and in his hair, then sipped on the scotch and sat back on the bed.

__The Serial Killer.__ Although we all don't agree, the consensus is that this man is in his early to late thirties. Some of us think he more likely is in his midforties, maybe more age appropriate for his victims. He gives the appearance of success—modest, but stable and successful. According to the description by those in the bar when victim no. 52 was killed, he is about five feet nine inches tall, muscular, with hazel eyes. He has no noticeable accent and in public appears to be quiet, maybe even shy. He doesn't stand out in a *crowd. He plans these murders down to the finest detail, and even when not necessary, unless time interferes, he will still do the same things every time.*

The picture at the last crime scene, Mark wondered, *was that part of his ritual or unscripted?*

Most serial killers, historically, were abused physically or sexually, or both, by female authority figures that transformed their lives. The child inside them, betrayed by that authority figure, is dead. They become someone else—someone they don't know, and someone they can't control. Sometimes the violent results occur immediately; however, in most cases, it takes years or even decades before they begin to kill. They are ticking time bombs waiting to go off. Sometimes it happens, and sometimes they mask the pain until they die, and it never happens.

In this case, we are not certain as to the nature of the abuse. Because of the profile of the victims, we do not believe the woman who raised him was his natural mother, but that is speculation. Clearly, there was a violent act that changed the course of his life, but we have insufficient information at this time to describe the nature of that act. We also don't know how he profiles his victims. We do believe that he is intelligent, dedicated and well organized. He will be difficult to find because of his intelligence and organizational skills.

Mark set the profile down on the blanket and saw the first gray light of sunrise behind the washed-out curtains over the windows. In the hallway, he heard the dull sound of something being dropped about every ten feet and realized it was the complementary morning newspaper.

What do I take from this? he wondered as he looked through the peephole, then opened the door and picked up the local paper. *How many of these did Tom read? How do I figure out what five professionals couldn't really understand?*

He opened the newspaper, then shook his head. He saw the story on the front page of the Seattle paper.

THE BIRDMAN—SERIAL KILLER

The byline was Pete Westport from the *New York News*, which meant it must have been picked up in every major newspaper in the country.

> *There is a new active serial killer the FBI calls "the Birdman." He has already killed fifty-three women in different cities across the United States. He kills, on average, every two weeks. Before he kills, he always gives his victims a present, a bird. He is now the most prolific serial killer in U.S. history. Joe Mosely, the director of the Behavioral Science Division, better known as the Serial Killer Division, refused to comment on this story. An FBI agent assigned to the case, Tom Anglen, was shot last Tuesday by the serial killer. At this time, we do not know if Tom Anglen was killed in the failed process of apprehending the killer or if the*

killer targeted the FBI agent. At Mr. Anglen's funeral, the reporter met two agents, Lou Mark and John Oliver, who were with Joe Mosely, the director of the Behavioral Science Division at the FBI. The News *does not know who will be handling this case after Tom Anglen's unfortunate death. The* News *does not have any information on how this serial killer works; however, unlike the Green River Killer, who only killed prostitutes, the victims of this man are normal, working women with families, which means anyone within his profile, anywhere in the United States, could be next. Only the killer and the FBI know what that profile is today. The source for this story told the news that all the victims are similar in appearance.*

For reasons no one understands, the United States produces more serial killers than any other country in the world. They become infamous celebrities with a following based on real fear and morbid curiosity. They are the monsters of this time and before, going back to Jack the Ripper, who was never caught. This man the FBI calls the Birdman—because the unique gift he brings with him—could be the worst yet.

"Jesus Christ. Cara!" he shouted. "Is she safe? Has she seen this yet? I have to call her."

He picked up his cell phone and started to dial the number when he heard Joe's voice.

"It's in every major newspaper in the country," Joe said. "You saw it?"

"Yes, sir. A few minutes ago. I need to call Cara now. I was dialing her number when . . ."

"Wait, I already called Schaeffer. She's safe. She's not even up yet. Don't make her panic. Help me figure out who leaked this."

"Leaked?"

"Maybe," Joe said.

"We don't call him the Birdman," Mark said. "Are you sure Cara's all right?"

"I promise." Joe paused. "You're wrong. People in the office have been saying that, calling him the Birdman."

"Really?"

"Yes, because of the birds of course . . ."

"There's something I need to tell you," Joe continued. "Two nights ago, I got a call from Pete Westport. He said he received an anonymous call from someone talking about this case. I should have told you. I'm sorry."

"You're right. You should have told me, sir."

"I know. I was afraid of scaring you. It was a lot at one time. I won't hold anything else back."

"What did you do?"

"I started looking for the leak," Joe answered.

"And?"

"I started thinking about who knows about this case," Joe said. "Oliver, of course, the profilers, the secretaries who type the memos. That's it. And I'm very careful about how much the secretaries know. I'm going to interview everybody until I find out."

"Someone is trying to sell the story," Mark said. "And whoever it is doesn't care about what happens to Cara."

"No, they don't," Joe said slowly. "I'll find the leak."

"Did our identity-recognition people come up with anything?" Mark asked after a few minutes.

"Nothing concrete yet. They only have three sketches to work with. They're working under the assumption that he makes small, fairly easy changes. A fake beard or mustache, different hats, clothing. They're focusing on the structure of his face, chin, nose, cheekbones, ears, jaw. I'll check on it again."

"Any prints on the picture?"

"Oh, yeah." Joe sighed. "More than a dozen sets of prints on and around the picture. More than forty different sets of prints in the room. We spent hours on this, and if he left a print anywhere, it will be difficult, if not impossible, to isolate it. Think about it. She was an attractive single woman. Interested male neighbors probably came over, female friends, dates. Some of which she could have missed when she cleaned. And because it was a brutal murder, Seattle cops were all over the crime scene. A home is a virtual museum of fingerprints. Anthropologists have found fingerprints in tombs in Egypt from thousands of years ago."

"I read the profile last night," Mark said. "I don't know what to take from it. I mean, some of it I knew or guessed already. They said they think he's quiet and shy. I don't know how that could be. And some of the woman fought back. I am wondering if one of them survived. I know we're going to get a lot of crank calls after the newspaper story, people claiming to be the Birdman or claiming to know him, or claiming to have been with him. But one or more of them might be real."

"I'll have our agents question them carefully," Joe said.

"There's one more thing," Mark said.

"What?"

"Thank you for protecting Cara—she is pregnant with our first child."

"I didn't know."

"Thank you anyway for taking care of her. I'm going to call her now."

"Try not to worry," Joe said. "I'll make sure she's safe."

CHAPTER 29

"**G**OOD MORNING, DEAR," she said. "Breakfast is ready."

"Thank you, Aunt Florence." Cara yawned, then stretched. "I always sleep so well here. Even now, when . . . Maybe that's why Lou wanted me to stay here until he finishes this assignment."

At the door to the bedroom, Florence stopped and turned back toward Cara, who was slowly getting out of bed.

"You didn't tell me what Louie's doing," she said.

"Working." She stood up.

"The newspaper, not the Sun Rise paper, the Des Moines paper, says he might be chasing a serial killer the FBI calls the Birdman."

"What? It said that in the paper?"

"His name is mentioned with someone named John with the FBI."

"Oliver?" Cara asked.

"Yes. Is that what he's doing now for the FBI?"

"What, yes. The Birdman? Lou's name is in the article?" She sat back down heavily on the bed.

"Yes, dear." She nodded. "He's killed fifty-three women all across the country. Please tell me what's going on. My brother-in-law was sure Louie had the gift, maybe stronger than his, but he still wanted Louie to be a lawyer, rather than a policeman. I don't know why Mr. Schaeffer is even here, but he walks the farm as if he were on guard duty several times a day, and he is always looking out the windows as if someone is coming."

Cara sighed. "Let me get dressed, and then I'll tell you what I know when I come downstairs. Is that all right?"

"Yes."

A few months after they started dating, Mark had taken her to his father's farm in Sun Rise, Iowa, for a long weekend. His father had been dead for many years, but his mother was fighting cancer, trying to hold on just long enough to watch Mark graduate from law school. It was a fight she was losing a little bit every day. That was when she had first met Mark's Aunt Florence, short and rail thin, with a sharp mind and sharp eyes. In her late sixties now, Mark's aunt didn't appear to have changed at all since the first time they had met.

Cara took off her dark-brown nightgown, then pulled a sweatshirt over her head and stepped into sweatpants. She looked out at the few hundred yards of space between the house and the barn and the cornfields that surrounded the house. Aunt Florence had hired a young family to farm the land, and they lived in a small house on the other side of the property.

"Schaeffer should be able to see anyone coming for miles," she said to herself. "And the family on the other side might hear him coming too."

They were engaged, she remembered, and Lou was only a matter of months from graduating from law school when the doctor called and said it could just be a matter of days. His mother had died two hours before they got to the farm, and Aunt Florence had been with her. Sun Rise was about eighty miles south of Des Moines with four small bars, a few more restaurants, and a total population of less than five thousand people. It was the heartland, she thought. Aunt Florence had told them how proud Lou's mother had been that Lou was going to be a lawyer.

"Lou thinks this is the safest place I can be now," she said to herself. "Am I? Who is this man? Is he after us? I have to call Lou."

She could hear Aunt Florence moving around in the kitchen downstairs and the deep voice of Schaeffer, who was respectfully thanking her for breakfast. *He would go to sleep now*, she thought. *He always works at night. I'll wait for an hour or so and talk to Aunt Florence.* When she saw Schaeffer outside the house, walking toward the barn, she left the room and walked downstairs.

"He works in the Behavioral Science section of the FBI. They catch serial killers," she said as she sat down at the kitchen table.

"That's the work he's doing now. Schaeffer is here to protect us if he figures out where we are."

"Is Louie in danger?" she asked.

"Yes, but he thinks this is the safest place I can be, or he wouldn't have sent me here."

"He was a lawyer. That's an honorable profession," Aunt Florence said. "Why is he doing this?"

"He was a good criminal lawyer," Cara said, "but he couldn't do it anymore, so he joined the FBI."

"I'm scared," she said. "This man has killed so many people."

"So am I. I'm going to call him soon when he wakes up, but I can't change what he learned. You knew his father."

"Until the end," she said.

"I can't stop him from doing this," Cara said. "And I can't leave him because I love him."

"And you're pregnant," Aunt Florence said.

"I was just going to tell you. How did you know?"

"I saw it when you got here. When?"

"I'm two months pregnant now."

"I'm scared for Louie." She stood up. "But you're right. My sister tried for years to get John to change, and she finally gave up."

She put scrambled eggs and bacon on a plate and set it down on the place setting in front of Cara. "You need to eat," she said.

Cara picked up the fork, poked at the eggs, then set it down.

"All right," she said, "you think I'm going to live the life of your sister?"

"I knew them all, dear. I knew his grandfather, Jacob, who became a writer after he quit the police force. He wrote mystery stories but never made much money at it. Pulp fiction, although I never knew what that meant, exactly."

"He just retired?" Cara asked. "Lou doesn't talk about him, much."

"In a way, he did," she said. "I knew Louie's father when he worked and after, after the accident."

"What was he like?" she asked.

"He was a brilliant detective. He could see things others couldn't. Obsessive when he got his teeth into something until it was over."

"And Lou?"

"Louie—I think Louie will be all right. I wish he had stayed a lawyer, but he'll be all right. I'm scared because of this man, but I think he'll be all right."

Cara looked across the table at the newspaper article. The story was on the front page, above the fold, and the title was "The Birdman—Serial Killer."

"Everything is okay," Schaeffer said as he came through the back door.

"Really?" Cara asked.

"Yes, Cara. Eat, you need to," Aunt Florence said.

"I'll call Lou in an hour or so. He has to find this man so we can go home."

When Mark awakened, he lay in the bed for a few minutes, turned, then sat on the edge of the bed.

"How does he do it?" he whispered. "How could anyone do this? It makes no sense."

He's quiet, shy, he remembered from the profile. *How?*

He rinsed water across his face and knew he had to call Cara, but he didn't know what to say.

He picked up the phone, and as he waited for her to answer, he turned on the television to the morning news.

"Hello, Lou."

"I'm sorry," he said, "I'm sorry about the newspaper article. There was nothing I could do about it. We think there might be a leak."

"You lied to me," she said.

"I didn't want to scare you." He sighed.

Mark saw something on the morning news, paused for a moment, then heard Cara's question.

"Am I safe?" she asked. "Is your aunt safe?"

"I wouldn't have sent you there if I didn't believe it."

"He knows about you now," Cara said.

"No, that's not true. He only mentioned my name next to Oliver's."

"But he'll know soon." Cara paused. "He targeted Anglen, didn't he?"

"I'm not . . ."

"Lou, you're lying to me." He could hear the beginning but unmistakable sound of crying. "You can't now, not now. Please not now."

"Yes."

"That can't be. No, it can't."

"It is, and you're right, it never happens."

"He could be here now. He could be waiting outside." She looked out the window of the bedroom at the cornfields across from the house.

"He's not. He doesn't know yet who I am. At worst, right now he's trying to figure that out. And I don't think he'll come after another agent. It's too dangerous. He got lucky last time. He's smart, and he knows that."

"But Lou, he could be here now, you know that."

"Listen to me," Mark said firmly. "He's here in Seattle now, I know it. He's only killed once here, and he won't leave until he finishes here."

"But you don't even know his name yet or what he looks like."

"He'll stand out in Sun Rise. He won't be able to hide there. Everyone knows each other. There isn't a tourist season. If I'm wrong, and he does target me, he'll never go anywhere near Sun Rise."

"I don't know what to do," she whispered. "If I asked you to quit now, it wouldn't help if he knows about you."

"I just saw something on a local television channel," Mark said, trying to remember.

"What?"

"I don't remember. It was quick, fleeting. But I think it might be important."

"You'll remember—you always do."

"We'll see."

"I'm sorry, Lou. I know I'm not helping. Panicking never helps very much, does it?"

"I don't really know what to say other than what I've told you already," Mark said. "I believe you're safe. I believe Sun Rise is the safest place I know of for you."

"I know what I have to do, and I know what you have to do. I have to be a patient as I can be, and you have to find him before he finds us."

"I will," Mark assured her.

"Do whatever you have to. I want to go home with you."

"All right. There's one other thing I didn't tell you."

"Should I be scared?" Cara asked carefully.

"No. At Tom's crime scene, Joe told me to kill this man when I catch him."

"Requested it?"

"No, ordered it," Mark answered. "I've never seen him like that."

"Do you think you can?"

"I'll protect myself, but I don't know if I can just kill him."

"Do it," Cara said after a minute. "Do whatever it takes to end this forever."

"I'll call you every day and, hold on, how are you feeling? I mean the baby."

"I'm healthy. Your aunt is going to take me to your doctor in town for a checkup tomorrow, but I'm fine. I love you. End this."

"I love you, Cara. I will call you every day."

Mark set down the phone, then paced around the room. *How do I end this quickly?* he thought. He heard the phone ring and saw it was Joe.

"Lou, I reassigned Oliver to the case in Houston in case he's the leak. He's there now."

"It might be him." Mark thought about it. "He knows almost as much as we do about this case, but I don't think so. I don't think money is why he does this."

"We'll see. I met with Hank Paxton, director of Domestic Terrorism here, and he loaned me his best analyst. His name is John Connor. They don't know anything about the case now other than what they read in the newspaper. Only three of us will be working on this case now. There won't be any more leaks."

"Good. I need to figure this out quickly, how he does it. I'm close."

"Any ideas?"

"A lot, but nothing concrete yet. I have to get ahead of him, and so far he's been way ahead of us. Cara's safe in Sun Rise, isn't she?"

"Yes," Joe answered quickly. "He'd be a fool to try there. You were right to send her there."

"I'll wait for your call." Mark put down the phone.

CHAPTER 30

E VAN WALKED SLOWLY through the dark house with
a penlight in his hand. It was a small town house in a
respectable, but certainly not wealthy, suburb of Washington. In
the kitchen, he saw two open bottles of wine in the refrigerator,
bread, eggs, and food.

He walked back through the living room and saw the den
just off the formal dining room. For a moment, he shined the
penlight around the room and saw a series of jury verdicts on the
wall, a bookcase, and a file cabinet.

At the foot of the stairs, he turned his head and listened
for a moment, then heard his weight on the first step. At the
landing, he saw two bedrooms and a bathroom between them.
He only spent a few moments in the secondary bedroom, as he
only saw nondescript-style furniture, but in the master bedroom,

he turned on the light on the nightstand next to the right side of the bed.

Mark looked like he was six feet in the photograph, and she looked like five-five, maybe 110 pounds with reddish-brown hair.

"She's not my type"—he shook his head—"but she's nice, really nice. What's her name? I like her green eyes."

He set the wedding photograph down and examined Mark. *He has eyes like blue-tinted diamonds*, he thought. After turning off the light next to the bed, he flashed the penlight around the room and saw the closet was open and that things were out of place, having fallen from the shelf above the clothes.

"It is so neat everywhere else but not here," he said. "Why?"

He looked at Mark's suits quickly, all dark and all conservative, then her clothes and stopped at the lingerie at the end of the closet. Not being able to feel anything through the latex gloves, he pulled off the glove on his right hand and slowly moved the tips of his fingers across her lingerie.

When he was finished, he pulled the glove back over his hand and walked over to the dresser. On the right side of the top drawer, he found her panties and bras.

"Someone left in a hurry," he said in a low voice. "Why?"

In the bathroom, between the two bedrooms upstairs, he stopped at the wastebasket and combed through the assortment of tissue-and-cardboard toilet paper rolls until he felt something firm, even hard, at the bottom. He shined the penlight on it and saw three letters—EPT—then dropped it back inside and smiled.

Halfway down the stairs, he thought about her again. "What does she do? They both look younger than I am, maybe early thirties. She must work."

In the den, he focused the light on the wall and saw a plaque from the FBI Academy dated a few years ago, which said Mark had graduated number 1 in his class, and Mark's law school degree. Next to the law school degree, he saw a teaching certificate for Cara Barone.

"Cara—that's her name, and she's a teacher."

Turning, he pointed the penlight at the desk, then walked over and sat down in Mark's chair. Brown leather and comfortable. *From his office when he was still a lawyer*, he thought. He opened the top drawer and saw nothing of interest, but in the second drawer, he saw two loose-leaf binders. When he opened the one on top, he saw a series of pencil drawings, almost like stick figures. On the flat surface of the wood desk, he didn't see even one pencil, and the drawings looked old, decades old. He flipped through the warped pages and saw people fighting, defensive positions, outcomes.

"Mark didn't do this," he mumbled. "Who did?"

On the last page, he saw the name John Mark and a date more than twenty years ago.

"His father." He nodded.

He leaned back in Mark's chair and thought about the second binder. *He's younger than I am, why would he care about Dr. Mengele?*

He looked, again, at the summary page at the beginning.

"My father said he was the most prolific serial killer in history. Thousands and thousands died by his hand. If I can understand Dr. Mengele, maybe I can understand evil. The material on Mengele was collected by Mark's father, why? I'll have to find out.

"John Mark, his father, teaches him how to see the crime," he said. "He runs away from it for a while, then embraces it. What happened to his father? Why did he kill himself?"

He closed the binder and carefully set it in the drawer, then the other binder on top of it, and closed it.

Pointing the penlight at the walls, he saw old newspaper articles and began reading them. There were three, and they were about Mark's father. He read the title on the first one his light found.

"John Mark, the Man with the Eyes, Solves a Twenty-Year-Old Crime."

He read the story, then turned off the light and sat in darkness in Mark's office. He had been to John Oliver's house first, which was on the other side of town. He was gone, as was his family. He had seen the accounting degree from a school in Ohio and was sure it had to be the other man, the other name, who had replaced Anglen—Lou Mark. Now he knew he had been right as he remembered some of Anglen's last words before he had killed him.

"I know that the man with the eyes will catch you and kill you."

"It's Mark," he whispered in the darkness. "It's him. Where is his wife? Where is Cara? He sent her away. Where?"

He found the bookcase with the light and walked over to it. He saw a series of old mystery magazines. He pulled one out, felt the glue on the book had split apart with age, and scanned it until he saw a story and the name Jacob Mark.

"His grandfather," he muttered, "it has to be."

After he scanned the story quickly, he picked up another magazine then another, until he came to the last one.

On the cover he read:

"Monsters," a story by Jacob Mark, his last.

He looked at it, then tucked it under his arm and walked out of the den.

"I don't think I can do what he can"—he shook his head—"but I can stay ahead of him for a long time."

"I need to go back to Seattle for a few days, then I'm going home," he said as he opened the front door, "to my birds, my cat, my home."

He walked about a block and a half to the car, then started it. "My father lost control, that's what happened to him." He nodded. "I won't. Besides, I'm going to see him soon."

He pulled away from the curb and looked at Mark's townhome one last time.

"I learned a lot about you tonight."

Slowly pulling away into the deserted streets, he added, "Now I just have to find where you hid Cara from me."

CHAPTER 31

MARK SAT IN the middle of the bed, with the profile on his left and a series of selected crime-scene photos all around him. He picked up the crime-scene photos of the body he had just seen in Seattle a few days ago and realized that he couldn't remember her name. He switched the photos to his left hand, then scanned through them. The position of her body on the bed was different from the others. Although her hands were still neatly crossed over her abdomen like a corpse in a coffin, her body was twisted, her right foot rested on the carpet, and her left hip was twisted toward the other side of the bed. "What happened?" he whispered. "He didn't arrange the body as he normally does." Mark stood up and placed the photograph in the middle of the bed, then walked around the bed several times, stopping every few feet.

"They're still alive when he has sex with them, after he hits them with a hammer or whatever, I'm sure of that," he said quietly in the empty hotel room. "Was she still barely alive when he left her? Why? Why would he take the chance?"

Mark picked up the photograph and sat back down on the bed.

"She might have been found and lived just long enough to identify him in some way. She didn't, but she might have. But she couldn't move her hands or she would have."

This is the first one after he killed Tom, Mark thought. *Did he feel rushed, scared, afraid? Did he feel Tom's presence in the room? When he learns that I replaced Tom, will he feel mine?*

He picked up the profile.

> *He plans these murders down to the finest detail, and even when not necessary, unless time interferes he will still do the same things every time.*

He has to confirm their dead before he leaves, Mark thought, *but this time he didn't.*

> *We do believe that he is intelligent, dedicated and well-organized. He will be difficult to find because of his intelligence and organizational skills.*

"She couldn't move her hands," Mark said, "because of the brain damage from the hammer, but for whatever reason, she could move her lower body slightly. She was trying to get up. She was trying to get away. Could she still see? Could she hear the door close behind him when he left her apartment?"

Mark closed his eyes and tried to place himself back in her bedroom. What did she hear? Did he talk about Tom when he thought she was dead? Did he talk about the next one?

He looked back at the profile.

> **Target victim.** *Age 35-40, blonde, and in good shape. Each of them was married once for a relatively short period of time. Each of them was childless.*

He picked up the photo again from the last crime scene, then looked at the other four on the bed.

"There must be something that all of you know that I don't know yet."

He dropped the photographs and thought about the church and Tom and the man standing about ten feet away from Tom, the boy, the man's hazel eyes, the burns on his fingers.

He walked over to the small desk against the wall in the corner of the hotel room and took the photographs of Vincent Crea's drawings from his briefcase. He quickly looked through each drawing in the Joanie series and stopped at the last one.

But if you think about it, I was like God just before I killed them. They'd do anything I wanted just for a chance at living, he remembered Vincent Crea telling him.

I just saw her. I saw her in the parking lot of a grocery store when I was delivering beer—Gods don't answer questions, do they? Mark remembered.

Mark remembered Anglen's words in the book:

> *This one has a place where he feels comfortable, safe, his home.*
> *He travels to kill, but he goes home each time with his trophy, a finger, and leaves it in a special place, almost like a shrine, as an offering. I need to find that place he calls home and drive him away. Then I'll catch him.*

Mark sat down on the end of the bed with his back to the photographs. *What did the last one hear? How do you do it?* He turned around, leaned on the bed, and shoved the photos onto the floor.

He dialed Cara's number and waited.

"Are you all right, Lou?" She'd been sleeping.

"Yes, I promised I'd call you every day. I'm sorry about the time."

"Nothing has happened yet?"

"No," Mark answered. "I can see all the pieces, I just can't put them together yet. But I think he's scared now—he did something, or didn't, that I think he did every other time."

"What?"

"I really don't think you want the details." Mark shook his head.

"You told me yesterday that you saw something, remember?" Cara asked.

"What do you mean?"

"You said it was fleeting, on television."

"Fuck!" Mark shouted. "That's it. It's the only thing it could be."

"You know now. Tell me. What did you see?"

"He has a profile, right? They all do. The victims of this serial killer look like sisters."

"Yes." She could hear the excitement in his voice, like when he'd been working as a lawyer and he finally figured out the best way to try a case.

"Yet he has killed pretty much all over the country, but he doesn't kill in the state where he lives."

"So?"

"He sees them before he even leaves his house, he has to. How does he do it?"

"I don't know."

"What I saw on television only for a second was an advertisement for an Internet dating service. I don't even know which one, but I know it's the only way he could do it," Mark explained.

"Don't millions of people use those services? I see the ads on TV. I'm trying to remember the names. They all sound the same. They promise a lot—romance, relationships, marriage sometimes."

"They never quite promised what this man delivers"—Mark paused—"he must see it for the profile. I don't know how he does it yet. I'm going to call Joe. Thank you."

"Lou, you said he was scared that you saw it at the last crime scene," Cara said.

Mark sighed. "He didn't confirm she was dead. I'm sure he did that on all the others."

"My god, she lived for a while after . . ."

"You can't ask me about any more details, you really can't. But now I might know how to stop him. There's one piece missing. I need to call Joe."

"Call me again tomorrow," Cara said quietly. "I won't ask you anything again."

Mark looked around the hotel room as he waited for Joe to answer the phone.

"Lou." He cleared his throat.

"He uses Internet dating services. He sees them at home on his computer, then meets them. Think about it," Mark said quickly, "it's the only way."

"I . . ." Joe coughed. "You're right. I don't know why we didn't see it before now."

"We were applying a historical model to a crime nearly as old as time. There were serial killers back in biblical times. We just didn't update the model for today, for the Internet. But there's something still missing."

"What?" Joe asked. "It has to be this—it can't be anything else."

"You're right except for one thing that will never need to be updated."

"I'm not following you."

"A serial killer has to see the victim to know she's the right one. Vincent Crea saw Joanie in a parking lot when he was delivering beer. He didn't say this, but he knew right away that she was the one he was looking for. Maybe it was the way she moved, the way her hair swayed across her shoulders, maybe her smile. Maybe her scent or the feel of her skin."

"But this one saw them on the computer."

"Right, but not in that way," Mark explained. "We can determine profiles in terms of age, appearance, etcetera, but we can't determine what only the serial killer knows instantly that she's the one and, for that moment, the only one."

"You're saying that he can't get that sensory component from a computer monitor?" Joe asked.

"Yes, absolutely," Mark answered, "except he has found a way to do it, and I don't know what it is."

"You lost me, Lou. He does use a dating service, but there's something else."

"He does use a dating service, without doubt. He has a very specific profile, and we know what most of it is, hair: age, body type, marital status. He has to see their photographs. What I don't know yet is what the other common element is. When I figure that out, I'll be able to track him to his family, and I should be able to find where he lives."

"What do you want me to do?"

"Please ask John Connor to look into this right now. I don't know how many dating services there are or which one or ones he uses. We should be able to narrow it down. We have fifty-three names, and we can start checking them on each database. Don't tell him anything more. Maybe we can still find out the source of the leak."

"Lou, don't millions of single people use Internet dating services?"

"I'm sure," Mark answered.

"Think about it. He knows what he's looking for, his profile, right?"

"Yes."

"And the dating services have already stalked these women for him without knowing it. And the database is probably tens of millions of women. That's what you're saying."

"Yes," Mark answered.

"Other than the one component you don't yet know."

"Yes."

"So," Joe continued, "we have an insatiable predator whose prey has already been identified and located by someone else."

"Like an endless line of sheep," Mark said.

"Clearly, he's found a way to hide himself in their world. You need to find the other component soon."

"I know. I'll call you."

Mark sat down on the edge of the bed. *He can't know yet that I took Tom's place. Do I still have time?*

CHAPTER 32

"**M**R. WESTPORT, I** have more information for you."

It was late at night, as the first time, but he recognized the voice immediately.

"You still won't tell me who you are?" Pete asked.

"I can't yet."

"What is it?"

He could tell that the man's voice was not being artificially altered like a *60 Minutes* interview with a whistle-blower or a mob informant. But he couldn't tell if the man was disguising his voice in another, simpler way.

"I need an advance," the man said.

"We're not supposed to do that," Pete answered quickly.

"Hell, you do it all the time. You buy news."

"How much?" Pete asked after a few seconds.

"Not that much," he said. "This story will sell a lot of papers."

"How much?"

"Fifty thousand."

Pete hesitated. "I'll talk to my editor. I'll call you back. Give me your number."

He heard the man laughing.

"All right, I'm sorry," Pete said. "When do you want to call me?"

"Thirty minutes," the man answered. "If you don't answer the phone in thirty minutes, I'll go elsewhere, to another newspaper. I'm offering you an exclusive on this, and I'll hold back some information for the book."

"Are you saying you know who he is?" Pete asked.

The man laughed again. "Of course not, but he'll be caught, probably killed. You're wasting my time, Mr. Westport, good-bye."

Pete walked down the hall and stopped at his editor's door.

"I got another call from our informant," he said. "He's going to call me in thirty minutes. He has more information, but he won't divulge it unless we pay him fifty thousand dollars. He's offered us an exclusive on this and other stories, as well as a book deal, potentially."

"And, obviously, you still don't know who he is?"

"No." Pete shook his head.

"We really shouldn't do this," his editor said.

"No, but if I promise, we might still get information from him."

"Tell me what you think about him."

"You mean, what? From his voice?" Pete asked.

"Yes, in part."

"I'm terrible matching voices with ages. But"—Pete shrugged—"he sounds mature, not old. I'd say forty or so. He's educated."

"Professional?"

"Could be."

"Does he sound like he has the training of an FBI agent?" his editor asked.

"I'd say the cadence of his speech is consistent with that kind of training. I'm not helping, am I?"

"Some. How would he know all this?" his editor asked. "Maybe he has access to internal reports at the FBI?"

"Maybe." Pete shook his head. "Are we going to do this?"

His editor nodded. "Get the information now, and tell him we'll wire the money first thing in the morning. If it's good, I want the story on the front page tomorrow."

"He does too. I need to get back to my desk."

At the door to his editor's office, he stopped. "Should I tell Joe Mosely about this, or should I call him as a source for the story?"

"Let's see what it is first."

The phone rang a few minutes after he sat down.

"Pete Westport."

"Do we have a deal?"

"Yes, but we can't wire the money until morning. Is that all right?"

"Yes."

Pete wrote down the information on the accounts.

"What is it?"

"He uses an Internet dating service," the man said.

"Say that again."

"He uses an Internet dating service to profile his victims. That way he can accomplish the profile quickly and move from one city to another, kill two, then move on to the next," the man continued.

"Millions of people use those services all across the country," Pete said.

"More than that," the man said.

"That's a major industry. I can't write that story without some corroboration."

"You have the same source you had for the last story."

"But this is different . . . Can I write that the source is the FBI?"

"Do you know that?" the man asked.

"No, goddammit!" Pete shouted, then turned in his chair and saw his editor standing behind his desk.

"You have a good source," the man said. "I guarantee the story.

"Can you give me anything else? Which services?"

"I'll call you within a week," the man said.

"Goddammit," Pete said after he hung up the phone. "The killer uses Internet dating services to profile the victims."

"Write the story," his editor said.

"Debbie!" his editor shouted across the room.

"Yes?"

"We did a story on Internet dating services not long ago. Find it. Give the basic facts, how many people use it, the disenchantment with the bar scene among today's singles, and what kind of revenues those services are generating. And what kind of promises they make. Give it to Pete for his story."

Debbie walked over to Pete's desk. "I can tell you," she said. She was thirty-four and had worked at the paper for four years after her divorce. "They claim to have professionals who devise a profile to match compatible people. That it is virtually guaranteed. They have testimonials from satisfied customers. They have pictures of engaged and married couples on their websites."

"Do they guarantee your safety?" Pete asked.

"No, but I never worried about it personally. I never thought that compatibility meant someone would hurt me."

"You use these services?" Pete asked.

Debbie nodded. "Yes."

"It's fucking ingenious," Pete mumbled.

"What?" his editor asked.

"What will we believe next? Millions of people believe that a third person can find your soul mate through a standardized questionnaire—without ever talking to either person—and guarantee the results."

"You need to make one more call," his editor said.

"I know," Pete answered. "I'm way ahead of you. Debbie, try to find at least one of the people we interviewed for that story. Ask them what kind of measures they use to protect their clients from the wrong kind of people."

"I will."

"Do you have any children?" Pete asked as she walked toward the desk.

"No, Pete."

"But you were married," he said.

She nodded.

"Are you still on a dating service?"

She nodded again.

"Get off it," Pete advised her, "at least until this one is caught."

"What's your headline?" his editor asked.

"Birdman Selects Victims through Dating Service," Pete said.

"Good, I like it. You don't have much time."

"And you're stealing it from me," Pete replied.

He incorporated the material Debbie gave him from the old story, and when he was at the end, he walked over to Debbie's desk.

"Well?" he asked.

"I found two executive types for two different services, and they both refused to comment on their security measures."

She was blonde and attractive in his opinion. He noticed that she wouldn't look at him.

"I don't think you fit his profile. Is that what you're thinking?"

"But I might," she said.

Pete still didn't understand why an attractive woman would agree to meet a total stranger. "Why do it at all?"

"They promise me a lot of things that I want. I don't want to be alone. Family. Someone who has similar interests who will listen. You know, happy."

"And instead, some of these women get a dead bird and a claw hammer." Pete shook his head.

"But it could happen at the bars too."

"Sure." Pete nodded. "But not for him. Debbie, you don't need that."

"I won't take any more dates from those services until he's caught."

"How many referrals did you get?" Pete asked.

"A lot. Hundreds."

"Over what time period?" Pete asked, surprised by the numbers.

"Well, as long as you pay, they keep updating the list. Six months, about," she said.

"These people, without ever meeting you or the guys, found hundreds of perfect matches for you in six months?" Pete asked.

She nodded. "That's what they said."

"How many were perfect?"

"I had dates with five or six."

"How many were perfect?" Pete asked again.

She shook her head. "None."

"I need to finish the story," Pete said abruptly.

He sat back down and typed that representatives from two of the largest Internet dating services in the country had declined any comment on the security measures they provide for their subscribers.

He felt a hand on his shoulder, turned, and saw Debbie.

"You scared the hell out of me," he said.

He hated writing about serial killers. Sometimes, it seemed like they were in the room looking over his shoulder, proofreading his story.

"Why don't we get a drink," she said, "or a cup of coffee?"

"Sure."

CHAPTER 33

PETE LIT A cigarette and looked around his living room in the faint glow from the match. His apartment was small and the furnishings sparse, considering that he had probably been the best crime writer at the *New York News* for the last twenty years. During that time, he had covered nearly every major crime story. He had won awards, written a few true crime books, and made real money, but two ex-wives, two children he rarely saw, and taxes had taken most of what he had accomplished financially. He was fifty-five years old now, six feet two, and 230 pounds. With the exception of a few strands of jet-black hair, his hair was white, and by his standards, he was a good ten pounds overweight. He still worked out, but he would have lapses when he drank too much, and then he would have to start working out again.

He found a clear spot in the nearly full ashtray, sipped from the glass of Jack Daniel's on the coffee table, then pushed a few butts aside in the ashtray and sucked on the end of the cigarette until the tip glowed, briefly, in the dark room. The older he became, the more anal he seemed to be.

"I should call him," he mumbled to himself. "I should tell him."

He preferred to work the night shift at the newspaper, when he bothered to go in at all, and his editor, Carl Flagg, understood, because his work was still good and sold newspapers. But his absence from work gave other, younger, crime writers opportunities they wouldn't have had if he had been there.

Carl had told him not to call Joe Mosely because it was pointless. After all, Carl had said to him, "He won't say anything, he never does." He put out the cigarette and leaned back against the old couch. *Carl's right*, he thought. Joe knew about the leak the moment he saw the first article.

He lit another cigarette and again looked around the living room of his small apartment and shook his head. No space remained in the ashtray, so he picked it up and, with his glass in his other hand, walked into the kitchen. In the tiny laundry room, just off the kitchen, he dumped the ashtray into a slightly larger one and poured another glass of whiskey.

As he sat down on the stained old leather couch, she said from the doorway to the bedroom, "Pete, I thought you were coming back to bed."

"I am, in a minute."

"Come back to bed now," she said and touched his leg, then moved her hand under the towel around his waist.

Debbie had just learned that she was pregnant, she had told him. She hadn't told the father and hadn't seen him since the only time they'd had sex. He had been a match from one of the dating services, and when she refused to have sex a second time, he had hit her until she gave in.

"I have to make a phone call first," he said.

"Can't it wait?" Debbie asked.

He laughed, "In a minute. I really do have to make this phone call."

They'd had drinks at an Irish pub around the corner from his apartment after the paper had been put to bed.

"Can I wait with you here?" she asked.

When they got inside his apartment, he had apologized for the mess and, in a way, the state of his life, and she had kissed him, and in a few minutes, they'd been in the bedroom. After, she had told him about the conception of her child and that she would never know if it occurred during consensual sex the first time with a man she thought was decent or the violent rape thereafter.

He had held her. "You went on other dates from this service after that?"

"Just one." He could feel her body shaking as if it were freezing in his apartment. "And I wouldn't have sex with him."

"Jesus Christ," he muttered. "Guaranteed results."

"I was never so scared in my life, Pete." She hugged him, and he could feel her cold fingers on his back. "He was a little rough the first time. Different than when we met. And I didn't want it again. And I didn't have a choice. He hit me three times."

"You'll be all right."

"No," he answered. "I need to be alone for this call. It's about the case. You already know more than you probably want to about this."

"Then you'll come to bed?" she asked.

"Yes." He nodded.

When she walked through the darkness into the bedroom in his apartment, he looked at the clock with the red LCD display across the room. It was five o'clock in the morning, and the paper would be on the streets in a matter of minutes. He looked up at the ceiling for a moment and remembered Joe's home telephone number.

"Joe, this is Pete Westport from the *News*."

"First, fuck you. You woke me up," Joe said. "And second, I still have no comment."

"I'm sorry, there's a story coming out in a few minutes. I got another call. I just wanted to warn you."

"What does it say?" Joe asked.

"He said that this serial killer uses Internet dating services to profile these women."

Joe got out of bed and walked out of the bedroom. "Why did you call me?" Joe asked.

"I wanted you to know," Pete answered, "before you read it this morning."

Who is it? Joe thought. *Who would leak facts on this case to the media, and why did he choose Pete?*

"If he calls you again," Joe asked, "will you call me before you publish?"

"I don't know if my editor will allow that."

"Will you let us tap your phone so we can get a voice print on him?" Joe asked.

"I'll ask Carl," Pete said.

"I'll get an order from a federal court judge!" Joe shouted.

"I called," Pete said slowly, "to give you a warning about this. I didn't have to. And the shield law will protect our sources. You know that—you're a lawyer."

"Anything else?" Joe asked.

"No. I asked. He basically said next time."

"I'll call you after I read the story."

Pete set the cordless phone down, lit another cigarette, and sipped on the glass of Jack Daniel's. As he watched the smoke rise over his head in the room, he thought, *I have a story that could make me millions. Why does the source really matter?*

In the bedroom, Pete lay down next to Debbie and felt her move toward him on the bed.

"I was never so scared in my life." She held him. "Never. You don't know what it's like to feel powerless."

He could feel her fingers gripping his shoulders and her breath on his chest.

"It's over," he whispered.

"He left the bed for a while," she said, "then he came back. I thought he was somebody else."

"Stop, it's over," he said again.

"Then he raped me, and I couldn't do anything to stop it."

"I'm sorry." He held her tight and felt her legs curl around his legs.

"It won't?"

"No, it won't happen again. I won't let anyone hurt you," Pete said.

"It was like, after he hit me and held me down, that there was darkness all around me."

"Debbie . . ."

"It was like I was dead."

"I won't let anyone hurt you again. I promise. Is that why you came home with me tonight? You were scared?"

"Yes, partly. I couldn't be alone tonight. But I've liked you for a while. I just wasn't quite sure how to tell you."

"You're safe now." Pete greatly touched her blonde hair. "Sleep."

CHAPTER 34

"**M**ICHAEL," SHE SAID. "I'm so glad you called."

They were at an Italian restaurant in Seattle.

"So am I." Evan smiled. "I thought after the *News* article yesterday that, you know, nobody would trust a dating service until they catch him."

"You don't look like a serial killer." She sipped from the glass of Cabernet he had ordered.

"I wonder what they do look like." He stared at the ceiling as he reached for his glass of wine. "I wonder if you could tell if you were having dinner with him or me."

"I'm sure I would know," she said confidently.

"I told you I work with birds. I write articles about them for the Audubon Society, among others. In a way, I guess I'm the birdman."

"Right"—she laughed—"you're the killer."

"How many matches have you had?" Evan said after a few minutes.

"A lot. They give me new ones every month, as long as I pay them thirty dollars. Of course, I can eliminate 90 percent just from their pictures."

She was thirty-seven years old, according to the bio on the computer, had been married once, and had no children. She did aerobics religiously, and he could see she was in great shape. She had blonde hair, was five feet six with long legs, and her name was Julie Phillips.

"I found your picture to be interesting because I couldn't quite make out your face," she said.

He'd had it taken at the shore near his home. He was wearing a baseball cap with the brim down, and he was standing in a shadow from the sun. He would only send the photograph after he had picked one out from the list of matches.

"But I could see your body," she said. "You're in good shape."

"I work out."

"How long will you be here?" She sipped from the glass of wine.

"I leave tomorrow for a conference in New York. But if things work out between us, I can come back in a few days."

"I'd like that," she said.

She was a computer programmer at Microsoft, and the photo she had posted had drawn his attention.

"I liked your picture," he said.

"I liked doing it," she answered. "I got an old boyfriend to film me, and then we had fun afterward, but you don't want to know about that."

"The past is just that." He shrugged.

She had been wearing the same low-cut black top she was wearing now, but in the photo on the service, the straps were hanging off her shoulders.

"I like sex," she said, "actually, I love it. And I like to experiment, but I'm running out of time."

"Aren't we all?" he said.

"I mean, I want a family. I don't have one now. My mother is a cruel, venomous woman, and my brother rarely talks to me. I want a chance to make it right with my own family."

"What about your father?" he asked.

She looked away. "I don't talk to him much either."

"I'm sorry."

"I'm going to change all this." She nodded her head positively. "It will be better."

"Sure. Do you want another glass of wine?"

"Yes. Thank you."

"What happened to your father?"

She kept her head down. "I don't like to talk about it."

"Tell me, please."

"He shot himself a year ago," she said. "It was tough. It was hard to understand."

"I'm sorry for your loss."

"I . . ." She hesitated for a moment. "I went to a friend's house that night. Someone I had been dating."

"Sure, of course you would." He sipped on the wine.

"He wouldn't let me in." She started to cry a little bit. "He said he was too busy, he was working."

"I'm sorry," he said again.

"Then I went back to him months later," she said. "We had chemistry, but it didn't work out. I suppose I never forgave him for not being there when I needed him."

"You still think about him?" he asked.

"Yes." She nodded. "But I shouldn't."

"So, why dating services? You shouldn't have any problems getting dates."

She waved her hand in the air. "I got tired of going to the bars. You meet the same people with the same bullshit stories about how successful they are. They screen them for me with their profile, so I don't have to take the risk of going home with a stranger who is going to beat the shit out of me or hurt me. They promise matches, and I believe in their system."

"I'm glad"—he lifted his glass and touched it against hers—"that they gave me your name."

At her home, an hour later, she smiled. "I want to give you some incentive to come back soon."

She undid the buttons on his white oxford shirt, then kissed his chest.

"Does that feel good?"

"Yes," he answered.

Then she undid his belt, pulled off his pants, and led him into the bedroom. After a few minutes, she straddled him and starting moving slowly up and down.

"That feels good," he said.

"Incentive," she whispered.

When they were done, he rolled to the other side of the bed and caught his breath.

"Wait here," he said. "I bought a present for you. It's in the car."

"What is it?" She gently rubbed his chest.

"You'll see in a minute."

He set the birdcage down on the counter in the kitchen.

"Julie, come here," he said.

"What is it?" She appeared totally naked and stared at the black cloth over the cage.

"See."

She pulled the black cloth off the cage, then dropped it on the floor.

"It's a bird. You're him!" she screamed and tried to run out of the room.

He grabbed her by the back of her hair and punched her in the face. The first two knuckles of his right hand landed flush on her nose. Then he picked her up and carried her into the bedroom. He looked at the blood flowing from her broken nose and nodded. *Ketchup*, he thought.

"Wait here," he said to her.

In her home office, he found a claw hammer. He waited by the side of the bed, holding the hammer behind his back until he saw her eyelids flutter.

"My father knew," he said.

"What?" she said. "Please don't hurt me."

"My father knew."

He smashed the point of the hammer into the orbital bone above her right eye. This time the scream was closer to a whisper, and her head slumped against her right shoulder.

"Wait," he said calmly, "I need to make a call."

In her living room, he sipped on a glass of red wine, then picked up her phone.

"Pete Westport."

"You know who this is?"

"Yes."

"I'm at a friend's house now," Evan said.

"My friend isn't feeling well. I'll call you back, Pete."

Pete heard the dial tone.

"What is it?" Carl asked.

"He just called me, said he was with a friend who's sick."

"What the hell does that mean?" Carl asked.

Pete shook his head. "I don't know."

"Where did the call come from?"

Pete looked at his phone then at Carl. "Seattle."

"Is he going to call you back?"

Pete nodded.

"Let me know when he does."

Evan set the phone down next to her, caressed Julie's stomach for a moment, and felt her body move slightly.

"Wait," he whispered to Julie.

In her living room, he opened the door to the cage on the kitchen counter and waited until the bird stepped off her perch onto his right index finger.

"It's time to sing."

He listened for a moment, then slowly crushed the bird in his hands, then set her body back in the cage.

Julie was starting to move a little more on the bed, but her movements were disjointed, like a watch with a badly broken spring. "You're like a soft-shell crab with a broken leg now."

He dialed Pete's number. "Pete."

He could hear a low moan in the background.

"Julie's not feeling too good," he said. "I think she has the flu. Let me get her an aspirin."

He set the phone down, picked up the hammer, and looked down at her. The orbital bone over her right eye was crushed, but she could still see out of her left eye.

He leaned over her face and whispered, "You gave me incentive. You never know, do you, when you're going to meet someone like me? It's time to sing."

Evan smashed the hammer over her left eye and watched as her head slowly fell over her left shoulder. Then picked up the hoof nipper, which was beside the bed, lifted her left hand, and cut off her ring finger.

"What was that?" Pete asked.

"I dropped a tray on Julie's hardwood floors. That's all."

"What the hell is going on?"

"You have a research person, Debbie? I saw her name in the last article."

"So?" he said, and heard three dull thuds like drumbeats.

"Nothing, really."

"What about Debbie?"

"I told you nothing."

"You're him. You're the killer. You're not from the FBI."

"Look at the caller ID on your phone," Evan said, then hung up.

Pete looked up at Carl. "It was him."

"I know."

"No, I mean it was the killer, not the FBI."

"You're sure?"

Pete nodded.

"He called from Seattle, Washington," Carl said. "Do we have a name?"

"Julie Phillips on the caller ID."

"What is it, Pete?" Debbie had walked over from her desk.

"He just called me again."

"What did he say?" Debbie asked.

"It's weird. He said he was at a friend's house."

"That's it," Debbie said, "he didn't tell you anything new?"

"No." Pete looked up at Carl. "Debbie, let me talk to Carl for a minute. I'm trying to figure this out."

"Give us a minute, Debbie," Carl said, "I'll get you a drink in the office."

"What is it?" Carl asked after he sat down behind his desk.

"It's him." Pete lifted his arms and shook his head. "From the first call, it hasn't been someone from the FBI, it's been him."

"Take a drink." Carl pointed at the glass on the front of his desk.

He watched Pete drink all of it, then poured another.

"Are you saying that we have a direct connection with the most prolific serial killer in U.S. history?"

"Yes." Pete nodded.

"This is one hell of a story."

"I know, but . . ."

"He's killed fifty-three women . . ."

"No." Pete shook his head. "I think its fifty-four now. The caller ID said Julie Phillips, and I'm sure she's dead now. I think I heard him kill her."

Pete took a drink, then set the glass down on Carl's desk.

"There's something else." Carl noticed Pete's hand was shaking as he picked up the glass.

"What Carl asked?"

"He mentioned Debbie."

"How could he know? You listed her as the lead researcher in the last article. Fuck."

"I know. I can't tell her, I can't protect her, and I don't even know if he's after her."

"Go back to your apartment. Take Debbie, and write this story. We have to do our jobs," Carl said.

"Joe Mosely? Should I call him."

"I'll do that, go."

In the elevator, Debbie clasped Pete's hand.

"What is it?"

"I think I heard him killing someone tonight, and it scared the shit out of me."

"What do you mean?"

"The killer has been calling me, not the FBI."

CHAPTER 35

MARK SQUATTED DOWN next to the bed and looked at Julie Phillips's body. On the chest of drawers, he saw a photograph of three women that he assumed were Julie and two sisters, and when he looked back at her on the bed, he couldn't recognize her face. Next to the bed was the claw hammer, clean, except for one strand of blonde hair clinging to the beveled edge on the point of the claw hammer. As with the others, her hands were crossed neatly over her abdomen.

"Why?" Mark whispered.

He gently pushed her hair away from her face.

"What were your last thoughts?" He looked at her body. "And what can you tell me?"

He walked around the bed and looked at the blood trails on the headboard and the wall behind it.

"He hit her once, then left the room. What did he do before he came back and finished it?"

Mark looked at her face again. Both of the bones over her eyes were crushed, as were her eyes.

"He did one first," Mark mumbled. "And then he waited in the other room until she regained consciousness so she could see him with the other eye. Why?"

He could almost see the look on her face as she squinted at him with her left eye. He could see her rub her right hand across the right side of her face and hear her cry, then see her blurred vision of the hammer coming toward her left eye before the room became dark and she was blind. But she was still alive.

He could feel her trying to understand why her life would end this way, then, as it lingered on, begging for it to end, begging for the darkness to fold itself around her.

"Lou," Joe said at the door to the bedroom, "what is it?"

"I just saw her die."

"And?" Joe asked.

Mark closed his eyes. "He crushed her right eye like a grape, but she could still see out of her left eye."

"She was still alive?" Joe asked.

"I think so, because of the blood trails on the headboard over the bed. Because of the brain damage from the first blow, I don't think she could tell right from left. I imagine she tried to touch her right eye, but she didn't know which hand to use."

Mark sighed. "It has something to do with his father, something that happened a long time ago."

"What?"

"Fuck!" Mark shouted, then leaned over and stared at the Berber carpet until the carpet fibers blurred together and became one. "What? I can't see it yet."

"You will," Joe said.

"He's going to see his father, or he just saw him in prison," Mark said. "He's the monster."

"The killer?" Joe asked.

"Yes, no, of course, but I'm talking about his father." Mark tried to catch his breath. "Maybe, one more, one more crime scene, and I'll see it."

"What else?" Joe asked.

"I think after he hit her the first time, he left the room, sipped on a glass of wine, then called someone from her phone. I think she's his next date. Please check her phone records and call her. He has a signature thing he says before he kills. It's part of the ritual, and it has something to do with the birds."

Mark looked out the window of the bedroom of Julie Phillips's home and saw the daily rain in Seattle. He could hear Joe on the phone.

"He called New York," Joe said after a few minutes. "The *New York News.*"

"Pete." Mark nodded. "But why didn't they call us? They knew before the Seattle Police did. I think he could hear him killing her."

"I'll find out," Joe said.

"The birds again," Mark said. "Always the birds."

Mark rubbed the palm of his right hand across the left side of his face.

"His photo was on her computer. I'm sure he erased it before he left. Can we retrieve it?"

"I don't know," Joe said.

"I want the computer and the bird flown immediately to Quantico, and I want our best people to look at them."

"The other one, here, didn't have a computer at her house," Mark continued, "which means his picture could be on the office computer. We need that too. I don't think he could have erased that photo."

"Other than killing a lot of people, what is he trying to do?" Joe asked.

"Did we get anything on his father?"

"In the last thirty years, during the time span we're talking about," Joe said, "in this country, more than three hundred men took a hammer to pregnant wives."

"Stepmothers, with a young stepson?"

"We're still looking at that," Joe answered.

"I wonder what those fucking dating services would do with that statistic."

"We should know more in the next few days," Joe said. "His father could have been executed."

"No." Mark shook his head. "He's seen him recently or will soon."

"I didn't forget what I asked you," Joe said.

"I don't know what he's trying to do yet. This is pure insanity." Mark lifted his arms. "We let people who don't know us match us with people they don't know. And based on a standardized test, they know what we want, what we dream about, and what's best for us. And this guy has tapped into that bullshit."

Mark walked through the narrow hallway into the living room and saw John Connor standing next to the birdcage on the kitchen counter.

"What is it?" Mark asked as he heard Joe stop next to him.

"I've never been at a crime scene before," he said. "I've just been an analyst for five years, and Mr. Paxton likes my work. But I've never been in the field."

Mark turned toward Joe, ignoring Connor. "It's just like in the profile."

"What?" Joe asked.

"She confided in him, I think," Mark said. "And he's quiet, shy, paranoid. He thinks people are looking at him when they don't even know he exists."

"I think I know, sir," Connor said.

Mark turned toward John Connor. "Tell me what you think you know."

"I did the research Mr. Mosely asked me to do on Internet dating services. It's big business. He can program what he wants if he's smart, and I think he is. He tells them what they want to hear and, because of their situation, they probably would confide in him. I read our profile on him, and their clock is ticking in their minds."

"Go on," Mark said.

"I found over one thousand websites on Internet dating services," he said. "There are mainstream heterosexual sites, gay websites, age difference sites, older man and younger woman or vice-versa, specialty things, like urination, and then the porno-style websites which are really disgusting. On some of those sites, which are owned by offshore corporations, you can get young boys or girls, I mean five years old."

"In this case," Joe said, "we're not looking for that."

"Maybe we should," Connor said seriously. "I saw a case in Phoenix where two middle-aged men contacted about thirty young boys through the Internet, had sex with them, and both men have AIDS."

"This case is not about a pedophile," Joe said, "and we do have a section in the FBI that devotes its time to catching sexual predators."

"I'm sorry, sir," Connor said. "I have two young boys, and the story scared the hell out of me because they're on the Internet all the time."

"Tell me about the business," Mark said.

"There are one hundred million single people in the United States," he said. "The biggest dating service claims to have nearly fourteen million subscribers, and the next four claim to have anywhere from two million to six million subscribers on each service. The total subscriber base, I think, is more than thirty-five million people."

"What do they gross?" Joe asked.

"These are mostly private companies, but based on the monthly subscription fees, it's a multibillion-dollar industry," Connor said.

"Who are the biggest?" Joe asked.

Connor rattled off five names.

"What about security measures?" Mark asked.

"They don't talk about that much. I mean they tell you to meet in a public place and be careful, but that's really it."

"Background checks?" Joe asked.

"No, none of them do it. But some of them claim they developed a multidimensional test that predicts better, long-lasting relationships. I doubt that any woman on that service would expect to meet a man who takes a claw hammer to her skull."

"Thank you, John." Mark pointed to the front door. "I want to talk to Mr. Mosely for a few minutes."

"Who did you tell about the Internet dating services?" Mark asked Joe.

"No one."

"It wasn't in any memo?"

"No." Joe shook his head.

"You can tell Oliver that he can forget about the Houston case and come back to work."

"It's not Oliver?" Joe asked.

"It's not anyone that works for us. It's the killer. He's selling his story to the *New York News*, to Pete."

"You're sure?"

"Yes." Mark nodded. "But I like Connor, and we need help. Let them work together, please.

"Arrange a meeting with the people at one of the largest dating services," Mark continued, "I want to meet the people who run it."

"I'll do it," Joe said.

Monsters, Mark thought, the title of his grandfather's last and best short story. Pulp fiction. They're not afraid of anything except the smallest of things, Mark remembered from the story.

"What are you going to do?" Joe asked.

"Go back to Quantico with you tonight," Mark answered. "He's done here. He's already gone."

"Did he take anything other than her finger this time?" Joe asked.

"I don't think so." Mark shook his head.

"Why?"

"I don't think he saw anything he wanted other than her."

"Have you talked with Cara today?"

"It's—he's a boy," Mark said. "She saw our old family doctor in Sun Rise today."

"Good, congratulations."

"Yes"—Mark smiled—"in about seven months, I'll have a son."

"You've changed since Tom's death," Joe said. "I can see it."

"How else am I going to catch the man that killed him?" Mark looked away.

"You're becoming your father, I think," Joe said.

"I am him, and it's how I'm going to catch this man."

"I knew him, and I respected him," Joe said slowly, "Could you hear her last thoughts?"

"I don't know." Mark shook his head. "I think she was trying to say the Lord's Prayer."

CHAPTER 36

"I 'M JOE MOSELY,** the director of the Behavioral Science Division at the FBI. This is Lou Mark, one of my agents."

They were in Los Angeles in a large ornate conference room in the corporate offices of one of the largest dating services. Across the table from them were three men.

"I'm Dr. Vincent March," the man sitting in the middle of the group said. "This is Dr. George Thompson, and this is our corporate attorney, Jack Andrews. Behavioral Science. Serial killers"—he paused—"is this meeting about the killer the paper calls the Birdman?"

Joe nodded.

"You believe he may be using our service?"

"Yes, we do," Joe said.

He looked like he did on television, Mark thought. *Kind, patient, and knowledgeable about human relationships.* He was somewhere in his sixties, Mark guessed, with thinning gray hair, and he was wearing the same kind of houndstooth sports coat he'd seen in the commercial.

"That's troubling." He took off his glasses and briefly rubbed the bridge of his nose.

"Troubling," Mark said sarcastically and started to stand up.

"Wait." Joe looked at him.

"I'm sorry, Mr. Mosely." Dr. March looked at Mark. "I didn't mean to minimize all of this. I take this allegation seriously. How can we help you?"

"We need to have complete access to your databases now," Joe said.

Dr. March looked first at his lawyer, then George Thompson. Behind him, Mark could see the sun setting.

"That's a lot more troubling. We have more than six million subscribers to our service. We have serious privacy issues. These people confide in us as they do with a lawyer or a doctor or a priest."

"There is no privilege here, Dr. March." Joe shook his head.

"We are only interested in one of your subscribers," Mark said and held up the index finger on his right hand.

"Jack"—Dr. March turned to his right—"what are your thoughts on this. You're our lawyer."

"I believe there is an expectation of privacy in our customers and that they rely on it. We promise it in our marketing and on our website. If you think about it, it's not that dissimilar from the right to privacy recognized by the Supreme Court in *Roe v. Wade*."

"They're fucking nuts, Mr. Mosely," Mark said. "The abortion case is like this business? The Supreme Court will never buy that argument."

"I agree with you, Lou," Joe said. "By the way, Mr. Andrews, we are both lawyers who worked in private practice before we joined the FBI. We need access now. We'll keep the information confidential."

"I asked George to be here today because he created the questionnaire, the matching index, and the profile we use. I believed then, and I still believe today, that we created something of value," Dr. March explained. "We're going to need a few days to evaluate your request."

"No," Joe said firmly, "I'm not going to give you the time or the opportunity to destroy evidence."

"That is an outrageous accusation," Jack Andrews said.

"Tell me about what you created here. What's the basis for your profile?" Mark asked.

"That is proprietary and copyrighted," Dr. March said.

"And I don't care," Mark replied. "What is it?"

Dr. March looked at his lawyer, who nodded at him. "It's complicated, but the MMPI is part of it. Do you know what it is?"

"The Minnesota Multiphasic Personality Inventory," Mark answered.

"You're right. It was created by scientists at the University of Minnesota to identify personality disorders such as manic-depressives, schizophrenics, sociopaths, etcetera. George and I changed the purpose and criteria."

Mark gripped the edge of the mahogany table, then looked at Joe.

"Are you saying"—Joe looked at Dr. March—"that you are using a test designed to identify people with mental and personality disorders to match people for dates?"

"No." Dr. March took off his glasses. "Of course not, we just use some of the same principles. For example, we repeat some of the questions to identify certain characteristics."

Mark pointed at Dr. March and leaned across the table. "Could you identify psychopaths through your questionnaire?"

"That's not really the purpose of our service." Dr. March shook his head.

"That's not what I asked you."

"Maybe, theoretically." Dr. March sighed.

"Could this man use your test to achieve his own ends?" Mark asked.

"That's . . ."

"Be careful how you answer that," Jack Andrews interrupted him.

"I was going to say that's extremely hypothetical."

Mark tapped his finger on the table as he looked out the window of the conference room.

"I wonder if he used his real name the first time before he knew what he was going to do eventually. If so, his name is on the computer," Mark said.

"Again, these are all extremely hypothetical questions. Assuming you're right that a serial killer is using a dating service, how do you know it's ours? I mean one of our competitors has more than fifteen million subscribers. It's more than twice our size."

"He's right," Jack Andrews said, "we would need some evidence before we open our computer to the FBI."

"If he has killed fifty-something women," George Thompson spoke for the first time, "shouldn't we help them?"

"There are other issues here, George," Jack Andrews said, "that we need to evaluate."

"Other issues? Really?" Mark said sarcastically. "It is more than fifty, Mr. Thompson, that we know about now. That number grows every two weeks."

After a few minutes, Mark pointed at Dr. March. "There is a way. Check two names on your computer: Julie Phillips in Seattle, Washington, and . . . Jesus, I never asked the name of the first one in Seattle."

"Sharon Morris," Joe said.

"We could research that for you and call in a day or so," Dr. March said.

"Check it now." Mark pointed at the computer in the corner of the conference room.

Dr. March started to stand up.

"Don't do it," Jack Andrews said, "not until we talk about this with outside counsel."

"Apparently you misunderstood me," Joe said slowly, and Mark heard the hint of his Southern drawl. "I thought I made it clear that either I have access to your computer now or I'm going to arrest all three of you."

"That's absurd," Jack Andrews said, "for what?"

"Obstruction of justice, violations of the Patriot Act," Joe answered.

"Patriot Act? Terrorism?" Jack Andrews laughed.

"What about fifty counts of accessory to murder?" Mark asked.

"I think we should help them," George Thompson spoke for the second time, "I don't want to . . ."

"That's blackmail," Jack Andrews said.

"I have two computer experts in your lobby who are also FBI agents. They can either look at your computers or arrest you. It's your choice."

Dr. March walked over to the computer in the corner of the conference room, "What were the names?"

"Julie Phillips and Sharon Morris," Joe said.

"They're here." Dr. March sighed after a few minutes. "They're on our system."

"Did you send them any matches today?" Mark asked.

"Don't answer that," Jack instructed Dr. March. "There are liability issues."

"Yes." Dr. March ignored him. "Eleven to Sharon, nine to Julie."

"You just found the perfect match for twenty men who apparently want a date with a corpse. I imagine Pete Westport would like that story, Joe?"

"I'm sure he would."

"We'll help you." Dr. March sat back down at the table. "We'll do everything we can. You can bring your agents in now."

"Thank you," Joe said. "Lou, call them please."

"I'm asking, no, begging you"—Dr. March lifted his hands in the air—"to keep all of this confidential. It will kill our business."

"We'll do what we can," Joe said.

The agents walked into the conference room, and Dr. March pointed at George Thompson.

"George will take you to our computer room and provide you with access to anything you need."

"He found essentially the same one," Mark said to Dr. March, "more than fifty times. How?"

"I don't know, how could I?"

"You know a lot more then you're telling me," Mark said.

On their way out of the conference room, Mark looked back at Dr. March and said, "I'll be calling you."

"You know, he says something to them before he kills them, every time or almost every time," Mark said to Joe outside the building.

Mark looked up and saw part of the sky through the smog in Los Angeles.

"He"—Mark rubbed the palm of his right hand across the left side of his face—"your never expect, no, you never know, yes. 'You never know when you'll meet someone like me.'"

"That's what he says?"

Mark nodded. "I think so. It's part of his ritual. These women don't have any idea who they will meet on an Internet date—soul mate or serial killer."

"Jason," Joe said from the backseat of the car, "take us to the airport."

Jason Weller was a field analyst whose work consisted primarily of collecting evidence.

"You're thinking about something else," Joe said to Mark.

"Yes, sir. There is something about this, the dating service, that Dr. March didn't tell us, and I don't know what it is yet."

"Should I set up meetings with the other dating services?" Joe asked.

"No." Mark shook his head. "He uses this one, I'm sure. He found something here that works for him. He has no reason to go anywhere else."

"Have you found the other component yet, how he selects his victims?" Joe asked.

"No."

Mark couldn't see the killer, but it was almost like he was whispering in his ear.

"*You never know, do you? You never know when you'll meet someone like me.*"

CHAPTER 37

EVAN WAITED IN the reception area in a small carrel, next to a dozen or so other people visiting friends or family. When he saw the guard bring him in, he smiled. Through the smudged Plexiglas, he watched him sit down, then pick up the black telephone.

"It's good to see you, Evan."

"It's good to see you, Dad."

He was dressed in the standard-issue gray prison jumpsuit. Now he was nearly seventy and had lived in this place for almost thirty years.

"I brought you a carton of cigarettes, and I put five hundred dollars in your account here," he said.

"Thank you, son."

Once a month, which is all the prison regulations allowed, he had come to this place since he was twenty-one.

"How have you been?" Evan asked.

"It's pretty much the same every day here," his father answered. "The boredom is like the electric chair on low wattage."

"I'm sorry," Evan said.

"I made the choice to marry her." His father shrugged. "I made the choice to stay with her."

His father was taller than he was, almost six feet one, and thirty years ago, other than a slightly rounded stomach from the beer, he had been in good shape.

"Have you found yourself a woman?"

"No." Evan shook his head. "I mean, I go out with women, but nothing permanent."

"God." His father shook his head. "I'd give anything to have one more before I die."

He had been very young when he first met Loretta, he remembered, when his father had introduced her to him as his new mother. She had been striking, he thought. Tall, blonde, with an exceptional body.

"Loretta was a bitch, but she was great sex," his father continued. "And she had perfect hands."

He had seen photographs of his mother but never met her because she died the day he was born. He still kept a photo next to his bed at his home of her and his father holding each other. He also kept a photo of Loretta, his stepmother, on the mantelpiece in his living room. Her hands were clasped together in the photograph, as if she were praying.

"I know, Dad." Evan looked away. "I know what Loretta was like."

"I want a child of my own," he could still hear Loretta shouting from their bedroom. "Not just your castoff from a dead woman."

"She died from complications at his birth—she bled to death," his father had answered. "He almost died. He lived in an incubator for a month."

"Well, maybe he should have died too."

"I should have done more," his father said, "to protect you from her anger."

"I think you did enough, Dad."

"Are you still working in your accounting job?" his father asked after a few moments.

"No." Evan shook his head. "You know I haven't done that for years. I write articles about birds."

"Right, Loretta again." His father shook his head.

"She taught me about the nightbirds."

"It's not true," his father said. "It's a myth."

"No," Evan said. "I found them. I have an aviary. You know that."

His father had been, before prison, a manufacturers' representative and made good money for that time. He had no use for birds or stories about birds that only sing at night after having sex.

"Are you doing well?" his father asked.

"Yes. I just got a fifty-thousand-dollar advance on a book I'm writing about birds," Evan answered.

LAWRENCE M. JAMES

"Good."

After his father started going out and didn't return home until hours after the bars closed, he remembered Loretta had come to him and talked about the nightbirds.

"When it's all said and done," he remembered Loretta saying bitterly, "when you're looking death in the face and waiting for God to take you, all that matters is loyalty. When I first met your father, I thought that was it. I gave him everything I had. But nightbirds are loyal."

"What are nightbirds?" he had asked.

"They mate for life. And they sing only at night and only after they have sex. Other birds sing like a mating call all day long, but not nightbirds."

"She wasn't nice to you," his father said.

"It was a long time ago, Dad."

"Some women just weren't meant to be mothers. Loretta was too jealous and selfish. That's why I did it when I found out she was pregnant."

"I know the story. I know what happened, Dad."

With words only, until his father learned that Loretta was pregnant, their fights were like brutal cage fights on pay-per-view television, and even though she came to him when his father was out with other women, she still called him a castoff from a dead woman when she argued with his father. When she and his father fought, they both drank, his father beer and his stepmother wine, by the gallon.

"I have a date with a woman named Jackie tomorrow night." Evan tried to change the subject. "I've seen her. She's very attractive."

"How did you see her if tomorrow is your first date?"

"Now there are computer dating services that match people. They sort of take the guesswork out of dating. They're experts. I tried one two years ago for the first time," Evan explained.

"Do you get any? I'd give anything . . ."

"Yes, Dad, I know." He sighed.

"Stay away from women like her," his father warned him.

"I know what I'm doing."

"Your father never understood loyalty," he could hear Loretta say. "It was nothing to him. But I got even with him."

"And if it doesn't work out with Jackie, I have matches with a lot of other ladies, including one named Debbie."

"Good, son, never put all of your eggs in one woman's fucking basket." His father laughed.

"Don't worry," Evan answered. "I learned a lot from you."

After it happened, he had moved in with his aunt and uncle, and they legally changed his last name to eliminate any association with what his father had done. He had gone to college, got an accounting degree, and for a while worked for a firm in northern New Jersey. His father's name was Michael Evan Wilkinson, and his name had been Evan Michael Wilkinson until his aunt and uncle changed it.

"You were always smart," his father said. "High IQ, the whole thing. When it happened, you were in the gifted group, way ahead of everybody else. I knew you wouldn't make the same mistakes with women that I did."

When his aunt and uncle died, he had inherited their home, as well as several hundred thousand dollars in cash. He had quit the accounting firm that same day.

"I'm very careful about the women I choose," Evan answered.

"That's good, son. But"—he laughed—"Loretta was gorgeous."

"I don't want to talk about Loretta anymore," Evan started to raise his voice. "She's why you're here."

"Fuck it," he said. "Fuck her."

For a while, he had dated randomly with little or no success, but then he had tried a dating service. On his first date, he thought he saw Loretta. She looked so much like her and acted like her. It had been two years ago, and after satisfying sex, he had killed her with a claw hammer he found in her kitchen. A long time ago, Loretta had told him that someday he would see her again.

"It's almost time," his father said. "After this much time in the joint, you can feel people coming up behind you."

He remembered that when he got home from school that day, there were police cars in front of his house and yellow-colored tape around the front porch.

"What happened?" he had asked one of the policemen.

"Who are you?" he had asked.

"This is my house," he had pointed out. "What happened?"

"I'm sorry, son. Someone got hurt. Wait here."

"No!" he had shouted and tried to run but felt the vise-like grip of the policeman's hands on his shoulders.

As the policeman held him, he had watched his father walk outside, in handcuffs, flanked by two other policemen.

"He's my son," his father had said. "I want to talk to him."

"I'm sorry, Evan," his father had said a long time ago. "She never believed me. She never thought I was loyal. And she never really accepted you."

He could smell the alcohol on his father's breath.

As he watched his father being taken away, he shouted, "Let him go!"

After the police car left, he had broken free and ran into the house. On the living room carpet, with a pool of blood around her head, he had seen Loretta. Next to her was the claw hammer they kept in a drawer in the kitchen. He could see the blood, hair, and tissue on the hammer. For a moment, before he felt strong arms pulling him away, he turned his head and looked at Loretta's face. He couldn't recognize her face anymore, but her hands were folded neatly across her abdomen.

He watched the guard walk up behind his father.

"It's time," he said.

"Sure, Joe, thanks."

Evan nodded at his father. "I'll see you in a month, Dad."

"You keep working hard," he said. "And you stay away from the wrong kind of women."

"I'll see you in a month, Dad." He nodded.

When he got home, several hours later, he turned on the light and walked downstairs into the basement. He had spent a lot of money building his aviary, and because of the nature of the birds, he had subdivided it into separate cages like condos once they mated. The main area was bisected by a trunk of a small tree, and those birds that had not yet chosen mates lived there and fought. The males would fight like pit bulls over a female, and sometimes one of them would die, but he understood. It was what they knew, and it was what they learned from other birds. He had now dozens of birds in his aviary. Upstairs, he could hear his cat Felix scratching at the door.

"My father is okay," he said and stepped inside the glass door. "I missed all of you."

He watched as two of the male birds sparred momentarily with each other, then flew to the opposite ends of the enclosure. They both wanted the same female and after a few minutes started again; at the end of the fight, one landed next to the female, and the other flew away.

"You've decided." He nodded and waited until both birds stepped onto his outstretched index finger.

"This is your new home." He placed them into an empty cage. "Enjoy your time together. You should never waste time."

He remembered Loretta telling him that no one should ever abuse time and that the nightbirds knew it instinctively. They came from China, and he had spent a lot of time finding an ornithologist who knew that the myth, as his father had described it, was actually reality.

"Her name is Jackie," he said to the birds he had just placed in their own home. "And I have a date tomorrow."

He smiled as he watched them turn their friendship into a relationship. They would be together until one of them died.

When he got upstairs, he made dinner; and while he ate the TV dinner smothered in ketchup, he looked at his new matches with Felix on his lap. There were fifteen new names. On average, he would get thirty new matches a month for each of the five aliases he used as long as he paid the bills. He had seen Dr. March's television ad two years ago, used his own name, and filled out the questionnaire honestly, he thought. The first "Loretta" had been the result. She had looked a little different in her photo on the Internet—it was a little out of focus. He really didn't understand until he saw her in person. It was perfect, and he had excused himself and walked into the men's room. He was alone there, and he had stared at his face in the mirror and saw the sweat on his forehead yet felt cold at the same time.

"How could I," he remembered saying to himself as he stared in the mirror, "take a psych test and find my perfect match is a woman who hated me? Who called me a castoff from a dead woman?

"How could my perfect match be the woman who put my father in prison for the rest of his life?"

He had remembered Dr. March on the TV ad talking about his personality profile, compatibility, and lasting relationships.

He had looked at the sweat on his face in the mirror and remembered what his father had said about Loretta, that some women should never have children. "It's simple," he remembered saying to his image in the mirror. *"Dr. March's questionnaire will find one Loretta after another. I'll never run out."*

As he scrolled through the bios and photos of the new matches, he remembered that he had returned to the table and complimented the first Loretta. They had gone back to her home, and during sex, she had rubbed her hands sensuously across his body. When they were finished, he told her he wanted to get some water, and in a drawer next to the refrigerator, he had found a claw hammer. Her name was Betty Lord, and she was thirty-six, divorced once, and childless.

"You should never have children," he had said as he stood next to the bed holding the claw hammer behind his back.

"That was nice. I'm sorry, what did you say?"

"You should never have children," he said again.

"Why? I want a baby," she said.

"I'm not a castoff from a dead woman!" he had shouted.

She started to get up. *"I think you should go. You're scaring me. I thought I got a match."*

"You did."

She didn't see the hammer in the dark room until a moment before she felt it crush the orbital bone over her left eye. She felt the second blow from the hammer over her right eye but didn't feel the last three at all.

He hadn't been prepared two years ago, he remembered, so he didn't leave a bird and hadn't brought the hoof nipper. Instead, he used a pair of garden shears he found in her garage. Before he left, he deleted his picture from her computer.

"It's simple," he remembered saying to his image in the mirror. "Dr. March's questionnaire will find one Loretta after another. I'll never run out."

Because there was no bird, he had never been given credit for the first crime, which was the only time he used his own name.

The birds were symbolic to him, he knew that; they always had been, but he thought that Mark would never connect the first crime with the Birdman because he had not left her his gift.

He got up from the computer, poured a glass of wine, and looked at his watch. It was nearly midnight, and in a few minutes, he planned to make a call.

Two months after the first Loretta, he set up five accounts with the dating service using fictitious names and multiple e-mail addresses. Evan picked up his cell phone and dialed Pete's number. After Loretta number 1, he had also set up multiple cell phone accounts with fictitious names and corporations.

"Pete Westport, the *New York News*."

"I have more information for you, Mr. Westport," he said.

"You're him, aren't you?" Pete said. "You talked about Debbie in our last call."

"Debbie?"

Evan found her photo on the service, looked at it, and smiled.

"Yes, Debbie," Pete said.

"I really don't know anyone named Debbie," he answered.

"Are you going to try to hurt Debbie?" Pete shouted.

"What's more important to you, Mr. Westport? Debbie or a story that only the FBI knows about?" he asked.

Carl, his editor, had walked into the newsroom when he had heard Pete shouting.

"Him?" Carl asked.

Pete nodded.

"What's the story?" Pete said after a few minutes.

"I'll need money the next time, but I'll tell you this for nothing. Mark's grandfather wrote mystery stories—pulp fiction."

"So what?" Pete asked.

After he pushed the red button on the cell phone, Evan whispered, "Debbie's a match."

"Anything?" Carl asked.

"Maybe."

"Then start writing the story," Carl said.

After Carl left the newsroom, Pete felt Debbie's hand on his.

"Did he say something about me?" she whispered.

"When?"

"This call or the last one."

"Of course not. I would have told you."

"Can I stay with you tonight?"

"Yes," Pete answered. "I want you to stay with me until Mark catches him."

"I care about you," Debbie said.

"I know," Pete said. "I feel the same way."

"What's more important to you, Mr. Westport? Debbie or a story that only the FBI knows about?"

"Let me write this story." Pete turned to his computer.

He typed on his computer, the words "Birdman Strikes Again" as his title.

When they were at his small apartment a few hours later, he looked at Debbie's body as she moved slowly above him.

"You feel so good," she said, "and I'm so close."

He moved his hands slowly up her arms, to her breasts, and rubbed them gently until he saw her take a deep breath, close her eyes, then exhale slowly.

In the brief time he had been with her, he had learned that her orgasms were long in duration, but internalized, like an implosion within her. Other women he had been with screamed, yelled, or twisted their heads back and forth on the pillow, but Debbie would always close her eyes just before, then exhale slowly.

"That was good," she said.

"Was it?"

"Yes." She kissed him on the forehead. "It always is with you."

Gently, he pushed her away, then got off the bed.

"You have to work?" she asked.

"Yes. I'll come back to bed in a few hours."

In the living room, he lit a cigarette and sipped on a glass of Jack Daniel's.

"What is more important?" he whispered as he remembered the words. "Debbie or a book that could solve my financial issues for the rest of my life?"

CHAPTER 38

"**D**R. MARCH, THIS** is Lou Mark with the FBI."
"Yes, Lou." Dr. March sighed. "You didn't need to
identify yourself. I won't forget you. How can I help you?"

"Our agents have come up with hundreds of names from
your database." Mark paused. "I want to narrow that down."

"Of course. Tell me what you need."

"Tell me about the process," Mark said.

"People either respond to our television ads or website,
or they are referrals from satisfied customers. They fill out our
questionnaire, we do a personality profile, and then we start
referring people to them as possible matches. There is no charge
for the questionnaire and the personality profile, but there is a
monthly fee after that."

"What's the nature of the questionnaire?" Mark asked.

"Generally, age, job, income, personal interests, how do they like to have fun, long-term goals," he said, "that sort of thing."

"What about physical characteristics?"

"Of course. If they wish, we'll post their photo on our website or they can choose to e-mail them directly to the potential match once they communicate with each other," he answered.

"What do the photos consist of?"

"That's up to the subscribers. They can give us a head shot, torso, or the entire person. Why?"

"Can you ask whether they have been divorced or if they have any kids?"

"Yes."

Mark looked down at the yellow notepad on the desk, then across the room. He was in an empty office at Quantico waiting to meet with Joe.

"The profile is age thirty-three to forty, blonde, attractive, and in exceptional shape. Divorced once and childless. Their goal is to get married and have a child. Did you get that?"

"Yes," he said cautiously. "But our system isn't perfect. I mean we try . . ."

Mark sighed. "You make some exceptional promises on your website, sir."

"It's a business," Dr. March answered.

"Really," Mark said sarcastically.

"That's really not completely fair," Dr. March said. "I worked with a team of psychologists on our questionnaire to identify personality characteristics and match people."

"And if you don't keep feeding them new names?"

"You're right. They would go to another service," Dr. March answered.

"Try that profile for now, and I want a list of the men you would match with those women."

"I'll talk to our computer people and our psychologists."

"Thank you, but there's something you're not telling me about the questionnaire," Mark said.

"What will you do with the list of new matches? There will be tens of thousands of names, maybe more." Dr. March ignored him.

"Let me worry about that," Mark answered. "Tell me about the questionnaire."

He still avoided the question. "It's proprietary and copyrighted. I've told you what I can."

"I'm waiting for you," Mark said, "and he's not waiting for anything. And I don't give a fuck about your dating service."

"Are you still protecting our clients' confidentiality?"

"You mean your business," Mark answered. "I will for as long as you help me."

"I was a clinical psychologist for thirty years," Dr. March said after a few minutes. "We learn a language of sorts, as we all grow up in terms of how we perceive the world. In theory, what the mental health care provider does is try to understand that language and help patients change. So I followed the model, but most of the time there were no lasting changes. People return to what is familiar to them even if it's not good for them. And most of the time, they never really understand it."

"So?"

"Our computer analyzes the information we're given by the subscriber," Dr. March explained.

"But don't most people lie?"

"Of course. A man who's five seven becomes nearly six feet. Women lose weight. Below-average golfers become class-A golfers. Income levels increase. It never ends. And nearly everyone lies about their past and their family."

"How does that help you?"

"Our questionnaire, which is a dramatically modified and shorter version of the MMPI, which I told you about at our first meeting, reveals patterns. The computer analyzes patterns in their answers in the lies they'd like to believe about themselves. On multiple-choice questions, the subscriber is given four possible one-word answers, and none of them are neutral. We also repeat some questions in a slightly different way with four different one-word choices. The lie reveals something to the computer."

"Give me an example," Mark said.

"Why don't I just e-mail you the questionnaire, and your people can analyze it."

"Send it to us."

"All right," Dr. March said. "There. It's on Mr. Mosely's computer. There are forty-nine questions thirteen of which relate to the subscriber's family relationships. They are spread randomly throughout the questionnaire. You'll know which ones."

"How does the computer determine that there is a match?" Mark asked.

"In the way I told you, by analyzing the information and the patterns. The computer makes the final choice. In some ways, the computer does what you do—it analyzes evidence and looks for patterns."

"Why the emphasis on family in your analysis?"

"Because the past defines the future, doesn't it? It's the best way to find a match."

Mark thought about the last few crime scenes and how each of the victims could have been sisters. "What if someone saw your TV ads and believed them, filled out your questionnaire, and went to his first date. He's smart, and what he sees is a ghost from his past."

"I wouldn't know without talking with him," Dr. March said evasively.

"Right." Mark laughed again. "You knew it the first time we met. What could it do to him if she were part of a catastrophic event in his life a long time ago or if she hurt him so badly that he buried it for a long time?"

"He could react negatively," Dr. March said. "But again, I don't know for sure."

"Negatively? He's killed more than fifty women."

"We're not responsible for what he may have done," Dr. March said defensively.

"Maybe," Mark answered. "I'm a lawyer, but I don't have any interest in suing you. Others may. I do know that each time he kills, your potential liability increases."

Dr. March was silent for a moment. "We've cooperated with your investigation, and I've been candid with you. I hope you will remember that."

Mark leaned back in the chair in the vacant office down the hall from Joe's office.

"It's there," Mark whispered.

"What?"

"If he used his real name first, before he met the first victim, then it's there in your database."

"But a little more than half of our subscribers are men. That's nearly three million names," Dr. March said.

"I know, and so does he."

Mark thought about the profile.

"He can hide in your subscriber base for a long time."

"Theoretically, yes. It could be like finding a needle in a haystack."

"I don't know why he's the first," Mark said, "it's perfect for them. Maybe he's not."

"I don't know that most of them have that kind of control," Dr. March said. "I think it was an accident. I think you're right, then he figured it out."

"An accident," Mark whispered.

"What?"

"What about their eyes?" Mark asked.

"What about them?"

"He can always see their eyes, right?"

"Yes, why?"

"In the crime scene photos, I can't see their eyes."

"Why?" he asked, then knew. "I'm sorry."

"They're gone," Mark said simply.

"I'm wondering if he saw something special in their eyes."

"Other than color?" Dr. March asked.

"Yes. Maybe a common imperfection that he recognized from someone in his past."

"I don't have your list of victims."

"You think he saw something special in their eyes?"

"Maybe. I know he saw something special in these women beyond the broad parameters of the profile, so he knew when he saw one on the computer that she was the one, and all of them have that special quality. I just don't know what it is yet."

"You might never find it," Dr. March said. "It might be so unique, that you'll never find out exactly what it is."

"No," Mark said firmly, "it was visible to him in a photograph, and I'll find it."

"He has a definite physical profile," Mark continued. "Would he deviate from that?"

"Has he?" Dr. March asked.

"No, at least not that we know about now."

"There would have to be a good reason, I would think," Dr. March said. "I know that's not much help, but . . ."

"No . . ."

"You gave me the profile of his victims. What does the woman you're thinking about look like?" Dr. March asked.

"Reddish-brown hair, petite, attractive, married, and pregnant," Mark answered.

"Your wife, I assume. You are probably the best reason he could find to deviate from his physical profile of the victims," Dr. March said finally.

"But they don't do that," Mark explained. "All the data we have, all that we know about them, tells us that they kill only within their profile. They are focused, obsessed on a look, a type of woman for their own reasons. The Green River Killer only killed prostitutes for example, and ..."

"You were concerned enough to ask me about your wife," Dr. March interrupted, "which means you already know the answer. You have a different kind of monster here. He takes real chances. It made no sense to confront Tom Anglen. Each time he kills, he gets stronger in his own mind. Now he believes he's invincible. That he'll never be caught."

"But it doesn't make sense," Mark said.

"I know you don't have much respect for what I did before this or what I do now," Dr. March continued, "but clearly he's serious and focused. I think he has taken the time to learn about you, for reasons I don't understand. Your wife is in danger, as is your unborn child."

Joe opened the door, walked into the office, and sat down on one of the side chairs in front of the desk.

"Cara?" Joe asked.

Mark shook his head.

"Thank you, Doctor, please call me after you input the new profile," Mark said.

"Of course."

Mark hung up the phone. "Dr. March."

"What is he doing?" Joe asked.

"He says he's helping us."

"Here." Mark handed him one piece of yellow notebook paper. "That's a narrowed profile. Please send it to our agents working on Dr. March's computers. They are getting hundreds of names."

"What else did you talk to Dr. March about?"

"Cara. Let me call Cara. I'll be there in a minute."

Mark picked up the black-colored phone on the desk after Joe left the room.

"Cara."

"Lou . . ."

"I think we may have a strong lead," he said.

"Good."

"You're thinking about something else," she said.

"No," he answered, "I just have a meeting in a few minutes."

"You're sure?"

"Yes. I'll call you tonight. You're safe."

Mark stood up and walked out of the room. *As long as he continues to kill,* Mark thought, *she's safe or he would have done it already, or does any of that even matter to him?*

CHAPTER 39

"THIS ALL HAPPENED** so fast, that I thought we should talk." Pete looked at her across the table.

"Okay," she said slowly. "Is this it?"

"No, I mean we started working on the Birdman story, we had sex that night, and now we're, in essence, living together."

"You're not happy with that?" she asked.

"No, that's not what I mean." He waved away the thought. "But I do think we should know more about each other than what we do in the office and what we do in the bedroom."

"All right."

A few awkward minutes of silence followed. "Thank you for bringing me here."

Pete looked out the floor-to-ceiling window in the building across from the offices of the *News*. "I always liked this

French restaurant. The view from the top of this building is extraordinary."

"I know it's beautiful."

"I just haven't been able to afford to come here in a long time," he said.

"What changed?" she asked.

"The Birdman," he said simply. "Carl gave me a good-sized bonus for those stories. I'm even thinking about moving out of that dump I live in now."

Pete sipped on a glass of wine and looked over at Debbie. She had blonde hair, deep brown eyes, a narrow waist, and stunning legs. Her face, although not exceptional like her body, was attractive. Like every other man in the room, he had noticed her when she first came to work at the *News* four years ago, but she was married then and he had just finished his second divorce.

"Can I ask you something?"

"Sure." He shrugged.

"Aren't you one of the highest-paid crime writers in New York?"

"I have been for a long time."

"And you wrote a few books. I read them."

"Yes, and although they weren't best sellers, I made a fair amount of money."

"What happened?"

"Two wives. A couple of kids. Bad money management. I don't care about money. I probably should, but I don't."

"Alcohol?"

Pete smiled. "That might have something to do with it."

"I asked about you a while ago," she said shyly.

"I didn't know," Pete said.

"Would you have done something about it if you did?"

"Yes." Pete laughed. "Of course."

"I was told that you would disappear from work for a while when you were drinking, and good stories would be assigned to others. Like Falcon and the story about the man who killed his entire family."

"That's true." He nodded. "That would have been my story. Falcon wrote the book, it was a best seller, and he left the paper. I never liked him much anyway."

"And Carl only keeps you around because he thinks you're the best when you work."

Pete lifted his hands in the air, then shrugged. "We've been friends a long time."

"But the book on the Birdman should change all that?" she asked.

Pete nodded. "I'm the only one he's talked to about this case. No one else can write that story. I already started it. It shouldn't take long to finish it after Mark catches him. But I'll still work at the paper. I'm a newspaperman. People like Falcon aren't."

"Have you met Mark?"

"Once." He raised his right index finger in the air. "I met him at Tom Anglen's funeral."

"What's he like?"

"Young, early thirties," Pete answered. "I think this is his first serious case. His father was a legendary detective in the Midwest. They called him the man with the eyes."

"Why?"

"Supposedly he could see the crime at the crime scene as if it were happening again in front of him, like a movie or old-style animation. I read about him. He had some stunning results, actually a lot. I don't know how he died.

"I talked to my publisher, and he's excited about this book," Pete said after a few minutes. "On one hand, we have the most prolific serial killer in U.S. history, and, on the other hand, we have a young FBI agent with a strong background just starting what could be a noteworthy career stopping serial killers. And Joe Mosely promised me an exclusive interview with Mark after he catches him."

"That's good, Pete." She nodded.

"Sure."

"Find out more about Mark's father, his cases, how he died. And the killer told me Mark's grandfather wrote short stories, mystery stories. See if you can find them and read them."

"Where should I start?" she asked.

"He said pulp fiction, so look at the paperback anthologies of mystery stories. *Ellery Queen's Mystery Magazines*, that sort of thing."

"What are you looking for?"

"I have no idea." Pete lifted his arms in the air.

"All right."

He changed the subject. "Enough about me. I want to ask you a question. You are a beautiful and intelligent woman. Why would you need those dating services?"

"I went to the bars for a while after my divorce. I didn't like it. I didn't like the guys I met there. I had sex with strangers on occasion because I love sex. But you know that." She smiled.

"Yes."

"I saw Dr. March on TV, and I wanted what he promised."

"Tell me again how many matches you got."

"Hundreds," she answered.

"Did you post photos?"

"Yes."

"Head shot?"

"No." She shook her head. "I had a girlfriend take a picture of me sitting in a chair with a bouquet of flowers on the table next to me. The picture was from my knees to my head. The flowers were blooming."

"Why did you get divorced?"

"He was a nice enough guy when he was sober, but verbally abusive when he drank. I finally had enough, although, like everyone else, we tried again and again."

"Is your family here?" he asked.

"No. I'm from Connecticut. My father died a few years go. My mother still lives there."

"What kind of matches did you get?" he asked.

"A wide assortment. I mean, there were a number that were similar in looks, temperament, common interests, that sort of thing. Why?"

"What kind of common interests?"

"Movies, books, romance, etcetera."

"There must be more," he said.

"I felt more comfortable with some of them than I did with others. I'm not sure why, but I knew it when we first met," she answered. "I want to go back to the apartment now."

"Did you feel chemistry with me?"

"Yes, I just told you, a long time ago," she said. "But I was married then, and I'm loyal. I want to go home."

A half hour later, in the bedroom, she stood in front of the mirror over the old dresser he bought shortly after his first marriage. "Take my clothes off," she whispered, "slowly."

He pulled her sweater over her head, then gently rubbed her arms, shoulders, stomach, and breasts.

"That feels good."

Then he unzipped her skirt and felt it fall slowly past his legs to her feet. For a few minutes, he continued to caress her body.

"You're driving me crazy," he said. "Let's get in bed."

"I know I am."

In bed, after sex, she whispered that she loved him, and he was quiet for a few moments.

"You know I feel the same way." He sighed as he gently pushed her away and got out of the bed. "But I need to work now."

"I know." She nodded. "I'll sleep."

At the door to the bedroom, he looked back at her and watched her adjust the pillow until she was comfortable. "It will be a little while," he said.

"I know," she said, "go work."

He sat down in front of the computer.

"What is it about Dr. March's service?" He typed on the screen of his computer in his living room. "And what does it have to do with this serial killer?"

He typed in the name at the top of the screen and pressed Go. In a matter of seconds, he was at that website. He read on the monitor the description of the questionnaire and profile and the promises, almost guarantees, of compatibility and long-lasting relationships.

"I wonder," he mumbled, "what deep compatibility means? How the hell can anyone guarantee that?"

He leaned back in the chair and thought about what Debbie had said about feeling chemistry with him before they even really met.

"I wonder," he said to himself, "if Dr. March found a way to tap into that."

He switched to a blank screen and typed in "The Dating Game." For the next hour, he wrote a follow-up story on Internet dating services and e-mailed it to Carl's computer.

"Carl, I wrote a story on Internet dating services. It's on your computer. Call me," he wrote.

Ten minutes later, Carl called him back. "I cut it a little—it was a little long—but I like it. We'll run it tomorrow. I like how you closed the story."

"Good. Thank you."

"You got a lot of this from Debbie?"

"Yes, and the website," Pete answered.

"If you're going to write about her, is it a good idea for you to get involved?"

"I didn't mention her name in this story." Pete shook his head.

"I didn't say that."

"I don't have a choice now, Carl. I'll see you tomorrow night."

He read the last paragraph of the story on the computer:

> *Dating services promise their customers the deepest compatibility, and the longest-lasting relationships. In a word, happiness. After divorces or a series of failed relationships, nearly everyone wants what they haven't been able to find on their own. Can these services deliver on their promises, or is it simply the latest scam in which we trust experts to manage our lives? Do they deliver something new or something old? In this case, one or more of these dating services have delivered a man standing next to a bed holding a claw hammer behind his back. Deep compatibility. Long-lasting relationships.*

Pete went back to the website, typed in Debbie's name, and saw the photograph. The flowers on the table next to her were pink and appeared to be roses, although he knew nothing about flowers. She was wearing a simple black dress that dipped slightly around her breasts and that appeared to stop just above her knees.

"Pete," he heard her say behind him and nearly jumped out of the chair, "I thought you were coming back to bed."

He felt her hands on her shoulders.

"Why are you looking at my photo?"

"I was doing research on dating services. You told me about it tonight, and I wanted to see it."

"Is it good?"

Pete turned off the computer and stood up. "I think you look terrific. Let's go to bed."

In the bedroom, he held her for a few minutes, then turned away, trying to get comfortable on the bed.

"What is it?" she asked.

"Nothing."

"Yes there is."

"What are you going to do about the baby?" he asked.

"I don't know yet. Does it matter?"

"Yes."

"What do you want me to do?" she asked.

"End it."

"I'll have to think about that," she said after a few minutes.

"Tell me when you make that decision."

CHAPTER 40

"**E**VAN, THAT FEELS good."

It was their second date. On the first, they had talked for hours at the bar, and then at her apartment, but she wasn't quite ready. Divorced once and childless, she was a paralegal at a local law firm, thirty-six, blonde, and attractive.

"Evan, I'm so close."

"Yes."

Her bio on the service was succinct, he remembered. *I want to travel with a lover who's my best friend. I want a family, a child.*

She worked out, and he could feel her strength beneath him as she finished. He could feel the muscles in her arms and in her legs stiffen around his body. After a few minutes, he felt her body relax.

"God, that felt good."

On their first date, she had talked about so many things—her marriage and then her divorce, her work, her family—and he had listened. Loretta had taught him to listen, and he had never forgotten.

He started to move faster above her, feeling her muscles tighten again, and then kissed her gently on her forehead after.

"That was great," she said.

"Yes, it was, Jackie." He smiled.

He twisted away from her, like a pretzel uncurling itself, then lay on his back for a moment before he got off the bed.

"You're coming back?" she asked.

He nodded. "Of course."

In the living room of her apartment, he sipped on the glass of red wine he had left behind when they went into the bedroom, then walked over to the window and looked at the lights of Manhattan. On their first date, she had told him that she had lived there forever and that she couldn't imagine living in any other city. She had lit a candle before they made love and set it on the dresser across from her bed. For her it was romantic; for him it meant nothing. *It meant so much to all of them—the lighting, the ambiance*, he thought, *like a stage production, like Loretta.*

"Evan?"

"I'll be there in a minute, Jackie," he answered.

From the window, he could see the *News* building, and he assumed that Pete and Debbie were working.

He'd told her he kept birds and wrote articles for the Audubon Society and other magazines, and it hadn't bothered her at all.

They had talked about movies they liked, and he had told her that he loved *Chaplin, The Kid, The Gold Rush,* and *City Lights.*

"Evan," Jackie said again.

He turned away from the window and saw her standing in the living room, naked and beautiful.

"What are you doing?" she asked.

"Thinking. I have a present for you downstairs in the rental car. Go back to the bedroom and let me get it for you."

She smiled. "What is it?"

"Go." He gestured at her with the wine glass. "You'll see."

When he got back up to her apartment, he set the birdcage on the counter and looked through the drawers in her kitchen until he found a ball-peen hammer, which he set on the counter next to the birdcage.

"Loretta, you can come out now," he said calmly.

"Loretta?" she asked.

"I'm sorry, Jackie."

"Who's Loretta?" She looked angry.

"An old friend."

Then she saw the birdcage, and the hammer next to it, and started to scream. That ended abruptly when he punched her in the face.

After he picked her up, carried her into the bedroom, and laid her on the bed, he saw the blood flowing from her broken nose.

In the living room, he lifted the black shroud from the cage and looked at his bird.

"It's time to sing."

He dialed Pete's number on his cell phone and waited until he heard his voice.

"Pete Westport, the *News*."

"I'm here," he whispered.

"Where?"

"I can see your building from her window," he said.

"You're in New York?" Pete sat up in his chair.

"Yes, Pete."

"Okay." He looked around the newsroom and saw Debbie working at her desk.

"Is Debbie with you?"

"Why? Why do you want to know?"

"I saw her photo. I liked the flowers. I liked it."

Pete could hear something in the background that sounded like a low, deep moan. "What is that?"

"I need to go now, Pete," Evan said. "I need to finish this. I'll call you later."

At the kitchen counter, he picked up the ball-peen hammer, then walked into the bedroom, stood next to the bed, and waited until she opened her eyes.

After he killed her, he washed off the hammer in the bathtub and the blood splatters from his chest, then set the hammer down, gently, next to her bed. In the living room, he talked to his bird and heard her sing until her voice was just a whisper, then silence.

"I'm sorry."

He took the hoof nipper from the inside pocket of his sports coat and walked back into the bedroom. Her face wasn't beautiful anymore, but he could still remember how beautiful she had been only a few minutes ago.

"You were so lovely," he whispered in her ear.

When he drove out of the underground parking garage, he looked up at the *News* building and dialed Pete's number.

"She's across the street in that apartment building east of you. Room 1211."

"Why are you doing this?"

"Because you're a good writer, Pete."

"No, I mean why are you killing all these women?"

"They want what they should never have," he said simply.

"What do you mean?"

"They should never have children."

I wonder if he knows, Pete thought, *I wonder if he knows Debbie's pregnant, but how could he?*

"You'll leave Debbie alone? Promise me?"

Evan laughed. "She's a match. What else can I do?"

"Please, I'm asking you," Pete said.

"She matters to you?"

"Yes."

"I'll think about it."

Pete heard him click off the phone.

"Who was it? Him?" Debbie asked.

Pete nodded. "I need to call the FBI now."

"Joe, he's in New York now," Pete said after Debbie was back at her desk. "He killed a woman across the street from our building."

"Give me the name," Joe said.

After he hung up, he watched Debbie working at her desk and wondered if his next story might be about her. He had no idea how he could protect her from a man who had killed more than fifty women.

He walked over to her desk, kissed her on the forehead, then crouched down next to her.

"A writer should never say this unless he's writing for daytime TV," he said.

"What?"

"I think it's good we finally got together. I think we're good together."

She didn't smile or even move, instead she asked, "He's here?"

Pete nodded. "The apartment building across the street."

"You lied to me," she said finally.

"No."

"Is he after me? Am I next?"

"No."

He held her shoulders and could feel her body shaking.

"Stay here in the newsroom."

She nodded slowly.

"It's just a precaution. Don't worry."

"All right."

Pete closed the door to Carl's office and sat down in one of the side chairs in front of his desk.

"He called. He's in New York. He killed again."

"What else?" Carl asked.

"She looks so much like the others."

"Debbie?"

Pete nodded.

"You think he's after her?"

"I don't know." Pete shook his head.

"What can I do?"

"I need to borrow a gun."

CHAPTER 41

"**WHAT WAS HER** name?" Mark looked at her on the bed.

"Jackie," Joe said.

"And he called Pete from her phone in this apartment?"

"Yes." Joe nodded.

"What did he say to Pete?"

"The usual, I guess, except he said Debbie, Pete's girlfriend, was a match."

"Meaning that Debbie is a subscriber to Dr. March's service." Mark nodded. "Then we might be able to find his name."

"If he's telling the truth. If it's not another game the killer is playing," Joe said.

"Let's see," Mark said.

Mark looked around Jackie's bedroom—simple, plain, and as quiet as she was now.

"I don't think he took anything from her, other than her finger," Mark mumbled to himself.

"She was," Joe said as he put the cell phone in the inside pocket of his suit coat.

"How long was she on the service?"

"She still is actually," Joe said. "Six months."

"How many matches?"

"Pete said a lot. He doesn't know how many."

"One minute, sir." Mark reached for his cell phone. "Dr. March, check the name Debbie Billings in New York. She works for the *New York News*. She's been on your service for about six months."

"Is she like the . . . is she dead?"

"No."

"She's on our service," Dr. March answered.

"How many matches?" Mark asked.

"A lot," Dr. March said, "hold on, more than a thousand."

"E-mail that to Mr. Mosely's computer right now."

"Hold on"—Dr. March paused—"it's done."

"Is he in this group?"

"Maybe," Mark said. "Thank you."

"How many?" Joe asked.

"More than a thousand. It's on your computer."

"I'll have Connor start reviewing it now."

Mark sat down on the bed next to the body. Carefully avoiding the dried blood on her face and around her head, he gently touched her forehead, then her cheek with the fingertips of his right hand.

"I thought it was your eyes," Mark whispered. "But I can't see them. What is it for him that makes it like he's there even though he's only seeing you on his computer monitor?"

Mark looked around the room again. "There are no photographs of you in this apartment. Why?"

"Does he even know why he chose you?" Mark seemed to be asking her. "Did he tell you? Did he focus on anything about you?"

Mark stood up, then turned toward Joe. With a half smile he said, "They thought my father was crazy too. Did you have Connor and Oliver look at photographs of the victims before this one?"

Joe nodded. "They didn't see anything special about their eyes."

"I don't think it is their eyes, although that would be the most obvious," Mark said.

"You'll find it," Joe said.

"Will I? I don't see anything different here, sir. I think you can bring in the crime-scene unit."

"You're going to the hotel?" Joe asked.

"Yes, sir. I'm running out of time, you know that."

"Yes."

"By now, I'm sure he's been to my house. By now, he knows everything about me. He knows where my father's farm is in Sun Rise. He may even know that Cara is pregnant. And I don't even know his name. Right now, he's disguised his appearance, his identity, when he was born, everything about him. And he's in a similar age group with hundreds of thousands of men, who were all matches for more than fifty attractive women."

"I understand, Lou, but she's protected, I promise." Joe reached over and gripped his forearm. "I call Schaeffer every two hours. Sun Rise is a small town with one main street and what, seven or eight businesses in the downtown area. I call your police chief every day to see if any strangers have come to town. He's met Schaeffer. He goes out to your farm every day. His name is Jake, right?"

"You didn't tell me that. Yes, Jake, I've known him since I was a kid."

"Lou, I lost not only my best agent, but one of my best friends. I'm not going to lose any one else, and this man is going to die."

"I appreciate all of that, sir." Mark said quietly. "It's just I should be there, and I can't be. He distracted us with the leak. We lost time, and he just kept killing. Now Cara is the distraction. It's the last one he has."

"Then he can't go after her now, can he?" Joe said.

"And that is a rational answer applied to a man who is insane. I need to find what allows him to turn a two-dimensional image on a computer screen into a memory from a long time ago. Something that's as real for him today as the day it happened."

"And you're sure it's not their eyes?" Joe asked.

"Yes. Whatever it is as much as anything, it's his fingerprint on each and every one of these crimes. When I find it, I can find him."

Mark walked toward the door to her apartment.

"I'm going to the hotel, sir. I'll call you in the morning."

After he walked inside the hotel room, he threw his suit coat on the bed, then placed both guns on the dresser.

In the bathroom, he slowly washed his face, then looked at himself in the mirror.

On the clock next to the bed, he saw it was nine-thirty in the evening and that the bottle of scotch next to it was nearly empty.

"The bar downstairs," he mumbled as he picked up his father's gun.

"I'm in town on a sales meeting," she said to Mark in the bar downstairs.

"Really," he said.

Other than the bartender, she had been the only person in the bar when he had walked in and ordered a scotch.

"Another one, sir?" the bartender asked.

"Sure."

She was blonde, attractive, and Mark guessed in her late thirties. She wasn't wearing a wedding ring.

"I'm sorry," she said to Mark. "I was just making conversation."

"Don't worry about it." Mark lifted his left hand from his cell phone.

"You keep looking at it." She pointed at the phone.

"You're right. I'm waiting for a call."

"Work?" she asked.

"Yes."

She looked a little like all of them. What do they think the first time they meet him? They've been told they have a match.

"What kind of work do you do?" she asked.

"I'm a cop."

"Here in New York?"

"Now, yes."

"A detective?"

"Yes."

"And you're working on a case now?"

"Yes."

She had been three barstools away from Mark when he sat down, and now she moved to the barstool next to him.

"A murder case?"

"I really can't talk about it."

"Of course," she said. "Your eyes are striking."

"Thank you."

"You don't say much, do you?"

"No, I'm just thinking about this case."

"And waiting for your call." She placed her hand on the face of his cell phone.

"Yes. Can I ask you a few questions?" Mark said.

"Sure. My name is Sarah."

"I'm Lou. Are you married?"

"No"—she smiled—"not now."

"Have you ever been?"

"Yes, biggest mistake of my life."

"How old are you?"

"Thirty-six, actually thirty-seven in three weeks. Why?"

"Kids?"

"Thank God no, not with him."

"What do you like to do?"

"Travel. Meet new people, live."

"What do you want?"

She shrugged. "What everyone wants. Family, kids, a man who cares about me. You sound like the questionnaire on that fucking dating service."

"Which one?" Mark asked.

He heard her say the name of Dr. March's dating service.

"Did you find anyone?"

She looked down. "Not yet."

"You're attractive, why do you need a dating service?"

"Thank you. For all the reasons they say." She ordered another drink. "It's hard to meet someone, that's all, who wants what you want."

"Do you read the *New York News*?"

"When I'm here," she answered. "I . . . do you mean the Birdman stories?"

Mark nodded.

"You're not him." She shook her head. "You can't be. I was thinking about . . ."

"No, I'm not. You were thinking about what?"

"Never mind."

"Tell me."

She looked down. "I was thinking about asking you to have a drink in my room. You have beautiful eyes. I saw them across the bar. You said you were a cop . . ."

"But you really don't know me, do you?"

"You're scaring me now."

"You're safe." Mark stood up. "I am a cop. But stay away from that dating service for a while."

"Can I see your badge?" She looked up at him.

"I hope you listened to me." Mark ignored her question. "I don't want to see you at a crime scene."

"No." She lifted her hands. "I heard what you said. But now I'm scared. Please have another drink with me. I don't want to go upstairs alone."

"My father would have, it was part of what he was, but I can't."

In the elevator, he thought it was absolutely brilliant—the killer's plan was focused, simple, targeted. *Why didn't I see this in the beginning?* Sarah, and so many others, could be his next victim.

He set his father's gun on the nightstand next to the bed, then turned on the television.

"Where are you?" he whispered. "How do I find you?"

He looked through a series of crime-scene photos he had in his briefcase, then set them down on the desk.

"I've done this"—he shrugged—"and I can't see it."

Sarah does look like them, he thought—blonde, attractive, in good shape, thirty-seven years old. It was the only time he'd seen one alive that looked so much like the victims. He wondered if Pete's girlfriend looked like she could be Sarah's sister. He tried to see her in a photograph on a computer screen, first her head, then her torso, then her legs. Then he closed his eyes and visualized her in a crime-scene photo lying naked on a bed with her face crushed, blood all around her, but her hands neatly crossed at her abdomen like a corpse in a coffin.

"I . . . I," he stuttered, "that's it. It has to be."

"Mr. Mosely . . . ," Mark said into the cell phone.

"Lou."

"Have our agents, no, have Oliver and Connor look at the photos on the dating service for each victim."

"I think our agents at the service already did that," Joe said.

"Have Oliver and Connor do it. I need to know if they're head shots, torso, or the entire person."

"Why?"

"Then modify the profile for the killer's father. A man who killed his wife with a claw hammer to her skull, who arranged their hands over her abdomen afterward."

"You think it's the hands," Joe asked.

"I know it's the hands. Check it, but I'm sure. When I said fingerprint a few hours ago, I didn't know how close I was. I can find him now, sir. I can end this."

CHAPTER 42

EVAN PARKED THE car in the driveway next to the house in front of the detached garage. Located across the river from the city in New Jersey, his house was relatively small, only fifteen hundred square feet with two small bedrooms and a den. At the door, he petted his cat, set a small box down on the dining room table, and walked into the bathroom in the master bedroom.

When he walked back into the living room, he saw his black cat sniffing and pawing at the box.

"Felix, get the hell away from that!" he shouted.

In the den, he took the finger out of the box, covered it with plaster, then placed it in the kiln for thirty minutes.

While he waited for the plaster to harden, he sat down in front of the computer and saw he had ten new matches from Dr.

March's service. As he scrolled through the photos and the bios, he stroked his cat, which had jumped on his lap.

"You miss daddy cat, don't you? You miss me when I work."

He stopped at one, read her bio, then studied the four photos she had posted on the website. "Maybe, Felix," he mumbled. "Maybe she'll work."

He noticed that she didn't live far away in New Jersey, about an hour's drive at most. Her name was Brittany. He glanced at her e-mail address. He typed:

> *Brittany,*
> *I just saw your name. My name is Michael. I looked at your bio and photos. I'd like to meet at a bar or restaurant to have a quick drink and talk.*
>
> *Michael*

After he sent the e-mail, he went into the kitchen and poured a glass of wine. When he opened the refrigerator, he noticed that he only had one bottle of ketchup left. Like a shadow, his cat had followed him into the kitchen, leapt onto the counter, and tilted his head as he watched the golden-colored liquid fill the wineglass.

"Remind me, Felix, we need to buy another case of ketchup. Chardonnay, Felix. Do you want some?"

Felix sniffed the top of the glass, turned away, and sneezed several times.

"I guess not." He laughed. "Come on."

He peered into the window of the kiln and watched the plaster hardening around Jackie's finger, then checked his e-mail.

"That was quick," he muttered.

> *Michael,*
>
> *I saw your bio about wanting a friend, a partner, a relationship, but I didn't see a photo. I don't like to think of myself as superficial, but I would like to see a photo before we make a date.*
>
> *Brittany*

"Sure," he said.

He found a photo he had not used for a while, in which he was wearing a hat and had a fake beard and mustache.

> *Brittany,*
>
> *Here it is. It's not a great picture. When would you like to get together?*
>
> *Michael*

He had made different but similar photos for each of the five aliases. When he was Michael, it was the hat and a fake beard and mustache. When he was Evan, it was a hat, a fake but thicker mustache, with a slight shadow over his face. For David, he took a photo of a movie star with dark hair, whom so many people had said he looked like, and altered the image slightly after he scanned it into his computer. For John, he had taken the same photo and altered it a little differently. And for Brad, he had gone back to Michael with the fake beard and mustache, but without the hat.

As he waited, Felix leapt off his lap and chased something into the corner of the den.

"No!" he shouted and grabbed Felix by the scruff of his neck, then threw him out of the room and closed the door. "We don't hurt small things, Felix. I know it's your instincts, but we don't hurt small things."

He picked up a tissue and waited until he cornered the lizard and grabbed it. It was about the size of half of his little finger, including its tiny tail. At the front door, he set it on the ground and watched it run away.

In the den he heard, "You've got mail."

"Come on, Felix," he said. "I think we have a date."

> *Michael,*
> *Let's get together. I can do it tomorrow night or Friday.*
> *Brittany*

It was Tuesday, and he thought about Debbie and, maybe, tomorrow night.

> *Brittany,*
> *How about Friday, seven, at the Green Gables Restaurant, in the bar.*
> *Michael*

He heard the buzzer go off on the kiln next to him and turned it off. After a few minutes, he set it carefully on the small platform he had built like a jewelry store display of a single finger with a ring on it. It was covered in gray velvet, with the back at a forty-five-degree angle and a single slot in the middle. At the bottom were her name and the date. He turned on the light in the cabinet, opened the doors, and set it next to Julie's finger.

He had chosen the cabinet carefully at a used-furniture store about two years ago. It was almost exactly like Loretta's curio cabinet he remembered from many years ago, made of dark, rich mahogany with glass doors and four shelves. When his father was out, whoring around according to Loretta, she would sometimes dust her possessions with a feather duster as she talked to him about the nightbirds. He now had more than twelve fingers on the first and third shelves, with exactly twelve on the second and fourth shelves. He looked at each of them, stopping at Julie's and Jackie's fingers for a moment, then looked down at the Bulova watch his father had given him many years ago, with the old brown leather band and smoked gray face. He nodded, then turned off the light inside the cabinet.

"You've got mail," he heard on the speakers next to his computer.

Yes.

Brittany

"Come here, Felix." He patted his lap and watched Felix leap at him, as if he were flying.

"I'm sorry I yelled at you." He petted him. "Look, I burned my fingers again. They're red."

He could hear and feel Felix purring, almost like music.

"What do you think, Felix? Pete likes Debbie. Should we do it now or wait?"

He continued to pet the cat as he stared at Brittany's last message on the computer monitor.

"He has to tell my story. People have to know. They can't be fooled anymore."

He turned off the computer, stood up, and set Felix down gently on the carpet in the den.

"I have to talk to my birds."

Felix followed him to the door to the basement.

"No," Evan said sternly. "You know you're not allowed in the basement."

He opened the door, turned on the light, and closed the door behind him. As he walked down the stairs, he could hear Felix scratching at the door.

"What do I do about Debbie?" he asked.

The birds had noticed the light as he came down the stairs, and some of them flew to the glass door to greet him. Others were involved in the complex pattern of mating and paid no attention at all to his presence in the room.

"Is she a distraction or an asset? Good or bad for Pete?"

He looked at the many separate cages for the birds that had mated for life, cages that were like condos or apartments.

"I could do it tomorrow." He nodded. "But should I? The FBI is going to post agents around her, but I'll get around them. I killed Anglen."

Smiling, he stepped inside the enclosure and felt four birds land on his shoulders. He held out his index finger, and a bird flew onto it. He lifted his right hand gently in the air, and the bird flew to the trunk of the tree he had placed diagonally in the middle of the enclosure.

"I want to feel the moment when Mark's father pulled the trigger and felt the bullet going into his brain."

He closed his eyes and remembered when he had been in Mark's house, in the den, and the newspaper articles on the wall about his father.

"Why would a famous man with a family kill himself?" he said to his birds.

"And what did his grandfather's story mean?" He tapped on the head of one of his birds. "Monsters. Who was the monster? And what about the little girl? What did it mean?"

He turned in the enclosure and brushed against the trunk of the tree in the middle.

"I think I understand the story, but Mark will have to tell me more someday."

He looked at the cages until he selected a bird for Brittany.

He shook the birds off his shoulders, walked out of the enclosure, and closed the door behind him. At the top of the stairs, he could hear the birds singing, and he smiled.

"Felix." He bent down and pushed him away from the door. "You can never go down there."

In the den, he turned on the light in the cabinet and looked at the fingers in the display case again.

He smiled softly as he gently touched the fingers. None of them knew why it was happening to them. He knew that for sure. After the first blow with the hammer, words were of limited use any way, he thought. When he heard the sharp crack of their skull and saw their blood splatter on the wall, the bed, and sometimes himself, words just didn't seem to matter much.

"Sure, I talk to them, Felix." He nodded, then scratched him behind his ear. "Because it's the right thing to do."

His cat stretched his paw out tentatively toward several fingers, and Evan slapped it lightly.

"No, Felix." He shook his head. "You can't touch daddy cat's things."

He took a feather duster and carefully brushed the dust away inside the cabinet, then turned off the light, and closed the double doors.

"There," he said.

He walked into the bedroom, used an off-brand mouthwash, then brushed his teeth. He always tried to save money. He smiled when he noticed Felix sitting next to him on the counter in the master bath.

"I should be as quick and as silent as you are," he said to the cat, "then no one would notice me until . . ."

He spit into the sink, then put the toothbrush on the rack inside the medicine cabinet.

"It's time for bed," he said. "I found a bird for Brittany."

He pulled the comforter over his shoulders and waited for the cat to find the spot he wanted next to him.

"I wonder if Mark figured it out yet. I wonder if he knows how beautiful their hands are."

CHAPTER 43

"**Y**OU WERE RIGHT,**"** Joe said. "You can see their hands on the photos posted on the dating service on every one of the victims."

"Good." Mark sighed and sat down on the bed. He was in the hotel room in New York.

"There's something else," Joe said.

"What is it?"

"The positioning of the hands on the dating service photos. If they are sitting, their hands are in their laps, one hand on top of the other. If they were lying on their backs, what's the word?"

"Supine, I think," Mark answered.

"If they were lying on their back, the positioning of their hands would be just like they are in the crime scene photos. It's the same if they were standing in the photograph."

"It makes sense."

"If the killer has the right software, he can enlarge details in the photo. Connor showed me. He could have enlarged their hands. That's what you were looking for, isn't it?" Joe asked.

"Yes. It explains how he knew they were the right ones just from a photograph on a computer."

"I don't see anything special about their hands," Joe said.

"And you won't. It's the one part of the model for a serial killer that never needs to be updated with technology or time. It's the part we'll never know because only they can see it. What about his father?"

"There was only one who arranged their hands that way after he killed his pregnant wife with a claw hammer."

"The name?"

"Michael Evan Wilkinson. He's serving a life sentence in a state prison in Pennsylvania. That's where it happened. I e-mailed you the newspaper story in the *Inquirer* from thirty years ago."

"Where is the prison?" Mark looked at the e-mail on his phone.

"It's just outside Philadelphia, maximum security. He's in his early seventies now. He's been there thirty years, and he'll be there for the rest of his life," Joe answered.

"He has a son, but they don't mention his name in the story yet." Mark kept reading. "You have more?"

"Yes. Since he was incarcerated in that prison, he's had one visitor, the same one, every thirty days for the last sixteen years. He signs in under the name Michael Stewart. He takes him money, in cash, cigarettes, food."

"When was the last time?" Mark asked.

"You're not going to like it," Joe said carefully.

"When? Tell me."

"Three days ago."

"Fuck!" Mark shouted.

"I told you . . ."

"And he can only have visitors once every thirty days, is that right, sir?"

"Yes."

"If I had seen this four days ago we'd have . . . whatever. We can't wait for him to come back to the prison, sir. He'll kill at least two more women and maybe Cara. Did you run the name Michael Stewart through the database at the dating service?"

"Of course," Joe answered. "We found five Michael Stewarts, but none of them could be him."

"You're sure?"

"Yes, Oliver checked out all of them. One Michael Stewart is nineteen and a biology major at UCLA. Another Michael Stewart is seventy-eight years old looking for a younger woman, according to his profile, in the range of fifty-five to sixty. He's not hiding behind those names, Lou, he's far too smart."

"They have video at the prison where friends or family visit inmates, right?"

"Yes, I'm having an agent in the Philadelphia office review that now. When he's finished, he'll call me and then send it to me."

"I want to see the family history." Mark continued going through the list in his mind as fast as possible. "I need the name of the boy and what happened to him after his father killed his stepmother."

"We're looking into all that now," Joe said patiently. "This is the way these cases go. You can never look back and think what If I'd done something else would it have been different."

"Give me a few minutes, sir. I want to read the newspaper story and think about this."

He pulled up the story on his phone and began to read it.

DEATH COMES TO LARCHMONT
By Edward Moore

> *Yesterday, after receiving calls from several concerned neighbors, the Larchmont police went to the home of Michael Evan Wilkinson. Mr. Wilkinson has lived in our community since shortly before his first wife died giving birth to his son. The son's name is being withheld at this time. About a year after his wife died, Mr. Wilkinson married Loretta Prince, a stranger then to our city. Yesterday, the police found Loretta Prince dead on the living room floor of their home. Mr. Wilkinson, who is presently in custody and being held without bond, is believed to have killed her through repeated blows to the head with a claw hammer he found in their home. Sources within the police department have indicated that Mr. Wilkinson has confessed to the*

crime. When the police arrived, Mr. Wilkinson was sitting next to the body crying, again according to police sources.

Neighbors have said that there was a history of heavy drinking and violence between them. One neighbor could not be interviewed at all by the police because he disappeared mysteriously several weeks ago. Neighbors said he was a regular visitor to the Wilkinson home doing the day when Mr. Wilkinson was at work. His name is George Allen Peterson, and he was an accountant who worked in Philadelphia.

This is the first murder in our small town in twelve years. This event hardly makes us like the big city we're only thirty miles away from, where murder is far too common, but it is a disturbing reminder of a basic tenet of the human condition that no matter where we live, raw and uncontrolled emotions will sometimes control our lives.

Mr. Wilkinson will be arraigned at . . .

"Nothing more about the boy," Mark mumbled. "And what happened to the accountant, George Allen Peterson, and does the boy know anything about it? When should I visit his father?"

Mark paced around the room several times, then crouched down near the door. *What would you do*, he looked up at the ceiling. *I should know.* He nodded. *I watched you work for years. I'm close and I can't lose him again. I can't lose him this time.*

"Sir, I appreciate your patience," Mark said into the cell phone. "I read the newspaper story, and I thought about it. I have questions."

"Go ahead."

"Have we checked the database of the dating service for the last name Wilkinson with any first name, but particularly with the first names Michael or Evan?"

"We're doing that now. Nothing yet."

"Anything yet on the video?" Mark asked.

"A few minutes ago, I talked with our agent in Philadelphia. It turns out that there is only one old camera, and the perspective is on the prisoner. It shoots from an angle over the visitor's shoulder, the concern apparently being contraband."

"Then we should be able to see him when he leaves?"

"Yes," Joe answered. "He hasn't seen it yet. I should have it in a few hours."

"I saw a little family history in the newspaper story," Mark continued. "His mother died giving birth to him, but there's nothing about the boy. Do we know how old he was when it happened, the murder?"

"No."

"Do we have any history yet on the stepmother, Loretta Prince?"

"Nothing yet, Lou. We did just learn this, you know that."

"Yes, sir."

"Most of these answers are going to be the same, but I have everyone working on it. I do have two agents at the prison dressed as correctional officers in the event he or anyone else visits Wilkinson."

"How many trials did he have?"

"Two, we think. He was given the death penalty the first time and life imprisonment the second time. We think the boy might have testified for his father at the second trial. The trial transcripts are at the archives for the Court of Appeals. I should have them soon."

Mark sipped on the scotch and set it down on the nightstand.

"Who is George Allen Peterson?" Mark asked. "The story intimated that he was Loretta's lover, friend, whatever."

"Mr. Peterson has been missing for thirty years. I don't know much more at this point, other than he was single, his parents died before he disappeared, and no one seems to know why he left suddenly."

"Maybe"—Mark paused, then looked at the door when he heard a low male voice in the hallway—"Wilkinson killed him because he was having an affair with his wife."

"That's what I think."

"Then where is the body?"

"I don't know. I'll have agents interview the neighbors tomorrow and see if anyone still lives there from thirty years ago. When do you want to meet with Wilkinson? I can arrange it for anytime you want."

"Not yet. I want to know more about George Allen Peterson first, how he died, where he is, and whether Wilkinson murdered him."

"What difference does it make now?"

"Because I believe Pennsylvania is a death penalty state, isn't it? I thought about this," Mark added.

"Hold on. You're right. If you care, there are now thirty-three death penalty states. But so what?"

"Now I can't threaten him with anything, but he hasn't been tried yet for the murder of George Peterson."

"You're right, Lou. You intended to use that as leverage?"

"I intend to do whatever it takes. I want you to leak Wilkinson's name to Pete. I want him to interview Wilkinson and make sure he takes Debbie."

"Why?" Joe asked.

"Because he'll treat Debbie like shit, and it will make Pete angry. But wait. Don't say anything. I'm sure she's been working on the story, and don't most people want to see the monster? Here she can see meet the father of the monster in a cage. She'll go."

"Leak it?"

"Actually, no." Mark thought about it. "Tell Pete I'm giving him an exclusive and I may want a favor soon."

"When should I tell him?" Joe asked.

"Now please, sir. Also ask Oliver to call Dr. March. I think this started as an innocent experiment for him in a way. He just wanted a date, then he met Loretta without intending it. He might have used real information for the first time, and there might have been a complaint filed by a subscriber. I want Dr. March's complete complaint file from the beginning of that business."

"Anything else?"

"That's all for now, sir. Thank you. I'll wait for your call."

He washed his face, brushed his teeth, then turned off the light in the hotel room. From the window, he could see the lights of New York City. Now he nodded, then turned away.

CHAPTER 44

"SIR, THERE'S A man here who claims he's Pete Westport with the *News*. He has a woman with him. He wants to see Wilkinson."

"What does he look like?" Joe asked.

The agent looked up at the television monitor in a room just outside the visiting area.

"Tallish. Dark, graying hair. Looks to be in his early to midfifties. A little overweight. The woman is good looking, probably fifteen years younger."

"Hold on a minute," Joe said.

Joe dialed Mark's cell phone number.

"Yes, sir."

"There's a man at the prison in Pennsylvania who claims to be Pete Westport. He fits his description. He's with a younger woman. He didn't wait long," Joe said.

"No, he didn't. After the next story, he'll know that he will never be able to see his father again," Mark said. "Please call me when Pete finishes."

Joe picked up the other line. "Check their credentials. The woman's name should be Debbie Billings with the *News*, then have Wilkinson taken to an interrogation room and videotape the interview."

"How long have we been waiting?" Pete asked Debbie.

"About an hour."

"It seems longer."

He paced around the room until a young corrections officer stepped inside.

"Mr. Westport," he said, "I'm sorry it took this long. We set up a separate interrogation room for you. Please follow me."

"Thank you," Pete said.

"We'll bring him here in a few minutes," he said.

The room was small with a single metal table in the middle of the room and three chairs around it. In the upper-left corner of the room, Pete saw the video camera.

"Did he look like a corrections officer to you?"

"No," Debbie said. "You're right, he's FBI."

"They were waiting to catch him here," Pete said. "And we're being recorded right now."

Pete heard the door open and turned. He saw a man who was about six feet one with gray thinning hair and a sallow complexion from spending decades in prison. To offset the steady loss of hair from his head, Pete assumed, he had a thick gray mustache. He was in handcuffs and leg shackles, and each step he took as the guard guided him to the chair was no more than six inches.

"Knock on the door when you're finished," the guard said, then closed the door behind him.

"I'm Pete Westport from the *New York News* and this is Debbie Billings, my research assistant."

"Yeah, deep research." Wilkinson eyes focused on her breasts. "I'd give ten years for ten minutes with her."

Pete sat down across from him and waited until Debbie sat down next to him.

"You must wonder why we're here," Pete said.

"I suppose, but I'm glad." He laughed.

"Sir, you can look at me occasionally, otherwise I'm going to ask Debbie to leave the room."

He turned slowly. "All right. Why are you here?"

"Your son."

"Why would the *News* be interested in my son?"

Wilkinson glanced toward Debbie and saw her hands gripping the edge of the metal table.

"God, you have great hands," he said.

"We believe he's the serial killer who calls himself the Birdman," Pete said.

"The guy who kills women he meets on an Internet dating service?"

"Yes."

"No, that's bullshit." He shook his head violently. "My son never had any balls. For a while, I thought he was a fag."

"He's killed over fifty women," Pete said. "He kills them the same way you killed your second wife, Loretta Prince."

"This is fucking crazy." Wilkinson stood up and leaned across the table. "He was just here a few weeks ago. He's a quiet, shy kid."

Pete didn't move, but he heard the legs of the metal chair Debbie was sitting on scrape backward across the concrete floor.

"He has sex with them." Pete stared into his eyes. "Then he takes a hammer, most of the time, and kills them by crushing their face, just like what you did to Loretta."

"You're fucking nuts!" Wilkinson shouted, then tried to raise his arms over his head.

"Pete," Debbie said, never taking her eyes off Wilkinson, "let's get away from here, now. Please now."

She imagined that the look on Wilkinson's face was identical to the look on his face years ago when he killed his wife.

"Then he has sex with them again," Pete said, "after he cuts off the ring finger on their left hand."

Wilkinson slowly sat down.

"My son." He looked confused. "My son has done these things?"

"Yes," Pete said.

"I'll have to talk to him about this." He nodded his head. "I taught him to be a good boy. I'll straighten him out, don't worry."

"It's a little late, sir. He's killed more than fifty women, all of whom looked like Loretta."

"I loved Loretta. You have to believe me," he explained.

"Sure," Pete said sarcastically, "that's why you're here. The FBI is after him."

"Who?"

"A young agent named Lou Mark."

"I don't know that name." He shook his head.

"I need background from you after you were incarcerated."

"Mark." He looked confused. "My son did this?"

"Sir, I need some background from you. What happened to your son?"

"He went to live with an aunt and uncle on his mother's side. His natural mother, she bled to death during childbirth." Wilkinson answered.

"What were their names?"

"Pete, like you, and Maria Morgan."

"Did he change his name?"

"Yes, legally. Pete and Maria did it. They never came to see me after I came here. It wasn't just my fault, you know. No one understood that. Loretta had one hell of a temper, and it got worse when she got pregnant."

He remembered how it felt each time he smashed the hammer into her face. He remembered the sex games they would play after they fought. It was like a carnival ride, he thought. He remembered waiting by her side after he folded her perfect hands across her abdomen, until the police took him outside and he saw his son in the front yard.

"So your son's name is Evan Morgan?"

"Yes." He nodded.

He looked around the room, then focused on Debbie for a moment.

"You look like her," he said, as if he were seeing his wife again. "You're not quite as tall, but you look so much like her. I still think about her, sometimes."

"Were you the father?"

"I don't know." His eyes darted around the room.

"Were you the father?" Pete asked again. "Or is that why you killed her, because another man was the father?"

"I said I don't know."

"Do you think Evan knew about the other guy?"

He knew, he thought, *the little fag knew. He watched them together, but he never told me. He betrayed me for a fag accountant Loretta called her nightbird.*

"I don't know." He shook his head. "I think he and Loretta were just friends."

"What was his name?" Pete asked.

"It's been a long time." Wilkinson looked away.

"You remember," Pete said.

Debbie watched his face and saw him nod.

"George, George Peterson. He was an accountant. Gentle type. For a while, I thought he was a fag."

"Did you talk to Evan about George?"

"No." He shook his head. "If Loretta was cheating on me, I didn't want him to know. I didn't want anyone to know."

"Loretta"—he paused—"was great sex, and she needed it on a regular basis."

"What did you tell Evan?" Pete asked.

Wilkinson looked away.

"What did you tell Evan?" Pete asked again.

"She was abusive," he answered. "She didn't hit him, but she would yell at me in our bedroom that Evan was just a castoff from a dead woman. I knew that Evan heard it. I tried to stop her, but I didn't until that day. She was a horrible mother, and she had no right to have children."

"And that was the explanation you gave your son?"

"Yes."

"What happened after you were incarcerated?"

"His aunt and uncle made sure he got a good education," he said. "He was the smartest kid in his class. He's gifted. He became an accountant and did that until first his aunt, then his uncle died, in the same year. They left him enough money so he didn't have to work as an accountant any more. He got interested in birds. Loretta always told him stories about the nightbirds. And now he keeps them and writes articles about them."

"Where does he live?" Pete asked.

"I really don't know that." He shook his head quickly.

"What are the nightbirds?" Debbie asked.

"I think it's bullshit." Wilkinson shifted on the metal chair. "These chairs are hard on your ass. Loretta told him nightbirds mate for life and are always loyal. They sing only at night, and only after they've had sex. I think it's bullshit. But my son spent a lot of money tracking them down, if it's true."

"He leaves a bird," Pete said.

"I know." Wilkinson lifted his hands. "I thought about this before. I just didn't want to believe it."

"You never asked?"

"No." He shook his head. "I don't like to think about what Loretta and I did to him."

"What does he look like?" Pete asked.

"His mother, a little. A little like me."

"That doesn't mean much," Pete said.

"You said the agent's name is Mark?" he asked. "I'm not going to help him find my son so he can kill him. Would you do that to your son?"

"Anything else?" Pete looked at Debbie.

"Is George still alive?" Debbie asked.

"I wouldn't know." Wilkinson looked away. "I've been locked up here for nearly thirty years. How would I know?"

"Has Evan mentioned him?" she asked.

"No. Never. Are we through here?"

"I think so," Pete said. "Unless you want to tell us anything else."

"I do have something," he said slowly.

"What?" Pete asked.

"Take these off me"—he gestured at him with his handcuffed hands—"and leave the room and leave her behind. It'd be like old times."

Pete stood up, walked across the small room, and knocked on the square Plexiglas window on the door.

"You're done, sir?"

"Yes."

"He's brand new." Wilkinson stood up and pointed at the guard. "He doesn't belong here. He's FBI. Tell Mark he'd be wasting his time talking to me."

Pete and Debbie watched him being led from the room, while he took small six-inch steps.

"He scared the hell out of me," Debbie said.

"I know," Pete said. "I shouldn't have brought you here. I should have come alone."

"I never want to meet that man's son." Debbie shook her head. "Never."

"You won't. Let's go."

"Maybe I should go away," she said. "He's going to be angry that he can never see his father again."

"We'll talk about it."

CHAPTER 45

"**B**RITTANY . . ." HE STOOD up.

"Michael," she said. "You look different than your photo."

"I shaved off my beard," he said. "Please sit down."

Evan had chosen a booth in the corner of the bar at the Green Gables restaurant, and he watched her skirt slide upward as she sat down in the booth.

"You look like your photo." He sat down across from her.

They were quiet for a moment as they evaluated each other visually.

"Have you had many dates like this?" he asked.

"Yes." She rolled her eyes. "Too many. I thought I told them what I wanted through their questionnaire. Then they sent me a bunch of . . . well, they didn't work."

"Yes, I had the same experience."

The cocktail waitress took their drink order and walked to the bar.

"A cosmo?" he asked.

"Yes. It's really all I drink, other than a beer or white wine occasionally. If I have more than two, I'm drunk. I'm kind of a lightweight."

"Same here."

She looked so much like her, he thought—the hair, the body, her hands.

"I've always found on these dates that there is an awkward moment in the beginning, when you wonder if they delivered on their promise." He reached across the table and touched her hand lightly.

"Yes?"

"I hope we can pass that moment," he continued, "that's all."

"Maybe." She smiled. "You're not like the bunch of geeks they sent me so I would keep paying their fucking bill."

Evan had read Pete Westport's article yesterday morning, with his coffee and Felix. His memory was close to photographic, and he would never forget the words.

"I know this sounds, excuse me, like bullshit, but you are stunning."

"Thank you."

"Tell me what you do," he said.

"Yesterday," he remembered the words, "this reporter met with the father of the Birdman. His name is Michael Evan Wilkinson. For the

last thirty years, he has been in prison for killing his wife and the baby she was carrying. The initial sentence was death, but on appeal, after a new trial, he was given natural life, which means he'll die in the place where he has lived for the last thirty years. He is, without doubt, the most crude and disgusting human being I have ever met. Shortly before he killed his wife with a claw hammer, a neighbor of the Wilkinsons disappeared. His body has never been found. Although Wilkinson was never charged with that alleged crime, it is possible that George Allen Peterson was the father of the child that his wife, Loretta Prince Wilkinson, was carrying, and he was killed by this crude and disgusting human being."

"Pete will be sorry," he mumbled to himself.

"What?" Brittany asked.

"Nothing. I was just thinking about what wine I wanted to order next." He knew he could never see his father again.

"Tell me what you do," he said.

"Pharmaceutical sales."

"That's a good job," he said.

"Yeah, they're hard to get. After my divorce, for a while, I thought I'd have to blow the district manager." She laughed.

He smiled. She even talked like Loretta.

"But I didn't." She finished her cosmo. "Maybe one more."

"Sure." He signaled at the cocktail waitress. "How long were you married?"

"Three years, but the last eight months, we were separated."

George, he thought, was a good man, and he had simply disappeared a few weeks before his father had killed Loretta. The police had looked for him everywhere except where he was—in a deep grave under the basement of their home. Loretta had told him one night, when his father was out, that George was loyal, like the nightbirds.

"He shouldn't have done it," he mumbled.

"Done what?" She looked confused.

The cocktail waitress set their drinks on the table.

"I'm sorry," he said. "I'm fighting with someone at work."

"What do you do?"

"I'm an accountant at a medium-sized firm. And we have this Enron-type issue now."

"A public company?" she asked.

"Yes, but I can't really say anything else now."

"I understand."

"Although it can be assumed that the Birdman uses multiple aliases," he remembered the words again, *"his name is Evan Morgan. Evan changed his name shortly after his father was incarcerated. What did his father and his stepmother do to this man that caused him to become the most prolific serial killer in U.S. history? What was it like growing up in the same home with two monsters? For almost thirty years, Evan flew below the radar screen, living what may have appeared to be a normal life. Then something happened, and he became someone else. The sins of the fathers always and ultimately rest with their children."*

"You know, I almost stopped," she said and sipped on the cosmo, "dating through them. The Birdman, you know."

"Yes. It's a scary time."

"But what are the chances of my meeting him? And they always promise me a fucking match," She laughed. "And even though they've never really delivered, it could happen."

"Maybe it has." He looked at her hands folded together on the table and touched them. "I know this was only supposed to be a brief meeting to see each other, but why don't we eat something?"

"Yes, that's a good idea."

"You have beautiful hands," he said.

"Thank you."

In the trunk of his car, his bird was waiting to sing, and after they shared several appetizers, he drove her to her condo.

"Come up for a minute," she said when he stopped in front of the complex.

He parked on the street, and when they got off the elevator, he watched her open the door and followed her inside.

"Do you want a drink? I have a Chablis."

She was drunk after four cosmos, and he nodded.

In the bedroom, about a half hour later, she told him she hadn't had sex for six months, the last being one of the dates whom she saw three times before she ended the friendship.

As Evan moved over her, he thanked Dr. March, in his mind, for providing him with so many women who were lonely. He never thought he was particularly good-looking, but if you were in shape and appeared to be successful, good looks seemed to be optional. Sometimes, sex happened on the first date. Sometimes, it would take three, four or five dates; and sometimes he had to persuade them by hurting them. But once, one had refused entirely, and when he had tried to force himself on her, she had hit him on the head with the brass lamp next to the bed. Her name was Hillary, like the former first lady, and he had felt the blood on his forehead.

He felt her body relax underneath him. "That was good."

"Yes." He turned to his left. "I have some flowers in the car I forgot to give you. Let me get them."

"That's nice," she said. "I'll be here."

"You freak!" Hillary had screamed at him, then kicked him in the stomach.

It had hurt, he remembered. She had kept screaming at him, and he heard people moving around in the condo next to hers. She tried to kick him again, and the second time, he had caught her leg, twisted it, then threw her on her back. As he watched her struggle to get up, he had wiped off the blood on his forehead from the lamp.

"You're a fucking bitch, Hillary!" he shouted.

"Get out of here."

He'd heard a timid knock on the front door of her condo.

"Is everything okay?" the man at the door asked.

"You're lucky," he had said to Hillary.

At the door, he pushed the old man aside and ran to his car. It wasn't until he was miles away that he felt safe again.

He got dressed, left Brittany's apartment, and took the elevator down five floors.

George had been good to him, he remembered, had started teaching him accounting, and when he disappeared, Loretta had confronted his father.

"What did you do to him?" she screamed.

"Why the fuck would you care?"

"He was a friend. He was a friend when you were out all night fucking cocktail waitresses and strippers."

"Nothing. I did nothing."

"You screw around on me. You stick me with this kid, this castoff from your dead wife, and you get jealous when I find a friend."

He could still hear the sound of his father's fist hitting her face and her head hitting the hardwood floor in their bedroom.

As he took the birdcage from the trunk of the car, he remembered that it was only two weeks later that he had come home and seen the yellow police tape stretched around the front porch of his house. But that night, like every night they fought, he had heard them having carnival-style sex in the master bedroom after the fight ended.

"It's really not flowers," he said at the doorway to the dark bedroom.

"What is it?"

"Get up and see."

Behind his back, he held the claw hammer he'd found in a drawer in her kitchen.

"I'm tired, Michael." She yawned. "Can't I see it in the morning?"

"Who is this man?" He remembered the words from Pete's story. "Who is this man who kills at will after a dating service provides him with the means? Is he as sick as the man who will spend the rest of his life in prison, balding, with a sallow complexion from thirty years of incarceration that I met today? And where is George Peterson, the probable father of Loretta's child?"

"Fuck," he muttered. "Fuck Pete."

"What, Michael?"

"No. I want you to see her now."

"Her?"

"Yes," he said. "Get up, then we'll go back to bed, and I'll hold you until you fall asleep."

He heard the bedsprings move, then saw her like a shadow walking slowly toward him from the dark bedroom. George had been good to him, he thought, and he knew where George had been for more than thirty years.

"What is it?" she rubbed her eyes.

"She." He pushed her gently toward the kitchen counter.

She took two small steps then turned to her right and tried to run. "You're him!" she screamed.

She felt the claw hammer on the bridge of her nose a moment later. In the bedroom, he laid her on the bed, adjusted the pillow under her head carefully, and waited.

"I can't see my father ever again!" Evan shouted, then hit her over her left eye with the hammer and watched her pass out. The impact of the hammer on her face sounded like a cannon shot in the dark and quiet room.

In the kitchen, he pulled the black shroud from the birdcage and said, "It's time to sing."

"Pete!" he yelled. "Pete. He did this, or was it Mark?"

"Pete," he mumbled, then dialed his number on her phone.

"Pete Westport, the *News*."

"I didn't like your story today," he mumbled.

"Evan?"

"I didn't like your story today."

"Evan, where are you?" Pete asked.

"I'll call you back." He could hear sounds in the bedroom, hissing sounds, like water escaping from underground plumbing fixtures. She was trying to breathe, but she was dying. "I need to finish this."

In the bedroom, he waited until her right eye opened, then hit her three more times before he walked into the bathroom and cleaned the hammer with water from the tub.

"I didn't like his story!" he shouted. "I can never see my father again."

He set the hammer down next to the bed and walked into the living room and, after he crushed the bird in his hands, deleted the photo he had e-mailed to her computer.

In the bedroom, he attached the hoof nipper to the base of her finger and squeezed, then after a few minutes with her in bed, arranged her hands over her abdomen. He could feel the blood splatters on his chest as he moved above her.

"I'm in north New Jersey, Pete," he said into her phone afterward. "You should be able to see the number on caller ID."

"This has to stop." Pete looked at Debbie standing at the doorway to the bedroom.

"I didn't like your story," he said again. "You're supposed to be writing about me, not the FBI and not Mark."

Evan hung up the phone, looked around the room, then walked out of the door to her apartment, locking it before he closed it behind him. It was the first time he had killed one of them in his home state.

Debbie, he thought, *it's time.*

CHAPTER 46

MARK STOOD AT the doorway, scanned the living room quickly, then walked inside. The bird was dead in its cage on the kitchen counter, and there was a trail of blood from that point to the bedroom.

Mark walked into the bedroom and saw the claw hammer next to the bed. He crouched down and rubbed the palm of his right hand across the left side of his face.

I can never see my father again. I can never see my father again. Mark could almost hear his voice in the room.

"Jesus Christ," Mark whispered. "He must have hit you a dozen times, some of them after you were already dead."

Mark walked around the bed, carefully avoiding the blood on the carpet. "He even hit you in the chest and shoulders," Mark observed, "and he's never done that before. What is it?"

Mark crouched down next to her, then stood up quickly. "He lost control."

Her hands were folded neatly across her abdomen, and the ring finger on her left hand, as always, was missing. He saw family photographs in the bedroom, a jewelry box on the dresser, a few inexpensive prints on the walls. It was so much like all the others, as was she. Mark crouched down at the foot of the bed and closed his eyes. He thought he could almost hear the sound of the first strike from the hammer in the dark, quiet room, a surprised and startled breath, then a low moan.

"Lou, what is it?"

"I could almost hear it." He stood up.

Earlier that day, at Joe's office, he had watched the video of Evan's last visit with his father at the prison. In the grainy black-and-white video, Evan was wearing a hat when he left and what Mark thought was a fake beard and thick moustache. He'd told the agent to run the video back, then forward a dozen or so times, until he had the clearest view of Evan's eyes. The look in his eyes then on the video was almost calm—he had taken care of his father and done what a good son should do. Here, his eyes had been angry.

"Hear what?" Joe asked.

"Evan killing her."

"Do you see anything else? Did he take anything?"

"No"—Mark shook his head—"he didn't take anything, at least I don't think so. But he was angry. I think he was remembering

Pete's story about his father. And she was the beneficiary of his anger."

Mark walked to the other side of the bed and stopped near the closet.

"Pete's story reminded him of the past. Each time he hit her, he thought about his father, Loretta, and Peterson. I think that's everything I can see here, but I know what to do."

"All right."

"I know Wilkinson killed George Peterson. He thought Loretta was cheating on him and that the accountant was the father of the child she was carrying. His ego couldn't abide the thought, and he killed him, brutally I'm sure."

"And you think Evan witnessed the murder?" Joe asked.

"No, I don't think so." Mark shook his head. "If anything, he was part of the burial. Maybe it was Wilkinson's sense of justice. I really don't know." Mark shrugged.

"You think George Peterson is in that old house? That's where he buried him?"

"Yes, in the basement, I'm sure, and he's been there for thirty years." Mark nodded. "I read part of the trial transcript last night, Evan's testimony at the second trial. Evan saved his life."

Mark remembered Evan's trial testimony.

"And how were you treated by Loretta Prince?" his father's lawyer had asked.

"She said I was nothing more than a castoff from a dead woman. My mother bled to death giving birth to me. I never knew her."

"And this is what Loretta Prince said?"

"*Yes. I could hear her when they argued in their bedroom.*"

"*Did they fight often?*"

"*Always,*" Evan had answered. "*And always about me.*"

"*So he did this for you?*"

"*Yes.*" Evan had nodded. "*I think so. He was trying to protect me.*"

"*From Loretta Prince?*"

"*Yes, sir.*"

Mark remembered the cross-examination and how inept the prosecutor had been.

"*Didn't your father kill George Peterson, your neighbor?*" he had asked.

"*No, sir.*"

"*Well, we can't find him, and we can't find a body. It's been nearly two years now.*"

"*He was friends with Loretta,*" Evan had testified. "*That's all I know.*"

"*Was George your friend?*"

"*Yes.*"

"*How did your father feel about that?*"

"*I think he thought it was all right,*" Evan had answered.

"*Wasn't George Peterson the father of the child Loretta was carrying?*"

"*I don't think so,*" Evan had shaken his head. "*I thought he was going to be my brother. It was a boy, I think.*"

"*He didn't kill Loretta for you, did he?*"

"*I think he was trying to protect me from her.*"

"He killed her because she was having an affair with your neighbor."

"No, sir."

"Think about Evan's testimony, sir. Evan said he thought Wilkinson was the father of Loretta's child, that he was going to have a brother. What if that were true?"

"But we don't know that, no one does," Joe answered.

"But what if it were true?"

"Then Wilkinson killed his own son and Evan's brother when he killed Loretta. I think I see." Joe nodded.

"Who owns Wilkinson's old house now?" Mark asked.

"An older retired couple. They bought it thirty years ago."

"We need a court order," Mark said.

"You want to dig it up?"

Mark nodded. "I think you can bring in our people. I've seen everything I can here."

Outside Brittany's home, Mark stopped next to their car.

"We're close, I think," Mark said to Joe, "it's almost sunrise in a way."

"You think we're about to catch him?"

"Yes. If we exhume Loretta's body, could DNA testing determine if the child she was carrying was the accountant's or Wilkinson's?" Mark asked.

"I don't know"—Joe shook his head—"It's been a long time. Jason's an expert on DNA."

"It doesn't matter." Mark dismissed the thought quickly. "Please get a court order, sir, for the exhumation of Loretta

Prince and her child. Make sure the child appears in the order specifically."

"Why?"

"Jason"—Mark got into the backseat of the car—"could DNA evidence determine the natural father of Loretta's child?"

"It's possible, sir," Jason answered. "It depends on how the evidence is collected, time, that sort of thing."

"Let's get the exhumation order," Mark said. "We may never need to use it."

CHAPTER 47

MARK KNOCKED ON the door and waited until he saw an older man peering through one of the square-paneled windows on the door.

"Yes?" he said after he opened the door.

"I'm Lou Mark, FBI, sir." He held up his badge.

"I'm sorry," the man replied. "What did you say?"

"I'm with the FBI," Mark said slowly. "This is Joe Mosely. He's the director of the Behavioral Science Division."

"Behavioral Science? What the hell is that?"

"It's part of the FBI. We have . . ."

"Why are you at my house?" he asked.

"We have," Mark started again, "a court order to search your home."

"I'm going to call my lawyer," the man stepped back. "I don't trust the government. I used to, but I don't now. They don't keep their promises. They lie to us. The war. Prescription drugs. Lies."

"Stop it." Mark raised his voice slightly. "This has nothing to do with you."

"It's my house," he said simply.

"Who is it, Sam?" Mark heard his wife ask from another room inside the house.

"The FBI. They want to search our house."

"Mr. Johnson"—Joe stepped in front of Mark—"this has to do with the family that owned this house before you."

Behind them were two agents each holding a dog on a leash.

"But we've lived here for nearly thirty years," he said. "I'm retired now. We don't know nothing about the family that owned the house."

Mark saw the man's wife walk around the corner from the dining room.

"Who are they, dear?"

"FBI. I told you."

"I'm Elaine." She looked at Mark and smiled.

"We have a court order to search your house," Mark said again. "We believe a murder occurred here more than thirty years ago. We know you had nothing to do with it. I think the body is buried underneath the house."

"There is a dead body under our house?" She looked scared.

"Yes, I think so."

"I still want to call my lawyer," the man said.

"Please feel free to call whomever you wish." Mark walked past them into the living room. "Where is the door to the basement?"

"Off the kitchen." She pointed.

Mark gestured at the two agents standing behind Joe. "Wait here for a moment."

"Why didn't they look thirty years ago?" the man asked.

"I'd like to know that more than you," Mark said. "If you want to call your lawyer, Joe will talk to him. You are not suspects, sir, please believe me."

Mark opened the door to the basement and turned on the light and, when he was about halfway down, saw that it was a concrete floor.

"Was it this way when you bought the house?" Mark asked Mr. Johnson who was standing at the top of the stairs.

He walked slowly down the stairs, stopped at the last step, and looked at Mark.

"No." He shook his head. "It was dirt then. Why do you have dogs with you?"

"They're cadaver dogs. They might be able to find the body."

"I don't like this at all." The man shook his head.

"I'm sorry for the inconvenience, sir. Please talk with my boss for a few minutes, and then I'll be up."

Mark looked around the small basement. There was some metal shelving on the walls with various tools, an old sewing machine, a television, a few chairs. Mark crouched down and placed his hands on the floor for a few minutes.

"I'm sure I'm right," Mark whispered. "Evan and his father buried George Peterson here one night thirty years ago."

Mark stood up and looked through the small windows at the top of the basement wall. *No one would have seen this*, he thought, *and I believe George Peterson was alive when Evan's father threw him in the hole. And Evan has had that image in his mind for thirty years. Evan can't stand people staring at him—he must be remembering George staring at him as he buried him. But where was Loretta, drunk, passed out, or did his father hit her? This was the punishment from his father for not telling him about the affair.*

Why didn't Evan's father pour concrete immediately so it would be George Peterson's crypt? *Time*, he thought, *he didn't have time because he killed Loretta a few weeks later.*

"I know he's here," Mark whispered.

"Sir," Mark said in the kitchen of the home, "they can go downstairs now."

"Go ahead." Joe pointed at the two agents holding the dogs.

"Will you be able to find him with that equipment?" Mark asked one of the agents.

"This is ground-penetrating sonar. Between it and the dogs, if he's there, we'll find him."

Mark turned. "Mr. Johnson, call your lawyer if you wish. But why don't we let them work?"

"He's my son-in-law," he said. "And he charges me for picking up the damn phone."

Mark smiled. "I know lawyers."

"Dear," his wife said. "What's his name?"

"I don't remember." he shook his head.

"Lou Mark," Mark answered.

"It's okay, dear," she said. "He's really an FBI agent."

"I know," the man muttered angrily at her. "I don't need you to tell me that."

"Can I get you gentlemen coffee?" Elaine asked.

"Thank you," Joe said.

"I don't drink it," Mark said.

"What about a soda?" she persisted.

"Sure," Mark said.

For a while, they sat at the kitchen table, and Mr. Johnson and his wife talked about their lives—their children, their grandchildren, and his work for Ford on an assembly line for more than thirty years until he retired a few years ago.

"I don't trust the government for a minute," Mr. Johnson said. "My medical benefits and my pension aren't there anymore, and my wife has Parkinson's disease. Look at her hands. I can't afford the medication, and the government tells me I can't buy it from Canada."

"I'm sorry," Mark said.

"They never deliver on their promises," he said. "You wait, someday they'll do it to you. They'll fuck you."

Mark heard one of the agents walking up the steps from the basement and turned.

The man nodded. "There is a body under the floor."

"How far down?" Mark asked.

"Six, seven, maybe eight feet."

"There's a body under our basement?" Mrs. Johnson asked.

"It must have taken all night to dig that deep," Mark said.

The agent shrugged. "I don't know."

"Evan must have helped him," Mark said. "But why didn't Loretta hear him?"

"I don't know, sir."

"Evan, Loretta? Who are they?" Mr. Johnson asked.

"Show me." Mark stood up, then walked downstairs.

"There, sir." The agent pointed at the concrete floor next to the air conditioning unit.

He watched as Mark crouched down next to the air conditioning unit and rubbed the palm of his right hand across the left side of his face.

"Sir, do you want us to open it up?"

"Yes," Mark said. "Try to find him by morning."

Mark could almost feel the dirt falling on George's body.

"Mr. Johnson, Mrs. Johnson," Mark said in the kitchen. "We located the body."

"A dead body?" Mrs. Johnson asked.

"The only kind you'll find buried seven feet in dirt," Mark said. "We're going to have to cut through the concrete to get to him. We'll pay to make everything right afterward."

"A dead body?" Mrs. Johnson asked again.

"Yes."

Joe looked at Mark. "Let's go outside."

"Mr. and Mrs. Johnson, we appreciate your patience this evening and tomorrow. Our agents should be done by morning," Mark said.

Joe followed Mark as he walked out of the house.

"What did you see?" Joe asked when they were outside on the front porch.

"I think he made his son help him and the man was still alive when they dropped his body into the hole. They covered him up with dirt, and a few weeks later, his father killed Loretta."

"Unbelievable," Joe said, then looked back inside the house. "How could he have done that to his son?"

Mark shrugged.

"You think Debbie might be next?" Joe asked after a few minutes.

"Yes."

"Why?"

"Because he can never see his father again." Mark shrugged. "Why he'd want to, I don't know."

Mark could hear the agents opening up the concrete in the Johnsons' basement with a jackhammer.

"Joe," Mark said. "I want you to move Cara."

"Where?"

"Your house."

"You don't think she's safe at your aunt's farm?"

"I don't know." Mark shook his head.

"I'll move her tonight and have one agent inside and one outside my house."

"Thank you. I'm going back to the hotel. I'll be ready in the morning," Mark said.

"I know."

At the hotel, he lay back on the bed and closed his eyes. He remembered that they'd had two dogs on the farm when he was growing up, and one was more aggressive than the other, stronger, and heavier. His father had put the male in a dog run near the house, and the female would taunt him every morning about 5:00 a.m. Once, he remembered, the male, who weighed well over one hundred pounds, got out, and he had watched his father separate the two dogs.

"See." His father had pointed at the male dog after he locked the gate to the dog run. "If you put an alpha male with an alpha bitch, they'll tear each other to pieces."

"Every morning," he continued, "she taunts him, drives him crazy. It's all they know. Watch them, watch her in front of the dog run. But believe it or not, they love each other."

He sat up on the bed as he remembered.

"What?" He looked around the room. "What do the dogs have to do with this?"

"He's dying." His father nodded. "There's nothing we can do."

"Nothing?" Mark had asked.

"No." His father shook his head.

"What about—?"

"No."

"I don't want him to go away."

"You watch," his father had said. *"After I do this every morning at about the same time, she'll look for him. She won't forget."*

"Why?" he had asked.

"You'll learn, you'll know."

"Won't she know he's gone?"

"No. Go in the house."

"Why?" he had asked.

"He's really sick. He's going to die, and I want to spare him the pain."

"Sick with what?"

"Cancer. He can't beat it. Go now."

He remembered the sound of that shot as he remembered the sound of the shot downstairs in the den when his father killed himself.

For weeks, maybe months, the female had looked for the male every morning and seemed surprised that he was no longer there. They were family, he thought—it never goes away.

For Evan, he thought, *his father would never go away no matter what had happened in the basement of their home more than thirty years ago. He would keep looking into that deep hole for the rest of his life.*

CHAPTER 48

"**C**OME HERE, FELIX." He patted his lap.

He was sitting at his computer, looking at new matches. The site was amazing, he thought, it was like an assembly line turning out one Loretta after another. They had the only secret to solid relationships—the past. He felt Felix purring on his lap.

"You sound like music. Daddy cat is home." He stroked Felix's head and back. "But I have to go away again tomorrow."

The cat's eyes shined back at him, and he remembered another set of eyes from a long time ago.

He saw the lead story on the *New York News* website and read the title.

THE BIRDMAN—THE SECRET TO A THIRTY-YEAR-OLD MURDER

"What?" Evan read on.

Yesterday, Lou Mark found the remains of a man who was murdered more than thirty years ago. The killer was the Birdman's father, and the victim was George Allen Peterson, an accountant who lived across the street from the Birdman's father and stepmother. George Allen Peterson was the father of the child Loretta Prince Wilkinson was carrying when she was murdered by her husband.

"What?" Evan looked at the screen. "How? My father didn't want anyone to know."

As Felix slowly cleaned himself on Evan's lap, he read the story.

Evan Morgan, the Birdman, assisted his father in dropping the body into the deep grave in their basement, then filling it with dirt. George Allen Peterson was buried alive.

"How does he know that?" Evan whispered to himself.

He looked down at Felix who was still cleaning himself.

"How, Felix? How could Pete know all this?"

Felix finished and looked up at Evan.

"I don't like this, Felix." Evan shook his head. "I don't like this story. Dad will be pissed."

Many people have said and written that to know where you're going, you have to know where you've been. Preserve the past because it defines the future. Was Evan Morgan made the night he helped his father bury an innocent man alive? Or did it happen a few weeks later, when Evan came home from school and found his stepmother's face caved in with a claw hammer?

"Dammit!" Evan shouted and Felix jumped off his lap. "Mark. It was Mark."

He closed his eyes and vividly remembered that night. He had always liked George, gentle and nearly neurotically passive. He would walk across the street at night while his father was out. For a few months before he stood at the edge of the deep hole, he could hear him sometimes with Loretta in his father's bedroom. They thought he was asleep, but he heard everything. Loretta was sex, and sex was Loretta. She could drive a man crazy with a simple gesture. It was all she really knew, and she took the gentle accountant to places he had never imagined. During the day when his father was gone, he remembered that George would talk to him about being an accountant.

"Did that fag come over here again today?" he remembered his *father asking when he came home.*

"Yes," Evan said, *"he told me about being an accountant."*

"You spend much more time with him, and you'll be a fag too."

It had been like lightning striking his father's brain when Loretta screamed at him one night that the fag was the father of her child. For days, his father drank and beat Loretta in between finishing a bottle of whiskey and sleeping it off. Once he had walked into their bedroom and saw Loretta standing next to the bed with a kitchen knife in her right hand. From the side, he could see her slightly distended stomach just below the blade of the knife. She had always believed that her body, even in her late thirties, was like a sleek and expensive racing car, built for speed and male attention.

"No!" he had yelled and saw his father's bloodshot eyes. "No, don't do it."

It was brutal. His father had grabbed her wrist, twisted it, then taken the knife from her hand and thrown it across the room.

"You're carrying that fag's child!" he shouted and punched her in the stomach.

His father had been in shape then, and strong, and he could almost hear the sound of the air crack each time he punched Loretta in the stomach.

"Bitch!" he shouted and punched her again. "You have no right to even think about giving birth to anything, not even an insect."

"Dad, stop."

Loretta's face was pale and she clutched at her stomach, then fell to her knees.

"How could you do this to someone you love?" she gasped.

"How could you fuck that fag?"

He hit her with the back of his hand, and Evan could still hear the sound of her head hitting the edge of the nightstand, and see the blood just below her hairline running down the left side of her face. After his father stopped the bleeding, she drank until she fell backward on the bed and passed out. That night was the night that his father walked across the street and invited George over for a drink.

"Felix, come back." He patted his lap and felt his weight on his thighs.

"Good cat. Daddy cat loves Felix."

He closed his eyes and could see the body next to the air conditioning unit and the sweat on Michael Evan Wilkinson's face.

"*Dig, dammit,*" *his father shouted at him.* "*You knew about this. You hid it from me.*"

"*Daddy . . .*"

"*Dig, you little son of a bitch.*"

Evan could see that he had beaten the man with a crowbar he had taken from the trunk of his car in the middle of the night, then wrapped the body in plastic. Loretta was drunk and had passed out hours ago in their bedroom, but Evan was awake and saw his father carry the body downstairs to the basement.

"*Dig, you son of a bitch.*"

"*Daddy, I'm sorry. She said he was loyal like the nightbirds.*"

"*Fuck her.*" *He placed his boot on the blade of the shovel, then threw the dirt in Evan's face.*

"*You won't forget now, will you?*" *he shouted.*

"*No, Daddy.*"

"*You'll always remember that Loretta was never fit to have children, like most women. They're just fucking whores.*"

"*Yes, Daddy.*"

"*Deeper!*" *his father shouted.* "*They're never going to find this son of a bitch.*"

He remembered he could feel George's faint heartbeat as he held his calves and his father held his shoulders, just before they dropped him into the hole. For him, watching George's body fall was like watching a Sam Peckinpah movie like *The Wild Bunch*, when in seeming slow motion, his body finally hit the ground. He watched George's body twist for a moment and then not move again. He didn't scream or yell when he felt his back snap; he just grunted and stared up at him.

Mark said that he was coming and that he would find him soon. Mark said the man with the eyes would catch him wherever he is.

Evan looked at Felix. "It's the man with the eyes again. We don't like that."

"Mark thinks he can stop us." He petted Felix. "But he's wrong."

"Bury him!" his father had shouted. "Bury that fucking fag."

"Dad, he's still alive."

He could see the plastic surrounding George's head sucked into his mouth each time he tried to breathe. He could see his right eye, wide open, begging for help.

"I don't give a fuck." His father threw dirt into the hole. "Bury that fucking fag."

Michael Evan Wilkinson is being questioned at this time concerning the death of George Allen Peterson. He could be tried for murder. And, if there's any justice in this world, he will be executed this time.

Evan stood up quickly, and Felix leaped off his lap.

"I need to talk to my birds."

"Bury him!" he remembered his father yelling.

George could move his head slightly, and even after the dirt completely covered his face, Evan still could see it moving back and forth until it stopped moving at all, when he finally died.

Downstairs in the basement, he stood in front of his aviary, and heard Felix scratching at the door.

He saw two birds on the trunk of the tree in the middle of the enclosure.

"They're in love," he said.

For a few minutes, he watched them, then walked inside and felt the birds land on his shoulders.

"It's time for Debbie, isn't it?"

He held out his finger and watched the hen drop down on it.

"It's time for Debbie," he repeated.

He set the bird back on the trunk of the tree and watched her mate drop down next to her.

"You're going to be a mother," he said to the bird. "You're loyal, you're good. You mate for life."

He turned and walked out of the enclosure. At the top of the stairs, he pushed Felix away from the door and closed it behind him.

At his computer, he went to the website, saw the photo of Dr. March, and typed in Debbie Billings.

"Your hands are perfect," he said as he looked at her photo. "You're beautiful."

He turned off the computer. "Pete will just have to understand."

"You can't do this, Dad," he cried and felt the back of his father's hand across the side of his face.

"Fill that fucking hole in now!" he shouted.

He remembered he had thrown a shovel full of dirt down the hole, and it had landed on George's face; he could no longer see his right eye, but he could hear him whispering "Please help me" for another few minutes.

"You're beautiful," Evan said again. "You're beautiful, Debbie."

In the bedroom, he brushed his teeth, then turned off the light in the bathroom and turned on the light in the bedroom. Since he was a child, he had been afraid of the dark. When he was a child, he thought he could see things, shapes, coming from the darkness around his bed.

"Come here, Felix." He patted the bed and then felt Felix jump up and lie down next to him.

"Debbie's beautiful, isn't she, Felix? I think she's a match."

He lay back down and closed his eyes.

"Maybe I should tell Pete about Mark's secret. I read his grandfather's short story."

He could still see George's face in the grave, and his eye looking at him, begging for help, as he fell asleep.

CHAPTER 49

"**DON'T YOU THINK** I know?" Debbie shouted at Pete.

"What?"

"For the last few days," she said, "I've seen the agents downstairs, the one who's pretending to be a doorman with the earpiece. This building doesn't have a doorman."

"Okay."

"I'm the bait," she said. "Aren't I?"

"Don't talk like that. The FBI wouldn't do that."

"All you want is the story, even if I'm the victim."

"That's not true." Pete shook his head.

"Jesus Christ." She sat down next to him on the old leather couch. "I finally find someone I care about, and it turns out that he will write my obituary."

"You're important to me, please believe me."

"Not as important as the story," she said sadly.

"Debbie, I'll . . ."

"No." She placed her hand firmly over his mouth. "Don't make promises you can't keep."

They heard a light knock on the door.

"Is it him?" Debbie asked staring at the door.

"I don't know." He reached for the gun he had borrowed from his editor. "Who is it?"

"Lou Mark. I need to talk to you, Pete."

Pete bent down and saw Mark through the peephole, then unlocked the door.

"Come in," he said.

"I'm the bait to catch this man, aren't I?" Debbie glared at Mark.

"No, of course not, but we have a good man downstairs watching this building if he tries."

Mark looked at Debbie and lifted his hands. "All right?"

"I don't know."

"You're a decent person," Mark said to her. "I'm sorry this insanity has to be part of your life."

She stared at his eyes.

"What is it?" Mark asked.

"Your eyes. You were right, Pete."

"What about them?" Mark sounded annoyed.

"They're deep blue and ice-cold, like death," she said.

Mark looked away. "Some people think so."

"No, they're beautiful and scary at the same time. It's how you see the crime, isn't it?"

"That's a long story and a complicated . . ."

"Can you see my crime scene?"

"I can't see them before," Mark answered, "but he won't get to you."

"If I'm not the bait, why are you here?"

"I have a story for Pete," Mark answered. "I wanted to tell him in person. Do you want us to move you? I can put you in a hotel room in another state with two agents. But Pete will have to stay here. I need him if Evan wants to contact him again, and I need him for another story."

"I'd have to leave Pete?"

"Yes."

"I don't know." She shook her head.

"Think about it," Mark said.

"I read some of your grandfather's short stories," she said after a few minutes.

"How the hell did you find them?" Mark asked.

"You didn't tell me that," Pete said.

"I just found them. Some I found on archives on the Internet from the magazines, and one I found on an estate sale on eBay. It was part of a collection of old mystery stories."

"Amazing," Mark said. "You're very smart."

"It was called 'Monsters,'" she said. "It was the best one I've read so far."

"It was the best story he ever wrote. He died the next day, but my father made sure it got published."

"What was it about?" Pete asked.

Mark watched her eyes.

"It was a murder mystery," she said.

"Do you know?" Mark asked Debbie.

"What it means?" she answered. "Yes, I think so."

"What was that?" Pete asked.

Mark looked at the door and whispered, "Quiet."

"What?" Pete said.

"Quiet," Mark whispered again.

He could hear someone in the hallway.

"There are two more apartments at the end of this hallway," Mark said. "Are they occupied?"

Pete shook his head.

"George," Mark whispered into the tiny microphone on the lapel of his sports coat. "George, are you there?"

Mark took the .38 from the shoulder holster.

"He's here," Mark said. "He's in the hallway now. Maybe we'll get lucky tonight."

"I have a gun," Pete said.

"You won't need it. Just get out of the way."

Mark looked through the peephole but didn't see anything. He could hear heavier footsteps now, then running. He yanked open the door and heard a shot that splintered the doorjamb next to his shoulder. A man was standing at the end of the hallway about forty feet away. He was wearing a hat and had a beard and mustache that Mark recognized. "It's him. Stay here and lock the door."

Mark aimed, and he disappeared behind the wall. Mark heard him shove open the door to the stairs and then heard him running down the metal steps.

"George," he said into the cell phone. "He's here. He's coming downstairs now. Be careful . . . answer me. Where the fuck are you?"

Mark ran to the elevators. All the way down he aimed the gun at the door. In the lobby, when the elevator doors opened, he looked around quickly and saw no one. Outside, he saw a few people on the street, but no one that looked like or was dressed like him.

The building had once been a hotel, and in the lobby was an old-style reception counter. Behind it, he found George lying sprawled on the floor. He put his hand on his throat, felt no pulse, and closed his eyes.

"Mr. Mosely."

"What happened?"

"He came here for Debbie Billings. He got away."

"George?"

"Dead."

Joe sighed. "I'll call our office and send a team over there now."

"He's gone. We won't catch him tonight."

Upstairs, the door to Pete's apartment was closed.

"Pete, it's me."

Mark saw the gun in his hand when he opened the door. "Put that down now. I don't want you to shoot anyone by accident."

"He got away?" Pete set the gun on the coffee table.

"Yes, and he killed George, the agent downstairs."

Debbie looked up at him. She was sitting with her legs up and her arms wrapped around them in the corner of the old couch.

"He would have killed me tonight," she said.

"I'm not sure you're right." Mark sat down next to her on the couch. "He may have followed me here. It could have been a warning after the story about his father."

"Where is he now?" Pete asked.

"I have no idea. Somewhere in the city, or on his way home."

"What did he look like?" Pete asked.

"He is five eight, five nine. He was wearing a hat low on his forehead and a fake beard and mustache, so I couldn't see his face. But it's funny, he was dressed up, matching coat and slacks, like he was on a date."

"What are you going to do?" Mark nodded at Debbie.

"I don't know."

"Weren't you scared when you saw him?" Debbie asked.

Mark nodded. "They're very scary people."

"Then how do you do this?" she said.

"Another time, we'll talk about it. Why don't you both pack what you need and we'll put you in a hotel for a few days?"

"You don't really think about it, do you?" Debbie turned toward Mark.

"I don't know what you mean," Mark answered.

"I think you do. It's what I saw in your eyes. You would have killed him tonight without hesitation."

"Of course. You really need to pack some things so we can get you in a hotel away from here. Go."

Mark leaned back on the couch and listened to them packing in the bedroom.

He heard a quiet knock at the door. "Sir, it's Special Agent Richard Todd. My partner is in the lobby."

Mark looked through the peephole, then opened the door.

"Mr. Mosely said you wanted to look at the crime scene. Neighbors called the police when they heard the gunshots and NYPD is here and they want in now."

"I'll be right down."

"Cara? Is that why he was here?"

He noticed his hands were shaking as he dialed Joe's number.

"Cara? Is she okay? Has there been anything?"

"No, why?"

"Maybe that's what he was trying to tell me tonight. Is she asleep?"

"Yes."

"Tell your men to be careful."

"They know," Joe said.

Mark set the phone back inside his sports coat and turned to talk to Pete who had just walked into the room. He could hear Debbie still packing in the bedroom.

"I want you to do a story, and I want it published tomorrow."

"Are you the source?"

"Say the FBI."

"What is it?"

"We exhumed Loretta Prince's body. The DNA analysis establishes that the child she was carrying, a son, was Michael Evan Wilkinson's," Mark said.

"He killed his own son. He killed Evan's brother," Pete asked. "Is that the story?"

"Yes. On the birds, six years ago, Evan Morgan ordered a matched set of nightbirds from a breeder in China. You can use that too, if you want."

"How did you know he would be here tonight?" Pete asked.

"I didn't." Mark shook his head.

"Then you were hoping he would try for Debbie. You are using her as bait, you son of a bitch."

"I know what it looks like, but it's not true," Mark tried to explain. "He profiled her long before I was given this case and before you started the relationship. Believe me. Please I need your help on this story. The best protection she can get is when I stop him."

"I don't believe you, but I'll do the story."

After Pete left with Debbie and Agent Todd, Mark called Joe.

"They're gone. I gave Pete the story."

"What did you tell him?"

"That we exhumed Loretta Prince's body and DNA established without doubt that the child was Wilkinson's."

"But I just got the exhumation order today, and we haven't done anything yet"—Joe paused—"forget that. You want to see Wilkinson tomorrow, right?"

"Yes," Mark answered. "And I need the exhumation order. You know it just might be true, sir."

"Does it matter?" Joe asked.

"No."

At the hotel, the FBI agent told Pete and Debbie that he would be outside, then closed the door.

Pete lit a cigarette then sat down on the couch in the room outside the bedroom in front of the television.

"This is nonsmoking room," Debbie said.

Pete smiled. "Really? I'm breaking the law?"

Debbie opened her suitcase and found the old mystery magazine, brown in color from age with the adhesive tearing away from the binding.

"Here." She put one of the hotel glasses in front of him with water at the bottom. "Look at this."

"*Ellery Queen.*" He tapped the cigarette into the glass and heard the ash simmer momentarily as it landed in the water.

"This is old," he said.

"Look at the list of new stories."

"'Monsters,'" he read. "The final mystery story by Jacob Mark."

"Yes," she said.

"This is what you were talking about with Mark? Jacob Mark was his grandfather?"

"Read." She nodded.

"This will take a few minutes," he said.

"Just read it."

He started, then read about ten pages. "A man beat his wife to death after a history of abuse, then put a kitchen knife in the heart of the neighbor who tried to stop it. Then he ran, and a police detective named John Murdock has been following him. Right?"

"Yes," she said.

"The Murdock character thinks the killer will come back to the scene of the crime one more time to retrieve something he left behind, and he waits for him each night, remembering his life and his career."

"Right." Debbie nodded.

"Isn't this fairly typical of mystery stories from this era? What's special about it?"

"I don't know what was typical, but read the end."

He was waiting in the small and dark house alone when he saw an old car stop in front and the headlights go out. The man got out of the car and looked furtively up and down the street. John Murdock took the gun out of the holster on his belt and waited at the side of the front door. Two months, he thought as he heard the key in the lock, two months since this man had killed his wife and his neighbor when he tried to stop him. Now he had come home. Murdock believed that one day he would come home, but he always wondered what would bring him back.

Murdock heard the door creak slightly, then saw his shadow from the streetlight. When he saw his head, he grabbed his hair, yanked him to his knees, and put the muzzle of the .38 at the back at his head.

"Police, if you move, I'll kill you!" Murdock shouted.

"Please don't hurt me," he begged. "I didn't mean to do it."

"Why did you come back here?"

"I wanted something," he whined.

"What?"

"Something she gave me a long time ago."

Murdock felt the point of the man's elbow strike his groin and pulled the trigger, but he had moved, and he missed. As he slumped to the ground, he saw him stand, pull a knife, and move toward him. He pulled the trigger three times before he fell back and dropped the knife.

"Now," Murdock said. "It's over. But he never told me why he came back home. What called him back?"

At home, Murdock sat up in a bed when he heard a shot downstairs.

"What is it?" he mumbled. "I killed him. I already killed him."

He looked at the dresser and didn't see his gun.

"Shit," he muttered, then ran downstairs to the living room. On the rug, he saw his son sitting with his gun in his right hand and his daughter lying on her side with blood around her head.

"Daddy, I'm sorry. It was an accident. I . . . I . . ."

Murdock touched his daughter's neck, looking for a pulse, and felt nothing. The bullet had gone through her left eye. He took the gun from his son and sat down on the rug in front of him.

"What happened?" Murdock started crying.

"You left your gun here"—he pointed at the table near the door—"when you came home. And, and . . ." His son could barely breathe. "We both touched it and played with it, and when she handed it back to me, I took it by the trigger, and it shot."

"She'll be okay, right, Daddy?" His son looked up at him.

Murdock wiped the tears from his face and shook his head. "She's gone, and it's my fault, not yours. I don't ever want you to think about this again. Just remember I was careless. Go upstairs to my room, and I'll be right up."

"Daddy," his son said at the foot of the stairs, "why won't she be all right? We were just playing."

"Go upstairs, please . . ."

"She touched me after, Daddy, she touched my face and my eyes, so I knew she was okay."

"Go, please . . ."

When his son was upstairs, Murdock cradled his daughter's head in his arms and tried not to let his son hear him. He could feel his body shaking inside and taste the tears on his face.

"I was careless, stupid, and I lost you because of it."

He looked around the room. He knew he had to call the station, but he still held her.

"You were special," he whispered into her ear. *"You could see things I couldn't see. Your eyes were your gift. Do you forgive him? Do you forgive me? Did you give him your eyes before you went away?"*

He set her down gently.

"I must be crazy now."

From the phone in the kitchen, he called the station.

"Harry, my daughter's been shot, she's dead. It was an accident. You need to come here."

"What happened, John?"

"I'll tell you when you get here."

In his bedroom, he saw his son huddled, crying, on the edge of the bed.

"She's all right now, isn't she, Daddy?"

He sat down next to him. *"I talked to her, and she forgives you. She even gave you something."*

He sat up. *"What?"*

"Remember her eyes? How she could see things?"

"Yes." He nodded.

"She gave them to you so you would always remember her."

"She did?" He seemed excited.

"Yes, some people will be here in a few minutes. I need to go downstairs. I'll be back."

He looked at his son, then closed the door behind him. At the bottom of the steps, he sat down and waited for his friends. What do I do now, *he asked himself.* What can I do for my son? *He thought about what the man had said to him hours ago as he lay on the floor of his small dark house, dying.*

"I came back," he coughed blood on the dirty T-shirt. "It was something she gave me. I . . . I . . . remembered it. It wasn't much, but it meant a lot to me . . .

Murdock remembered that the man who had killed his wife and neighbor died then without telling him anything more. Will my son be all right after this, *he wondered,* and how will this story about her eyes affect his life? She did have a gift, maybe she did give it to him. Who was the monster tonight, *he wondered,* the man who killed his wife and his neighbor or me . . . ? *He heard cars in front of his house, then voices.*

Pete looked up at Debbie. "This is what you found. This is what you were talking to Mark about?"

"Yes."

"Mark's father . . ."

"Yes, Pete."

"Mark's father killed accidentally, his . . ."

She nodded. "Maybe."

"And then, the eyes?"

"Yes."

"Do you think it actually happened?" Pete asked.

"I don't know."

CHAPTER 50

"FELIX," HE SAID as he felt him rubbing against his leg and heard him purring. "I met an FBI agent tonight."

Evan set the gun down on the dining room table, walked into the master bedroom, and turned on the light. He always wondered if he'd see someone standing in the room, staring back at him. Not two weeks ago, he thought, as he sat down on the toilet seat, a house only a few blocks away had been burglarized.

"It's not safe here anymore." He flushed the toilet. "I'm going to have to move to protect my birds and my cat."

On the dining room table, he saw Felix sniffing the gun.

"No," he said gently and picked up the gun. "Let's see what matches we have today."

In the den, Evan sat down in front of the computer, and within a minute, he was on the website.

"I like her, Felix, but she's too far away."

Felix had jumped up on his lap and watched as he scrolled through the photos and the bios.

"Too old," he muttered.

"Too sweet. There, maybe."

He always read the bio after he looked at the photos.

"Divorced," he mumbled. "Even better. Family. Wants a child."

He looked down at Felix, scratched him behind his left ear, and felt him purring again.

"She wrote that she want it to be excited about a man again. She wrote that she wants them to deliver the perfect man. Maybe we can deliver. Besides, she has beautiful hands."

> *Melanie,*
> *I got your name from the service. You look interesting.*
> *I have enclosed a photo.*
>
> *David*

"I haven't used that name since"—he turned and looked at the cabinet behind him—"was it Barbara? Since Barbara. It was three months ago, no, four months."

"You've got mail," he heard.

David,

You look interesting too. Why don't we try a short meeting and see how it goes. I'm pretty much free this week. Send me an e-mail.

Melanie

"Amazing. It's just too easy," he said to Felix.

Melanie,

How about tomorrow at Maxwell's in the city at seven?

David

He looked at the confirming e-mail. "Good."

He gently set Felix down on the carpet and stood up. "Wardrobe."

In the walk-in closet, in the master bedroom, he looked at his sports coats. His father had told him a long time ago that the first impression you made was important.

"She has a decent job," he mumbled, "conservative."

"This, I think." He hung the navy blazer in the corner of the closet and selected a pair of khaki slacks and a light-blue oxford shirt, and hung them next to the blazer.

"Good. Felix, I need to talk to my birds."

After Felix followed him out, he closed the door to the closet. He didn't like seeing Felix's black hairs on his clothes.

There were two large fir trees in his backyard, and sometimes at night, when he would walk outside, sit on a patio chair, and look at the sky, he could hear birds singing, and he wondered if they were an American variety of Chinese nightbirds.

Years ago, after contacting breeders on the Internet, he had found an unsophisticated website of Chinese origin that made the claim that the nightbirds were not a legend, but there were only a handful of legitimate breeders. He didn't really know why he'd thought about the birds then, other than he had thought about Loretta that day and her story about the nightbirds and was feeling curious. She claimed that her mother had told her about the legend of the nightbirds.

"Evan, my mother told me about the nightbirds."

"What, Mom?"

She was the only mother he would ever know, and his father was out, again.

"They're loyal. They mate for life, you know. They protect each other. Some people think it's just a legend, but sometimes I hear them at night while I'm waiting for your father to come home. You can only hear them sing at night. For them, it is private and personal."

He remembered reading on the website that they were smart birds, and once you established trust with them, they were like family that would stay with you until they died. He had ordered two, a male and a female, and had visited his father at prison the day they arrived. His father had laughed at him and said only fags raise birds, but he had done it. He had finally found the nightbirds.

"Why do you call me a castoff from a dead woman?" Evan *remembered asking Loretta.*

"I never said that."

"You're lying," Evan answered. *"I hear you say it every night you fight with Dad."*

"Forget it." She had patted him indifferently on the head. *"You're not a bad kid."*

The first time he had given one as a gift, it hadn't been easy to feel a friend who loved and trusted him die in his hands. But he had to give them something else to look for because his real name was on Dr. March's service. Now it didn't matter, he thought. He remembered what his father had said after they had dropped George into the hole.

"Look"—his father had pointed at George—"he's alive, he's moving his head, but that's it. He must have broken his back in the fall."

He had watched his father smile. "Good. Bury him."

Evan could hear faint sounds coming from the bag around George's face and see his right eye staring up at him.

"Start with his fucking head!" his father shouted.

"Dad . . ."

"I said shovel dirt on his fucking head."

Evan had picked up a spade full of dirt, then dropped it in the hole and watched it fall around George's face. When the dirt hit the plastic around his face, he heard George scream, "No!"

"He doesn't like that, does he?" His father had grinned. "Do it again. That's what Loretta's fucking nightbird deserves."

For a long time, he had forgotten about it, except for periodic nightmares. His aunt and uncle never allowed him to talk about it with anyone. They didn't know that he had helped kill George.

Nobody knew other than his father and later Loretta, and she had taken that secret with her when she died.

His father was the only family he had left after his aunt and uncle died in the same calendar year, and over the years, when he visited him at prison, his father seemed more interested in his life and his career. The Loretta voice in his mind, which he tried to ignore, always said that his father just had nothing better to do while in prison then finally care about his own son.

When he met Betty, his first date from the service, it all returned. While he was in the men's room after he met her, he could hear his father and Loretta screaming in his head, just as they had done more than thirty years ago.

He opened the door to the basement and went downstairs.

"I saw Mark tonight, but I got away."

He felt the same four birds land on his shoulders.

"I'll see him again, but I have a date tomorrow night. Melanie is her name. And I don't have to take one of you this time. Mark knows. He is trying to find us now."

Whenever he walked inside, they all stared at him. They were family.

"We have to move. It's not safe in this neighborhood," he explained to his birds, "and Mark said he's coming, but it will take him awhile to find us. I need money. I'll call Pete, and after Melanie, we'll go."

He was afraid that the FBI might find him before he moved.

"You're my family." He could feel tears in his eyes. "I can't imagine not seeing you again before the darkness takes me away."

CHAPTER 51

"**I DON'T WANT TO** be insulting, and I mean that," Evan said and turned onto his side on the bed. "But you don't do this with all your dates, do you?"

"No, of course not. I haven't had sex in two months."

She'd been looking forward to the date all day long, and now she turned on her side and looked at him through the mirror on the wall.

"You have mirrors on each wall," he said. "The only thing missing is the ceiling."

"So . . . ?" she said insulted by the implication.

"I'm sorry." He gently touched her left shoulder. "I did hurt your feelings."

His hand moved slowly, sensuously down her left arm, then touched her stomach and finally stopped at her breasts. In the light from the candle over the bed, he watched her eyes follow his hand.

"I'm not a slut." She yanked his hand away from her breasts. "I won't fuck somebody for an appetizer and a few drinks."

"I'm sorry." He moved his hand back to her breasts. "But you like watching me touch you."

"Yes, it's erotic."

"Loretta was that way." He moved his hand down between her legs. "Does that feel good?"

She began to relax and closed her eyes. "Yes, that feels good. Who's Loretta?"

"An old friend," he said. "You like to watch?"

"Yes." She sighed. "Yes."

"I'm surprised you didn't cancel." He turned her over slowly and rubbed her ass. "You have a great ass."

"Keep doing that." She moaned slightly. "It feels good. Why would I cancel?"

"The Birdman."

"Why would he want me?"

"You're his type."

"How . . . do you know?" She pushed up on the bed.

He pushed her back down. "Relax, I just read it in the paper."

Slowly, he massaged her back, then her shoulders and neck.

"I'm tight there, push harder."

He watched her eyes in the mirror and smiled. "He's in the city, according to the story today," he said.

"I didn't read it. I was busy at work. But why are you talking about this?"

"Loretta liked people to watch. She even let me touch her a few times."

"A girlfriend?" she asked.

He lifted her hips off the bed and heard her gasp.

"I like watching you," she said.

"She let me touch her," he said as he moved behind her.

"What? Who?"

"Loretta."

"Your girlfriend?" she asked.

"No, Mom."

He could feel her body stiffen beneath him, but he was stronger and held her down.

"You had sex with your mother?" she yelled. "Let me go now. You're sick."

"No." He smiled and moved behind her. "But I drilled a hole in the wall, and I watched them together. She liked it this way."

His voice was soft as he remembered.

"Let me go!" she yelled again.

"Just watch. Just enjoy the feeling. My father used to say that."

She continued to struggle underneath him, and in the mirror on the wall to the left, he could see tears form in her eyes.

"Please," she begged.

"Sometimes, Loretta cried too."

"My god!" she screamed. "You're him. Help, God help me."

He shoved her facedown into the pillow to muffle the screams until he finished a few minutes later. When he released her head, he could hear her ragged breathing.

"Please . . ."

He drew his fist back, waited until she started to scream again, and punched her sharply in the back of the head.

"You like to watch, don't you?"

He put his hands around her neck gently to see if he had broken it and felt her heart beat under her jawline.

"Good."

In the living room, he sipped on the glass of wine that she had poured him after she had invited him into her home. *Home*, he thought, *soon I'll have a new one.* That day he had found a new house several miles from his home. It was about the same size, and he knew Mark would never suspect that he was so close to where he used to live. It was a for sale by owner, no brokers, and he had signed a contract that required him to close in seven days. He had already called the movers and told them he had special cargo.

He could hear her moaning into her pillow and unplugged two lamps and ripped the cords from them.

"Are you all right?" he asked.

He tied her hands to the brass headboard with one cord, and her feet to the legs of the bed with the other. When she started to scream again, he took a dirty handkerchief from his pocket, opened her mouth at the jaw, and shoved it in her mouth like a bit on a horse.

"I haven't finished your wine yet," he said simply.

"You know, Lou Mark thinks he has me." He shook his head. "He's wrong. I'm moving."

Her eyes were wide open, and he could see the tears on her cheeks.

"And she wasn't my mother, you mirror freak," he said with controlled anger. "She was my stepmother."

He could hear the muffled word "no" over and over again.

"And I didn't have sex with her. It was just when my father was out . . ."

He slapped her lightly on the right side of her face. "I'll be back in a few minutes. Wait for me."

He sat back down on her couch and sipped from the glass of wine, then poured another glass. Once, he remembered, his father had caught him.

"What is that?" he asked Loretta.

"Your fucking son."

"I thought he was going to be a fag. Wait."

"He likes to watch me." Loretta smiled at him from the bed. "He's not a fag."

"But he's just a kid."

"At his age, kids know about sex."

"He's just a fag."

He remembered that his father had burst through the door to his bedroom, picked him up, then had thrown him several feet in the air. He still remembered the sensation, like flying, until he felt his back on the bed and his head hit the oak headboard.

"I'm going to fill in that fucking hole." His father was close enough that he could feel his spit on his face and smell the alcohol on his breath. *"Do you understand?"*

"Yes, Dad, yes."

"If it happens again, I'll beat the fuck out of you, you little fag."

His father, he remembered, liked to hurt people, and he had seen him get rough with Loretta, but she seemed to like it.

Years ago, before the nightbirds, before Dr. March, he met a woman who seemed to like him, and she never understood why he visited his father at prison religiously every thirty days.

"Calling him an animal degrades any species," she had said. "He's a monster."

"He's my father," Evan had said. "He's the only family I have left."

After a while, he grew tired of her commentary on his father, and one night, he punched her flush on the nose. She hadn't called the police, but she had never come back. When he told his father, he remembered, his father had been proud of him.

He could hear moaning in the bedroom. In the kitchen, he found a claw hammer in a drawer next to the refrigerator.

"It's time to sing." He looked down at her, then hit her over her left eye with the hammer.

"I thought I had a match." She squinted at him through her right eye. "I thought I, a match . . ."

"You did," he said flatly, then dropped the head of the hammer on her right eye.

He picked up the cordless phone in her living room and dialed Pete's cell phone number.

"Do you see the name and number on your phone? Call Mark. I'll call you later."

"In seven days I move," Evan said to himself as he carefully locked the front door to her home. "I have a lot of work to do."

CHAPTER 52

THE OLD MAN sat on the edge of the bed in his cell, looking at the piece of paper he had received only a few minutes ago. Tomorrow, he would be arraigned for the premeditated murder of George Allen Peterson more than thirty years ago. First-degree murder, he thought, the death penalty. Like a dog, they would strap him to a gurney, swab his arms with alcohol, like it really mattered, then stick needles in his arms until he couldn't breathe anymore.

"My son." He set the paper down on the bunk. "My son unearthed a thirty-year-old secret. How could he do this to me?

"He was always a worthless little fag just like that fucking accountant," he said bitterly.

He looked down at the piece of paper, an indictment for a thirty-year-old murder.

"I got him." He gritted his teeth. "I got that fag."

For sixteen years, since he turned twenty-one, Evan had come to see him once a month, he thought. It wasn't his fault that Mark had found something no one else could see.

"You have a visitor," the guard said.

"My son?" He looked up.

"No." The guard shook his head.

"You're right it couldn't be." He shook his head. "Who the fuck wants to see me?"

"Someone from the FBI."

"I don't have anything to say to the fucking FBI."

The guard nodded at another guard to open the cell. "Come with me, now," he said.

"What, no handcuffs?" He held up his wrists.

"Just go," the guard said.

The guard opened the door to one of the private interrogation rooms and shoved him inside. In the corner, he saw a man with his back turned.

"What the fuck do you want?" he asked.

"Mr. Wilkinson." Mark turned. "Sit down."

Mark waited until he did, then walked across the small room and leaned across the table.

"Where does he live?"

"You're Mark. You're after my son."

"Yes, were does he live?"

"Who?" He smiled.

"I'm not going to ask you again," Mark said.

They had the same eyes, Mark thought, hazel with gray flecks in the pupils, and without the false beard and mustache, he looked like an older version of Evan standing at the end of the hallway at Pete's apartment building, smiling at him.

"My son?"

Mark nodded. "You wouldn't tell Pete when he was here."

"I really don't know." He shrugged.

"You killed George Peterson," Mark said. "You're going to stand trial for it, and this time, I can virtually guarantee it will be the death penalty. This time, your son won't testify for you."

"I'm not going to rat him out," he said defiantly.

"The next person he's going to try to kill," Mark said slowly, "is the woman Pete brought here."

"She was hot. I wanted to fuck her." He laughed.

"Sure. And the next one will be the woman who's carrying my child."

"I don't know where he lives." He shook his head.

"I just left a crime scene. Her name was Melanie. She was young, late thirties. Your son had sex with her, punched her in the back of the head, then shoved a dirty handkerchief in her mouth to muffle her screams." Mark paused. "He tied her to the bed with brown electrical cord, then slowly beat her to death with a hammer."

"I still can't believe . . ." Wilkinson shook his head.

Mark leaned back, then slapped the left side of Wilkinson's face. "You're not listening."

"You can't do that, there are cameras in here."

"They're not working today. You're not hearing me. I'm not going to let him kill Debbie, and I'm not going to let him kill Cara. I'm not going to let him kill anyone else. Tell me where he lives."

"Fuck you," he said.

Mark punched him flush on his nose and watched the chair tip backward slowly, and then Wilkinson fell on the concrete floor.

"I need to know where he lives." Mark saw the blood flowing from Wilkinson's broken nose.

"Fuck you." Wilkinson wiped the blood off his face. "I'm not going to rat out my son."

Mark pulled the chair out from under him and threw it across the room.

"You are going to tell me!" he shouted.

"I got rights," he whined.

"Fuck you and your rights."

Mark saw the guard watching him through the Plexiglas window on the door to the interrogation room and waved his hand at him. After the guard walked away from the door, Mark made a fist and hit Wilkinson on the nose three times.

"You're going to tell me!" Mark shouted at him again. "You're going to tell me before I leave here."

"Fuck you, I can't breathe." Wilkinson coughed several times.

Mark reached into the inside pocket of his sports coat and found the exhumation order.

"We exhumed Loretta's body," Mark said slowly.

"Ex what?"

"Dug her up. Do you know what we found?"

"No." He shook his head.

"You killed your own son. You were the father of the child Loretta was carrying. You killed Evan's brother."

"I don't believe you. Loretta said . . ."

"Loretta lied to you. You killed your own child."

"I don't believe it," Wilkinson said. "Women know these things."

Mark threw the exhumation order at him. "Read it."

"But she told me it was that fag accountant," he said.

"DNA doesn't have a reason to lie," Mark said.

"I don't believe it," he stuttered.

"You're going to die like a dog for killing your own child," Mark said. "They shave the hair off part of your forearm, then they stick a needle in it, and you can watch the juice drip slowly over your head. You'll get sleepy, but you'll fight it for a while. The juice will feel warm, even hot, in your veins. And then you will disappear as if you never lived. The darkness will take you."

"You can't do this," he whined.

"Who's going to stop me?" Mark shrugged. "Nobody cares about what happens to you."

"I have rights, the Constitution," he said.

"Not that I can see." Mark looked him in the eyes. "Are you going to tell me?"

"Yes." He nodded slowly. "I can't believe Loretta lied to me. I can't believe . . ."

Mark helped him up, then handed him the chair.

"You'll make sure I don't die that way?"

"I'll do what I can," Mark said.

"My son, thank you, was always kind of fruity, gay, you know," he said. "Like that accountant."

"Where the fuck does he live?" Mark shouted. "I don't care what you think."

"Please"—he held up his hands—"please let me tell you."

Mark nodded impatiently.

"Loretta needed sex all the time," he said. "And . . ."

"I don't have time for this. I need his address." Mark shook his head.

Mark watched him sniff, then wipe the blood from his nose.

"You broke my nose."

"I don't have a lot of time," Mark said.

"Has he really killed that many?" he asked. "I don't believe it."

"More than fifty women. Believe it."

"Why?"

"He had a good teacher," Mark said.

"I didn't do this." He shook his head.

"You made him an accomplice to a murder when he was only seven years old."

"He watched Loretta with him through that hole in the wall, and he didn't tell me," he explained. "He watched her having sex with that fucking fag accountant. His loyalty should have been to me."

"So you made him bury a man alive."

"Yes." He nodded firmly. "It was his punishment."

"Unbelievable. I just need to know where the fuck he is, and I'll leave you alone with your perception of the world."

"He watched them together," he continued. "He got off on it. She had a great body, great tits. She showed them to him or let him touch them, but she wouldn't admit it no matter how many times I hit her."

He looked around the small room as he remembered.

"Mr. Wilkinson, I'm not enjoying this time I'm spending with you," Mark said.

"Just please, just let me talk for another minute," he stuttered.

Mark nodded.

"After he turned twenty-one, he started coming here every thirty days. He leaves money in my prison account. He loves me. He testified for me. He saved my life."

"I read the transcript," Mark said.

"He was so scared that day. I mean he wasn't even ten yet. They tried to get him to talk about that fag accountant, but he wouldn't. He kept our secret all this time, until you found the body."

Mark sighed. "All I need—"

"God, she was great sex." He looked up at the ceiling, remembering. "It was my downfall. Too much testosterone or something. But my son loves me."

"I need the address."

"I was good to him." He nodded. "That's why he comes to see me."

"Now." Mark lifted his hands in the air.

"You're going to kill my son, aren't you? I don't have any other family. I might as well be dead."

Mark stood up and lifted his hand. "Now."

"Don't hit me again." He put his hands in front of his face. "I'll tell you."

"Where?"

"It's a small suburb in north New Jersey. I'll write it down for you."

"I'll remember. Just tell me."

Mark listened, then knocked on the Plexiglas window on the door.

"You'll make sure I don't get the juice?" he said at the door. "I don't want to die like a dog. I told you what you wanted to know."

"I'll do what I can." Mark motioned to the guard. "Get him the fuck out of here."

Mark took the cell phone from the pocket of his sports coat.

"He lives in New Jersey at . . ." Mark gave Joe the address. "We should have agents stake out the house."

"Sure. How did you get the father to talk, or do I even want to know?"

Mark ignored him. "No recommendation of leniency. If anyone should die . . ."

"You sound tired," Joe said.

"It was a long interview." Mark paused. "My father would have killed this man if he'd caught him. He could identify the monsters, and he knew that if you don't cut their heads off, they'll spawn new generations."

"You are tired," Joe said.

"I'm tired of living in their world."

"Louie," he remembered his father saying a long time ago, *"the monsters always come back. You know sunrise, sundown. They spawn others."*

"Spawn?"

"Create."

"Oh . . ."

"They start with children, their own, and they imprint them for life."

"Imprint?"

It was after, after he'd been shot in the back and was confined to a wheelchair.

"Sometimes I just killed them," his father said, then tilted the bottle of whiskey and drank from it. *"There was nothing else to do with them."*

"Was it right?" he had asked his father.

"It wasn't about right. It was an obligation. If you let them live, they would just create others like them."

"What do you want me to do with the exhumation order?" Joe asked. "Do you want me to dig her up now?"

"There's no reason to now," Mark answered, "it worked."

"You told him he was the father . . ."

"Of course."

"You lied to him."

"Absolutely. I needed the address." Mark shrugged slightly.

"I understand."

Outside the prison, he climbed into the backseat of the car.

"Do we know?" Jason asked.

"Yes."

"What's he like?"

"You saw the videotape," Mark answered.

"I mean . . ."

"Somebody should have killed him a long time ago. Take me to the airport."

"Yes, sir."

Jesus Christ, Mark thought as he looked out at the bleak countryside surrounding the prison, *I just did the same thing my father would have done.* He started to ask himself if it was right or wrong and realized that he already knew the answer, that it didn't really matter.

"He was the man you saw in the video." Mark turned toward Jason. "And the son has become just like the father."

CHAPTER 53

"**H**E LIED TO me," Wilkinson said. He looked around his cell and shook his head. For thirty years, his life had been defined by a room that was barely larger than a walk-in closet, with grayish-green walls, a bed that was more like a cot, and a steel toilet next to the bed.

"That man's not going to help me. I'll be tried now, lose this time, and then I'll be put down like a dog."

He couldn't forget Mark's eyes, deep blue and cold like death, he thought, but alive and angry when he hit him.

"I'm sorry, Evan," he whispered. "He scared me. But it's Loretta who did this to us. I'm sorry I killed my own son."

After a few minutes, he grabbed the edge of the bed hard with both hands and looked up at the ceiling of his cell.

"Loretta, if you hadn't fucked around on me, we could be having sex now. I'm going to be killed like a dog now."

He remembered how Loretta would put her hands above her head when he was doing her, how she would arch her body upward and stare into his eyes even when she was pregnant with that fag's child. He remembered what she said, sometimes, after sex.

"He's not mine. As far as I'm concerned, he's a fucking orphan who should have died when his mother did."

"He almost did," he said. *"He was in an incubator for a while. He was tiny and blood red when he was born, like someone had poured a whole bottle of ketchup over his head."*

"Do you think I care?" she asked. *"You know that accountant across the street is always watching me."*

"I'll take care of that," he said.

"He comes over here when you are at work. I can't stop him." She shrugged indifferently.

"I'll take care of him."

He leaned forward, and from a tear in the mattress, he pulled out a belt he had stolen from the machine shop. *Loretta lied to me,* he thought, *she made me kill my own son.*

"I'm not going to be executed," he said. "But what will it do to my son? What will he think if I leave him again, for the last time?"

"What does that fag do?" he remembered asking Loretta.

"He just wants to talk, but he looks at me when he's here. He looks at my body."

"And you like that?"

"I can't stop him, can I?" She smiled. "Come back to bed. I like looking at you when you stand next to the bed after we have sex. It turns me on."

"Are you, I mean, have you been with the accountant?"

"No, hon. I'm faithful like the nightbirds."

"The nightbirds are bullshit," he said.

He draped the belt over a hot water pipe in his cell and stood on the edge of his bed.

"He'll understand." He nodded. "He'll understand that I couldn't let them kill me like a dog."

"The nightbirds are just a legend," he said as he shoved himself inside her.

"No," she said. "The nightbirds are an ideal that we can't seem to duplicate."

He remembered again that she had put her hands over her head, as if she were tied up, and arched her hips upward and smiled.

"Do you want me to talk sexy to you?"

"Yes."

He looped the belt around his neck.

"Evan, I'm sorry," he whispered. He could feel the bed tilt underneath his weight. "You have to understand that it's not about you."

"No. When the accountant comes over, he touches me. I can't help it."

"I'll kill him!" he shouted.

"No, I'll tell him to stop. You know, your son watches."

"I'll fix him."

"You should."

He felt the belt tightening around his neck and the bed swaying back and forth underneath him.

"Evan, you have to understand." His voice was hoarse.

When he was certain that the accountant was the father of the child Loretta was carrying, he had punched her in the stomach until she was bleeding inside, and he could see blood on her lips and chin, and when she was screaming at him to stop, he had found the claw hammer in the kitchen. She had run downstairs, and he had barely caught her at the door, then he had thrown her down on the hardwood floor in the living room and heard her head hit the floor like a gunshot and then lifted the claw hammer over his head. Afterward, he had folded her hands over her abdomen and sat next to her until the police took him away.

He felt the belt tightening around his throat and the bed moving like a carnival ride under his feet like sex with Loretta.

"You have to understand, Evan," he whispered, "I didn't mean to rat you out. I just couldn't die like a dog."

The bed flipped over. He felt his body fall as if he had dropped off the side of a cliff and the belt tighten like a vise around his neck. He gasped for breath for a moment, then heard his neck snap to the left and whispered the words, "Good-bye."

CHAPTER 54

MARK SURVEYED THE exterior of the small old house.

"Has anyone been inside?" Mark asked.

Jason raised his hands defensively. "Only to see if he was there. We didn't touch anything."

"Good."

The neighbor from the west side walked into the front yard. "Is there something wrong?"

Mark pointed at him. "Take care of him."

"I'm Jason Welles with the FBI, sir. I'm going to have to ask you to leave the property."

"Is there something wrong? Is Evan all right?"

"Sir, you need to go back inside your house." Jason guided him away from the property.

"I just wanted to know why all of you are here," he explained.

"Of course you do"—Jason nodded—"and we appreciate it. You're a good neighbor."

Jason watched Mark walk inside.

As Mark glanced around the living room, he saw a black cat leap onto the back of the old couch. "Come here." He held out his hand.

He scratched the cat behind his left ear and read the tag on the collar.

"Felix Morgan Wilkinson. He gave you his actual last name."

The furniture was old but clean. On the mantelpiece over the fireplace were a series of framed photographs—Evan's father flexing next to a swimming pool; his natural mother, Mark assumed, with his father by the pool; his aunt and uncle who had taken him in; and Loretta, lying in bed with her hands crossed over her abdomen, as if she were lying in a coffin.

Mark picked up the photo of Loretta. She was attractive, blonde, with a spectacular body, but it was her eyes more than anything else that drew his attention. She was wearing a low-cut black top with spaghetti straps that lay over her breasts like a thin veil and a short skirt. Her eyes were half open or half closed, and she was smiling.

Mark closed his eyes.

"He still remembers it." Mark could almost see Evan looking through the hole he had cut in the wall between his bedroom and theirs. "He'll always remember Loretta, but for her, it was just a game."

In the kitchen, he looked in the refrigerator and found a loaf of bread, cheese, lunch meat, and several bottles of white wine.

Mark closed the refrigerator and walked down the hallway. In the first bedroom, he saw the cabinet, the fingers, and a computer. For a few minutes, he looked at the cabinet and the fingers inside as he rubbed the palm of his right hand across the left side of his face, then sat down in front of the computer and felt Felix on his lap a few seconds later.

Mark found his Internet connection and saw the website for Dr. March's dating service.

"Is this what you did?" Mark looked at Felix. "You'd sit on his lap when he selected dates."

Mark stared at the website, then went to e-mails. He scrolled through them until he saw one to Dr. March and stopped.

"Dear Dr. March," he read, "You promised me matches. I need more like Judy, blonde . . ."

"The date of this e-mail is more than two years ago," Mark said. "Dr. March didn't mention that."

Mark set Felix down on the carpet and walked to the front door. "Jason, come in here!" Mark shouted. "Look at the computer. You know more about it than I do."

"What do you want me to find?" Jason asked him inside.

"It looks to me like Evan was in direct communication with Dr. March two years ago. See what else you can find. And afterward, find a cage for the cat."

"What are we going to do with him?"

"Look at the computer," Mark said. "I'll tell you later."

Mark walked into Evan's bedroom and saw a double bed, a used handkerchief on the nightstand next to it, and a photograph of his father and what he assumed was his natural mother on the dresser. In the closet, he saw a varied wardrobe with different-colored sports coats, shirts, slacks, and suits.

"Wardrobe," Mark whispered in the closet. "He always changed. He knew what they wanted to see from the bios on the website."

"Yes." Mark looked down at Felix. "His strength, his gift, is to give them what they expected, what they wanted."

In the kitchen, he opened the door to the basement and watched Felix run down the steps ahead of him. At the foot of the stairs, he saw the aviary and Felix eyeing the birds inside like they were lunch.

"It's like a little city, with condos and a playground area in the middle," Mark said and watched Felix leap at the glass.

"No." Mark picked him up and walked upstairs. "Nightbirds. He kept an aviary of nightbirds."

"What did you find?" Mark asked Jason at the door to the smaller bedroom.

"He's been in regular contact with Dr. March, telling him what he wants, under multiple aliases."

Mark set Felix down.

"Jesus Christ." Jason pointed at the fingers in the display cabinet behind the computer. "How could he do that?"

"Did Dr. March give us this information?" Mark ignored him.

"Jesus Christ," Jason said, "I turned the light on inside and brushed against . . ."

"Answer me, dammit," Mark said.

"No." Jason shook his head. "He hid it or deleted it. I checked with our agents who searched the database."

"I wonder how many other people talk to Dr. March," Mark said.

"He's on TV all the time," Jason said. "He kept those files from us. Don't you want to look at the fingers?"

"I already did," Mark answered.

"I'm sorry, sir, it's just that I've never seen . . ."

"I know."

"What do you want me to do with the cat?" Jason asked. "He's a good boy."

Jason petted him and felt Felix purring like music.

"Take him to the local Humane Society," Mark said.

"They'll euthanatize him in three days if no one claims him," Jason said.

"I know." Mark nodded.

"You think . . ."

"Have two agents there in case he tries to save him."

"He didn't do anything. I mean . . . I'll take him."

"You don't understand. Just take him to the Humane Society."

"But, sir, I . . ."

"Just do it, goddammit!" Mark shouted.

Mark walked outside and saw Joe on the front porch. "Have you been inside?"

Joe nodded. "I saw all of it."

Jason walked outside with the cat in a small cage and looked at Mark.

"Jason, take that cat to the local Humane Society as soon as we leave here," Mark said.

"Are you sure?"

"Yes."

"I will."

"Sir, please call Pete," Mark said to Joe, "and tell him Evan's cat, Felix, will be killed three days from now."

"What do you want to do?"

"We have someone to arrest," Mark said.

"Who?"

"Dr. March. He concealed material evidence. He's been in contact via e-mail with Evan for years. He obstructed justice. Have Jason arrest him tonight."

"What will that accomplish?" Joe asked. "We won't be able to make it stick."

"Maybe, maybe not. Jason, get a news crew. I don't care which one, they're everywhere. Open the cages in his aviary on camera. Those birds are like pit bulls. They'll fight and kill each other. At least that's the legend."

Before he had looked at Evan's computer, he had turned on the light inside the display cabinet and had seen the ring fingers of more than fifty women. They looked like they were in a display cabinet at a jewelry store, white from the plaster, straight, and perfect. *Evan, fingers, hands,* he thought, *Loretta.* He remembered Anglen's words from his book, *He travels to kill, but he goes home each time with his trophy their finger and leaves it in a special place, almost like a shrine, as an offering . . .* Anglen had been right, Mark thought, the shrine was the cabinet for his father and each finger was an offering.

"What about the fingers?" Jason asked.

"Let Pete look at it for his story," Mark said. "And then move it to Quantico."

"I've never seen anything like it," Jason said again.

"I know," Mark said.

"Everything is all right at your house?" Mark asked as he watched Jason set the cage in the car. "Cara?"

"Yes," Joe answered. "There are two agents there at all times, and I'm going back there now. She's safe."

"Good." Mark nodded.

"I came here because I wanted to know why I lost one of my best friends, why I lost Tom. And what I saw was a cat and what, fifty ring fingers. You'll finish this now, Lou."

"He'll go after Debbie next, then Cara. I'll be at the hotel where we put Pete and Debbie tonight. I'll finish it there."

CHAPTER 55

EVAN SAT IN total darkness in the middle of the empty living room, with his arms folded around his legs and his knees flush against his chest. Slowly, he rocked back and forth.

"The movers were coming," he whispered. "I had everything ready."

He stood up and looked at the fireplace in the moonlight. Several miles away, his cat, his birds, and his computer were trapped inside his house. He would never see them again. And his father was now nothing more than a small pile of ashes in a cardboard box.

He'd read Pete's article. The headline read:

BIRDMAN'S FATHER COMMITS SUICIDE

He started to cry from a place deep inside him a time long ago.

"You gave me up," he whispered, "but I forgive you. I know Mark made you do it."

"You did the best you could. You were family." He wiped the tears from his face.

He walked through his new house and looked at the kitchen, the bedrooms, and then through the window at the backyard. His cat would have liked it here; his birds would have felt at home in the basement. He could feel the agents in his house and on his computer.

"Shortly after he met with Lou Mark yesterday, Michael Evan Wilkinson hung himself with a belt from a hot water pipe in his cell. Michael Evan Wilkinson is the father of the serial killer who calls himself the Birdman. His name is Evan Morgan. In two nearly simultaneous acts of betrayal, Mr. Wilkinson told Lou Mark all about his son and then abandoned him forever by taking his own life. According to Mark, he justified his brutal treatment of his son as punishment for not revealing the affair his wife was having with a quiet, shy, accountant who lived across the street. What was that punishment? Forcing his son to bury George Allen Peterson alive."

"Mark!" he screamed suddenly and heard the echo in the empty room. "He did it. He took my father from me, my cat, my birds, my life."

He felt his body convulsing like he was having a stroke, then he felt tears again on his face.

"Family," he cried, "that's what matters, and now I'm alone."

He walked outside to his car. He had work to do, he had purpose; first Debbie, then Mark's wife. As he started the car, he muttered, "My father couldn't have killed my brother."

He remembered that part of Pete's story.

"The FBI says DNA analysis on Loretta Prince's unborn child revealed that it was Michael Evan Wilkinson's child. That means that Michael Evan Wilkinson killed his wife, his unborn son, and the brother of his living son, Evan Morgan. With a few swings of a hammer thirty years ago, Michael Evan Wilkinson wiped out his entire family with the exception of Evan, who became the most prolific serial killer in U.S. history. After he learned this, he hung himself in his cell."

"I know you couldn't have killed my brother, Dad. The FBI is lying. I'm going to miss you, Dad. You did the best you could. Mark and Pete are going to pay. They're going to learn what it's like to lose everything."

"I would like to rent a car," he said quietly.

"What kind?"

"An SUV."

"We have Ford Expeditions, Explorers, Land Rovers, if you want to spend the money," he said.

"I think the Expedition will be fine." He set a credit card on the counter.

"Evan White," the man said, reading it. "Mr. White, I need to see your license, run your card, and you'll have your car."

"Is there a tool kit in the SUV?" he asked.

"Yes, sir," he answered. "Here's your credit card, Mr. White."

"Is there a hammer in the tool kit?"

The rental agent looked up. "I think so, yes, you have to screw it together. It has a metal handle, sort of small, with a little bit of rubber at the end on the handle. Why?"

"I just moved. I have some pictures to hang in my new house," he said.

"Are you all right, sir?"

"Quite, I just have a lot of work to do tonight, and I'm tired from moving."

The clerk stared at him, apparently expecting a further explanation.

"I'm sorry," he added, "I have pets."

"What kind?"

"Pets," he said again, "and it will take them a while to adjust to their new home."

"Sure. Here are the keys. The car is on the preferred lot, right around the corner."

"I'll find it." He took the keys and turned away.

"What was wrong with him?" the clerk asked the woman standing next to him at the rental car counter.

"He's busy." She shrugged.

At the car, Evan found the tool kit next to the spare tire in the well and slowly screwed the small hammer together. After sitting down behind the wheel, he set the hammer on the seat next to him, along with a roll of duct tape. He then drove to the *News* building and waited outside.

"I miss you, Felix," he whispered. "I miss my birds. And Pete is going to pay."

"I like it, I like your story, but it's sad." Debbie leaned over and kissed him on the cheek. "The father is a monster, and yet he killed himself. Was it because he betrayed his son, or he didn't want to die by lethal injection? Or was it because he killed his unborn child?"

"It's what the story is about." Pete turned off the computer. "I really don't know. I don't even know if Mark told me the truth."

He rubbed her forearm gently.

Carl walked out of his office and nodded. "Is Mark going to catch him soon?"

"He thinks so." Pete stood up and put his coat on. As Debbie straightened the collar, he said, "We're going to the hotel."

"Be careful," Carl said.

"The FBI agent is at the hotel," Pete said. "We'll be safe."

In the elevator, Debbie hugged him and put her head on his chest.

"It'll be over soon?"

"Yes." He nodded. "When this is over, when the book is finished, we will be getting a big check from my publisher. My agent is working on the movie rights now. He's talking big numbers."

"You don't seem happy," she said. "You don't seem to be excited about it. This is good news."

He watched the elevator doors open. "I'll feel better when it's over."

Pete opened the door to the driver's side of the car, then walked around the car and opened the other door.

"Thank you," she said.

"It's what you do," she said when he sat down behind the wheel. "It's your job."

"No." He shook his head. "I used to be a newspaperman. That was my job. Now I'm going to be a rich man who writes about a psychopath and his collection of fingers that will probably end up being auctioned off on eBay. What the fuck is wrong with us? Do you know that you can buy cards, like baseball cards, with photos of famous serial killers—Dahmer, Gacy, Bundy, and others? Evan Morgan is a fucking celebrity, like a movie star."

"We can have this discussion afterward," Debbie said. "I just want it to be over."

Pete nodded. "Yes, I do too."

When he drove through the open gate to the underground parking garage beneath the *News* building, he didn't notice the Ford Expedition behind him.

"Where are they staying?" Evan mumbled. "Not at his apartment anymore."

He followed a few car lengths behind Pete's car.

"Mark will be sorry, and so will Pete." He nodded. "My father's life had value, and they took it away. His ashes are in a cardboard box, and they'll be thrown away like cigarette butts in an ashtray because I can't claim them."

He saw the right blinker flash on Pete's car and slowed down, then followed him around the corner.

"My birds," he whispered.

At the hotel, he had seen the video. His birds were fighting like sharks over a dead corpse cast into the ocean. Mark had separated his couples and had taken them from their condos, and the fights between them were death matches. He knew Felix would be euthanized in a few days.

"He'll pay." Evan nodded. "He can't stop me."

At the light, at the dark intersection, he saw no one, and he let his right foot slip slowly off the brake of the Expedition until it gently bumped Pete's car.

"Now," he whispered as he watched the interior light come on in Pete's car. "Time's up."

"What is it?" Debbie asked.

"Nothing." Pete sounded annoyed. "A minor accident. We'll just go."

Pete heard a gentle knock on the window and turned.

"I'm sorry," he heard a man in a hat with a beard and mustache saying. "I wasn't paying attention."

Pete rolled the window down. "Don't worry about it. It doesn't matter."

"It does for my insurance company. Those bastards run the world."

"It's all right," Pete repeated.

Evan yanked the door open, then grabbed Pete's hair and pulled him out of the car. Three times, he smashed Pete's face downward onto his right knee before Pete collapsed on the asphalt.

"Loretta, it's good to see you again." Evan bent down and peered into the car at Debbie.

"No!" she screamed.

He reached inside and punched her flush in the nose, then walked around the car, picked her up, and carried her to his rental car. At the back of the Expedition, he opened the hatch, set her inside, and wrapped duct tape around her wrists, ankles, and mouth.

He had left his car across the street from the rental car lot, and after about ten minutes, he could hear her moaning in the back of the Expedition.

"We're almost there, Debbie." He looked in the rearview mirror. "Just be patient with me."

He parked the rental car next to his car, then got out and opened the hatch. Her eyes were wide open when he stared down at her.

"I wish I had more time," he said and ripped the duct tape from her mouth. She looked around for help, but all she saw was the darkness of the night and the occasional car passing the parking lot.

Evan touched her stomach through the white sweater, then moved his left hand slowly up to her breasts.

"You were going to be one of my dates." His voice was hoarse.

"You can do whatever you want," she said desperately.

"No." He smiled and shook his head. "I don't have time, and it won't help you."

Behind his back, in his right hand, was the hammer from the Expedition tool kit. With his other hand, he touched her hair gently, then her neck.

"Your hair has nice texture, and your skin is soft," he said quietly. "But I lost everything."

"I found someone I care about," she said.

"So?"

"It's so hard to do that," she said. "I'm begging you. It matters to me. I don't want to die in the back of a rental car."

He shrugged. "I'm not responsible for this."

"Mark?" She looked up.

He nodded. "Yes. He made my father rat me out. He made my father kill himself. My cat, my birds."

"I'm pregnant," she cried. "I'm going to have a baby. You can't kill my baby."

She remembered her last discussion with Pete about her pregnancy.

"I want to keep him. I don't have any children. Maybe I never will again. It's not his fault who his father is."

"Are you sure?" Pete had asked.

"Yes." She nodded.

"Then we'll do it."

"You can't kill my baby," she begged.

"I used to know someone who did that."

He lifted the hammer from the tool kit over his head and smashed it into the orbital bone over her left eye. She let out a scream that pierced the silence in the dark parking lot.

"No screaming allowed." He hit her again.

"I'm blind," she mumbled in agony. "I can't see anything."

"My cat." He hit her again.

"My birds." He smashed her teeth.

"My father." He hit her again and again until he heard the last deep sigh of her life.

With the duct tape he had ripped from her mouth, he wrote the name Cara on the ceiling of the rental car with the blood he had wiped from her face.

"You really never know, do you? Pete is right. You really never know when someone like me might come into your life. It's chemistry."

He smiled at the irony and, as he walked toward his car, began planning his next trip.

"It'll drive Mark crazy," He stepped into his car.

He needed to buy gas, he thought, as he looked at the gauge. But first, sleep, at the hotel.

"Mark will know soon"—he nodded—"what it's like to lose everything."

CHAPTER 56

"THANK YOU, AUNT Florence," Schaeffer said. "That was good."

Schaeffer was, she guessed, about Cara and Lou's age, a few inches taller than Lou, and a good thirty pounds heavier. He had dark hair, a pleasant and respectful smile, and had been with the FBI for six years. From his appearance, she thought he was strong, physically, with a somewhat simplistic view of his job—he was given a job, and he just did it—but he had never worked in the Serial Killer Division before now.

"You're welcome," Aunt Florence answered. They were having dinner in the kitchen.

"Is Cara sick, ma'am?" Schaeffer looked at Aunt Florence.

"What do you mean?"

She took the plates over to the sink and rinsed them off. In the western sky, in the direction of the barn, she saw lightning flash in the sky, long and jagged like a broken piece of glass.

"Before she left, I could hear her throwing up some mornings," he said.

"There is a storm coming," Florence said, ignoring his question. "A big one, I think."

"You don't have to answer me," he said and stood up from the table.

He looked out the window and saw the lightning in the sky for a moment over the dark barn. There was the sound of light rain now on the roof, and he could hear the wind blowing.

"I like the storms we have here this time of year," Florence said. "But it's so dark around the house at night in the field."

"I understand, ma'am."

"Lou likes the darkness," Florence said. "I think he's always felt most comfortable here at night. It reminds him of where he came from and his father."

He could hear the rain now pelting the roof and the gusts of wind. Again, he saw the lightning over the barn and heard the thunder seconds later.

"It's close," Schaeffer said.

"The lightning is a good five miles away," Florence said, "although it looks like it's on top of us."

"The storm is getting worse," Schaeffer said from the doorway to the kitchen, then walked across the kitchen and looked out the window.

"Was there a light on in the barn earlier?" Schaeffer asked. "I don't remember that."

"No," Aunt Florence said, "we don't turn the lights on in the barn at night."

It was the only light in the dark field for what seemed like miles. "I'm sure it's just the storm," Schaeffer said, "but I'll check on it."

"Cara's pregnant," Florence said. "That's what you thought, and you were right."

"Thank you, ma'am. I'll be back in a few minutes."

Florence watched as Schaeffer walked the few hundred yards to the barn and opened one of the doors.

He felt the blow on his back near his shoulder blades and fell facedown into the barn.

"What's your name?" he heard someone ask.

"Jeff Schaeffer, FBI," he mumbled.

"Yeah," he heard the voice again, "I know all about the FBI."

He felt his gun being taken from the holster on his belt and then felt his head spinning as he was turned over on his back.

"Who are you?" He asked.

He thought he could hear a bird somewhere in the barn.

"Tell me about Cara," the man asked.

"Who are you?" He asked again.

He was stunned, but his vision was clearing, and to his left he could see a medium sized-black-colored bird and to his right, a man standing over him holding an axe. For a moment, he blinked, then thought he saw the man drop the axe and take something from the inside pocket of his sports coat.

"Tell me about Cara," he said again. "She's pregnant, isn't she?"

"You're him?"

He felt the bone near the knuckle on his left little finger break first, then screamed in pain. Outside, he could hear the storm and the thunder. Then he felt pressure like a tooth being pulled on the ring finger of his left hand, and screamed again.

"You only have eight left now," he heard the man say above him. "And I don't have a lot of time. Tell me about Cara. She's pregnant, isn't she?"

"Mark would kill me," he mumbled.

"Now," the man said slowly. "You have seven fingers left."

"I'm an FBI agent," he muttered.

"You're nothing now."

He could hear the bird singing and tried to move the fingers on his left hand.

"You're stubborn," the man said. "That's six. And now you can't even pick up a fork with that hand."

Schaeffer tried to make a fist with his right hand and felt the man grab it, open it, and he screamed out loud again.

"Stop, please," he begged.

"What do you know about Cara?" the man asked.

"She gets sick in the morning," he whispered.

"Good." The man dropped his right hand. "I knew she was pregnant with Mark's child."

"Is she waiting for me in the house?" he asked.

"No." He shook his head slowly. "The fingers on my left hand hurt."

"You don't have any left. Don't waste my time. I saw someone in the house. Who is it?"

"Mark's aunt," he mumbled.

"Where the fuck is Cara?" he shouted as he heard the thunder, then saw the lightning over the barn.

"She left," he whispered, "a few weeks ago. Mark moved her."

"You haven't told me where." He applied the hoof nipper to the middle finger on his right hand.

"No, please, not again."

"Then tell me."

"She's staying at Mr. Mosely's house."

"Are there are agents around the house?"

"Yes, I think so."

"How many?"

"Two."

"Thank you," Evan said.

Evan grabbed his face and turned him toward the sound of the bird.

"Do you see that?" Evan shouted.

"What?" Schaeffer mumbled. "No, what?"

"The bird."

"I hurt," he gasped.

"I know. That was my last bird. I brought her to my new house. She is pregnant. I lost my other birds."

Schaeffer tried to get up, but when he pushed off the dirt floor of the barn with his left hand, he screamed in pain.

"You see," Evan said slowly, "I want you to understand why I'm doing this. Don't you want to know?"

"Please let me go," he begged.

"I'm sorry I can't do that, Mr. Schaeffer, but Mark will know why I was here."

As he lay there, he felt relief for a moment when the man stopped talking until the sharp edge of the axe cut through his right arm at the elbow, then his shoulder and as he was passing out from the pain, he felt the sharp edge of the axe on his right knee.

"I knew it," he said, after he finished with Schaeffer.

At the door to the barn, he looked at the house for a moment.

"No," he whispered. "She can feel the pain like I did. And Mark can wonder as I kill him if I'll come back here one more time."

"Lou, there was a light on in the barn and Schaeffer went out, and he's not back. And . . ."

She spoke quickly, without breathing at first, then he could hear her nearly hyperventilating.

"Slow down," Mark said.

"I think he's here."

"Are you all right?"

"Yes."

"Lock yourself in the master bedroom and wait for me. Take the shotgun with you."

"Lou, I think he's here," she said again. "I think he killed Schaeffer."

"Move fast. And I'll get there in a little more than an hour. I love you, be careful."

"What else," Mark whispered, after he hung up the telephone. "What else can I do now, from here?"

He closed his eyes and remembered Jake's number.

"Jake."

"Lou?"

"Yes, please get over to my house right now."

"All right," he said. "Why?"

"And take your deputy. Don't go in the barn. One of you wait outside, the other in the living room where you can watch both the front and back doors," Mark continued. "Make sure you're armed and make sure you're careful."

"Why?" he asked again.

"I'm sure he killed the FBI agent who was watching my aunt," Mark answered.

"In the barn?"

"Go now."

"Aunt Florence, Jake and his deputy are on their way over now," Mark said. "And I'll be there soon. One will be outside, and the other in the living room. Don't leave the room no matter what you hear."

"I'm scared, Lou," she said.

"So am I," Mark said.

"My aunt called. I need a plane now," Mark said, "right now. I know he killed Schaeffer. What if he's killing her right now? I can't do anything about it. I . . ."

"Stop," Joe reached up and touched his shoulder. "Why would he do that?"

"To hurt me. I took everything away from him, and now he's trying to do it to me."

Joe looked out the window of his dining room. "He's smart. He doesn't want your aunt. He thought he'd find Cara at your farm. Whom did you call in Sun Rise?"

"Jake, you know, the chief of police," Mark said.

"Sit down, wait until he calls," Joe said.

"I need a plane, now," Mark said.

"You need to be here because he's coming here, and you know it."

Mark sat down at Joe's dining room table. "Cara?"

"Yes, Lou."

"He wants to kill her first, then me. Then he thinks he can go back to his life, the birds, another cat, and a computer."

Mark sighed. "Send Jason now and another agent who's a little more physical than he is."

Mark heard his cell phone ring, looked at it, then picked it up.

"Jake," Mark said, "tell me."

"You aunt's fine," he said, "other than this whole thing scared the hell out of her. But she'll be all right. She's tough. The agent, whatever his name is . . ."

"Schaeffer."

"He's dead. I'm out in the barn now. My deputy Hank is in the house with your aunt. I've never seen anything like this. I don't think I will again. Jesus Christ."

"Is he gone?" Mark asked. "I need to know."

"Yes. Your aunt saw a man running across the field. Then saw a car. He's not here."

"Is she all right?" Joe asked.

Mark nodded. "Tell me about Schaeffer."

"There's blood, like red wine, all around him. I almost slipped in it. He cut off his fingers, or most of them. He cut off his arms at the elbows, his legs at the knees, and his head. He left the axe next to the body. There are flies all around the body parts. I almost threw up when I came in here."

"He knows," Mark whispered.

"I found something else, a blackbird."

"Dead?"

"No, alive. I've read the newspaper stories, Lou. As a cop, my guess is he left him for you."

"Thank you. Please stay with her. Two agents will be there within two hours. I can't tell you how much I appreciate this. Thank you."

"Sure, Lou." He heard Jake cough, then clear his throat.

"And please take my aunt to your house."

"You're right," Mark said to Joe after he closed the cell phone. "He's coming here."

"Lou," Cara said from the living room. "He's coming here?"

"I'm sorry, I didn't know you were standing there," Mark said.

"Lou, I'll be out back with Jason," Joe said.

"Thank you," Mark said.

"Here?" She pointed down.

"Yes."

"When?"

"I don't know." Mark shook his head.

"Where is he now?" Cara asked.

"I don't know." Mark shrugged.

"I read Pete's story." Mark saw her hands trembling. "I know he wrote my name over her in that car."

Mark walked toward her and hugged her. "I wish you wouldn't read Pete's stories. I wish you could stop thinking about it. You know I'll make sure he never hurts you."

"You said that about Debbie, Lou."

"I know. I regret her death. She was truly a decent person."

"What are you going to do?"

"I don't know yet. I don't know where he is. When I decide what to do about this, how much do you want to know?"

"I just want to know that we're safe. I'm scared for you, me, and the baby," Cara said.

"You couldn't be in a safer place. Please go upstairs while I talk to Joe."

"That's what you said about your aunt's farm," Cara said.

"I know."

"And he's there now, isn't he?"

Mark looked away.

"He didn't kill her, did he?"

"No, my aunt's safe, please go upstairs."

"Cara?" Joe asked after Mark walked outside.

"Scared to death," Mark answered. "And she should be. I promised myself, Pete, and Cara that I would catch him before he got to Debbie and I almost did, but that doesn't help her much now."

"What are you going to do?" Joe asked.

"I don't know. I think I did everything my father and Tom would have done."

"Lou," Joe said. "We don't catch these people overnight. It took twenty years to catch . . ."

"I know, sir, but if I don't catch him soon, he will kill Cara and my son, next week, next month, whenever. I can't watch her all the time and chase him."

"I only want one agent here, and I want him to be conspicuous in a car across the street." Mark pointed. "And I want you and Elaine to stay somewhere else for a few days."

"Are you sure about this? You're going to try to finish this here and now."

"Yes." Mark nodded. "If I don't catch him now . . ."

"You told me," Joe said.

"How are you going to?"

"I'm going to do what you asked me to do. I'll call you every two hours."

CHAPTER 57

"WHO IS HE?" Evan looked at the waitress and pointed at the man on the bicycle outside. It had taken him three days to drive from Sun Rise, Iowa, to Virginia.

"Skip," she answered. "He's homeless. We try to help. We feed him when the kitchen closes. You know, what's left."

"So what about the flowers?"

"He sells them," she said. "I don't know where he gets them. He's a Vietnam vet, and none of us thinks he's quite all there."

"Good. Thank you. A little more coffee, please," Evan said.

"Certainly, sir."

Evan watched him rearranging the flowers in the bins attached to his bicycle. Occasionally, he'd examine one that appeared to be brown and dead and then throw it away. He was not far from Joe Mosely's house, at a place that served breakfast all day. He could see the sun setting on the west side of the restaurant.

"There you go, sir." The waitress poured the coffee.

She wasn't terribly young, but not old either, with dark hair and a small-stoned wedding ring on her left hand.

"How long have you been married, if you don't mind?" Evan asked.

"No, of course not, sir. Ten years. We're expecting our first child now."

"Congratulations."

"Thank you, sir." She smiled. "I can't wait."

"You know you've got me curious about Skip. Is that his name?"

"Yes."

"Does he sell those flowers in the neighborhoods around here?"

"Yes, sir. He tries."

"It's good to see someone trying, not just packing it in and living off the government."

"I agree, and Skip does try hard, which is why we help him."

"I'm going to give him some money on the way out. Congratulations on the baby."

He continued to watch Skip reorganize his inventory and smiled.

"Its sundown," Cara said, while she looked out the front picture window at the agent in the car across the street.

She was wearing loose-fitting brown slacks and a brown sports coat. On her left hip, she could feel the gun Mark had given her, and in the right pocket of her slacks, she felt the weight of the cell phone.

"It's almost time, isn't it?"

"I think so."

"Do you think he's here?"

"Not yet." Mark shook his head.

Her voice quivered slightly "What did your father say about sundown?"

"It was really my grandfather who said, wrote it first, as the opening to his last short story. At sunrise, the monsters run away hiding from the light, but at sundown, as the light wanes, they return."

"Right."

"Sit." Mark gestured at her with his right hand. "This should be finished soon."

"I hope I can hold out." She sat down on a chair to the right of the picture window.

"You can."

The agent looked in the side mirror of the car and saw what appeared to be an older man riding a bicycle on the sidewalk. He was dressed in ragged, old clothing and was wearing a safety helmet. He saw him in the driveway a few houses behind his car and watched him walk to the front door.

He felt the cell phone vibrating in the inside pocket of his sports coat.

"Yes, sir," he said.

"Anything?" Joe asked.

"The street is empty except for the old guy who sells flowers door-to-door on a bicycle. He comes through here, three, four nights a week. He looks harmless enough, Mr. Mosely."

"Be careful, and call me in one hour."

"Yes, sir."

"Lou, I talked to Fitzpatrick," Joe said.

"Is that his name?" Mark said into the cell phone.

"Robert Fitzpatrick," Joe answered. "The street is quiet. People are in their homes, probably watching television. The only person on the street is the flower guy."

"The flower guy?"

"He's a homeless person who sells flowers door-to-door. He was in Vietnam near the end of the war. His name is James Howard, but he goes by Skip. He has some neurological problems, but he's harmless. He's about seventy now. Maybe it won't be tonight."

"Cara won't make it through another day. It has to be tonight," Mark said.

He looked over at the car parked down the street, then stopped in the driveway. He laughed as he remembered that he had actually sold some nearly dead flowers a few houses ago for ten dollars.

"Hi, I'm Skip. I'm a Vietnam War vet. Would you like to buy some flowers?" He asked at the door.

Back at the restaurant, he had talked to Skip.

"They told me about you inside," he had said. "I'd like to buy some flowers. I think it's good you're trying to make it on your own."

"Thank you," Skip had said, "these are nice."

He held it up in the air and saw aphids crawling on the leaves and a price tag from a grocery store.

"No," he said and handed them back to Skip. "Can we move over there? I think I'll be able to see better."

"Sure." Skip wheeled his bike toward the corner, and Evan had followed.

"Do you like these?" He held up a small bouquet and looked inside. He could see her husband sitting in an easy chair watching television and a little girl sitting on the couch.

"I don't know," she mumbled. "Hon, should we buy some flowers? It's Skip."

"Yeah, sure, whatever you want," he said.

When he looked at her husband, he thought about Skip again.

"I like those." Evan had pointed at a bouquet in the back bin. "I'll give them to my girlfriend. How much?"

"Ten dollars."

When Skip reached into the bin, Evan grabbed the strap on the safety helmet, whispered, "I'm sorry," and then drew the razor across Skip's throat.

"I'm sorry," he said as he dragged the body to the garbage cans in the back.

"I truly am sorry," he said again as he took the safety helmet from Skip's head and the worn-out old jacket from his shoulders. After he had piled garbage bags on his body, he put on the jacket, then the helmet, and rode away on the bicycle.

"How about these?" she asked. "How much?"

"Ten dollars."

"Hon, I need ten dollars," she said.

"I'm watching . . . whatever." He got up, pulled out his wallet, and, at the door, handed him a ten-dollar bill.

"Thank you, sir," Evan said and handed the flowers to his wife. "With the war now, thank you for helping out a veteran."

"Sure," he said.

While he was putting his wallet in his back pocket with his head turned toward the television, Evan took out the razor and slashed the left side of the woman's face first, then the right side of the man's face, and, as he stumbled backward, slashed the razor across his fat stomach and watched him fall. After he shoved the woman to the floor, he turned and stared at the little girl sitting on the couch.

"Mommy, Daddy!" she screamed.

"Scream your head off," he said, then ran through the house and left through the kitchen door.

"Lou, what is that?" Cara asked.

He could hear the loud screaming of a child.

"I don't know." Mark drew his gun. "Go upstairs now."

"Lou . . ."

"Now!" he shouted. "Do everything I told you to do."

Mark saw Fitzpatrick get out of the car and run toward the sound of the screaming.

Mark waited until he heard Cara lock the door upstairs, then walked outside, and saw Fitzpatrick at the front door of the house. He walked slowly across the neighbors' yard until he reached the driveway.

"Fitz . . . Robert!" he shouted. "What is it?"

"They're okay. They're cut, but okay. They said the flower guy went nuts. I think it's okay."

Mark saw the bicycle on the front porch and the flowers.

"The flower guy," he whispered. "Fuck . . ."

He turned and ran toward the house.

At the bedroom door, he knocked gently and muted his voice. "Help me. You need to take me to the . . ."

"Lou," Cara said.

"Help me." His voice was deep and hoarse.

Cara unlocked the door, opened it, saw the stranger's face, and screamed. He kicked her hard in the abdomen and watched her fall backward.

"Just like Loretta," he said.

He could hear someone open the door downstairs and turned his head.

"Mark," he said. "He's coming to save you."

"God, it hurts." Cara clutched at her stomach.

She could taste what she thought was blood in her mouth, and as she looked up at him, she thought she saw two men, standing side by side.

"Good, we can finish this tonight." He closed and locked the bedroom door. "He'll be here in a minute. You'll be able to hear him running like a madman up the steps."

"Lou!" she screamed.

"Good, scream your fucking head off, and I'll kill him when he comes through the door."

She heard Mark's shoulder hit the old hardwood door twice before the lock broke. As it flew open, she took the gun from her belt under her coat, and with trembling hands, she shot Evan somewhere in his back.

Mark heard the shot, saw Evan stumble backward, and fired three times into his chest before he collapsed on the floor. He kicked the gun Evan had dropped across the room and took the other gun from the inside pocket of his coat and the razor from his pants.

"Are you all right?" Mark knelt down next to Cara.

"I need to go to the hospital," Cara whispered. "He broke something, I think, when he kicked me."

Mark called Joe. "We need to get someone here immediately, fast," he stuttered. "An ambulance for Cara, now."

"I'll do it. Is it over?" Joe asked.

"Evan Morgan is lying on the floor. Cara shot him once, and I shot him three times. Get me a fucking ambulance."

"Can you stand up?" Mark asked.

Cara shook her head. "I don't think so. He's the monster, isn't he?"

"He was."

Mark saw the blood in the corner of her mouth roll slowly down her chin. She looked pale, and he was sure she was dying.

"He broke something, Lou. It hurts."

"You'll be all right. I promise."

When he heard the siren minutes later, he looked at Evan and saw the smile on his face.

"I did it, didn't I?" He smiled. "I hurt you."

"We'll see."

Mark smashed the butt of his father's gun down on Evan's nose and watched his eyes roll back, then close.

Cara heard footsteps on the stairs.

"Please move away, sir," the paramedic said as he knelt down and placed his hand over her heart.

"Is she all right?" Mark asked. "Please tell me she is."

"I don't . . . Yes, sir."

"The baby?"

The paramedic looked up quickly. "She's pregnant?"

"Yes." Mark nodded.

"We need to get her to the hospital now. What about him?" The paramedic pointed at Evan.

"He's gone. We'll call the coroner."

"Dead?" The paramedic continued to stare at Evan.

"Yes, dammit!" Mark shouted. "Get her to the hospital, now."

"Maybe I should look at him."

Mark showed him his badge. "Lou Mark, FBI. Get her to the fucking hospital now. She's bleeding inside."

"Yes, sir."

"She can't die," Mark said after they left. "She can't."

"Sir, what can I do?" Fitzpatrick stood at the door.

"You can leave the room, Robert. Wait for me downstairs."

"Is that him?" He pointed at Evan. "Is that the Birdman?"

"Yes. I'll see you downstairs in a few minutes."

"I can't move," he heard Evan whisper after Fitzpatrick left the room.

"What?"

"I can't move, I said." He looked up at Mark. "One of your bullets must have hit my spine, or maybe Cara's did."

Mark looked down at him and remembered the first time he'd seen him at Pete's apartment. "I should have killed you then."

"I'm like George now."

"The accountant?"

"He broke his back on the fall. My father had a lantern next to the grave in the basement. I could see his eyes through the plastic around his head. He could see the dirt dropping toward his face and tried to get away from it, but after a while, I couldn't see his face anymore, and his head stopped moving. The look in his eyes was like my matches, my women, when I stood next to their bed and lifted the hammer over them."

"It's finished now," Mark said.

"I know. I can't believe I'm like George now. But I found Loretta over and over again. A long time ago, she told me I'd meet her again."

Mark looked at the three bullet wounds in his chest, which were shaped almost like a triangle.

"I read your grandfather's story again last night," Evan said.

"We don't talk about it."

"I know. But your grandfather wrote it. Whose fault was it?"

"It wasn't anybody's fault. It was an accident," Mark said.

"You're going to kill me, aren't you?" he mumbled after a few moments.

Mark nodded. "Yes."

"Because I killed your baby and maybe Cara? I want to give you something." Evan coughed.

"What?"

"My watch. It's the watch my father gave me."

"I don't—"

"Please," Evan begged.

"It's time to sing," Mark said.

Mark grabbed Evan's hair, lifted his head off the floor, and punched him in the face with his fist like a hammer until he couldn't lift his right arm anymore. He didn't know how many times he hit him; he just knew he was dead.

For a few minutes, he leaned over and stared at the hardwood floor next to Evan's body and tried to catch his breath, then reached over and took the old watch from Evan's wrist.

Across the room, he picked up the cell phone and looked out the window.

"You can call the coroner," he said to Joe. "He bled to death. I'm going to the hospital now."

"I'll see you there."

"She'll be all right, I know she will," Mark said.

"What did I do, Dad?" he whispered. "What have I done? I'm afraid, Dad. I'm afraid I'll lose Cara." He felt his hands shaking uncontrollably.

Downstairs, he saw Fitzpatrick.

"You caught and killed the Birdman," he said. "You're famous now. What can I do?"

"You can take me to the hospital."

CHAPTER 58

MARK LOOKED OUT the kitchen window and smiled as he watched the puppy near the barn playing with the young boy. He was a German Shepherd.

"He's the son of the family that farms our land?" Mark pointed at the boy.

"Yes. His name is Bobby," his Aunt Florence said.

"How old is he?"

"I think he's five. I'm sure he'll be more his dog than mine, but thank you."

"Sure," Mark said. "Jake's deputy has a German Shepherd, and she had a litter, and I asked for one."

"Louie." She touched his arm. "Don't you want to talk about all this?"

"No, not now."

Mark walked outside to the barn. "They're amazing, aren't they?"

"Puppies?" The boy looked up.

"Yes." Mark nodded. "I'm Lou Mark. My aunt and I have this farm, and your parents take care of it for us."

"Yes, sir." He nodded. "I know. My daddy said you're a famous FBI agent. That you caught a bad man."

Mark knelt down and held his hand out toward the puppy, which ran toward him.

"You know what's really great about them, Bobby?"

"What, sir?"

Mark felt the puppy's teeth and claws like needles and razor blades on his forearm. "They trust you because no one has hurt them yet."

He watched the boy pet the dog.

"I want you to do me a favor," Mark said. "Will you?"

"Yes, sir."

"I'm not here all the time," he said. "I want you to help my aunt with the puppy. Will you help her with him?"

"Yes, sir. I'd like to do that."

"Good. I think my aunt has some treats for the dog and you too. Why don't you go to the house?"

Mark walked into the barn and looked at the old, heavy bag and the axe. He saw the boy, with the dog running behind him, near the front of the house. He had told Jake to kill the bird Evan had left behind when he killed Schaeffer.

"I'm home, Dad." He looked up at the rafters in the barn. "It took a while, but I've come home."

Joe had stayed for nearly a week and left only a few days ago. He'd told him that Dr. March had plead guilty to a misdemeanor, paid a small fine by his extravagant standards, and had gone back to his estate.

One night, he remembered, he and Joe had seen his new ad on television.

"We still have the same questionnaire," Dr. March said. "We still have the same multilevel matching criteria. And now we do background checks on every subscriber to increase your safety. We are about relationships and connections, and if you want that, call now. Our operators will tell you about our specials for new subscribers."

"Unfuckingbelievable," Mark had said to Joe. "Fifty-eight women later, two FBI agents, Tom, and he hasn't missed a beat. Do you think he might make even more money?"

"There's nothing you can do about it," Joe said.

"We'll see." Mark pointed at the television.

"What are you going to do?"

"You'll see."

"I'm glad you refused to talk to *Time* magazine for their cover story. It's because you made a promise to Pete?"

"Yes, in a way," Mark answered.

"And Debbie?" Joe asked.

Mark nodded. "I gave Pete the story, or part of it."

"Bookstores can't keep his book on the shelves, and he sold the movie rights for millions, I think," Joe said. "Have you read it?"

"No."

"What did you do with his watch?" Joe had asked.

"I gave it to Pete."

"I thought you might keep it."

"No." Mark shook his head. "I knew I'd give it to Pete when I took it from Evan. We both gave something up, Pete and I, didn't we, because of the choices we made."

Mark walked back toward the house and thought about the *Time* story that had come out yesterday. Jake had dropped off a copy.

His name is Lou Mark, he is thirty-two years old, and he catches serial killers for the FBI. Less than a week ago, he caught and killed Evan Morgan, called the Birdman by the media and the FBI, who was the most prolific serial killer in United States history. Lou Mark is a private person who declined our request for an interview.

Lou Mark's father was John Mark, a distinguished detective in the Midwest until he was shot and paralyzed from the waist down by a man who killed his wife and his neighbor. Today, John Mark's son is the most famous law enforcement officer in this country.

Mark stopped about ten feet from the front porch and looked upstairs and, for a moment, thought about Debbie and Pete.

Mark felt his cell phone vibrating, looked at it, and saw it was Joe.

"You got him, in a way," Joe said.

"I think I know what you mean, but tell me."

"A class-action suit was filed today against Dr. March and his business, seeking millions of dollars in damages."

"How did you find out so fast?" Mark asked.

"Ironically, Oliver found the headline on the Internet," Joe said.

"Really?"

"Tell me what you had to do with that?" Joe asked.

"Joe, all I did was give a friend of mine a list of the names of the victims. He did the rest himself," Mark answered.

"Ninety percent of the families joined in the lawsuit. I read the complaint. He's suing for wrongful death, among other things. He alleged that Dr. March communicated directly with Evan two years ago. He also wrote that he matched men with dead women. How did he know that?"

"I don't know. Good work?" Mark smiled.

"Maybe we should have shut him down."

"I thought about that, but then he just would have moved to another service, and we'd still be looking for him."

Mark thought about Sarah, the woman in the bar, after he found Jackie in New York.

Mark could hear the puppy barking inside the house.

"I don't think that's the only reason you called me," Mark said.

"Oliver found something else." Joe paused.

"What?"

"He found twelve women who were all killed in the same way in various cities across the country."

"How?"

"All we know right know is that he pours gasoline over them and burns them alive," Joe answered.

"Sex?"

"We're looking into that now," Joe said, "but I doubt we'll find anything."

"The same profile like Evan?" Mark asked.

"Not in terms of physical appearance, but in terms of a relative age range, yes."

"Married? Single? Divorced?"

"All of those," Joe said.

"You want me to do this?"

"Yes."

"I don't know if I can now. I'll call you in a day or so."

Mark walked inside the house and saw the puppy chasing Bobby around the dining room table.

"Bobby," Aunt Florence said sternly, "we don't do that in the house. Take him outside now."

"Yes, ma'am."

Mark smiled and petted the dog just before the dog chased Bobby out the front door.

"I'm too old for a puppy," his aunt said.

"He'll grow up soon enough. Do you think she's awake?"

"I don't know anyone who could sleep through that barking," she answered.

"After his first murder case, was Dad ever the same?" Mark asked her.

Florence turned toward him. "I don't know that it was the first murder case, but I know he wasn't the same after he caught the famous serial killer who'd been a fugitive for many years."

"I remember some of it," Mark said.

"You're wondering if you can ever go back?" she asked.

Mark nodded.

"Whatever you did, whatever you're questioning today, you did it to protect your family. And you stopped a killer."

"But I did things I never thought I could do."

"Your father had doubts at times too. But he had his own sense of justice, and right and wrong weren't really part of it. Whatever he thought before, it changed forever after he caught the man who made him famous. Now you have the same choices."

Mark nodded, then walked upstairs, remembering when Fitzpatrick had dropped him at the emergency room.

"Is she going to be all right?" Mark had looked down at Cara in the hospital bed.

"I think so," the doctor said. "What happened?"

"She saved my life. The baby?"

"No, I'm sorry," the doctor said quietly. "You didn't tell me what happened."

"*She shot a serial killer.*"

"*The Birdman? What did he do to her?*"

"*He kicked her before I got inside.*"

"*I'm sorry,*" the doctor said. "*Then it was the kick that killed the fetus.*"

"*Can she?*" Mark asked.

"*Yes. There's no reason why she can't conceive again.*"

"*Thank you.*"

Mark walked through the door and saw her sitting up in bed.

"I'm sorry about the noise," he said and sat down next to her.

"It's all right." Cara smiled. "I'm well now. I just like it here. It's safe now."

"Joe called. He said the families of the victims filed a class-action lawsuit against Dr. March."

"I don't want to talk about him." Cara turned away. "I don't care what happens to him."

"I'm sorry." Mark touched her hand. "It's just when I saw how badly he hurt you—"

"What else did Joe want?" Cara asked.

"I'll talk to you later about it."

"Another case?"

"Yes, I want to tell you something."

"What?"

"Her name was Julia. They called her Julie," Mark said. "She was my father's sister. She was a little more than a year older than he was."

"You're going to tell me now?"

Mark nodded. "People thought she was special. She was very smart, and she could see things. She could put things together with her eyes."

"You never met her?"

"No, she died long before I was born. She was eight when it happened, and my father was seven."

"Did your father tell you about her?"

"No"—Mark shook his head—"not while he was alive. I saw photographs of her. Her eyes were unusual. I asked about her, what happened. But my mother and my aunt didn't say much until after my father died. My grandfather was a cop, like my father, like me now. He came home from work one day and left his gun on the desk downstairs in the den, and my father picked it up."

"You've never told anyone this story, have you?"

"No. He pulled the trigger by accident, and the bullet went through her left eye. My father dropped the gun and ran toward her, and she touched him on the left side of his face, and then she died."

"Is it"—she pointed at the .38 on the dresser—"is it that gun?"

LAWRENCE M. JAMES

"No." Mark shook his head. "My grandfather destroyed that gun. But my grandfather believed that she forgave my father before she died, but he blamed himself for the rest of his life."

"Your grandfather?"

"Yes, and I'm sure my father did too. My grandfather told my father that Julie gave him her eyes. And when he became a cop, they called him the man with the eyes because of what he could do."

"What happened to your grandfather?" Cara asked.

"He quit being a cop the next day and worked this farm and, after a few years, wrote mystery stories. But he waited until he knew he was dying to write 'Monsters.' My father sent it to the magazine after the funeral."

"You saw this after your father died?"

"Some of it." Mark nodded. "It was his last thought. It was the first time I thought I could do it. And it was the only thing in his life that ever really scared him, other than not being able to walk again after he was shot. He tried to bury the moment when the accident occurred all of his life, but he couldn't. It was his last thought before he put the gun against the side of his head and killed himself."

"Your father thought he had to use the gift from Julie, from his sister?"

"I think so." Mark nodded. "But it was something my grandfather made up at that moment to make my father believe that Julie forgave him."

"Are you sure? Are you sure you don't believe it too?"

Mark rubbed the palm of his right hand across the left side of his face, then smiled. "I don't know."

Mark stood up, walked over to the window, and saw Bobby playing with the puppy outside.

Cara got off the bed, walked over to Mark, and hugged him from behind.

"What are you going to do?"

Mark lifted her hands and turned, facing her.

"We have to talk more about what we lost." Mark looked at her eyes.

"I can't now." She looked away. "It will take a long time."

"I know." Mark nodded as he saw a single tear form in her left eye.

"I asked you what you're going to do. I mean, is it sunrise or sundown? What your father said."

At sunrise, the monsters run away, hiding from the light, but at sundown, as the light wanes, they return. Never forget that, Louie, Mark remembered and didn't answer her.

"You've changed," Cara said.

"Have I? I suppose you're right, or maybe I just found something that was always there. But I know that next time it will be easier to do whatever it takes."

"Not that long ago you didn't know if you could do what Joe asked of you after Tom was killed."

Mark nodded. "I know."

"What are you going to do?" Cara asked again. "I have to know."

"I'm going to tell Joe to send another agent on the new case. If he can't find him, I may do it, but not now."

"I can't live through that again." She shook her head.

"You won't have to. They don't normally target the people trying to stop them."

"Promise me?" She looked up at him.

"Yes, it's sunrise. For now, they're gone."

Made in the USA
San Bernardino, CA
08 September 2013